THE UNHOLY DECEPTION

Also by L. A. Marzulli

Nephilim

THE UNHOLY DECEPTION

THE NEPHILIM RETURN

L. A. MARZULLI

ZONDERVAN™

GRAND RAPIDS, MICHIGAN 49530 USA

ZONDERVAN™

The Unholy Deception
Copyright © 2002 by Lynn Marzulli

Requests for information should be addressed to:

Zondervan, *Grand Rapids, Michigan 49530*

Library of Congress Cataloging-in-Publication Data

Marzulli, L. A. (Lynn A.), 1950-
    The unholy deception : the Nephilim return / by L. A. Marzulli.
      p. cm.
    ISBN 0-310-24064-6
    1. Human-alien encounters — Fiction. 2. Antichrist — Fiction. I. Title.
PS3563.A778 U54 2002
813'.54 — dc21
{B}   2002011429

Interior design by Laura Klynstra

Printed in the United States of America

---

02 03 04 05 06 07 08 /❖ DC/ 10 9 8 7 6 5 4 3 2 1

Prelude:
Somewhere in the Middle East

There are evil spirits here—bad jinn—I can feel it, the aged shepherd thought, pressing his back against the stone that towered above him.

He gazed into the night sky and called out the names of constellations, trying to ease his fear, then muttered a prayer to Allah.

Yes, bad jinn in this place, the old man thought, running his hand over the face of the stone, feeling its weathered surface. His father had told him that the jinn had erected these gargantuan rocks in a semicircle in the time before the great flood. On certain nights the jinn were said to visit, and woe to any traveler who found himself there when they did.

Allah protect me and this fool of a nephew, he thought as he listened to the tinkling of bells from his goats. He looked at the sky again and whispered another prayer. It was through the carelessness of his nephew, now fast asleep, that they found themselves in this unholy place. The young man had allowed his small herd of goats to wander beyond their traditional grazing area and out to where these giant rocks stood. In the morning they would leave this place to the jinn and other spirits.

Far in the distance, a single light caught his eye. The old man sat upright and grabbed his staff. He watched as the light moved toward him, growing larger all the time. And then he heard it, the sound of many swords in the air. It was an expression his father had used to describe the sound of a helicopter. His father had been just a boy when he'd first heard a helicopter and had thought it was an evil jinn, come to get him.

The old man wondered what a helicopter was doing out here in the wilderness.

His nephew stirred.

The boy will never be any good, he thought, rising to his feet.

"Uncle?" the boy asked.

"For the love of Allah, get up and make sure the goats don't loosen their tethers."

"Uncle, what's that noise?"

"Many swords in the air," he snapped.

The boy watched the growing light as the helicopter grew closer.

"What is it going to do, Uncle?"

"What?" the old man grunted, pretending not to hear.

The helicopter descended, and as it did, a brilliant beam of light shot out from under it, playing over the vast expanse of desert sand.

"Let's get out of here!" the old man yelled.

"Uncle—"

"Get the goats! Untie them, you worthless son of a jinn!"

The boy hurried to the goats.

The old man grabbed his staff tighter and offered another prayer to Allah.

"I have them all, Uncle," the boy cried out.

The old man took one last look at the helicopter, then ran to join his nephew. He grabbed the tether of the lead goat and headed into the darkness, away from the giant rocks. Away from the helicopter and the bad jinn.

* ○ *

Flying close to the desert floor, the helicopter began to crisscross over the large outcroppings of rock from which the goatherd and his nephew had retreated. Its spotlight played over the area, but kept returning to one large megalith of stone, the one in the center of the half circle. The chopper hovered over it for a moment, then began to descend. It landed, creating a sudden sandstorm from its whirling blades.

The engine shut down, a side door opened, and a dozen men clothed in gray jumpsuits scrambled out. A few moments later, artificial lamps were switched on and the area at the base of the rock was illuminated in garish light.

One man worked a sonar device. He walked, holding the wand in front of him, listening for any reaction in his headphones as he monitored the display screen.

He passed over an area in front of the megalith. The needles jumped, and his headphones responded with a constant chirping. He backed away a few steps, then moved forward, checking the same area. The needles jumped again and the chirping resumed.

"I think I've located it here," the operator called. He took a canister of spray paint from a pouch on his belt and marked a rectangle ten feet square in fluorescent orange. Moments later, the rest of the men began to dig. They worked in shifts of four. Each group would dig for exactly two minutes. Then they were replaced by the next four, who would continue for another two minutes, and they in turn would be replaced by the next group of men. As the sand and debris were removed, the hole in the desert floor began to deepen. Aluminum panels, held in place with hand-pumped hydraulic cross braces, were used to shore up the sides.

When they had reached a depth of ten feet, one of the diggers struck something solid with his shovel. He cleared away a portion of the sand from the object. The three other men in his crew dropped to their knees and brushed away the sand with their hands, while those from other crews helped, using brooms to sweep away the remaining sand. Soon an outline emerged of a large square stone.

The supervisor took out his walkie-talkie. "I think we've found it, sir."

The man's walkie-talkie crackled. "You *think* you found it or you *did* find it? Which is it?"

The man hesitated and looked down at the uncovered stone. He swallowed hard and replied, "Did, sir."

"Splendid. We'll be right down. See that all is ready, Mr. Sanders," came the reply.

Sanders shouted to the men, who began to construct a ladder down into the pit.

* ○ *

Arthur Bernstein, archaeologist, was sweating. He was nauseous, too, from the erratic flight of the chopper. He pawed at the collar of his shirt, trying to loosen it, and popped a button off in the process. He attempted to wiggle his toes in his boots, then realized, to his consternation, that his feet were swollen and numb. He took a deep breath and hoisted himself up, using the strap hanging from the roof of the chopper that he had held onto during the flight. Two of his hand-picked assistants, Jim Gleason and Bob Haney, both experienced archaeologists, eyed him.

He nodded at the men.

"What did he say?" he called to Mr. Wyan, the leader of the expedition, who handed the walkie-talkie to an assistant.

"They've found it, Dr. Bernstein," Wyan stated.

Bernstein forgot about his swollen feet and shuffled his way past crates of equipment until he came alongside Wyan, who towered over him. "Are we going down, then?" he asked, wiping another gush of sweat from his forehead.

Wyan smoothed back his dark slick hair. "As soon as you're up to it, Doctor," he said in a derogatory tone.

Bernstein wiped his forehead and signaled Gleason and Haney to join him. "We're ready, Mr. Wyan," he said, shifting his bulk from one leg to the other.

Wyan looked at him with cold, unblinking eyes. Bernstein felt his nausea increase as those eyes bored into him. He looked away. *He's got the eyes of a shark—merciless,* he thought. *And that nasty scar above his left eye only adds to the effect. I wonder how he got it?*

"Guarding this site has been a primary concern of our order," Wyan said, as Bernstein's two associates joined them.

Wyan had been standing in the cargo bay door of the chopper, and as he moved away Bernstein's team got their first real look at the site. "Incredible," Bernstein said, looking out the cargo door at the lighted megaliths of stone. Gleason, who served as Bernstein's photographer, snapped several pictures.

"The last time the stone was uncovered was just after Constantinople fell to the Turks," Wyan said. "Over five hundred years have passed."

"But we still can't be sure the site hasn't been compromised," Bernstein said.

"The Arab tribesmen believe that there are evil jinn out here. They avoid the place at all costs," Wyan stated.

Bernstein turned to Gleason and Haney. "These megaliths, some of them weighing over thirty tons, predate the Arabs by centuries. When these were placed here, our ancestors were running around in loincloths and living in caves."

Wyan arched a hand skyward. "Your team should be aware that these giant stones were put here by our friends, the Watchers."

"And will we be able to complete all the necessary arrangements before the reemergence of the Bethlehem star?" Bernstein asked.

"The star will emerge during the full lunar eclipse next month, so you should have plenty of time for your excavation. But we must utilize the time we have, so . . ." Wyan gestured toward the giant stone megalith, then added, "Mr. Kenson will accompany us."

Bernstein saw Kenson emerge from the partition separating Wyan and his associate from Bernstein's team and the rest of the crew. Kenson was a striking young man, just over six feet tall with neatly trimmed premature gray hair, dark brooding eyes, and a genetic abnormality of his hands that Bernstein battled constantly not to look at.

He's one of the most detached people I've ever come across, Bernstein thought as he shifted his bulk on his aching feet. *I wish he wasn't with us. The guy makes me uneasy,* he thought, avoiding eye contact with Kenson.

"Doctor, if your team will follow me," Wyan instructed, stepping on the gangplank that led to the desert floor.

Bernstein led his team toward the megalithic rocks that protruded, like misplaced towers, in the otherwise barren landscape. "They're enormous," Bernstein remarked to Gleason and Haney, who flanked him.

"Do you know what's buried beneath it?" Haney asked.

"No," Bernstein said, "only that it somehow links the alien presence and the reappearance of the Bethlehem star."

Wyan and Kenson stopped near the excavated pit; Bernstein and his associates hurried to catch them.

"You see how the shifting sands of the desert have concealed this place," Wyan began. "I'm of the opinion that the site has remained undisturbed since members of our group last checked on it. Mr. Sanders, have your men remove the cover."

"Yes, sir," Sanders answered from the bottom of the pit.

Haney, whose specialty was the cataloging and dating of artifacts, came close to Bernstein and whispered, "I just hope we're not compromising the site by entering it."

Bernstein nodded, concerned, as he watched Sanders point to two men with crowbars, who went to work prying the large stone. One of the crowbars slipped and flew back, smashing into the workman's shin and producing a nasty cut. The man cursed, then picked up the crowbar and went back to work. Other men stood ready with larger bars.

"Be careful not to nick it—we want it kept as pristine as possible," Bernstein admonished, nervously rubbing his fleshy fingers together.

Gleason shot a series of pictures as one corner of the slab was raised a few inches into the air so larger bars could be inserted. Wooden blocks were placed at each corner, and the same process was repeated at the opposite end of the slab. Leather straps were slipped under the slab. A metal tripod was erected above the hole, with a hand winch attached. A wire cable was lowered from the winch, and the leather straps attached to it.

Two men operating the winch began to turn the handle, and the stone slab inched upward off the wooden blocks.

"Easy . . . easy," Bernstein coaxed, as he watched the slab move unsteadily upward.

The slab moved slowly and stopped when it was at least eight feet over the newly revealed opening.

"If you'll follow me," Wyan directed, reaching for the ladder leaning against the side of the pit. "Mr. Sanders, do you have the lights?" he asked. Bernstein couldn't help noticing that there was less than a foot of space between the top of Wyan's head and the rough bottom of the stone slab that hovered above them.

"Yes, sir, right here, sir." The man produced several high-powered lanterns.

Bernstein saw Wyan take a lantern and climb the rest of the way down the ladder, followed by Kenson. It was his turn.

"Here's your lantern, Doctor," Sanders offered.

"No. Throw it to me when I reach the bottom," he said as he grabbed the ladder. He tested it with both hands before placing one of his boots on the top rung, gradually letting his weight rest on it. Satisfied that it would hold him, he moved his other boot and began to descend.

First Haney and then Gleason joined him at the bottom. Gleason snapped several photos before he even stepped off the ladder.

"Keep an eye on things here, will you, Mr. Sanders?" Wyan called. Sanders followed with a crisp, "Yes, sir." Then Wyan disappeared down the ancient staircase followed by Kenson.

Sanders tossed Bernstein a lantern. He switched it on and, holding it in front of him, placed his foot on the first stone step. "Incredible, isn't it?" he whispered to Haney, who was running his hand over the surface of the stone above their heads.

"The steps assume the same degree of angle in their descent as the Grand Gallery inside the Great Pyramid at Giza," Wyan called from below. "In fact, the smooth limestone walls you see are the same casing stones that once covered the outside of the pyramid."

"Make certain you take samples and see if they match the remaining casing stones in Giza," Bernstein instructed Haney.

"Sixty-four, sixty-five, sixty-six steps," Wyan commented as he reached the end of the staircase. "The number of man."

Bernstein's team followed and came to a halt next to Wyan and Kenson.

"Dr. Bernstein, take note of the materials used in the construction of the staircase. And do you see how the stones of this chamber seem to melt away and become another material?" Wyan pointed out, holding his lantern above his head.

"How did they manage it?" Bernstein asked.

"The technology used here is still unknown to the human race . . . at least officially. But let us proceed." Wyan pressed forward.

Bernstein reached out and touched the wall of a perfectly cylindrical tube. "Any idea of what it's made of?" he asked Haney. "So smooth, and yet it seems to have the durability of granite."

Haney examined it, then shook his head.

"You'll find that it's many times stronger than granite," Wyan called. "This passageway continues for another thirty meters, and then you shall see a wonder before which the discovery of Tutankhamen pales."

The men continued and soon joined Wyan and Kenson at the bottom of the steps. "It looks like we've hit the end of the tunnel," Bernstein announced, as his team shone their lights against the wall that now stood directly in front of them. "This can't be all there is."

"Appearances can fool you," Wyan replied. "Look there." He pointed toward a section of the wall. Sunk into the wall was the outline of a human hand with its palm facing outward, human in its appearance except for one very important difference. This hand had six fingers.

"Document that," Bernstein ordered.

Haney produced a tape measure and held it next to the impression of the hand.

Gleason snapped several pictures in rapid succession.

"What lies just behind this partition has been kept secret for almost two millennia, but this is the window in history where our secret must be revealed. We have announced to the presidents and heads of states of all the countries of the world that a special sign will be given, demonstrating that we are not alone. That sign is the reappearance of what, two thousand years ago, was misconstrued as the Bethlehem star. It will herald the return of the Christ consciousness and an evolutionary leap for the spirit of humankind," Wyan said. He turned. "Mr. Kenson, I believe we need your assistance."

Bernstein watched Kenson approach the wall. He reached toward the imprinted hand in the wall and paused for a moment so that his hand with all its fingers outstretched stopped a few inches from the imprint. He looked directly at Bernstein and spoke for the first time. "Almost a perfect match. Wouldn't you agree, Doctor?"

Bernstein nodded uneasily as Wyan placed his hand in the imprint on the wall. Though the print in which his hand rested was larger, all six digits were accounted for.

What's he doing? Bernstein wondered. Kenson allowed his hand to rest in the imprint for half a minute before withdrawing it.

"In a few moments we will see what's on the other side of this partition," Wyan announced, as Kenson stepped back from the wall.

At first nothing happened, but then the edges of the wall began to shimmer and vibrate, emitting an almost imperceptible low-frequency hum. The wall moved upward into the ceiling, where it vanished, revealing a hidden chamber thirty feet square.

"Incredible," Dr. Bernstein gasped.

"How did it rise of its own accord?" Gleason asked, while Haney recorded it all on film.

"The physics of sound and vibrations. Everything has a frequency in which it resonates. That is how the ancients were able to move the stones of the Great Pyramid," Wyan explained. "But there is much more to it than that, and in any case what the ancients knew was borrowed, of course, from the Watchers."

The group stepped into the chamber.

Bernstein looked around him. "What is that?" he asked, his voice shaking with excitement. In the center of the room sat a large glasslike container from which a dull yellow light emanated.

"See for yourself," Wyan said.

Bernstein hurried past Wyan and Kenson. "Astounding," he whispered as Haney came up beside him.

Gleason changed rolls of film and began a new series of pictures.

Bernstein took a tentative step toward the container. "It appears to be a high-tech sarcophagus," he exclaimed.

"And the body looks perfectly preserved," Haney added.

"Correct on both accounts," Wyan answered, "but take a closer look."

Bernstein felt Wyan approach and tower over him. "Look at the scars on his hands and feet," Bernstein said, pointing to the hands that were folded together on the naked body's abdomen, and then to the feet.

"Yes, and there." Wyan pointed. "That ugly scar in his side made by the spear of Longinus, the Roman centurion."

"The marks of crucifixion," Kenson stated. He pointed toward the dead man's shoulders. "Some of the scars from the whipping, where the three strands of the whip curled around the body and tore into the chest area."

"Over forty lashes, according to the texts," Bernstein added.

"See how the skin has been pulled and stretched there," Haney commented.

"Now you see why we have guarded this place so very carefully for two millennia," Wyan said.

"Look, Doctor," Haney said, pointing to the forehead. "The row of scars from the crown of thorns."

"It really is him, isn't it?" Gleason said from behind his camera as he snapped away.

Wyan walked to the front of the sarcophagus. "You see the bas-relief here?" He directed Bernstein's attention to the glasslike cover.

"Yes, it looks like a map," Bernstein remarked as he ran his fleshy hands over the cover of the sarcophagus.

"A stellar map, Doctor, if I'm not mistaken," Haney stated, pointing. "Here's our Sun, Venus, Mars, Earth, and the Moon."

"And it indicates very clearly that whoever left this here originated from the planet Mars," Bernstein added.

"Look at these artifacts that lie next to the body. I've never seen anything like them," Haney said.

"Yes," Wyan remarked, "and when we reveal this to the world, we will be able to link Jesus together with the alien race that built this sarcophagus and this chamber, for it was they who aided in his resurrection and enabled him to become the Christ in the first place."

"This is the body of a man well over thirty-three years old, and the wounds have healed over into scars. So it is true, then, that he lived through the ordeal of crucifixion?" Gleason asked, letting his shutter finger take a rest for a moment.

"Correct, he never succumbed to death," Wyan said. "I mentioned Longinus, the Roman centurion in charge of the crucifixion. He did not allow the spear to penetrate very deep. After Longinus pronounced him dead, Joseph of Arimathea took him down from the cross and carried him to the tomb, where the Watchers resuscitated him. Are you aware that there is a holographic film of the entire event from the beginning of the crucifixion until the resurrection?"

"I've heard of that from other members of our group, but never spoken to anyone who's seen it," Bernstein remarked.

"We'll have to arrange a viewing for you," Wyan replied, then continued, "Jesus then recovered, married, and sired children."

"The *Desposyni*, or heirs of the Lord, his descendants, are alive today," Kenson added.

"You'll find certain DNA matches will be very interesting," Wyan declared. "We've arranged a sample from the Shroud of Turin to compare it to . . . unofficially, of course. We must be careful, however, in how we present this."

"But that is why we're all here, isn't it?" Bernstein replied. "We've been trained for something like this by your group for a long time, even though we didn't begin to grasp the full picture until now." He gestured toward the lifeless body. "The tomb, the body, and these artifacts, coinciding with the reappearance of the Bethlehem star, should sway the delegates."

"That is what we're counting on," Wyan began, "but men are primitive in their beliefs. They cling to their established religious doctrine with its many falsehoods. Some have helped suppress the truth—the extraterrestrial intervention with the human race—out of fear and their desire to avoid panic. There are some who will try to hinder all that we are trying to accomplish."

Silence settled in the tomb as Bernstein and the members of his team mulled over what Wyan had said.

Wyan broke the silence. "There is one last matter: an area near here that must be excavated immediately. I have a rough approximation of where I want you to dig, based on aerial radar photography. I'll give the information to you before I leave, but when you find this particular artifact, let me know."

"And what is that, sir?" Bernstein asked.

"An ancient altar. Now, gentlemen, I must go." Wyan said. He and Mr. Kenson left the chamber to Bernstein and his team.

1

Interrogation Room

You've had a break with reality, Mr. MacKenzie, a psychotic episode resulting from your belief that you encountered extraterrestrial life forms."

Art MacKenzie eyed his inquisitor and brushed back a sweaty lock of dark hair. "I know what I saw, Ms. Scrimmer. They were demons. They were horrible, and if I hadn't had help from the angel that appeared, I wouldn't be here to talk to you about any of this."

Scrimmer toyed with a lock of shoulder-length dark brown hair and tapped her pen on her pursed lips. She countered in a patronizing voice, "There you go again, Mr. MacKenzie. You say it was an angel? How can you be sure? Had you ever *seen* an angel before this encounter? Did you have anything to compare this . . . this apparition to? How do you know that the extraterrestrial life forms didn't project the thought into your mind?" Scrimmer was perched on a stool in front of Mac, so that she looked down on him. She reached forward to a small table between them, retrieved a glass of water, took a sip, then set the glass back down.

Mac eyed the water. He had been at least twenty-four hours without food or water or sleep . . . just interrogations filled with questions from Scrimmer. Followed by a brief recess during which he would sit on the only chair in the room or lie down on the concrete floor and try unsuccessfully to sleep. He sucked his cheeks and pressed his tongue against the roof of his mouth. "How about some of that water? I want the water." He started to rise from his chair. Immediately, the two armed guards stationed on either side of the door moved toward him. Mac eased back down into his chair.

Scrimmer glanced at one of the guards and smiled.

She's flirting with him, Mac thought.

She crossed one black nylon-encased leg atop another, scribbled something on the clipboard, and asked again, "About the angel then, Mr. MacKenzie."

Mac tried to forget about the water and let out a deep sigh. "For crying out loud, I've been through this ten times with you and at least that many with the guys who debriefed me the first time. Why don't you compare notes with them? You'll find my story to be consistent."

Mac saw the neck muscles bulge on the guard Scrimmer had been flirting with, making the man's collar tighten.

Scrimmer shifted on her stool and looked down her pointed nose at Mac. "The angel, Mr. MacKenzie . . . how did you *know* it was an angel?"

Mac realized that his inquisitor could outlast him ten times over. He could see that she enjoyed, in a perverse sort of way, everything that she was doing. She would take a life-time, if necessary, to wear him down both physically and mentally. She wanted the truth—but that was the problem. Mac *was* telling the truth, and no matter how long she kept at him, he would not deviate from it. He looked at the attractive woman perched above him, and wondered how she'd ever found her way into such a bizarre occupation. "It was an angel," Mac began again. "It couldn't have been anything else. It was good. No, it was beyond good, it was holy. It was also the most powerful encounter with anything I've ever had in my life."

"Thank you, Mr. MacKenzie, but words like *holy* and *good* are just subjective, aren't they?" Scrimmer replied. "You thought you saw a *holy* angel, but it could have been a hallucination, perhaps caused by an extraterrestrial biological entity." She paused a moment, eyeing Mac, then continued, "You mentioned that the angel had . . ." She paused, allowing herself to smile. ". . . wings?"

Mac wiped some sweat from his forehead. "Look, I know how this sounds. But it's true, it had what looked like wings."

"Why is it that no one can corroborate your story, Mr. MacKenzie?" she queried, tapping her pen on the clipboard.

Mac slumped down in his chair and tried to get comfortable, but the rungs dug into his back. *The chair's deliberate*, he thought. He sat upright again, leaned forward, and replied, "Because the only other *human* person to see the angel was my father, who vacated the area after the angel appeared."

"Mr. MacKenzie, you realize that your father's murder is a well-established fact. He has been deceased for years. Surely someone else would know about your father being alive, if that were the case."

"You know who else saw him, Ms. Scrimmer, so why don't you quit playing games," Mac said, the anger rising in his voice.

"Oh. Yes. I'm sorry, Mr. MacKenzie, that's right, you did explain that to me." She searched her notes. "Here it is. General Roswell, whose real name is Nathan but also, when certain 'situations' deem it necessary, goes by General Black?" She cocked her head to one side and asked, "Mr. MacKenzie, which is it?"

Mac realized that this woman believed nothing he had said or would ever say. He eyed the partially filled glass of water, ran his tongue over his dry lips, and said, "Roswell was there. He saw my father, and you and I both know it. He testified to it during his debriefing."

"Did Roswell see the angel too, Mr. MacKenzie?"

"No," Mac mumbled.

"I couldn't hear you, Mr. MacKenzie," she scolded. "You know you have to speak up for the tape recorder."

Mac countered, "If I could have a small drink of that water, it would aid in my ability"—he raised his voice—"TO SPEAK A LITTLE MORE LOUDLY!"

Scrimmer shot a glance at the burly guard she'd been flirting with, then back to Mac. "I don't think that your behavior is productive, do you, Mr. MacKenzie?"

"I don't think not being able to eat or drink in who knows how long is very productive either. What do you say to that, Ms. Scrimmer?" he shot back.

Scrimmer tightened her lips. "Mr. MacKenzie, let's get back to the question I've asked. This angel that appeared to you with wings. Did it speak to you?"

Mac nodded.

"Mr. MacKenzie, the tape recorder can't detect a nod. Kindly voice your answer, please."

Mac cleared his throat, and using the hoarsest voice he could produce, replied, "YESSS."

"And how did the angel communicate with you, Mr. MacKenzie?"

"Telepathically," Mac mumbled, so that the last half of the word was almost inaudible.

"Tele, what, Mr. MacKenzie?" Scrimmer asked, annoyed at his antics.

"Tel-e-path-ic-al-ly," Mac replied, happy that he'd managed to rile her.

Scrimmer set her clipboard on her lap, eyed Mac, and without saying anything more, swiveled on the seat of the stool so that she faced the burly guard. She uncrossed her legs and dismounted. "Keep an eye on him," she instructed and left the room.

Mac looked at the burly guard. "She's just using you. Can't you see that?"

The guard ignored the taunt and stared at the wall behind Mac.

Mac leaned forward a little in his seat. "Yep, she's just playing with you," Mac challenged. When the guard didn't respond, he continued, "Oh, I see. You actually *believe* she's interested in you, for crying out loud."

He waited for a reaction, but none came.

Well, at least this was a way to get back at them for hurrying him away from Maggie and the kids, in the middle of dinner two nights ago—under the pretense of national security.

"So how much do they pay you here, buddy?" Mac asked. "You think Scrimmer's gonna go for somebody who makes what you do? Huh?"

The guard continued to ignore him, but Mac could see the color rising from the folds of skin that protruded from his collar. "Nope, she's just playing you. Using you to keep her flirting skills honed."

Scrimmer returned, and what she carried in her hand made the bile rise in Mac's throat. He pressed his back into his chair.

Scrimmer nodded toward the burly guard and said, "Would you be kind enough to assist me, Harold?"

The guard's face broke into a devilish grin. He motioned to his partner, and they took up positions on either side of Mac.

Scrimmer eyed Mac and said, "I was hoping that you would cooperate, Mr. MacKenzie." She stopped next to her stool.

"I thought I was," Mac replied with a false look of sincerity.

"Oh, look here, Mr. MacKenzie," Scrimmer said, holding her hand toward Mac with her palm open so that Mac could see the syringe.

Mac tried not to show any change of expression, but he could feel the sweat forming at his temples.

"Yes, Mr. MacKenzie, I was hoping that you would be more cooperative. But you aren't, and now I'll have to resort to other means."

"We could always try again, Ms. Scrimmer," Mac offered.

Scrimmer shook her head and began to walk toward him. "Harold, will you see that Mr. MacKenzie doesn't move about?"

Both Mac's arms were grabbed and pinned behind his back.

"Harold, turn him so that his shoulder faces me," Scrimmer asked.

Harold yanked on Mac's arm, which caused Mac to jerk upward in his seat.

"Thank you, Harold," Scrimmer said, flashing a smile. "Now, Mr. MacKenzie, this is a very potent drug. Of course, what makes it particularly interesting is that it is still somewhat experimental."

Mac tried to move away, only to have his arm yanked on again, which made him wince with pain.

"It's a very powerful truth serum, a little dangerous because of some of its side effects, but very effective. It will allow me to access anything that you have stored in your memory. And, Mr. MacKenzie, if you try to resist, you will feel very intense pain. The makers of this drug built that little feature into it. The more you resist, the more pain you will feel. The convicts that we used as test subjects confessed to things they never would have under normal conditions."

She took another step closer, so that now she was beside Mac.

He could smell her perfume which, in his hungered and dehydrated state, made him dizzy.

Scrimmer pulled the syringe cap from the needle. She inserted the point into the vial containing the drug and pulled back on the plunger, watching with satisfaction as the liquid seeped into the cartridge. "Now that should do it—twice the normal dose, with just a pinch more for good luck." She tapped the side of the syringe, turned it upside down, and eased a little of the liquid from the needle. "We don't want any air bubbles in this, do we, Mr. MacKenzie?" She stepped away from Mac and set the syringe on the stool seat. She unbuttoned the sleeve of Mac's shirt and rolled it up, then reclaimed the syringe.

"Now, Mr. MacKenzie, think of this as a journey to find the truth," she said, as she held the point of the syringe above Mac's upper arm.

2

Philadelphia

Helen Mintzer lay on the couch of her therapist's office. She pushed her shaggy, dishwater-blonde hair out of her face and tried to relax, but somehow couldn't keep from chewing one of her fingernails.

"Are you okay, Helen? You seem anxious today," Dr. Jacobson asked in a fatherly tone.

Helen adjusted herself on the couch and answered, "Yeah, I guess so. I feel . . . like this will never get any better." She grabbed a few strands of hair, put them in her mouth, and nibbled the ends.

Dr. Jacobson nodded. "But we've made some progress, wouldn't you agree?"

She sighed. "Yes, but they still come and get me."

"So the abductions are continuing?" he asked, jotting a note in her file.

Helen fought back the tears. "Like always, Doctor. They just do whatever they want."

Dr. Jacobson jotted something else and said, "Remember, Helen, you're not alone in this. There are others. You've even met some of them at our encounter group."

"Yeah, I know, but I don't want to live like this anymore. And neither you nor anybody else seems able to do anything to stop them."

Jacobson adjusted his glasses, then passed his hand over his graying hair as he settled in a worn armchair. "Why don't you tell me what happened since the last time we met?"

Helen folded her arms and stared at the curtained window. She could hear the sound of Philadelphia below her, a distant police siren, a garbage truck lumbering up the street, a kid shouting an obscenity at a passing car. Reluctantly she turned back toward Dr. Jacobson, but didn't answer.

"Did you have another encounter since the last time?" Jacobson asked.

Helen turned her head toward the back of the couch, away from her doctor. "I think so, but like the other times it's all blurry."

"Do you want to try to go under and talk about it?"

Helen thought for a moment, then nodded. After all, that's what she had come here for. She paid a good deal of her hard-earned salary to this man, but still the encounters continued. "Do you know what I could buy with the money I give you, if I didn't have to come here?" she said, only half joking.

Jacobson chuckled. "All right, this one's for free. Okay?"

"Really?"

"Really. Only let's get you under because I have another patient in forty-five minutes."

Helen relaxed and took a couple of deep breaths. She recalled the first time Dr. Jacobson had tried to put her under. She had resisted, and he had spent most of the session just trying to get her to relax. That had been a little more than a year ago. Now being hypnotized seemed very natural. She took another deep breath and closed her eyes.

"Now, Helen, I'm going to turn on the tape recorder and count to ten, and I want you to count with me. I want you to relax and breathe normally. Okay?"

"Okay."

"Ready, one, two, three . . . Helen?"

"Yes."

"Where are you, Helen?"

"I'm in my bedroom . . . sleeping."

"Alone?"

"No, my boyfriend is in bed with me."

"Are you both asleep?"

"Well, I'm almost awake. I'm trying to sleep, but they're in the room already."

"Who's in the room, Helen?"

"The aliens, the grays. Just like always."

"And do you try to move, to cry out?"

"I just want them to go away."

"What are the aliens doing, Helen?"

"Well, they're coming closer to the bed . . . coming to take me back to the ship, like always."

"And your boyfriend?"

"They switched him off."

"What do you mean by 'switched him off'?"

"I don't know. They do something . . . so he won't wake up. They're all around me, and I'm making a fuss. I don't want to go. Ronnie isn't waking up."

"Then what happens?"

"They float me out of the room . . . through the window."

"Is the window closed or open?"

"It's closed."

"And do you feel yourself going through the window?"

"No . . . I don't know how they do it, but we just go through."

"Then what happens?"

"We go to the ship . . . like always."

"Where is the ship?"

"I don't know. It's up above the apartment house."

"Are you in the ship?"

"I don't want to talk about it."

"It's okay, Helen, you're with me, remember? Dr. Jacobson. You're in therapy, and no one is going to hurt you."

"I don't know."

"Helen, it's all right to talk about it."

"Okay . . . I'm in the ship."

"And what's happening?"

"They're doing the exam on me."

"And what exam is that?"

"It's where they check out my vagina. I hate them. They're rough with me this time. They're mad or something."

"Why are they mad?"

"Because I keep coming here to see you, and they don't like that."

"Now what's happening?"

"One of them, he's like a leader or something . . . the others are afraid of him and he has a face like a . . ."

"What is it, Helen?"

"No, I don't want to look, but he's leaning his face so it's real close to mine. All I can see is his eyes. I hate those eyes. I try to look away, to close my eyes, but I can't. He holds me there, and then he starts to put thoughts . . . pictures into my head."

"And what does he say to you?"

"He tells me I have a very important task. I was chosen from a lot of women, and that I must trust him."

"Does he tell you what the task is?"

"No, he just shows me in a mind picture. A lot of people are gathered in this huge place, and they're all clapping together. I'm on stage, and I can see all of these people clapping. It's not for me. But I'm on stage, and the people are applauding. The alien tells me it's my son that everyone is clapping for."

"Do you have a son?"

"I don't know . . . they tell me I have a son, and that he's very important to them."

"Do you believe them? That you have a child?"

"I don't believe anything they say to me anymore, because they lie."

"So you don't trust them?"

"No, not anymore. When I was little I did, but not anymore."

"Have you ever seen your child?"

"He's not my child. He's their child."

"So you have a child, Helen?"

"I don't want to talk anymore . . . they lie all the time. And they hurt me. I just want them to stop."

"All right, Helen, that's enough for now. It's going to be all right. Let's get you up, okay?"

"Okay."

"Ready? When I clap my hands, you're going to awaken and will feel fine."

"Okay."

Helen's eyes popped open, and she looked around the room.

"You okay?" Dr. Jacobson asked.

She nodded.

"I'm going to play today's tape for a colleague of mine, if you don't object," Dr. Jacobson stated.

Helen sat up on the couch and wrapped her arms around herself. "I don't mind, if you think it will help."

"I'm not promising anything, but let's try it."

"Same time next week?" Helen asked.

"Yes. But I know you're struggling with your job, and who can blame you with all you have to deal with. I'm here to help you, Helen," Dr. Jacobson said, "so don't worry about the money, just come. And if you need me during the week, don't hesitate to call."

She almost smiled. "I promise."

He extended his hand and she took it, rising from the couch. They embraced.

"See you next week, Doctor."

"Next week, Helen."

Helen showed herself out and avoided looking at the young girl in the waiting room. She walked down the carpeted staircase, opened the door at the bottom, and stepped out onto the slate stoop of the building. The sun was almost gone from the sky, and the streets were clogging up with cars as rush hour got underway. Though it wasn't cold, she pulled the collar of her coat around her neck, folded her arms in front of her, and hurried down the sidewalk to her car.

3

Interrogation Room

Every muscle in Mac's body tensed, anticipating Scrimmer pushing the needle into the exposed flesh of his upper arm. "You can't do this," he said.

"Can't do what?" Scrimmer asked, moving the needle away from his arm, obviously enjoying the cat-and-mouse game she was playing.

"You can't inject drugs into people without their consent. I have *rights*."

Scrimmer smirked. "Right now, Mr. MacKenzie, you haven't any rights." She moved the syringe closer.

Mac was bracing himself for the inevitable when a booming voice exploded from the hallway outside the room. "Where in thunder is he?"

Scrimmer turned toward the commotion. "Harold, see what's going on."

"In here?" the voice from the hallway growled.

Mac looked at the doorway; Colonel Austin's stocky frame appeared. MacKenzie made eye contact with him and Austin nodded in return.

"Take your positions, men," Austin ordered as he stepped into the room. Half a dozen soldiers in black jumpsuits, toting a barrage of weaponry, followed him.

Scrimmer was clearly shaken by Austin's presence. "Can I help you, sir?" Scrimmer asked.

Austin ignored her. "You all right, MacKenzie?"

"I'm okay, Colonel, but I sure could use something to drink."

Austin nodded at Mac, then eyed Scrimmer and said, "I have orders for you to release Mr. MacKenzie."

Scrimmer pushed the point of the needle closer so that it almost rested on Mac's skin. "Who are you, and what right do you have to interrupt my interrogation?" she demanded.

"Your interrogation is about to come to an end by a direct order from the Joint Chiefs of Staff. Release Mr. MacKenzie under my recognizance, now."

"This man is a danger to himself. He's delusional and is a threat to national security, based on his alleged experience with extraterrestrial life forms," Scrimmer shot back.

"Well, that's one opinion," Austin growled. "But the orders I carry are very clear. Now we have only one choice here, and I suggest you option for it. Release Mr. MacKenzie."

Scrimmer didn't answer, and the needle remained poised above Mac's arm. He wondered if she had the nerve to defy Austin and inject him anyway.

Austin and his men remained stiff as the standoff continued.

Mac watched Scrimmer from the corner of his eye, and to his relief, saw her withdraw the needle.

"All right, Colonel," she said in a very icy tone.

"Now if you'll step away from Mr. MacKenzie."

Scrimmer took a small step away from Mac.

"If you men will be kind enough to release Mr. MacKenzie's arms."

Mac felt the grip on his arms loosen, and the two goons stepped away.

"Mr. MacKenzie, my men and I will escort you," Austin announced, gesturing toward the door.

Mac came to his feet and steadied himself a moment. Then he made a beeline for the glass of water. He snatched it from the tabletop and in two gulps finished it off. He placed it upside down on the table, took one last look at Scrimmer as he buttoned the cuff of his shirt, and walked out of the room.

Austin followed him. Mac gave a sigh of relief, glad to be next to Colonel Austin, the commander of an elite group of carefully selected and trained men that officially didn't exist. Mac felt with Colonel Austin the sense of kinship that comes to those who have survived great danger together; it was Austin and his men who had helped Mac rescue his children when they were abducted and taken to a secret underground base in the Nevada desert.

In the hallway, Austin's men formed a protective shield around Mac and Austin, two in front, two behind, and two on either side.

"How did you find me?" Mac asked.

"Not now. Let's get out of this place first." Austin quickened his pace.

4

Philadelphia

Helen pulled her beat-up VW Bug to the curb a short distance from her apartment building. A crunching sound came from beneath the front left tire; she had probably run over a soda can. She turned the motor off, but the car coughed and sputtered for a full ten seconds before it died.

She grabbed her purse and set it on top of the bag of groceries she had belted into the passenger seat to prevent them from spilling out as she drove. She got out of the car, reached back for the grocery bag, then leaned her elbow on the door lock and, using just her foot, slammed it shut. She held the bag in front of her and walked toward her apartment building.

In the elevator, out of habit, she breathed through her mouth. Someone had vomited in the elevator a week or so ago, and the stench had lingered, although now it was joined by a variety of deodorants and cleansers, all of which had failed to take the odor away. The elevator arrived at the eighth floor. She got out and walked down the worn path in the carpet to her apartment. Setting her bag in front of the door, she found her keys and opened it. She glanced down at the pile of mail that had spilled onto the carpet through the mail slot, then made her way to the kitchen, where she set the bag on the Formica counter. A cockroach scurried behind the toaster and disappeared. She went back into the living room, locked the door, gathered her mail from the floor, sat cross-legged on a saggy couch, and began to examine it.

"More bills," she complained as she sorted the mail.

One bulky manila envelope caught her eye. She picked it up and noticed that there was no return address on the front.

That's weird, she thought. She pawed at a loose edge with her chewed-to-the-quick, unpainted thumbnail, and after several attempts succeeded in tearing it open. She turned it upside down, allowing the contents to spill out onto her lap.

A picture caught her eye, and she felt the muscles in her neck tighten. *What is this?* She reached for the picture, and her eyes searched every detail of it. "No, " she blurted out. Still holding the picture, she picked up the only other thing that had fallen out—a letter, folded in half. She opened it. It was written in a cramped, scratchy hand. She looked for a signature and gasped as she found it. She looked at the picture, then at the letter, back and forth. Letting them fall to her lap, she brushed her hair back from her face with both hands.

"This can't be," she moaned. "It can't."

5

Edwards Air Force Base

Mac slid into the middle seat of a black Suburban, let his head collapse against the headrest, then felt his body melt into the leather seat. Colonel Austin followed after him. Two of Austin's men climbed into the rear seat, while another two occupied the front. In moments the car was underway.

"Where's Maggie?" Mac said. "Is she all right?"

"I've got four of my best men with her and your children, MacKenzie," Austin replied.

"Right, but how *is* she? Let me use the cell phone, I want to call her."

"In a minute, Mac, first things first. She's safe, and you'll have to hold any phone calls till we're off the base," Austin replied.

Mac let a stream of air whistle through his closed teeth. "All right, so what's going on, and who are these people?" he asked.

Austin took off his black beret and scratched his balding head. "Not sure, but that Scrimmer dame had a high-security clearance. I think she's Black OPS."

"What?" Mac yelled. "These goons drag me out of my house in the middle of dinner, separate me from my wife and kids, and keep me locked up in a stinking isolation room for who knows how long, and then to top it off, this Scrimmer dame, as you put it, is about to inject me with who knows what, and all you have to say is you *think* it's Black OPS? For crying out loud . . ."

Austin grinned. "Good to see you again too, MacKenzie. I didn't expect a show of gratitude, but remember—another couple of minutes and you would have been in la-la land."

Mac sighed, then nodded. "You're right." He thanked Austin and his men, and then, aware of the incessant growling in his stomach, asked, "Do you have anything to eat?"

"Sergeant, what chow you got up there?" Austin asked.

"Nothing, sir," the soldier answered.

"Can you get me something to eat?" Mac repeated.

"As soon as we're off the base," Austin replied.

"So how did you know where to find me? Roswell?" Mac guessed.

Austin nodded, and his face grew serious. "It was one of the last things he handled personally."

"Last things? What's that supposed to mean?" Mac asked.

"General Nathan—Roswell, as you call him—succumbed to cancer yesterday afternoon."

"For crying out loud," Mac whispered. He leaned forward and cradled his head in his hands.

"I'm sorry, MacKenzie . . . I'm not real good at this sort of thing," Austin mumbled.

"How did he find out about me?" Mac asked.

"He called Maggie's Vineyard looking for you. Had a favor to ask. He knew he didn't have long."

Mac picked his head up. "A favor?"

"I'll get to that in a moment. As I was saying, Maggie answered, and was hysterical about your being taken away. The general had to have his daughter, Laura, calm Maggie down. He made some calls, found out what had happened, and here we are."

The Suburban pulled up to the guard gate, and the driver showed the sentry his credentials. The man saluted, and the Suburban left the base.

"Where are we anyway?" Mac asked.

"Edwards Air Force Base," Austin replied.

"They transported me in a van with painted-out windows; I had no idea where I was," Mac informed him. "So Laura talked to Maggie, and she got the info to Roswell, and he made some magic phone calls, and presto! Here you are. But why isn't Uri with you?" Mac pressed, wondering where the ex-Israeli commando was. Only a short time ago, Uri Ben-Hassen had enticed him into flying to Jerusalem, where he was shown the remains of a giant skeleton, the Nephilim, which was a creature that had resulted from the union between fallen angels and earthly women. It had been found underneath the Temple Mount.

Austin looked out the window for a moment, cleared his throat, and said, "Uri flew back to Israel yesterday. To be with his grandfather."

"What?" Mac had a very uneasy feeling in the pit of his stomach.

"His grandfather had a stroke. He's in a coma. He's not expected to live."

"Elisha? A stroke? What's going on?" Mac stammered. "He was supposed to fly here and meet Uri and me."

"Almost seems like all of this has been orchestrated," Austin offered.

MacKenzie frowned and locked eyes with Austin. "It's not just a coincidence, is it?"

"The general didn't think so. He had a pretty good idea what was going on—and that's where his 'favor' comes in. He died a broken and disillusioned man, Mac. He had lost faith in everything. But he loved his country. He loved what it stood for, and the freedom that it offered humanity."

"But he saw it changing, didn't he?" Mac asked.

"Yes, he did, and it made him old before his time."

"The alien agenda?" Mac whispered.

Austin nodded.

"Scares me too ... more than I want to admit," Mac replied.

"There's more," Austin said. "First we're going to get you fed—and then, Peru."

"Peru?" Mac repeated.

"Part of the general's last request, if I can use that term."

"Why Peru?" Mac asked.

Austin frowned and shook his head. "They found Cranston."

"Cranston?" Mac's stomach flipped as he remembered the last time he saw his former editor, screaming for help from inside the belly of a UFO. "How is he? Where did they find him?"

"Hiding among the ruins of Machu Picchu. He was naked, and his body was covered with what the doctors think are radiation burns."

"Machu Picchu?"

"An ancient city high in the Andes. Roswell believed it was built by extraterrestrials."

"What do the archaeologists say about that?"

Austin shrugged. "I don't know. I don't investigate this stuff or ask too many questions, I just follow orders. And I'm supposed to get you to Peru, to help bring in Cranston."

"Listen," Mac said wearily. "I've done my part. My family needs me. I want to see Maggie and my children."

"The entire trip will take less than twenty-four hours. That's a promise."

"How are you going to get us down there and then back here in that time?" Mac asked, not sure he wanted to hear the answer.

"In the BlackBird."

"The BlackBird?"

"The SR71 BlackBird. She'll fly faster than a bullet fired from a .30–06. And she'll do better than Mach 3!" Austin grinned, which rearranged the wrinkles on his face. "Radar can't detect her, and you're so high up, you have to wear a space suit."

"What? Austin, you're crazy! I don't even like to fly in a 737. I'm not going!"

Austin ignored him. "She goes so fast, her skin gets hot and the paint turns blue." He started to laugh. "The engines cause a shock wave 125 feet long. Mac, you're in for the ride of your life."

Mac folded his arms in front of him and glared at Austin. "No way, I'm not going. You can send me back to Scrimmer for all I care, but I'm not going."

"You're just hungry and tired, that's all. After you've eaten some food and gotten some sleep, you'll be fine," Austin coaxed.

Mac mumbled something, then asked, "Why do I have to go? What's so important about my being there?"

Austin grew serious. "Listen, MacKenzie. Cranston's cracked up. Keeps talking all sorts of weird stuff, like the end of the world. Whatever went on in that UFO did a number on him. The general believed if you talked to him, you could maybe help bring him back to reality. He might have information."

"And if I don't?" Mac asked.

Austin scratched his head again. "I can't make you go, Mac."

"What about Maggie and the kids?" Mac pressed.

"As I said, I have four men stationed out there helping with the harvest and keeping an eye on things."

"You guys think of everything, don't you," Mac huffed. "And Uri, Elisha?"

"I don't know. We can call later if you like."

Mac looked out the window and sighed. "Let's get something to eat first, and then I'll let you know."

Austin stifled a grin. "Pull over at the first decent place you come to, Sergeant."

"Yes, sir," the driver said.

"BlackBird," Mac huffed, and stared out the window. He wondered about Roswell's death and Elisha's stroke . . . *Coincidence?* he asked himself, then answered his own question. *Not in a month of Sundays.*

* ○ *

Early the next morning, refreshed by the food he had gorged on and ten hours of sleep, Mac stood on the tarmac of the Point Mugu Naval Air Command. He had called Maggie, but that had only made this trip to Peru seem that much worse. He yelled, "Why is it leaking, Austin?" as he tried to get comfortable in his space suit.

Colonel Austin winced and replied, "You don't have to yell, Mac, I can hear you just fine." He adjusted the mouthpiece on the helmet that covered his head. "You'll get used to it; just talk normally."

"I am," Mac yelled again, which made Austin cringe a second time. "You haven't answered my question. Why is the stinking plane leaking fuel all over the place? I'm not getting into that thing." Mac waved a gloved hand in dismissal at the plane.

"It's supposed to do that. The tanks seal themselves when the BlackBird reaches operational altitude."

"How high is that again?" Mac asked, then added, "Never mind, I don't want to know."

"This plane has one of the best safety records in the Air Force," Austin stated.

"Well, then we're just about due for a change," Mac countered.

Austin shook his head. "Trust me, Mac, I've spent almost as much time in the air as I have on the ground."

"That explains a lot about you, Colonel."

Austin gestured at the plane. "Let's get aboard. I've got a checklist to go down; it'll take some time." Austin started for the plane and was ready to climb the entry ladder when he turned around, looking for Mac. "Come on, Mac!"

Mac's booted feet remained welded to the tarmac. "You didn't tell me the half of what this was going to be like, Colonel. You know I hate to fly, and that's an understatement." He tried not to notice some of the ground crew who were grinning at him. "Besides, you didn't tell me about the fuel leaking."

"MacKenzie, it's nothing. The tanks seal themselves when you reach opera—"

"Yeah, you told me that," Mac interrupted. "But what if *all* the fuel leaks out *before* we reach that height? Then what?"

Austin closed his eyes and pressed his lips together so that all the color was squeezed out of them. "Listen, MacKenzie, do you have any idea of how many hard-earned taxpayers' dollars we're spending while you stand here and ask these questions?"

"I'm one of those taxpayers, Colonel," Mac reminded him.

"The plane has one of the best safety recor—"

"You told me that," Mac interrupted.

"We'll be less than two hours in the air," Austin said, trying a new tack.

Mac just stared at him, let a few seconds go by, then asked, "No stunts?"

"Not a one," Austin replied, with the sincerity of a monk.

"No tricks? No upside-down stuff?" Mac pressed.

"Promise."

"No funny business?"

"I'm just going to fly the plane, Mac. She'll do the rest."

"That's what I'm afraid of," Mac mumbled. "All right, let's get out of here."

"Now you're talking, Mac," he said, and his face beamed through the glass of his helmet.

The men walked toward the SR71. Mac pointed at the leaking fuel all over the runway and shook his head. Austin boarded first, then the ladder was moved back, and Mac ascended into the other cockpit. A technician helped him adjust his harness strap and hook his oxygen supply to his suit.

The tech finished and gave him the thumbs-up sign before he left.

Mac held up his gloved hand and repeated the gesture.

"You okay back there, MacKenzie?" Austin's voice crackled over Mac's headset.

"Yep," Mac answered.

"Hang on for a few minutes, then I'll kick her in gear."

"Okay," Mac answered, then closed his eyes and thought again of Maggie. If he let his imagination go a little, he could even smell the scent of her hair.

He was startled from his thoughts as the plane lurched forward.

"Get ready for the ride of your life, MacKenzie," Austin chuckled.

The plane taxied down the runway of the Point Mugu Naval Air Command.

"BlackBird, you're cleared for takeoff." Mac heard the voice of a flight controller in his headset.

"Ready to go," Austin replied. "Hang on, MacKenzie."

Mac braced himself. The plane picked up speed as it made its final turn on the tarmac and pointed its nose down the long runway.

"Here we go," Austin announced.

Mac heard the engines whine as the plane started down the runway. *Not bad,* he thought as the plane's wheels left the tarmac. And then it happened. The plane rocketed forward, the force of it pushing Mac back into the cushioned seat. Her nose tilted up, so that Mac was now looking at the blue canopy overhead, as the BlackBird streaked skyward.

"Whoowee, I love this!" Austin yelled.

Now it was Mac's turn to cringe at the volume in his headset. He didn't respond. Instead he grabbed his shoulder harness, closed his eyes, and prayed that it would be over soon.

The plane shot upward faster than Mac could have imagined, and then, when it seemed like it would never end, the BlackBird leveled out.

"We're at operational altitude, Mac," Austin informed him, "about 87,000 feet."

Mac wet his lips. "Thanks for reminding me, Colonel."

"Don't blink or you'll miss Los Angeles . . . oops, you missed it." Austin cracked up.

Mac forced himself to open his eyes and looked around. *Space . . . I'm in space!* He looked above him and saw a handful of stars. He gazed below and to his amazement, found he could see much of the American Northern Hemisphere. "Look at that, will you," he exclaimed. "That's incredible . . . it doesn't seem real."

"Pretty amazing, huh?"

"I feel like an astronaut."

"You are one. You're weightless, you know."

"What?"

Austin chuckled again. "MacKenzie, see the clipboard in front of you?"

"Yeah."

"Take the pencil that's velcroed to it, and let it go."

Mac did as he was instructed. "For crying out loud, will you look at that . . . it's floating," Mac exclaimed.

"Look out your left side, we're about to go south of the border."

"Already?"

"We'll be in Peru in less than an hour. I told you you'd enjoy it. This isn't so bad now, is it?"

"You're right, Colonel. This is amazing," Mac agreed.

* ○ *

Several hours later, Mac found himself in the office of Dr. Sanchez, head of the psychiatric department in the hospital located a short distance away from the U.S. military base near Lima, Peru. He stood by a display case housing pre-Columbian art. "Nice collection, huh?" Mac said.

Austin shrugged.

The door behind him opened and a heavyset man Mac assumed to be Sanchez came into the room. Introductions were made, and Mac took a seat in one of the chairs in front of Sanchez's desk.

"I noticed you were admiring my artifacts," Sanchez said, pleased. "I found each one."

Mac nodded. "Are you an amateur archaeologist?"

"Of sorts," Sanchez replied. He let a moment pass. "Thank you both for coming down . . . for Mr. Cranston."

"Tell us, where did you find him in Machu Picchu?" Mac asked, glad, as his journalistic instincts took over, to be doing something that felt familiar.

Dr. Sanchez swiveled in a well-worn leather chair behind his desk, grabbed a folder, and, laying it down in front of him, pulled out a photograph. "A group of touristas found Señor Cranston hiding near this stone wall, here." He used a pencil to point out the area on the photograph.

"Did he say anything when he was found?" Mac asked.

Sanchez nodded. "The man was terrified. He kept looking up at the sky, repeating, 'Do not let them take me, do not let them take me,' over and over again."

"Do you have any idea who Cranston was talking about?" Mac asked.

Sanchez frowned, which caused his thick lips to turn downward, their corners disappearing into his prominent jowls. "Señor MacKenzie, Señor Cranston has had a very bad experience. It has made him most unmanageable, so that we must keep him sedated most of the time."

"I understand, Doctor, but did Cranston say anything that might indicate who did this to him, who is responsible?" Mac pressed.

Sanchez cleared his throat, "He said some things. *Loco* in the *cabeza*—crazy in the head—kind of things."

"And just how wild were they?" Mac pressed.

Sanchez folded his hands on his desk, leaned forward, and whispered, "He talked about UFOs taking him and performing experiments on him."

"Did you examine him to see if there was any evidence to corroborate his story?"

"Yes."

"And?"

"We found what may be radiation burns covering most of his skin. We also found marks in his flesh where tissue had been taken."

"And what did you make of that?"

Sanchez adjusted himself in his chair. "That's why you're here, Señor. We fingerprinted him and passed the information to your country. It was reported to us that he was listed as a missing person. So we want him back where he belongs . . . in his own country."

"When can we see him?" Mac asked.

"Immediately, of course. I will call ahead to make sure all is ready."

Sanchez picked up a pair of heavy-rimmed glasses and scoured a worn, plastic-laminated office phone directory. He found the number he wanted and dialed it. While he waited for a response, he said, "You'll see Dr. Espinoza. She is the physician who has been assigned to Señor Cranston. She has been with him since the first day, nearly a week ago." Mac listened to a short, one-sided conversation, as Sanchez conversed in Spanish. He set the phone in its cradle and said, "I will arrange for someone to take you to her. If you will follow me, gentlemen." He grunted as he hefted his bulk out of his chair, and motioned for the men to follow him.

* ❍ *

Cranston's room was private and windowless and in desperate need of a coat of paint. "Oh, boy," Mac exhaled, as he got his first look at the man. "He looks like he's aged ten years."

"I wouldn't have recognized him as the same man who was at your vineyard, MacKenzie," Austin added.

Mac nodded, then asked Dr. Espinoza, "Did he say anything to you?"

Espinoza nodded and spoke with just a trace of an accent. "Señor Cranston has said many things while he has been under my care. Most is jumbled and fragmented, but I have been able to put together some detail of what may have happened. I find that if we allow him to regain full consciousness, he becomes so terrified that he is unmanageable." Espinoza went to a nightstand next to the bed, opened a drawer, and produced a small notebook. "I have made notes and entered them into my computer. I have taken repetitive words and parts of sentences, and attempted to reconstruct something intelligible out of it. It is just guesswork, but here are the results." She handed the notebook to Mac.

Mac scanned the pages. "Very interesting. Listen to this, Colonel. 'Flying, ocean, eyes, terrible eyes, touching, mind numb, eyes and eyes, they're inside me, mind's eye, burning, end the world, God help me, darkness, black eyes, Aba? Too much, too much, too many eyes, help me.'"

"You have a partial word here," Mac said, pointing to the paper.

"Yes, Señor, I couldn't make it out."

Mac forced himself to say the name. "Was it *Abaris*, by chance?"

Espinoza brushed away a wisp of black hair. "Maybe."

Mac began to read again. "'The end of the world,' that doesn't sound very reassuring," he joked. Then he asked Dr. Espinoza, "Can we bring him to?"

Espinoza looked uneasy. "Yes. It will take some time, though."

"In the meantime we could get something to eat," Austin suggested.

"Sounds good," Mac replied.

"The cafeteria food is . . . well, not so good," Espinoza said, "but there is a nice restaurant not far from here. I could arrange to have someone show you the way."

Mac looked at Austin, who nodded his agreement of the idea. "Sounds great. How long do you think it will be before he's able to talk?" Mac asked.

Espinoza thought for a moment. "Maybe an hour or two. If something happens sooner, I will send for you."

"All right, that's workable," Mac said.

"This way," Espinoza said, and they left the room.

6

✳ ◉ ✳

Tel Aviv, Israel

Uri BenHassen looked at the comatose body of his grandfather, Elisha BenHassen, and forced himself to hold back the tears. He counted at least half a dozen tubes attached to IVs, and several more hooked to monitors. A white tube protruded from Elisha's mouth, helping the stricken man to breathe.

"Can I get you anything, Mr. BenHassen?" a nurse asked, as she poked her head into the private room.

Uri shook his head.

"No change?" she asked.

Uri's shoulders dropped a little lower, and he shook his head again.

She closed the door and was gone.

It's hopeless, he thought, studying his grandfather for any sign of improvement. But there was none.

The door opened abruptly, startling him. A man entered whom Uri recognized as Solomon Wiesenthal, called Major by all who knew him. He and Elisha had fought side-by-side in the Israeli war of independence. Afterward, the Major had turned his energies to hunting down and bringing to justice Nazi war criminals. Every prime minister since the birth of the tiny nation had sought his counsel.

Uri stood up. "Good to see you, Major, I'm glad you could come," he said as he embraced the older man.

"How is he doing?"

"No change."

The Major sighed. "I told him not to see the Nazi guard face-to-face. That is why we arranged the room with the two-way mirror. But he insisted."

"And now he's here," Uri lamented.

"From what I've been told, one minute they were talking, the concentration camp guard and your grandfather. Then that crazy camp guard started swearing and cursing at Elisha. He went at him, calling him a dirty Jew. And then he laughed in his face and said he would be glad to do it all over again."

Uri looked puzzled. "Do what all over again?"

"Kill your grandfather's brother. 'One less Jew to pollute the earth,' he said."

"That Nazi guard is an animal. It should be him here instead of my grandfather," Uri muttered.

"They told me your grandfather didn't say anything to the guard. Didn't raise his voice. He just grabbed his chest and collapsed onto the floor. The Nazi spit on him as he lay there. The guards grabbed the crazy man and hustled him back to his cell."

"And then they bring my grandfather here," Uri stated, nodding toward his helpless grandfather.

"I asked the head surgeon about his condition," the Major said.

"I know . . . I know," Uri said, "he's not to be expected to live through the night."

"We must hope for a miracle . . . but if his time has come, well, he has had a good life, and is loved by all who know him."

"I wish I believed in the miracles," Uri confessed. "Things would be better, but you know I don't believe in the super-natural."

The Major nodded. "You should get some rest. I can stay for a few hours."

"No, if he died while I was gone . . . I will stay." Then he added, "I could use something to eat. Rebecca could only come this morning. The children, you know."

The Major nodded again. "Yes, I know. I'll go across the street and get you a falafel. They make good ones there."

Uri nodded. The Major left, and Uri returned to his chair to resume his vigil.

A few minutes went by, and the door opened again. Uri turned toward it, expecting another nurse.

The man who stood in the doorway was someone Uri did not recognize. "Who are you?" he asked.

"My name is Johanen. I am a friend of your grandfather's. I'm here to help," the man said in a soothing voice.

Uri could feel his heart beating faster—this was the man he'd heard so much about from his grandfather. This enigmatic man, Johanen, headed the Spiral of Life organization, which was a select group of men and women dedicated to fighting the rise of a global government that they believed would be headed by the Antichrist.

"You are Johanen?" Uri repeated, unsure what to say.

Johanen stepped into the room and closed the door. He went to where Elisha lay.

"Has he regained consciousness at all?" Johanen asked.

Uri didn't answer. He just stood looking at the man, suddenly aware of an overwhelming feeling of . . . what was it— peace? Well-being? Goodness? He forced himself to answer, "No, not since the stroke. The doctors are saying he's not going to make it through the night."

"Oh?" Johanen replied.

Uri saw Johanen's blue eyes gleam and saw the hint of a smile at the corners of his mouth.

"Let us see if we can make a difference," Johanen said as he came closer to the bedside.

7

✦ ◉ ✦

Philadelphia

Helen picked up the picture again. There was no mistaking her mother, but next to her, with his arm around her waist, was a man she'd never seen before, a man who claimed in this letter to be her father. Her mother had served as a nurse in the Air Force, so it was no surprise that this man would also be in uniform. She knew nothing of military rank, but whoever this guy was, he looked important, with lots of medals and decorations on his uniform. She grabbed the letter and began to read.

"Oh," she exclaimed and raised her hand to her mouth, searching for a fingernail to chew. She finished the letter, then read it again. She got up from the couch and hurried to the kitchen, where she made some hot tea, then returned and read the letter yet again. Looking inside the envelope, she found the key that the letter told her would be taped there, a key to a safe-deposit box. The letter also contained the necessary information she would need to access it.

She found herself growing so angry she wanted to scream, wanted to hit the man who'd written this. But it was too late, for this man was dead, or so the letter indicated.

He cheated me even in death ... what a coward! she thought. Her eyes found again the part of the letter that, even with the hot cup of tea steaming in her hands, sent a chill to the depths of her soul.

So he's connected to them, she thought. *How could he do that to me ... to my mother? What a monster!*

She clutched the key in her hand and squeezed it so hard that the scored part of it left an impression in her palm. She reread what bank it belonged to, and the safe-deposit box it opened.

She heard someone unlocking her front door—her boyfriend, Ronnie. For some reason, she didn't want him to see any of this. She gathered the photo and letter, stuffed them back into the envelope, and slipped it under the cushion of the couch. She pushed the key into the pocket of her jeans, grabbed a magazine off the cluttered coffee table, and pretended to read.

"Hey, you home?" Ronnie called as he opened the door.

"Yeah." Helen tried to sound normal.

"How was your session?" Ronnie asked.

She shrugged. "Same as always."

"Does he help you?"

Helen nodded.

"I don't understand why you can't tell me what it's all about."

Helen tucked her legs under her. "I can't, Ronnie, that's all."

"Maybe I could help." He raised his eyebrows and held his hands out to her.

"No, trust me, you couldn't. Hey, you want to go out for pizza?" she asked, changing the subject.

"Pizza sounds good. Let me take a quick shower and we'll do it," Ronnie called as he headed toward the bathroom.

She didn't answer. Instead, she waited until she heard him moving around in the shower.

She jumped off the couch, retrieved the manila envelope, then put the key back in and went into the bedroom. She opened the top drawer of her bureau, the one she kept her panties and bras in, and put the envelope at the bottom of it.

She put on a little lipstick, brushed out her hair, and scolded herself for chewing the ends of it. Then, thinking of the letter, she bit off another nail as she set the brush back on her bureau top.

The shower stopped running.

"You almost ready?" Ronnie called from the bath.

"Yep."

"Let's have the pepperoni and mushrooms, okay?"

"Okay," she answered as she bit off another nail—below the quick, making her finger bleed. She put the finger in her mouth to stop the bleeding and mentally counted the hours until the bank would open in the morning.

8

* ◉ *

Peru, South America

He is coming around," Dr. Espinoza said, as she held Cranston's wrist and checked his pulse.

"How coherent will he be?" Mac asked.

"It is hard to know for certain. People react to the medication in different ways." She shook her head. "But he is a frightened man, and his fear overrides the dosage of what we would give a 'normal' person to keep them sedated."

"So you don't know what to expect?" Mac pushed.

Dr. Espinoza folded her arms in front of her. "Señor MacKenzie, that is why we have the straps to restrain him— as a precautionary measure, both for the staff and Señor Cranston's own protection."

Mac nodded and looked at Cranston. "He seems to be coming around."

Cranston's eyes fluttered. He mumbled something, then began blinking rapidly. "Where . . . where am I?" His eyes darted around the room.

"You're safe, Jim," Mac said. He saw recognition in the man's eyes. "You're okay. It's me, Mac. We're going to get you home. It's all right."

"Mac," he mumbled, then a little louder, "MacKenzie?"

"I'm right here, Jim," Mac answered.

Cranston began to sob. "Oh, Mac—Mac, don't let 'em take me again," he said. His speech was slurred.

Dr. Espinoza glanced at MacKenzie and readied herself to start the IV again if necessary.

"Let who take you?" Mac asked, knowing the answer.

Cranston's eyes bugged, and he strained against the straps. "Aliens. They were horrible, Mac . . . and they did this to me." He tried to point to somewhere on his body, but since Cranston's wrists were fastened, Mac had no idea where he was pointing.

"He means the marks," Dr. Espinoza explained.

"Don't let them do it, Mac," Cranston blurted.

"The marks?" Mac repeated, and glanced at Colonel Austin, who shook his head.

"Here," Dr. Espinoza answered. She lifted the blanket that covered Cranston and showed him a scoop mark where a sample of flesh had been taken from the man's thigh.

"Those rotten . . . ," Mac huffed.

Cranston was trying to pick his head up off the bed so he could see better. "Mac!" he called, "Mac, do you see what they did to me?" Cranston's face contorted with rage.

"You're safe now, Jim," Mac said, but wondered if it were true. "What did they say to you?"

Cranston's face contorted and he began to sob again. "I don't . . . I can't think . . . think about it. Mac, it drives me crazy to think about it."

Mac patted Cranston's arm. It was clear that Jim was in pain, but they needed answers. "Come on, Jim," Mac said encouragingly. "Get a grip on yourself, and tell me what they said to you."

Mac watched as Cranston struggled to find his courage and his right mind.

"I don't know, Mac," Cranston said at last. "They're so horrible. They showed me what was going to happen—they showed me in here," and he lifted his head. "They showed me everything, Mac, and it was so horrible!"

"What was horrible?" Mac pressed.

Cranston choked back tears. "The end of the world. They showed me how the world is going to end. It was horrible, Mac . . . so horrible."

"The end of the world?" Mac repeated.

Cranston sobbed. "Yeah—the Apocalypse. Millions are dying. The four horsemen, Mac . . . unless we stop them . . . the aliens want this . . . want this planet . . . for themselves . . . for breeding, Mac! They're breeding . . . the hybrids . . ."

The hair on Mac's neck bristled, and for a moment he remembered the pungent odor when he had been deep underground at the secret desert base, in a sort of breeding room. He forced the thought from his mind and said, "What hybrids, Jim?"

"They used me, Mac. They made me have . . . sex . . . with one of them . . . a female. But I had to! They look in your eyes . . . and you have to do what they tell you. They get inside your head, and you have no choice. Oh, Mac!" Cranston began to cry.

Colonel Austin cleared his throat and asked, "Mr. Cranston, why did they let you go?"

Cranston looked confused and alarmed by this new voice. "Who are you?" he asked, and his body began to shake.

"It's okay, Jim," Mac said, his hand on Cranston's arm. "He's with me and he's a friend."

"He's . . . what? Who?" Cranston looked dazed.

Mac repeated Austin's question. "Why did they let you go?"

Cranston rolled his eyes, and his body began to tremble.

Dr. Espinoza was clearly growing increasingly concerned. She checked his pulse and announced, "I do not think he can take any more of this, gentlemen. His pulse is racing. I am going to put him under again."

Mac just stared at the shell of the man who had once been his editor. Jim Cranston, the powerful editor of the *Los Angeles Times,* had been reduced to a hysterical, cowering stump of a man, and all because of a UFO . . . and the demons that inhabit them.

Dr. Espinoza started the IV again. Cranston's body gradually stopped convulsing. Mac took his hand. "You're going to be okay, Jim. We're going to get you home."

Cranston rolled his eyes, focused on Mac, and just before he succumbed to the drugs, he mumbled, "Don't let them get you, MacKenzie . . ."

9

* ◉ *

Tel Aviv, Israel

"What are you going to be doing?" Uri asked, concerned for his grandfather as Johanen leaned over the motionless figure.

"I am going to pray for him, Uri," Johanen said, "and I believe that the God of heaven and earth will heal him."

Uri was stunned. *How can he believe that? And how did he know me?*

As if he could read Uri's mind, Johanen spoke but without taking his eyes off Elisha. "Your grandfather showed me your picture when last we met. He loves you like a son."

Uri nodded, and his jaw muscles tightened as he fought the tears back. Johanen closed his eyes and began to pray in what sounded like a strange dialect of Hebrew. Uri could understand some of the words, but many were different from those spoken by Uri and his fellow Israelis. Also, Johanen's accent was unfamiliar. Uri could place almost any Hebrew accent, having lived in Israel all of his life, dealing with the profusion of immigrants pouring in from all over the world, each bringing their distinct accent. But Johanen's was different.

He listened, catching a few phrases as Johanen prayed aloud.

"Oh, Great God of the Universe . . . Elisha, your servant. Heal him . . . Touch his life . . ."

Johanen placed both his hands over Elisha's heart and continued to pray. Then something strange happened. A green halo emanated from Johanen's hands, flowing out of them and into the body of Elisha. Uri rubbed his eyes, blinked hard, and looked again, but he wasn't seeing things. His mouth opened in astonishment. "What . . . ," he whispered.

Johanen continued to pray.

Elisha's left index finger moved. Then it trembled, curled in on itself, and stretched out again.

The green halo turned deeper in color, and spread so that it enveloped the entire bed.

Elisha's eyes blinked once, and then again. His breathing, which had been so labored, began to change, growing stronger. The old man's chest filled with so much air that the bed sheets rose a couple of inches.

Uri was dumbfounded. He saw Johanen reach forward and gently pull the plastic breathing tube out of Elisha's throat. He glanced at Uri. "This will make it easier on him."

A sudden flurry of thoughts flashed across Uri's mind. *How can I trust this man? I don't know him. What if taking out the tube will kill my grandfather? I'm not sure what I'm seeing. Is this hypnosis or something?*

Then to Uri's amazement, Elisha opened his eyes. He looked like a man back from the dead, but he was awake, and as he moved his eyes between Johanen and Uri, he seemed to be aware of what he was seeing.

Elisha grasped Johanen's hand and began to weep tears of joy.

"Go easy, my friend," Johanen said.

"Uri . . . Uri, I'm going to be all right," Elisha said in a halting voice, seeing his grandson at the foot of the bed.

"You need to rest now," Johanen said.

Two nurses came into the room. "Dr. BenHassen," one of them began, but they both stopped suddenly near the doorway, staring, their mouths open.

The green halo had almost disappeared, but the outline of it was still visible.

The second nurse gasped, "Oh—what *was* that?"

Johanen ignored them.

"I'm going to be fine," Elisha called from his bed.

Uri sprang from his chair and ran to embrace his grandfather, not caring who saw him cry.

10

Peru, South America

Mac leaned against the roughly plastered wall outside Cranston's room and asked Colonel Austin, "So, you've arranged for a military medical transport plane to take him back to the States?"

Austin nodded. "I just have to clean up a few things on this end, and he'll be off. You know, Mac, I haven't spent much time around him. But I barely recognized the man in there." He jabbed a finger toward the room where Cranston lay.

"They've destroyed him," Mac agreed. "Do you think the doctors can help him back in the States?"

"That's part of why General Roswell wanted you here, Mac. Cranston kept asking for you, mumbling your name, as he went in and out of consciousness. Roswell hoped that your being here would bring him around, and maybe give us some insight into what happened to him. And that happened, at least to some extent."

Mac nodded, then asked, "So when does he leave?"

"Tomorrow. Day after at the latest."

Mac closed his eyes. "When do *we* leave?"

"About six hours. We'll go back to the base and sack out, then head back home."

* ◊ *

Mac awakened to someone shaking his shoulder.

"Better wake up, MacKenzie," Austin said.

Mac cracked an eye open. "We're leaving now?" He yawned and stretched to a sitting position.

"Soon," Austin replied. "Thought you might like to shower before we take off."

"Yeah, I'm starting to stink," Mac agreed, managing a weak laugh.

"Mac." Austin sat down on one of the folding chairs. "Something's come up."

Mac met his gaze. "What?"

Austin's forehead creased in horizontal lines. "It has to do with your father."

Mac's stomach flipped, and his hand balled into a fist. "He's *not* my father."

Austin continued, "They've found him. He's alive, but in a trancelike state. He doesn't respond to anything. It's all here." He handed Mac the decoded message on a piece of paper.

Mac read it, then let his hands and the paper fall to his lap as he stared at Austin.

"I'm sorry, MacKenzie."

"You promised me. You said we'd go right back to the States."

"I didn't expect anything like this. No one did," Austin mumbled. "It's only three refuelings, and before you know it we'll be there."

Mac shook his head. "I don't want to get involved in this again. I'm way beyond my comfort level just coming here."

"He's your father, Mac," Austin reminded him.

"The *body* is that of my father, but whatever inhabits it now has nothing to do with the man who sired me."

"He's not dead."

"He's dead to me," Mac stated.

"Listen, MacKenzie, this is a way to corroborate your story about what happened at the underground base. Only you and General Nathan had contact with him."

"And I wish I hadn't. Besides, what do I care if I corroborate my own story?" Mac added.

"He was supposed to have been murdered, right?" Austin asked.

Mac gave the barest of nods.

"But he wasn't, was he?" Austin reminded him.

"Look, I know you believe me, because you were there at the base and you saw what I saw, and it terrified you too. But how do I know this isn't some sort of elaborate trap that my so-called father has set up?"

"They have the entire area cordoned off." Austin pointed to the sheet of decoded paper in Mac's lap.

Mac shook his head.

"All they want is a positive ID on him," Austin insisted. "Just an ID on him, MacKenzie. Heck, Mac, you owe it to those of us who want to try to stop all of—"

"All of what?" Mac interrupted. "The alien presence that our government declares doesn't exist?"

Austin tightened the muscles in his jaw. When he spoke, his voice was barely audible. "MacKenzie, you listen to me. I've been around, and I've seen almost everything a man can see, and most of what he should hope not to. You're right about what you said earlier, about being scared at the base. There wasn't a man with us that day who didn't have to change his underwear after what we encountered." He leaned forward and spit out his next few words. "And your father was partly responsible for it. Help us, Mac." Austin pressed further. "We'll take the BlackBird, make positive ID, answer a few questions, and back we'll come." He clapped his hands together.

Mac shook his head.

"You *have* to go," Austin replied.

Mac stared at Austin. "Why can't you go, and I'll escort Cranston back to the States?"

Austin didn't answer.

Mac tried again. "You go and do a video linkup. I'll view it and make the ID that way."

Austin shook his head ever so slightly.

Desperate, Mac thought of one last possibility. "Have them fly him back to Edwards."

"Can't do it, Mac, they want to study his body."

"But you said yourself, he's not dead yet."

"Mac, I need an answer, and I think you know the only one I want to hear."

"I really don't have a choice, do I?"

"'Fraid not, MacKenzie."

Mac stared at the four walls of the pathetic officers' quarters and mumbled, "I'll go. And I hope I don't end up just like Cranston."

Austin rose from his chair. "Everybody that's been involved is scared, Mac. Everybody." He walked out of the room. "You got half an hour," he called over his shoulder as he closed the door.

"Right," Mac replied.

He read the decoded letter one more time, smashed it into a wad in his fist, and threw it with all his might against the wall.

11

Arlington National Cemetery

Laura Nathan adjusted the black veil that covered her face and wished the driving rain would stop long enough to allow her father the burial she'd planned in accordance with his wishes.

The priest cleared his throat and began to read. "Ashes to ashes, dust to dust, for naked I came into this world, and naked I go from it." The wind blew a flurry of raindrops down the back of his starched white collar. He looked impatiently at his assistant, who tried to steady the umbrella over his head against another gust of wind, and began again. "Our Father, we are here to set at rest the body of General Daniel E. Nathan. May you keep his soul and watch over it until the day of your great judgment, when you will awaken those who have tasted the sting of death, and bring some to everlasting life and others to eternal damnation."

Laura shifted on her high heels and pushed a soaking wet strand of her long dark hair back under her hat, staring at the mahogany casket draped with the American flag. *He was afraid to die,* she reminded herself. *Even though I was with him until the last, he seemed so alone and hopeless.*

She looked at her older siblings who had flown in from various parts of the country to help with the funeral arrangements, wondering, *How could we have grown so far apart from each other over the years?*

The priest sprinkled some holy water on the casket, made the sign of the cross over it three times, and stepped back.

In the distance, the mournful sound of taps struggled through the driving rain, only to dwindle away among the endless rows of tombstones at Arlington National Cemetery.

Laura's body jerked in response to the first volley from a twenty-one-gun salute.

She stared at the casket and let the tears roll down her cheeks. The last shot faded, and she dabbed her eyes with the rain-soaked handkerchief. She looked around at the crowd of military and government officials that had come, in spite of the weather, to pay homage to her father, and nodded to several who caught her eye. They began to lower the coffin into the ground.

Laura threw the flowers that she was holding on top of the casket and whispered, "Goodbye, Daddy. I love you. And if there *is* something after this, I hope to see you there." She walked away and climbed into the limo that waited near the graveside.

The driver, an elderly black man, asked, "To the memorial dinner, ma'am?"

Laura looked through the tinted glass window and saw two men, one whom she recognized as a CIA operative. They had been following her from the hotel to the church, and now here they were at Arlington. *It doesn't stop even after he's dead,* she thought. "No, I want you to go back to the hotel for a moment," she answered. She picked up her purse, got her compact out, and began to repair the damage the rain had done to her makeup.

"Yes, ma'am," the driver drawled, maneuvering the limo past rows of tombstones.

"Horrible day for a funeral," Laura stated as she freshened her lipstick.

"Yes, ma'am, it most certainly is," the driver replied.

The limo left the cemetery and wound its way through the nation's capital, following the perimeters of sprawling government buildings whose marbled fronts glistened from the rain.

The grand architecture gave way to more modest structures, and they arrived at her hotel. The driver pulled under a large expanse of forest green canopy that led to the lobby.

He looked in his rearview mirror. "Ma'am, I think somebody is following us."

Laura was waiting for this, so she feigned innocence. "Really? Are you sure?"

The driver looked again. "I'm sure, ma'am. That black sedan been a few cars back ever since the cemetery."

"Oh. Well, my father was an Air Force general, you know. I'll only be a few minutes. Just wait here, okay?"

"Yes, ma'am," the driver replied.

Laura pulled her veil down over her face and waited for the concierge to open her door. She took his hand, got out of the limo, and walked up the red-carpeted steps into the lobby of the hotel. She went right to the elevators. "Fourteenth floor, please." The operator nodded, surveyed the lobby, and closed the doors.

Laura stepped out on the fourteenth floor. She opened her purse, found her room key, walked to her room, and opened the door.

"Who's that?" a shrill voice with a cutting New York accent called out above the blaring television.

"It's me, Laura. It's okay," she replied. "Are you ready?"

"Huh?"

Laura turned off the TV. "Put on your veil and your hat."

The woman did as she was told.

Laura said, "Your wig's on crooked. Come here. That's better," she said as she straightened the wig that matched her own dark brown hair. "The limo's out front. The driver is going to take you to the memorial dinner for my father. All you have to do is sit in the car."

"And what happens after I get there?" the woman whined.

"Go to the ladies' room. Take the wig and your veil off, then find your name at the table and enjoy the banquet."

"I'm not sure I like any of this," the woman moaned.

Laura dug into her purse and produced a wad of bills. She put a crisp, fifty-dollar bill in the girl's hand. "Everything is going to be fine. You're from an escort service, right?"

The woman nodded.

"You're getting a ride in a limo and a free dinner, not to mention your fee, plus my generous tip." She put another fifty in the woman's hand.

"I'm not going to get in trouble, am I?"

Laura put yet another fifty in the woman's palm. "I promise, just enjoy yourself. That's all you have to do. Now let's get you out the door."

As they walked toward the door, Laura realized that her dress was damp and wrinkled from the rain, but her double's was not. "Hold on—come in here first." She led her into the bathroom.

"What are you going to do?"

Laura turned on the faucet. "Your dress is dry and mine is wet." She gathered water in her hand and patted the dress. After going back and forth from the sink to the dress half a dozen times, they looked reasonably the same. She stepped back and looked at their reflection in the mirror.

"Great, let's get you out of here." She led the woman to the door. "Now what are you going to do?" she prompted.

"Get in the limo, and change in the ladies' room when we get to the dinner. Oh yeah, and have fun."

"Leave the wig and veil in the trash can in the ladies room," Laura reminded her.

Laura put one last fifty in her double's palm and pushed her out the door. She watched with satisfaction as the woman got into the elevator and vanished from sight.

Laura hurried into the bathroom, where she changed out of her wet dress. She pulled her suitcase from the closet and got the special laptop computer that her father had given her. It had a built-in wireless internet connection. It also contained an encryption device that allowed her to send scrambled messages, which, because of the prearranged code that changed every twenty-four hours, were almost impossible to crack.

She logged on and went to the Spiral of Life website, which, if one knew the proper passwords, was a direct connection to Johanen. She used the prearranged code and informed whoever was monitoring the site of her flight information, and more importantly that she was carrying the disk, as her father had wished, directly to Johanen. She sent the message, closed her laptop, and tucked it away in her handbag.

Half an hour later, she left her room carrying a single bag, and walked to the elevator.

She rode down to the lobby and called for a bellman.

"Can you get me a cab, please?" she asked.

"Ri'way," said the young man as he hurried out of the lobby.

Moments later he returned. "Cab's outside. Get your bags, ma'am?" he asked.

Laura smiled and nodded.

He led them through the lobby. On the way Laura looked at her reflection in the large beveled mirrors on the walls of the lobby, and thought, *I've always thought I looked great as a redhead. And the hair goes so well with my green eyes.* She blinked, feeling the unfamiliar green contact lenses.

Laura tipped the bellman as she got into the cab.

"Where to?" the driver smiled, not concealing his delight at having such a beautiful fare.

Laura smiled. "Dulles Airport, please." She crossed her legs and settled back in the seat, sure that she had given the slip to the men who had trailed her. *I wonder when they're going to catch on,* she thought.

The cab pulled out from under the canopy and was met by a downpour of rain mixed with hail. "Lousy weather, yeah?" the cabbie commented.

Laura shifted in her seat and folded her hands on her lap. She felt the disk that she had taped to the top of her panty hose, and wondered for the thousandth time why her father had waited until after his death to reveal its existence to her. What secrets did it contain? Is that why her own government had sent two men to follow her every move? Had they somehow found out about it?

Only hours after the death of her father, the same two men who had followed her to the cemetery had knocked on her door, produced the appropriate warrants, and confiscated many of General Nathan's papers. They never found his secret room, though, which contained highly classified information he had gathered during his career.

She would deliver the disk to Johanen as she had promised. Then it would be decoded, and she would know the answer to the mystery.

12

※ ⦿ ※

Cornwall, England

How many more of these are there?" Mac asked, as they went through their fourth checkpoint operated by special British military forces.

Captain Ian McAllister, who was Mac and Austin's British connection and head of the team researching the crop circle, glanced in his mirror at MacKenzie. "Won't be long now, we're almost there." He accelerated the Mercedes down a wooded stretch of road in the southern part of the English countryside, near the coastal city of Cornwall.

The car slowed as they came to yet another checkpoint. McAllister showed a pass, and they were let through.

"How do they keep all the locals out?" Mac asked.

"Cover story. Toxic chemical spill," Austin grunted.

"What about the farmer?" Mac queried. "Does he have a family?"

Captain McAllister clicked his tongue producing a slight tick. "He's very upset, of course. Apparently he saw the UFO as it left the field. He's been paid quite a sum of money to keep this to himself. We've relocated him and his family, at least for the present."

"Neighbors?" Mac asked.

"All civilian personnel have been evacuated from the area."

"Is there any, uh . . . change in . . ." Mac cleared his throat. "In him?"

"He's in a trancelike state, similar to what the yogis in India achieve," McAllister answered.

"Oh," Mac replied.

An awkward silence followed, then the captain spoke up. "It happened in a field similar to the one over there." He pointed out his window.

Mac leaned in front of Colonel Austin, trying to get a better look.

"It looks like wheat," Mac said.

"Yes, Mr. MacKenzie, wheat it is. The circle is in the next field over, just past that hedgerow there."

The car swung into a rutted driveway up a small hill and Mac got his first look at the site. "You guys don't waste a minute, do you?" he commented, as he eyeballed the tent city that swarmed with military and scientific personnel.

The car turned into a field used as a parking lot and pulled up alongside a hospital ambulance.

"They've got a medical team monitoring the subject," Austin said, referring to Mac's father's body.

McAllister shut off the engine. "If you'll follow me, I'll get you suited up."

Mac threw a look at Austin. "Suited up?"

"Prevent any contamination to, or from, the subject," McAllister answered, leading the way. "Just a precaution, Mr. MacKenzie."

McAllister led them into a tent that billowed out like a monstrous white pumpkin, inflated by forced air supplied by a nearby generator.

"This way," McAllister said, as he disappeared inside.

Mac followed and found himself in what he imagined was the control center. An array of large video monitors were set on desks, arranged in a semicircle, with half a dozen technicians in front of them. They all showed the same picture but from different angles: a naked body resting face up in the center of a crop circle in a field of wheat. "There he is," Austin grunted.

Mac just stared.

"We've got aerial photos as well," McAllister said. "As soon as you're suited up, I'll give you a look-see."

"I can't wait," Mac muttered to himself.

"Try this one," McAllister said, handing Mac a one-piece white suit.

Mac was surprised how light the material was.

"The suit is made from a variety of synthetic materials," McAllister expalined. "Very strong, but lightweight. It's the same suit we use when handling victims who have contracted Ebola. Keeps those nasty microbes out. Just slip it on over your clothes."

Mac did as he was instructed.

"Leave off your hood and filtration mask until we need them," McAllister said. "I've selected some stills from the video." He nodded toward a woman sergeant who sat in front of several small monitors, each corresponding to a different camera, which she controlled remotely.

Mac and Austin followed McAllister to the monitoring consoles. "This is Corporal Smythe. She's responsible for all the video and camera data, from the first shots we took until the present." Captain McAllister turned to the technician. "Corporal, go to the aerial photos first and zoom in from there. And please pay special attention to the location of the body as it relates to the crop circle."

Mac and Austin crowded around and watched. The screen went dark, and a moment later Mac got his first look at the crop circle.

McAllister took a pencil and pointed on the screen. "This is an aerial view of the crop circle or pictograph taken just before we sealed off the site. The field itself is about twenty acres and the pictograph in the center covers almost two acres. It's a very complex one, showing the planets of our solar system and the lunar eclipse. But look here." McAllister pointed to the space between Earth and the Moon. "What does that look like to you?" he asked Mac.

Mac stared at the object placed between the Moon and Earth in the crop circle. "Maybe a star?" Mac responded.

"But of course there is no star there. By the way, a total lunar eclipse is due this month, with the point of greatest eclipse appearing somewhere in the Middle East. So the timing appears to be no accident."

Mac stared at the image, trying not to notice the small white spot in the center.

"And here's the subject . . . at the center of what would correspond to earth," McAllister said. "You know, Mr. MacKenzie, I've been studying these for nearly twenty years. This one is unique."

"Because of the subject?" Colonel Austin asked.

"Yes," McAllister agreed.

"Are they all like this?" Mac asked. "So intricate?"

"Some are simple in design, a circle in a field of wheat or rape seed, while others, like the one here, are very complex."

"How do you know that my father's body and the crop circle are linked together? The crop circle might have been first, then his body added later," Mac suggested.

"No," McAllister said with certainty. "Remember, we have the farmer's own testimony of the UFO sighting."

"So he saw the UFO put the body there?" Mac asked.

McAllister shook his head. "No, not exactly, but when the UFO left he went out to get a closer look at the circle, and that's when he saw the subject . . . gave the old bloke quite a start." He paused for a moment. "Let me give you a bit of information on the formations in general, if I may."

Mac folded his arms and waited.

"At first when these crop circles were spotted, most people thought them to be hoaxes, and indeed, two men came forward and announced that they were the ones making some of the circles, using string and boards."

"So the mystery was solved?" Mac asked.

"Hardly. It was a cover story that *our* government used to keep the lid on the UFO phenomena in general, and to insure that our population wouldn't begin to panic at the thought of extraterrestrial involvement. Are you aware that the plants themselves have been tested and have been found to undergo chemical and biological changes?"

"Such as?" Mac asked.

"Well for one, the plant inside the circle takes up more nitrates than those outside."

"Anything else?"

"There are electromagnetic anomalies. Compasses spin, batteries often lose their charge."

"Are there electromagnetic anomalies in this instance?"

"Yes, especially around your father's . . . sorry about that. Around the body." He clicked his tongue again.

Mac saw Corporal Smythe fidget in her chair. He stared at the picture of the crop circle, paying attention to the star-like image between Earth and the Moon and wondered what it could mean.

McAllister continued. "As I was saying, there is a record of a circle dating as far back as 1678. It took place in Herefordshire. It's a woodcut showing a circle in a field of oats . . . and the devil mowing it."

Mac eyed the man. "Do you believe that? In a literal devil mowing it?"

McAllister chuckled. "Well, of course not a *literal* devil. Superstition and all of that, MacKenzie."

Mac shook his head and glanced at Austin. "You'd do well to take a second look at that woodcut. I think it is the answer to who's behind all of this."

Captain McAllister looked puzzled. "Well, I'll take your suggestion to heart, Mr. MacKenzie. Now look here. Corporal Smythe, please zoom in on the subject."

The body grew larger on the screen. Mac saw an elderly man with thinning gray hair. The skin was smooth and hairless and the body had very little fat on it.

McAllister began again. "As I said earlier, it's almost as if he were asleep."

Mac nodded and leaned closer for a better look. "That's him. This proves I wasn't making things up. I'm exonerated." He turned to leave.

Austin put out his hand. "Not yet, Mac. Give them a chance."

"Look, I've just made a positive ID on him, okay? So we can go now. I'm finished here."

McAllister looked concerned. "Mr. MacKenzie, I appreciate how you must feel, but—"

"You can't possibly understand anything about how I feel," Mac shot back.

"I'm sorry, of course you're right," he apologized. "I believe, Mr. MacKenzie, that whoever put this here is trying to tell us something . . . to send us a message, if you will."

"Your point being?" Mac asked.

"Well, Mr. MacKenzie, it points one toward the unthinkable."

Mac turned so that he was face-to-face with Captain McAllister. "Let's go back to the woodcut," he said. "It shows the devil cutting the circle, right?"

McAllister nodded.

"That's your unthinkable," Mac stated. "Captain, you're looking at the supernatural. It's not aliens that are doing this. It's the same guy who's in your woodcut—and his buddies."

McAllister didn't conceal his scorn. "I appreciate what you're saying, Mr. MacKenzie, but really, the thought of a devil—well, much of that rubbish died out long ago, thankfully, with the dawning of the Age of Reason."

"Look at the body, Captain," Mac challenged. "He should have been dead by now. Look how young the skin appears. And I'll tell you something else." He lowered his voice. "The last time I had actual contact with him, or maybe I should say 'it,' was undoubtedly the worst moment of my life. I can guarantee you that whatever, or whoever, inhabits his body, his shell, isn't human."

"So you're saying that it's not your father?" McAllister asked.

"The body is, but not the soul."

McAllister nodded. "Well, let's have a look at it then, shall we?"

Mac looked at Austin, hoping for a reprieve. Austin's face remained a study in stone. Mac took a deep breath. "Okay, let's get this stinking thing over with."

"You'll want to put your hood on and make sure your breathing mask is tightly fastened," McAllister instructed.

They suited up then walked to the side of the tent and passed through a shower of steam, and then proceeded into a tube that extended into the field.

"The steam has disinfectants in it . . . sterilizes any contaminants," McAllister explained, as he and Mac waited for Colonel Austin to pass through the steam bath. "We have the area around the body isolated. This tube keeps an artificial air supply pumped to the larger tent that covers the center of the crop circle, keeping the temperature at a constant. It's several hundred yards away, so it will take some time for us to reach it."

The men walked in silence. When they exited the tube Mac was under another air-inflated tent. "What are they doing to him?" he asked, as he noticed a variety of medical equipment surrounding the body, connected to it by tubes and wires, and a series of monitors set up on a table a short distance away.

"Monitoring his heart and vital functions."

They walked closer, and Mac was now just a few feet away from his father's body.

McAllister pointed to a machine hooked up to the body. "His heartbeat is very slow, and it appears that he's in a sort of suspended state."

Mac forced himself to look at the face. He nodded his head. "It's him."

"He was supposed to have been murdered years ago, right?" McAllister asked.

"Yeah."

"And you're sure it's him? No mistake?" McAllister asked.

"Yep."

"What connection might he have with the crop circle phenomena?" McAllister asked.

"He's connected to it in every way possible," Mac stated.

"How so?"

"Didn't Colonel Austin tell you guys anything?" Mac asked.

"Only that you claimed to have had contact with a man, presumably your father, who was supposed to have died years ago."

"Then you don't know what you're dealing with here," Mac stated.

"What do you mean, Mr. MacKenzie?"

Mac continued. "This is what I've been able to piece together . . . from him," and Mac nodded toward the body of his father, "and also General Nathan."

McAllister raised his eyebrows. "General Nathan?"

"The man who, along with my father, had contact with the ETs at Roswell."

"The UFO crash in 1947?"

"Yes, '47," Mac confirmed. "My father handled one of the surviving bodies and established a relationship with it telepathically. As the creature lay dying, it asked to inhabit my father, to share his shell. He agreed, and when he did, the aliens changed his name to Abaris. His murder was then faked by some rogue wing of our government, and my unsuspecting mother and I buried somebody else in his place."

"All these years passed, and you had no contact with him?" McAllister asked.

"Nothing, until General Nathan became involved in my life. And I have to tell you, there are times when I wish the whole thing were nothing more than a bad dream."

"Well, the body isn't a dream," McAllister replied.

"I'm not certain of the way this whole thing is put together. I don't think anyone is. But I'll tell you something. It's a deception. It just sucks you in, and you start to believe that there really are aliens. ETs from who knows where. Captain McAllister, they're not what you think. It's all a clever ruse . . . to deceive us."

Mac was interrupted by a doctor standing next to the body. "Captain, something's happening here."

"What is it?" McAllister asked.

"His heart is beating faster," the doctor replied.

Mac felt his stomach flip. He turned to Austin. "That's our cue. Let's get out of here."

"His respiration is quickening," a woman called out.

A soldier emerged at a run from the plastic tube. "Captain, we have an unidentified object on radar, and it's approaching fast."

Mac looked at the body of his father and noticed that the chest was now heaving. He backed off a few paces toward the tube. "Colonel, I don't want to be around if he wakes up. Let's get out of here now."

"My word, what—" McAllister began.

The tent shot up into the air and disappeared. In its place, directly above, was the orange glow of a UFO. The wheat began to dance in all directions from the cyclonic wind emanating from the saucer.

McAllister stared bug-eyed at it, unable to move.

Mac took one slow step backward before everything went berserk.

An intense beam of white light shot out from the craft and hit the body of Mac's father, pulling it to a sitting position.

Abaris's eyes flicked open.

A woman holding several vials of drawn blood screamed as she backed away, bumping into Mac and dropping the vials.

Abaris reached down and tore the monitoring tubes and wires off his body. He glared at Mac.

Mac took another step back and came alongside Austin, who was transfixed by what was taking place.

Captain McAllister stepped forward with his palms turned out in a gesture of peace. "Who are you, and how can we help you?" he shouted.

The beam intensified, and Abaris began to rise in the air. He floated toward McAllister, who remained with hands outstretched. Without warning, Abaris reached out, grabbed McAllister by the throat, and began to choke him. McAllister's eyes rolled back in his head.

Austin ran to help McAllister, but Mac was frozen with fear. He stared at his father's bulging yellow eyes and felt as if he was in a nightmare. All he wanted was to be far away from what was happening around him.

Abaris threw McAllister aside as if he were made of straw; the soldier disappeared into the wheat.

"My son! My son!" Abaris yelled, reaching toward Mac.

Mac willed himself to move and managed a few steps backward, but too late; his father had hold of him.

Mac's fear turned to rage. He came to life and punched with all his might, but the blow went wild and glanced off Abaris's shoulder.

Abaris's yellow eyes bulged. Still holding Mac, he yelled in his face, "I am the harbinger of the New Christ! Behold, he is the way!"

Terrified, Mac twisted in his father's grasp as his father pulled him upward; in no time he was dangling several feet above the ground.

Colonel Austin dove at Mac, tackling him around his legs. The extra weight broke Abaris's grip.

Mac tumbled to the ground, stunned by the impact.

"He is coming! The true might of the world! And he is terrible to behold!" Abaris shouted.

Austin grabbed Mac's shoulder and dragged him to his feet. "Let's go! Let's go!" he yelled.

The wind from the saucer was growing in intensity, whipping the cables that had been attached to Abaris into a flurry of Medusa-like tentacles. One of the monitors vibrated on its base, then hurtled through the air, taking out a portion of the plastic connecting tube, which collapsed. People fled in all directions.

Mac and Austin ducked into an undamaged piece of the tube and ran toward the control center.

"Where is it now, Smythe?" a technician who had fled alongside Mac yelled as they entered the control center.

"Hovering in the same place," Corporal Smythe answered.

"Do we have any of this on film?" a senior officer asked.

"Everything," Smythe answered.

Audio crackled over the speakers that were set directly next to the monitors. Above the sound of the whirling wind, Mac heard his crazed father utter a string of vile obscenities at the top of his lungs.

"Turn the speakers off!" Mac yelled. As he tore off his face mask and hood, he saw someone enter the tent. Mac elbowed Austin and pointed.

The man was stout of build, with broad shoulders and short, sturdy legs. A great mane of white hair, combed straight back from his forehead, hung almost to his shoulders, contrasting with his tanned, weathered face.

The man met Mac's gaze with two piercing blue eyes. He walked toward Mac, stopping a few feet from him.

"You have forgotten your most powerful weapon," were the first words from the stranger's lips.

"What?"

"You have forgotten to take authority over what is out there, MacKenzie. As you know by now, *you* are no match for

what is taking place in the field. But he who resides in you is."
The man gestured toward one of the monitors, which showed
the UFO increasing the chaos in the wheat field.

"How did you know who I—" Mac started to ask.

"I am Johanen," the man said, cutting him off. "Now we
must not waste anymore time. MacKenzie, Colonel Austin—"
He dropped to one knee, and pulled Mac down with him. Johanen stared at Austin who, speechless, bent down on one knee.

Johanen stretched out both his hands, and with his eyes
blazing cried out, "In the name of the most holy God, you
have no claim on this land or these people. You must leave. In
the power of the Lord, you are driven from here."

Mac's eyes darted from Johanen to the crowd around the
monitor—how crazy this old man must look to them!

"Look, something is happening!" the woman operating
the remote video cameras cried. "The UFO is wobbling."

"Is it about to crash?" Smythe asked.

The officer next to Smythe looked up, noticed Mac and
the others kneeling, and was just walking toward them when
two terrified people, dragging Captain McAllister between
them, burst from the tube.

"He's out cold!" one of them yelled, as they lay McAllister
down on the floor of the tent.

The officer hurried toward McAllister. Mac turned his
attention back to Johanen, who continued to shout out in his
strong voice, "In the name of Jesus of Nazareth, the Lord
rebuke you, for you have no power here and must leave."

At least the swearing stopped, Mac thought. The crazed
voice of his father had finally ceased.

"Focus yourself, MacKenzie. Pray as best you can," Johanen admonished. "Use the authority you have been given."

Mac didn't know where to begin, too caught up in the
craziness around him.

"It's leaving, sir!" Smythe yelled out.

"Where is the body?" the officer who was bent over McAllister shouted.

"It floated up into the belly of the craft . . . but wait. I'm having trouble seeing it. Something else is happening," Smythe answered.

Then Mac heard it—a torrential downpour of rain that engulfed the tent.

"Look at that—the storm came out of nowhere," Smythe said.

Johanen tugged Mac to his feet. "Follow me, MacKenzie, Austin. It's time for us to go." He turned and hurried out of the tent, followed by a bewildered Mac and an equally confused Colonel Austin.

13

National Defense Ministry,
Tel Aviv, Israel

Deep below the streets of Tel Aviv, an Israeli air defense radar operator sipped from his coffee mug as his eyes continued to scan the monitor in front of him. He had another fifteen minutes before his relief and he looked forward to it. It was past four in the morning and he was tired. All the operators worked only two-hour shifts. This lessened the chances of error, as studies had found that after two hours of staring at the radar screen, eyestrain and mental fatigue began to set in. The Israeli armed forces maintained constant readiness, as the threat of war hovered over the small country like an unwanted specter. Because of the ongoing threat of war, they had designed and built two special underground aircraft hangars, one in the north and the other in the south of the country. A series of bunkers were constructed next to a long runway. Each bunker could hold up to four jets and had ramps that led up to the runway. But in certain designated hangars one jet would have its turbines on and its pilot suited up and at the ready in the cockpit, twenty-four hours a day, seven days a week. In the event of an intruder into Israeli airspace, the pilot could taxi up the ramp and be on the runway and airborne in less than a minute.

Shlomo sipped his coffee again, and his eyes darted to something on the edge of his screen. Whatever it was moved very fast and on a straight trajectory. He cleared his throat. "I've got something . . . a bogey on my screen, and it's approaching our air space," he said to the woman next to him, who monitored a screen of her own.

"Are you sure?" She threw a glance toward Shlomo's screen.

Shlomo adjusted his monitor. "It's coming in very fast."

"Maybe a missile?" the woman suggested.

Shlomo pushed the red button that was next to his console. Moments later an Israeli colonel rushed in.

"Sir, I have a bogey on the screen . . . here." He pointed at the red blip that had now moved into Israeli air space.

"Missile?" the colonel asked.

"I don't think so, sir. It first appeared here"—he pointed—"the Mediterranean. No radio contact. I've confirmed it as unidentified. It's on a descending trajectory."

"Speed and projected target?" the colonel asked.

"Mach 3, and it appears to be headed here." Shlomo let his index finger swirl above the screen corresponding to the Negev desert in the southernmost part of Israel.

The colonel frowned. "Let's scramble an intercept."

"Yes, sir," a woman officer answered, and immediately relayed the order from her console.

Shlomo switched his screen to the view from the satellite which the United States had launched for Israel. Its orbit was in GEO synchronization over the country and it aided the Israelis in keeping a watch over their hostile neighbors.

"Looks more like a comet of some sort," the colonel muttered. "Look at the trail it's leaving."

Shlomo scanned the screen again. "That could be rocket exhaust, sir."

The colonel grabbed a chair and slid next to Shlomo. By now other officers and operators had crowded around Shlomo's station.

"I think it's slowing down," another operator said.

"Yes, I see it," Shlomo agreed. "It is . . . slowing down."

"What could possibly do that?" The woman operator was also monitoring the bogey.

"We have two jets that are headed toward the bogey," Shlomo stated. He pointed toward two blips on his screen moving toward the bogey. He did a few calculations using the special protractor that was part of his screen. "Estimated time till visual, seven minutes."

"Look at that—what just happened?" the colonel said.

Shlomo stared at his screen, then rubbed his eyes to make sure he wasn't seeing things.

"I think the thing has stopped . . . I think it's landed . . . in the desert."

"Terrorist maybe," someone suggested.

"No, no, look," Shlomo said. "It seems to be moving again."

"I'm confirming that the bogey is moving," the operator next to Shlomo agreed.

"Do we have a visual yet?" the colonel asked.

Shlomo shook his head. "Negative, sir. Our planes are too far out."

"Will you look at that?" someone exclaimed behind Shlomo.

Shlomo stared in disbelief at his screen. "Impossible . . . nothing can accelerate that fast."

"Incredible," the colonel agreed. The cluster of people stared at the red blip on the screen.

"Switch back to the satellite view," the colonel ordered.

The group watched as whatever it was headed out of the earth's atmosphere and disappeared.

A moment's silence, then the colonel said, "Give me a printout of the exact location where the thing landed. I'll turn it over to the ground forces and let them see if there is anything out there."

"Yes, sir," Shlomo said.

* ◦ *

In a desolate part of the Negev desert, a hooded figure watched the trail of what might have been mistaken as a comet until it disappeared in the millions of stars overhead. He knelt down and picked up a handful of sand. *It is good to be on the earth again,* he thought, as he let the grains slowly fall away between his fingers.

14

✦ ◉ ✦

Vatican City, Rome

A young priest with a shock of red hair and a boyish face knocked on the carved door of Cardinal Fiorre's private study, deep inside the cloistered sanctuary of the Vatican. "Cardinal Fiorre? I brought the manuscripts you asked for," he called from the doorway.

Fiorre glanced up and pushed his reading glasses down the bridge of his nose to get a better view. "Is that you, Father Thomas?" Fiorre squinted again, recognizing the familiar face of his aide. "Here, Thomas, let me clear a place for them." Fiorre rose from his velvet-backed chair and moved one pile of papers and several manuscripts to the side of his desk. "Set them here." He patted the top of the desk with his palms.

"Do you think there's something that will give you a clue to the puzzle in these?" Thomas asked, as he laid the manuscripts on the desk.

"One never knows, Thomas. His Holiness has exhorted me to leave no stone unturned, and that is what I intend to do with all my resolve."

Thomas nodded and took his seat at the edge of Fiorre's desk. "You were going to show me something yesterday and never did," he gently reminded the cardinal.

Fiorre grinned at the younger man, seeing through his attempts to mask his impatience. "Yes, Thomas, but you must promise me that what I will show you will not leave the sanctity of this room."

Thomas placed his hand on the crease of his dark trousers and leaned forward. "Your Eminence, you know you are like a father to me."

Fiorre chuckled. "And you like a son, Thomas. Now look closely, and remember that what I am about to show you is not conclusive, but it is what I've been able to amass, at least for the present."

Thomas nodded and waited as Fiorre moved several stacks of papers out of the way. He opened the top drawer of his desk, pulled out a black binder, and set it in front of him.

"Thomas, look here." Fiorre opened it to the first page showing a black-and-white photograph.

"A party," Thomas offered.

"Yes, but a very special one, and it was in fact, a gala hosted by this man." Fiorre turned the page, the picture showing a man towering over several other men who gave him their undivided attention.

"He has a noticeably ugly scar over his eye. Who is he?"

"His name is Anton Wyan, and he is a very wealthy man. He was throwing this gala. But it was more than just a party, for he was seeking donations for the Leukemia Foundation."

"A fund-raiser then?" Thomas queried.

"Most definitely, and an expensive one at that. Look here." Fiorre turned another page. "In this picture he's shown donating a very large sum of money, and here's the oversize check so that all can see and of course follow his example and contribute."

Thomas pointed to the many onlookers in the photo, who were applauding. "He seems well intentioned and generous with his money. A man to be extolled for his charity."

Fiorre nodded. "Appearances can fool you, Thomas. What if I were to tell you that a close protégé of his claims to be a direct descendant of our Lord?"

Thomas's face clouded over, and he looked confused. "By that do you mean that he is somehow able to trace his lineage to James, the Lord's brother?"

"A very good guess, Thomas, and theologically sound, but Wyan has indicated that his associate, this man"—and Fiorre turned the page to show a picture of a good-looking young man standing next to Wyan—"is *Desposyni*, or of the blood-line of Jesus himself."

"Impossible," Thomas muttered.

"Of course, impossible to those of us who cling to the true faith, but nevertheless this man believes it, and flaunts it when the occasion suits his purpose. It is what is called the Monrovingian heresy," Fiorre informed the younger man. "Wyan believes that he is of the true lineage of our Lord. You are aware that many crowned heads in Europe trace their ancestry to the alleged offspring of Jesus and Mary Magdalene."

Thomas shook his head. "Hasn't the church condemned this?"

"Yes, but it has a way of resurfacing and has done so periodically for almost two millennia. It is a heresy, and a damnable one at that."

"Do you think that he is the one you have been looking for?" Thomas asked.

Fiorre shrugged. "One can never tell, but look here, Thomas." He went to the middle of the book. "Here is another shot taken later that evening."

"A magic show?" Thomas asked.

"Yes, I suppose you could call it that, but a very interesting one."

"This is the same person who is doing the trick?" Thomas asked.

"Yes, and his name is Kenson. I assure you that the photograph is not a trick . . . at least not one that you've seen before."

"He's just doing a levitating trick . . . I think Houdini did a similar feat in one of his shows, if I remember correctly," Thomas offered.

"What if I were to tell you that he really did it. That the woman who is 'floating' in midair was wide awake, that several people pressed down on the body and couldn't move it, and that Kenson managed to somehow float her around the room, much to the astonishment of the guests."

"Incredible," Thomas gasped. "So he may have real power. Is he the one then?"

Fiorre adjusted his reading glasses and leaned forward to examine the next photograph, ignoring Thomas's question. "I'm preparing this for his Holiness."

"His Holiness will be very troubled by your communiqué," Thomas stated.

"That is why I must be sure. Look here at this close-up of Kenson's hands." Fiorre gestured toward another photo.

"The man has six fingers," Thomas said. A look of astonishment passed over his face.

"I see you're troubled, Thomas, but I applaud you on remembering what I told you . . . more than two years ago, wasn't it?"

Thomas nodded.

"Six fingers on each hand, Thomas. He's one of them, of that I am sure, and although I'm not certain that he is the one, I am confident that he is a hybrid or, if you prefer, one of the Nephilim."

"I can't believe it, Your Eminence. It is almost too fantastic."

"And yet we see the possibilities of such, here in the photographs."

"And what now?" Thomas asked.

"Those manuscripts you brought for me may prove to have some insight into Kenson's true lineage."

Thomas looked confused again.

"But while I peruse the manuscripts, can you make me some tea?" Fiorre asked.

"As you wish, Your Eminence." Thomas rose from his chair and left the room.

＊ ○ ＊

Ten minutes later, after Thomas had brought the tea and left, Fiorre rose from his chair and locked his door. Going back to his desk he withdrew a manuscript from a false bottom in the second drawer. He turned to the first tattered page and crossed himself before he began to read. He slowly turned the pages, crossing himself every time. He came to a series of photographs that had been taken with a very high-powered infrared telephoto lens. They showed the incredible transformation of a man into what Fiorre considered an abomination. Although the photos were taken as the man was getting into a car and therefore didn't document the entire transformation, enough of it was caught on film for Fiorre to know that the man he had come to know as Wyan was something far more sinister.

He finished reading, replaced the manuscript under the false drawer bottom, and adjusted the monitor of his computer closer to him. He logged on and typed in *www.spiraloflife.com*. He waited for the image of Michelangelo's finger of God, with the double helix of DNA emanating from the extended finger. *Ah, the gift of life,* Fiorre mused, as he looked at the logo. He had prided himself in keeping abreast of the important scientific breakthroughs in his lifetime, and was well acquainted with the complexities of deoxyribonucleic acid, or DNA. He clicked on the index finger and entered the site. He unlocked the top desk drawer, pulled out a series of codes, and looked at the date corresponding to the grid of numbers. He punched in the correct data, and was admitted.

He had met the man who ran the organization, Johanen. He had marveled at his knowledge of Scripture, and shared his love of their Savior, Jesus. He began to type his message, which included the pictures he had scanned, and added the proper encryption code. He watched as his message was scrambled into a hopeless jumble of numbers and letters ten times as long as he actually had written. He closed his computer down and went back to his studies with the satisfaction that Johanen would soon receive the important news.

15

Philadelphia

Helen clutched her purse and hesitated a moment before climbing the steps that led to the bank. She opened the door and stood just inside the entrance. She assured herself that this was the right bank, the same one indicated in her father's letter, stuffed in her purse.

It was the noon hour, and Helen had skipped lunch at her workplace, driving instead to Center City in Philadelphia where the bank was located. She was unsure of what to do next, not having accessed a safe-deposit box before, and felt nervous as she walked up to one of the tellers.

"Can I help you?" an Asian woman with bright red lipstick asked.

Helen put her purse down on the counter. "Yes, I think so. I want to check on a safe-deposit box."

"May I see some ID, please?" the teller asked.

Helen fumbled in her purse, produced her ID.

"What number?" the teller asked, as she handed the ID back.

"What?" Helen looked confused.

"The number of the safe-deposit box."

"Oh . . . wait a minute." Helen looked in her purse again. She brought out her father's letter along with the key. "Number 33062," she said, reading the numbers off the key.

The teller punched the numbers in her computer. "If you'll follow me." She closed her window and walked to the side of the counter.

Helen followed. The teller opened the door, let her in, then locked it again.

"In here." She pointed to a large open vault with a barred door that she opened with another key.

"What was the number again?" she asked.

Helen looked at the key in her hand. "33062."

The teller found the box and set it on a table in the vault. "You can stay here as long as you like. Just let me know when you're done." She smiled at Helen and left the vault, locking the door behind her.

Helen stared at the box in front of her. She had barely slept and was practically useless at her job. Her mind was a jumble of conflicting thoughts and emotions.

She looked through the bars of the door out into the bank and realized, to her relief, that no one was paying any attention to her.

She stared at the key she held in her hand, so tight that the ends of her fingers were white. *I'm afraid,* she admitted. She placed the key next to the box on the table. *I'll just sit for a moment and catch my breath.*

A minute passed, and a middle-aged black man wearing a finely tailored suit stopped in front of the barred door, looked at some papers he was holding, and then disappeared from view.

This is stupid, she said to herself. *I'm just going to open this now. I don't care what's in it. It can't possibly mess up my life any more than it is already.* She shivered as she pictured herself being examined aboard a UFO. *What can possibly be worse than that?*

She picked up the key and inserted it into the keyhole. Then she took her hand away and stared at it again. She realized that her throat had gone dry, and her temples were glistening with sweat.

She wiped her forehead. "This is ridiculous, Helen," she scolded herself aloud.

She sat forward in the chair, and with one quick motion sprang the lock and opened the box.

"Oh, my," she gasped. She quickly looked out the barred door to the vault. Reassuring herself that no one was watching, she picked up one of the stacks of hundred dollar bills that were inside it. *How much is in here?* she wondered. She counted the stacks and realized that there was a good deal of money in front of her. *There's got to be well over a quarter of a million dollars,* she told herself.

She explored the rest of the box and found another sealed envelope. She set the wad of bills back in the box and opened the letter. There were more pictures of this strange man who claimed to be her father, with her mother.

"Why didn't she tell me about him?" she mumbled angrily.

She opened the letter and began to read, sometimes rereading the same sentence two or three times to make sure she understood everything.

She finished the letter and started to cry. She covered her face with her hands and turned her chair so that it faced away from the door.

"Are you ready yet?" She recognized the Asian teller's voice calling her.

She choked a sob back. "No, not yet." She waited a moment, and checked to see if the woman was still there.

Satisfied that she was alone, she read the last page of the letter again. She transferred some of the money into her purse along with the letter. Then she closed the box, locked it, and slid it back in place on the wall in front of her.

She walked to the door. "I'm finished," she called.

The teller came over, opened the door, and Helen stepped out of the vault.

"Did you get everything you needed?" she asked.

Helen nodded, too stunned to answer.

"Good. Have a nice day," the teller said, as she let Helen out from behind the counter.

Helen walked on her low heels, pausing at the door of the bank. For the first time in her life she felt a new emotion. There was lightness, too, in her heart. She stepped outside the bank and felt the noonday sun hit her full in the face. *Is this what hope is?* she wondered, as she began to walk toward her car.

16

England

"Wait . . ." Mac yelled as they ran down the driveway. He dropped to his knees and vomited.

Johanen and Austin, who were several yards ahead of Mac, turned and hurried back to him. "Are you all right, Mac?" Johanen asked.

Mac shook his head and stood up. "No. Seeing him again and feeling the evil . . . It was like I was reliving the encounter at the underground base all over again."

Johanen rested his hand on Mac's chest. As he did, Mac felt as if a weight had been lifted from him. His mind cleared.

"Is he okay?" Austin asked.

"He will be," Johanen reassured him. "Come—we must hurry, Mac."

"How did you know where to find us?" Mac asked, as they began to run again down the gravel driveway of the farm.

"Not now, Mac, let us get to the boat first," Johanen called over his shoulder.

He's in incredible shape for someone his age, Mac thought as he struggled to keep up with the older man.

Mac reached the end of the drive and crossed the road. By now he was soaking wet from the rain, but he didn't mind, for it helped to keep his head clear.

"Over here," Johanen yelled. He parted a hedge and disappeared.

Mac and Austin followed, and found themselves in a field of potatoes.

"This way," Johanen instructed, setting off at a jog. They reached the end of the field, which was several hundred feet above the English coast.

"Careful, it is a bit of a drop," Johanen cautioned, as Mac and Austin caught up with him.

Mac looked over the edge. "How do you plan to get down there?" he asked, pointing below.

"There is an old trail not far from here. A little treacherous in places, but it will get us to my boat."

"Which is where? And how did you . . . I mean, where did the rain come from? And why did the UFO disappear?" Mac asked.

"All in good time, MacKenzie. Now, we must be off before you're both missed and they come looking for you." Johanen began to jog along the cliffside. "Here it is, just up ahead," he called out.

Mac got his first look at the goat trail, which descended to a small cove where Johanen's boat was anchored.

"There it is, let us go." Johanen led them down the trail.

Half an hour later they reached the cove's sandy beach.

"Can you row?" Johanen asked.

Both Mac and Austin nodded.

"Then put your backs into it," Johanen joked, as they got in. He pushed them off from the shoreline and jumped in, just as the bow left the sand.

Mac and Austin began to row while Johanen made his way to the stern of the wooden dinghy.

"You must learn to wield the authority you have over the Evil One. That, and to use your most powerful weapon, which is prayer, MacKenzie," Johanen admonished. His eyes bored into Mac.

Mac was angry. "I was too caught up in the moment."

Johanen ran the fingers of both hands through his thick white beard, combing it out from the rain. "You must understand, MacKenzie, that you might have been destroyed back there. And Colonel Austin must realize that you need to be protected, for there are those who want to take your life."

"My life?" Mac asked, astonished.

"The entity that inhabits your father's body, for one. But there are others who are part of a greater and much older cause," Johanen said, cryptically.

"What do you mean by older?" Mac asked.

"Older than the first man, Adam," Johanen replied.

Mac stopped rowing, and the dinghy began to turn off course.

"Careful, set her straight," Johanen admonished.

Mac timed his stroke with that of Austin's and the boat got back on track. "I don't know what you're talking about," Mac admitted.

"I was hoping to send Dr. Elisha to mentor you in the Way, but the same evil that would destroy you almost did the very same to him."

"Colonel Austin told me he had a stroke."

Johanen sighed. "And if not for the healing touch from the Ancient of Days, he would be dead by now."

Mac shot a glance at Austin and waited for Johanen to continue.

"As I said, evil is afoot and will stop at nothing to have its way. It is a mystery. The Mystery of Iniquity."

"Mystery of Iniquity?" Mac repeated.

Johanen continued, "Yes, led and orchestrated by the Prince of the Power of the Air. It was he who was once the most anointed angel, until iniquity was found in him and he rebelled, leading a third of the angels with him. Hold up now, and we'll drift the rest of the way." The dinghy came alongside the larger boat. "Give me the rope, and I will tie her off." Johanen climbed up the rope ladder that hung over the ship's side, holding the dinghy's mooring rope in one hand as he did so.

Mac and Austin followed, finding themselves on the deck of Johanen's boat.

"It's a converted lobster boat with a custom lead keel. She will right herself like a cork in the heaviest of seas," he commented, slapping the freshly painted gunwales.

Mac noticed that the boat sported a variety of high-tech navigational gadgetry. "What's all this?" he asked.

"Radar, global positioning, sonar, depth finder, radio, CB, shortwave, and of course, two onboard computers," Johanen stated. "Come up to the bridge, and we will continue our conversation there." Johanen bounded up an enclosed staircase that led to the bridge. He fired up the twin diesel engines, then hit the control that hoisted the anchor. The boat turned toward the opening of the cove, and moments later, crested the waves of the open sea.

Johanen took a reading from his global positioning monitor and checked it with a map. "We have a few hours before we arrive at our destination," he said.

"And just where is that?" Mac asked.

"Off the coast of France. Then we fly to the Italian Alps."

Mac gave Austin a woeful look. "There's that word again, *fly*."

"At least we're safe, Mac," Austin reminded him.

"As I was saying, the Mystery of Iniquity," Johanen began, "sometimes referred to as the Secret Power of Lawlessness, has been at work for centuries."

Mac gave Johanen a troubled look. "For centuries?" he asked.

Johanen nodded. "And it continues to this present day. You see, Mac, civilization has such a thin veneer of order and decency, manifested through the arts, science, education, and in your country, democracy. But all one needs to do is take a casual glance at history, even recent history, and one will see just how thin that veneer is."

"Like the concentration camps? Or the butchery that took place in Rwanda?" Mac asked, following Johanen's train of thought.

"Precisely," Johanen replied, "and much of this is orchestrated by the Evil One."

"So why does God allow it?" Mac asked.

"People have free will to worship God Almighty and his Messiah, or not to."

"And if they don't?" Mac asked.

"All one needs to do is look at a newspaper to see examples of that," Johanen said.

"So when will this iniquity, as you call it, end? Or does it?" Mac asked.

Johanen checked the boat's course on the global positioning monitor. "Mac, history *will* end at some point. The linear progression of humankind, as we know it, will come to a close, and the Messiah will return and rule the earth from Jerusalem."

"And the evil will end?" Mac asked.

"It will, but before it does, the Man of Lawlessness will rise to power, and he will display false miracles that will deceive many. I have begun to call it the 'Great Deception,' a name taken from a portion of Scripture which says, 'The coming of the lawless one is according to the working of Satan, with all power, signs, and lying wonders, and with all unrighteous deception.'"

"And who is that man?" Mac asked.

"No one knows, MacKenzie, but many of us feel that his time is drawing near."

"And how do the Nephilim and my father figure into this? Or do they at all?"

Johanen brushed his shaggy wet hair back from his forehead. "Yes, I believe that the Man of Lawlessness will boast of what I will call an alien connection; perhaps he will be a hybrid, the product of fallen angels and earthly women. At any rate, part of the deception will be to make people believe that the aliens have come to help usher us into a golden age, a new age of world peace and harmony. Of course, many will be deceived by the miracles and signs and wonders which will accompany this." Before Johanen could say anything more, he was distracted by something that appeared on his radar. "Something is coming toward us very fast," he snapped. "Look here." He pointed at the screen.

Mac and Austin drew nearer.

"Whew! It's moving all right," Austin exclaimed.

"It is close enough that we should be able to see it," Johanen said.

"Look out," Mac yelled, as something that looked like an orange fireball streaked past the boat, making it rock back and forth.

"I believe it is the same ship that hovered over your father," Johanen said.

"Yeah, it had the same insignia on its bottom, an inverted V with three horizontal lines at the base. It's him. He found us . . . we're not safe anywhere." Mac trembled.

"Not true, MacKenzie. It streaked past us, but I promise it can do little more than that."

"Why?" Mac asked

"MacKenzie, we are surrounded by the hosts of heaven. Although you can't see them, they are near."

Mac shot Austin a look of disbelief, which Austin returned with an I-don't-know-what-he-means-by-that-either look.

Johanen continued, "The Mystery of Iniquity is at work, but it is not all-powerful, and those who serve it cannot come and go and do whatever they please, unhindered."

"Yeah, but they do seem to have the upper hand most of the time," Mac shot back.

"Only from your perspective, MacKenzie. The enemy knows his time is near. It is a time of lawlessness, when the Son of Perdition—another of the many names for him—will have power to do amazing things, but his power will be from Satan himself. He will use it to destroy and lead people away from the Holy One of Israel and direct them toward himself, instead."

The radar blipped again.

"Here it comes," Austin shouted.

This time the craft came in very slowly, hovering a few hundred yards to the starboard side of the boat. Then, without warning, it plunged into the sea and vanished.

"It's gone," Mac cried.

"At least for now, MacKenzie," Johanen replied. "He is restrained, and will be so, until he that restrains him is taken out of the way."

"Until *who* is taken out of the way?" Mac asked.

Johanen smiled and tapped Mac lightly on his chest. "The same Spirit that resides in you, MacKenzie."

17

＊ O ＊

Rome, Italy

Laura checked her makeup and applied some fresh lipstick. Alone in the bathroom of the plane, she adjusted her wig and put some drops in her eyes to ease some of the discomfort from the green contact lenses she wore.

The warning bell sounded, followed by a steward's voice instructing the passengers to take their seats and fasten their seat belts.

She found her way back to her seat and buckled up—next to the middle-aged man with the bad dye job to cover his gray who had tried hitting on her a couple of times during the flight from Washington. Laura had responded with some well-placed quick and witty refusals, and he had stopped his advances, much to her relief.

She stared out the window. It appeared that the Italian weather was as dismal as what she had left in the States, raining and overcast. *What could be so secret that Daddy would never have even made a brief mention of it,* she wondered. He had kept secrets from her before, after all, most of what he had allowed her to share in was classified above top secret.

There had to be areas that she would not be privy to. *But this is different*, she pondered, *whatever is on this disk haunted him at the end.* She saw him in her mind, wide-eyed and fearful in the final moments of his life. *He wasn't in pain*, she thought. *The morphine drip took care of that. No, it was something else.* She remembered that just before he died, almost at the last instant he had had a change of heart about something. *He wanted to tell me something, but didn't have the strength to*, she thought. *No, that's not it either*, she corrected herself. *He was desperate to tell me something, and it has to do with this.* She rested her hand on the disk that was taped to the top of her panty hose.

She was jostled out of her reflections as the plane bounced on the tarmac. The plane taxied and connected to the loading tube. As soon as the seat belt sign was turned off, she stood and grabbed her bag from the overhead compartment.

"Let me help with that," Dye Job offered.

"No thanks, I can manage," she answered, flashing him a polite smile. The line of people slowly filed out of the plane. She checked her bags and went through customs.

She looked for the small airline that was her connecting flight to the Alps along the Swiss and Italian border. Her Italian was terrible, and she was relieved when the foreign exchange clerk smiled and replied to her in English.

"Will not leave for an hour," he said. "Is a most beautiful part of the world."

"Oh, how so?" Laura answered, making conversation.

"The mountain air hazaway," he groped for the right word, "has a way of making you feel clean, like a new snow." He laughed good-naturedly.

Laura smiled and handed the man a wad of American dollars.

He shook his head and chuckled, "You make my job so tough." He quickly made the calculations from dollars to Euros.

"There." He handed her back the new currency.

"You wait over there." He motioned toward a row of uncomfortable-looking chairs.

"Thanks for your help," Laura said, going over to the chairs.

She sat down, crossed her legs, and pretended to read the magazine that she had purchased before boarding the plane in Washington. She read for a few minutes, then, putting the magazine back in her purse, grabbed her carry-on bag and headed toward the ladies' room. She walked into one of the stalls and waited for the second hand of her watch to circle two times before she went back out. She glanced in the mirror, then followed an elderly woman wearing a hat to the door. "Let me help you," she said, as she opened the door for the woman.

"Oh, you're so sweet," the woman said as she shuffled her way out of the rest room.

Laura used the woman's hat to shield her face. As she walked next to the woman, she was able to peek around the hat. *Oh no*, she thought, *I'm definitely being followed . . . but how? And by whom?* She thought, *It makes no sense. There is just no way.* Then she thought of the fake ID. *Maybe they figured it out, but how?*

The short balding man with a trimmed beard stood across the waiting room. She had first noticed him when she'd gotten off the plane, and paid little attention to him. But now, she realized, he was aware of her every move. She went back to her seat, took her magazine out, and pretended to read. She glanced at her watch. *I have about ten minutes before they board,* she calculated.

She got up again and walked to the ladies' room, rolling her carry-on bag behind her. She went into a stall, took her wig off, and began to undress. She opened the bag, took out a pants suit, and threw the dress and wig she'd taken off in the bag. She changed her heels for low-cut shoes and exited the stall.

What a mess, she thought as she looked at her waist-length hair piled on top of her head and pinned in place. She grabbed a brush, laid it on the counter next to her, and began unpinning her hair. She tossed it behind her back, ran her fingers through it a couple of times to loosen it, then brushed it out. *Oh no, the contacts,* she thought, and took them out of each eye. *The bag! What about the bag?* She started to panic. She calmed herself, and looked at the bag. *Wait, I can tuck the handle back into the suitcase and carry it instead of rolling it.* She looked at herself in the mirror.

It'll work, she thought with satisfaction. *It just depends on me. I have to be confident, and I have to find the right person to be with . . . I have to get lucky here.*

She glanced at her watch. *Almost three minutes since I entered, I've got to go now.*

She walked toward the bathroom door and cracked it open so she could get a glimpse of people who were passing by. A married couple passed in the midst of an argument. *No way,* she thought. Then a mother with a newborn in her arms passed by. *It might work. I could pretend to be her sister,* but she dismissed the prospect. Two students with backpacks. *No way.* And then she couldn't believe her luck. It was the man who had sat next to her on the plane, Dye Job. Without hesitation, she put on her best smile and walked briskly out the door, pulling some of her long brown hair in front of her. She walked up to the man. "Oh, I'm so glad you made it." She kissed him on the lips. The man was stunned and confused, but she continued to kiss him. She pulled away from him, tapped his lips with her index finger, then grabbed his arm and snuggled next to him as she led him to the revolving doors to the outside.

She counted each step as she grew closer to the doors and the outside where she knew there would be taxis.

We're almost halfway. Please don't stop . . . don't say anything, she pleaded to herself.

"Look, who are you, missy?" Dye Job said, as he leered at her.

Laura snuggled closer. "Just keep walking. It doesn't matter who I am. I'm in trouble, and I need you to get me outside . . . okay?"

The man responded by putting his arm around her.

The doors were almost in reach.

Just a few more steps, she thought, and she began to feel hopeful.

"Let's have some more of that honey," the man said. He stopped, and this time took Laura in his arms, bent her backward, and kissed her full on her mouth.

Your life's at stake here, so enjoy it, she commanded herself, and even uttered a little sigh when the guy brought her to a standing position. He leaned forward again but she stopped him. "Not now, studly, let's wait till we get to our motel." She took his arm and made a dash for the doors. She went through, and there were at least ten cabs lined up waiting for fares.

She hurried over to the closest one, dragging the man with her. She opened the door, threw her bag in, and made like she was about to give the guy another kiss, but instead pushed him away and jumped in the cab, slamming the door shut.

"Hurry, go, hurry . . ." she tried desperately to think of the Italian for "Let's go." Finally it came to her. *"Andiamo! Andiamo!"* she shouted, and pointed forward with her hand.

The driver responded with a flurry of Italian, and the cab sped away from the curb.

* ○ *

The balding man who had watched Laura was growing anxious. *She's been in there too long,* he thought. He checked his watch and waited another couple of minutes. He ground his teeth together and eyed the door to the ladies' room impatiently. He checked his watch again, then realizing that something wasn't right, hurried over to the ladies' room. He looked around and not seeing any airport security, went in.

"What are you doing?" stammered a startled woman who was fixing her hair at the mirror.

The man ignored her and began to look underneath the doors of the stalls. He came to the last one, slammed it against the side of the stall, and cursed, glaring at the startled woman as he left.

He looked around the lobby, racking his brain trying to remember who had come out.

"The one with the long hair that kissed the guy," he muttered. He slammed his fist against his open palm and hurried to a phone booth.

He took his cell phone from his coat pocket, and his finger stabbed at the numbers.

"Yes," a voice answered.

"She's not on the plane," the man huffed into the receiver.

The man on the other end swore. "Can you do anything?"

"Not a thing . . . it's on the runway, and going to take off any moment. We're going to have an international incident because of this. What do you want me to do?" the balding guy asked.

"She has the disk. We need to get it or destroy it."

"Look, everything your man said checked out; her flight from the States then the connecting one. We know that Nathan wanted her to carry it to Johanen."

"But she eluded you, didn't she?"

The balding man gritted his teeth. "Look, she was clever . . . but what about the flight? I can't stop what's going to happen."

There was a pause. "When is it set to blow?"

"As soon as the tires leave the runway."

"Well then, I suggest you get out of there and call me later." The receiver went dead.

The balding man hung up the phone, buttoned his blazer, and calmly headed for the airport exit. He climbed into a cab, gave an address, and looked at his watch.

The cab pulled away and started picking up speed.

A loud explosion startled him. He looked through the rear window and saw a black cloud above the airport in the distance, where the runways were. Then he heard the wail of sirens . . .

* ◦ *

"Right." Laura pointed her index finger toward her side of the car. The cabby rattled off something in Italian that she didn't understand, and pulled the cab over to the curb. He turned around and said in very bad, broken English. "Lady, where is you wanna go?"

Laura thought for a moment. All she had was the address of the pickup spot where she was supposed to meet someone from Spiral of Life.

"Lady, come on?" the cabby whined.

Laura looked at him, then dug into her purse, handed the man a Euro note, and said, "Silencio." She muttered in English, "I need time to think."

The cabby smiled, showing a set of capped teeth, shrugged his shoulders, looked at the bill in his hands, and said, "You the boss, lady."

She sat back, took a deep breath, then tried to sort out what might have happened. *I need to think this through,* she thought, *Somehow they followed me. But who? Could they have found out about the girl from the agency that I hired as my double? Maybe airport surveillance . . . they could have monitored that? What if there were two sets of agents, and I only gave one the slip?* All of these were possibilities. *I wonder if anyone is on me now.* She looked behind her at the tangle of cars coming out of the Rome International Airport.

The rain eased up, and in the distance the clouds had cleared to reveal an azure sky.

"You the boss, lady," the cabby repeated again.

Laura was startled to hear the wail of sirens as two police cars streaked by.

The cabby plugged one ear with his finger, then gave a quick shrug, indicating that to him, this was an everyday affair.

Laura opened her purse and dug out the special laptop computer that her father had given her. She powered it up, then went again to the Spiral of Life website. She clicked on the index finger from the painting of Michelangelo's Sistine

Chapel and entered. She clicked where she knew a hidden icon would be, and after the password box came up she entered the password for the day. She related the incident at the airport, indicating that she would wait for instructions as to how to proceed.

As she was closing the laptop, she glanced at the rearview mirror and saw that the cabby was very interested in what she was doing.

"My son has the computer," the cabby said proudly.

Laura smiled, closed the laptop, and put it back in her suitcase.

"I don't want to use it." He tossed his hand in the air.

"Take me to a good hotel. Okay?" Laura asked.

"The best hotel for you . . . yeah?" He threw the car in gear and pulled out into traffic.

On the way Laura stared trancelike at the statuesque fountains, ornately decorated buildings, the remains of ancient aqueducts, and the parade of people that bustled on the streets.

The cab swung into the driveway of the hotel and stopped under a red awning that domed out over the entrance.

Laura paid the fare, included a generous tip, which made the cabby beam, then walked into the hotel lobby.

Twenty minutes later she sat in her room and stared at the screen of the laptop. She took the disk from her pantyhose and laid it next to the laptop. She ordered a meal from room service, then settled back and waited for an answer.

18

❖ ◯ ❖

Philadelphia

A boyfriend who won't make a commitment," Helen read aloud from the list she had just completed. "A dead-end job. A car that's about to die." She thought of the problem she had starting the old VW Bug when she left the bank an hour ago. She crossed her legs underneath her, adjusted the pillow behind her back, and continued reading the list as she sat on the couch in her apartment. "No *real* friends. No immediate family." Then she wondered, *I wonder if my fath . . .* and couldn't make herself say the rest of the word. *I wonder if he told my half sister.* She reached into the envelope she had taken from the safe-deposit box, grabbed the pictures, and looked at them again. *She's pretty,* she thought, as she stared at her half sister with the waist-long brown hair. She went back to the list. "Dr. Jacobson, my therapist. He counts a lot. But what if my fath . . ." and she stopped again. "What if *he's* right? What if I travel halfway around the world and find this Johanen." She looked at the letter again, wondering why he thought this Johanen would be able to help her, rid her from the abduction experiences that had plagued her life for as long as she could remember.

She had been crossing out each item on the list, and now her pen hovered over Dr. Jacobson's name. *He's helped me cope, but the same thing happens over and over again. Nothing works. They always come back,* and with that said, she crossed his name out.

She looked at her watch. *Ronnie will be home in less than three hours.* She stared once more at the picture of Laura, gathered the photos back in the envelope, and jumped up from the couch. She hurried into her room, searching her closet for the only suitcase she owned, a battered second-hand one she'd bought from a thrift store. She paused, then threw the suitcase back into the closet. She looked across the room at her purse, with those big wads of money still inside, and she smiled. Her mind was made up.

* o *

Helen looked in her rearview mirror at the stack of boxes of new clothes she had purchased along with a new suitcase to put them in. She stopped at a light and changed the CD in the player. She closed her eyes and inhaled the wonderful new car smell from her four-door Honda Civic. She giggled when she thought of the expression on the salesman's face when she pulled out several wads of hundreds and paid for the car in cash.

She looked at herself in the rearview mirror. There was only one more thing to do. She pulled into the Hilton and allowed the bellhop to park the car. She started to take her packages from the back seat but the bellhop suggested she check into her room first, and then he would bring them up.

She went to the front desk, paid for a deluxe suite, and asked, "Where's a good beauty salon?"

* o *

An hour and a half later she was watching in the mirror as the stylist blow-dried her new hairstyle. The woman had cut the chewed ends off, giving her a chin-length bob, and then had rinsed her hair with henna, giving it subtle red overtones.

"I love it," Helen said.

The stylist, a severely bleached blonde with painted-on eyebrows, stopped chewing her gum for a moment. "It makes you look like you're ready for the runway," she kidded. "It's a great look for you, and we got rid of your chewed ends. Promise me you won't nibble?" The stylist chided her like a mother.

"Promise," Helen replied, smiling at the woman.

Helen looked at herself again and wondered if Ronnie or Dr. Jacobson would have recognized her. When the stylist finished she left a generous tip and hurried to her car. She decided to go back to her hotel, call room service, and dine in her suite, a luxury that until now had been in the realm of fantasy.

* ○ *

Helen sat propped up on big, fluffy pillows, lifted another succulent mouthful of curried chicken, then sipped from a glass of white wine. She felt like a princess. She watched the last portion of a newly released movie, then began to channel surf, stopping at the shopping channel. For a moment she considered buying the diamond bracelet being offered at incredible savings. Other items were displayed, but she wasn't interested in any of them, so she changed the channels again and found a talk show. "Boring," she said out loud, and took another sip from the wine glass. She flicked to another channel and she froze as she heard: "You're wrong, UFOs have been seen by millions of people and—"

The man was interrupted as an older man with jowls shot back, "You'll have to prove that with some hard physical evidence."

The first man held up a picture, and the camera panned in close. "Here's your evidence. This was taken by a policeman in Ohio this past fall."

"That doesn't prove anything. It's just a light in the sky."

"No, it's *not* just a light. Here's an enlargement of the picture." He held it up. The audience applauded.

"It's real all right, you idiot," Helen said aloud.

"That photo could have been faked. Has it been analyzed?" Jowls countered.

"Faked by a policeman?" the other shot back.

"He might want the publicity."

"Here's another of the same craft shot by a citizen, the same night, in the next town over." The audience applauded again.

The camera panned to the host. "We'll be right back, and when we do, we're going to bring out a woman who claims she's been abducted by aliens, so don't go away."

Helen drank the rest of her wine in one gulp. Here was someone like herself, who had been taken against her will.

She had met several other abductees through Dr. Jacobson. She had even gone to a support group several times. Everyone there had had one thing in common: they had been abducted, and they had been powerless to stop it.

The program came back on, and the host read from a three-by-five card. "Our next guest is Mrs. Elaine Hunt, who claims to have been abducted by aliens and taken aboard their ship, where they performed gynecological examinations on her."

Helen clutched one of the pillows in front of her.

The camera panned to Mrs. Hunt, a woman in her late twenties, who walked onto the stage to the applause and fascination of the audience.

"Mrs. Hunt," the announcer began, "you claim to have been abducted by aliens, who performed gynecological experiments on you. Will you elaborate on this for our audience?"

"It started several years ago," she began, rubbing her hands together. "It was in the middle of the night, and I was asleep with my husband. Suddenly I was aware of this bright light coming into my room. At first I thought I was dreaming, but I knew I wasn't because I looked over and heard my husband snoring. After that I couldn't move. It felt like I had been paralyzed by something, and then they came and took me away."

"Who came and took you?" the announcer asked.

"Oh, I'm sorry," she began. "Four gray, alien beings with black eyes, something like this."

The camera panned in as the woman held up a sketch she had drawn.

"Were you on any medication at the time?" Jowls asked.

"No, sir, I was not," the woman replied.

"Had you been drinking or using any drugs?" Jowls pressed.

"No, Mr. Cass, I did not," the woman replied.

So Jowls has a name, Helen thought. Out loud she said, "I'd like to see how terrified you'd be, Mr. Cass, if they came for you."

Cass fired another salvo at the woman. "How are we supposed to believe you, Mrs. Hunt? What evidence do you have?"

Someone in the audience booed.

The woman looked at Cass and replied, "I only wish it had never happened. It was the most terrifying episode in my life."

"Did you try to resist?" the other man on the panel asked.

"You can't resist. It's impossible," Helen blurted out.

"You can't resist them." The woman echoed Helen's words.

"What happens then?" the announcer asked.

"Well . . ." She began wringing her hands. "They somehow make it so I can't move. I can't even speak, and then we go to the ship."

"And how do you get to the ship?" Cass asked.

The woman hesitated a moment. "We float through the air and go up to their ship."

"Through a window?" Cass pressed.

The woman shook her head. "No, not through a window." She paused, then stated, "We go through the wall, somehow."

Someone in the audience laughed.

"Don't laugh, you idiot," Helen shot back, hugging the pillow harder.

Cass continued his line of questioning. "Mrs. Hunt, how can I believe that you defy the laws of physics and go *through* the wall?"

The woman shrugged.

"This is a very common occurrence to people who have had the same or similar experience," the other guest said, supporting Mrs. Hunt.

"The lady's telling the truth!" Helen shouted at the screen.

"You can't have thousands of people from all walks of life, from every ethnic and social background, have the exact, same experience without some truth to it," the other guest continued.

"But there's not one shred of solid evidence," Cass stated. "Show me something tangible and then I'll believe."

Several people in the audience responded by clapping. The camera panned to the show's host. "Mrs. Hunt, for the sake of argument, let's believe what you just told us is true. What happens next?"

Hunt looked down at her hands and didn't speak. Her lips began to tremble, and finally she broke down. The camera zoomed in on her, and Helen heard the audience murmur in sympathetic tones.

The announcer handed her a Kleenex, and Mrs. Hunt dabbed her eyes.

She began in a subdued voice. "Like I said, they bring me aboard, and then they put me on this table, and they remove my clothes." She stopped and dabbed her eyes again. "Then one of them comes over, looks into my eyes, and he tells me that everything is going to be all right, and the examination won't hurt."

"How does it feel when the alien looks in your eyes?" the announcer asked.

"Well, it's horrible because you can't think when that happens, and all sorts of images and pictures and things that he wants you to see just take over."

"Is it similar to hypnosis?" the host asked.

"I don't know, because I've never been hypnotized before, but when the alien does it, you can't do anything but lie there."

"You can yell at them," Helen called out. "At least you can tell the creeps that you hate what they're doing to you."

"And then?" the host prodded.

"They examine me and take samples. Sometimes one of them will bring in another abductee, a man that I don't know." She broke down again and cried.

"Take your time, Mrs. Hunt, we understand how hard this is," the announcer said, and the audience applauded to show their support.

"Well, like I started to say, they bring a man in, and he's scared to death too. I can see how scared he is. One of them looks into this poor man's eyes, and he calms down a bit. Then they take his arms and help him onto the table where I am, and then . . . .and then he . . . " She lifted her hands to cover her face and started to sob.

The camera panned in on the host, who gave the camera his best compassionate look and said, "We'll be right back with our last guest, Mr. Joe Jackson, who claims that he knows how to stop alien abductions."

Helen just stared at the TV, dumbfounded. *No one knows how to stop them,* she thought. She got up and moved to the end of the bed, closer to the TV.

Five commercials went by with Helen barely noticing them, then the host introduced his final guest. "Give Mr. Joe Jackson a warm round of applause, will you?" The audience responded, and Mr. Jackson walked out and took a seat next to Mrs. Hunt.

"Welcome to the show, Mr. Jackson, nice to have you here."

"Thank you."

The host read from another card. "Mr. Jackson, you say that you have evidence supporting your claim that you know how to stop these alien abductions."

Jackson nodded. "Yes, I do."

"Would you care to explain?" the host asked.

Jackson smiled. "I have been researching the abduction phenomena for the last fifteen years. At first it seemed like there was nothing anyone could do to stop it. Many of the people I interviewed and examined have stories almost identical to Mrs. Hunt's." He reached for a glass of water and took a sip. "One person I interviewed, however, told me a very unique story ... different because he was able to stop his abduction."

Helen sat still, hanging on every word.

"And how was he able to do this?" the announcer asked.

"He called upon the name of Jesus Christ."

There was some laughter from the audience.

Jackson looked at the audience. "You've just heard this woman's shocking story"—he gestured to Mrs. Hunt—"and most of you believe her, right?"

A majority of the audience applauded.

Jackson turned to Mrs. Hunt. "May I ask you a personal question?"

"Yes, you can," Hunt said.

"What's your religious background?"

"I don't have one, but when I was a little girl, we went to the Baptist church."

"Do you believe in God?" Jackson asked.

"Yes, I believe in something greater than ourselves."

"Have you ever asked for help while the abduction experience was taking place?"

"There is no help from anywhere!" Helen shouted.

Mrs. Hunt shook her head.

Jackson turned to the audience and continued, "The man that I spoke about has sworn, in a signed affidavit to me and my associates, that his story is true. The man was having almost the same experience as Mrs. Hunt and most of the other people I have interviewed, except that he stopped the abduction just when he was about to be taken from the room. He felt himself start to rise or float above the bed. Like Mrs.

Hunt here, he was terrified. The only difference is, at that moment he cried out to Jesus Christ to save him. The man was a Christian. He was able to force himself to call out, 'Jesus save me,' and the abduction experience was stopped cold. He fell back into the bed, and as he looked around he realized the alien beings were gone."

"That's a fantastic story," the host said.

Helen recalled the words in the letter about the man her father claimed could stop the experiences, the man whom she knew only as Johanen. Isn't that why she was here now? Isn't that what had started all of this, the car, the clothes, the new hair, and the hotel room? *And that's why I'm leaving tomorrow morning. To find Johanen and maybe get free from all of this.*

"We've heard from a fascinating group of guests tonight, haven't we?" the host announced as the camera panned back, showing all the guests, and then the audience applauding. Then back to a closeup on the host. "But that's all we have time for on this show. And we leave it to you, our viewers, to decide." The host looked serious as he stared for a moment at the camera. "You've heard the evidence, and now it's up to you to decide for yourselves about UFOs—fact or fiction?" The audience applauded, and changing moods like a chameleon, the host's face beamed at the camera as he continued, "Join us tomorrow as we explore the benefits and risks of plastic surgery. We'll have as our guests . . ."

Helen turned the TV off. The room was very quiet.

I wonder if what that Jackson guy said was true . . . about Jesus, she thought. *Impossible. Nothing can stop them. Not Jesus, or anything else.*

She turned off the light, crawled into the queen-size bed, and buried herself down under the sheets. Holding a pillow, she curled herself as tightly as she could around it and went to sleep.

19

✦ ◯ ✦

Rome, Italy

A diverse group of men, known collectively as the Cadre, were seated at an ebony conference table that had an inlaid red dragon curled in on itself in the center. The windowless walls were covered in crimson curtains that riffled at the air flow from the climate control system.

"Here's another." Mr. Wyan's voice came from the far end of the table as a picture came up on the large screen providing the only light in the otherwise darkened room.

"What's the date?" an elderly man with a thick German accent asked.

"Eighteen sixty-five," Wyan answered.

"Where was it taken?" asked a man with part of his nose bandaged due to an ongoing battle with skin cancer.

Wyan answered again, "In America, right after the Civil War. I believe the location is Appomattox."

"Yes, but are you sure it's the same man?" the German asked.

"Yes," Wyan said. "Compare that to a more recent picture." He hit a key on the computer, and the picture that appeared on the screen was much clearer than the one preceding it.

"The face is the same," the man with cancer said.

"I agree," the German added.

"Go back to the first one, will you please?" an elderly Japanese man asked.

Wyan pushed a key and the picture changed.

"Look there," the Japanese man said. He rose from his chair and walked toward the picture. "There seems to be a light around him."

Wyan nodded. "Yes, I've made a note of that. It seems to show up more in the daguerreotypes than the newer photos."

"We've managed to trace some of his finances," Mr. Kenson added, speaking for the first time.

"He's managed to conceal most of the records, but we did find this," Wyan said, changing the picture again.

"I'm having trouble seeing it," the German complained, as he slipped on a pair of glasses.

"They're bank statements we purchased from someone inside his organization," Wyan said. "Note the date on the top. It's faded but still legible."

"Sixteen forty-two," the Japanese stated.

"Impossible," the German added.

"Impossible? Yet we have proof that it is the same man," Wyan countered.

"But that would make him almost three hundred and fifty years old," Skin Cancer protested.

"True, but we have other records that would make him older," Mr. Kenson added, nodding toward Wyan, who changed the picture.

"A parchment from the year 903," Wyan said.

"He has an interesting way of signing documents. He uses a very distinctive symbol," Kenson stated. "The symbol is identical, both on this document from the year 903, and this one from last year."

Wyan clicked the computer, showing the two symbols next to each other. "Now watch what happens," Wyan said. "The next image shows the symbols on top of one another. For clarity, one has been colored blue and the other red." He clicked again.

"Almost a perfect overlay," the Japanese man declared.

"And you're saying that it was this man that helped bring about the ruination of our plans in Germany during the war?" the German asked.

"The records are sketchy. He has a masterful way of covering his tracks. But the answer is yes. Both Mr. Kenson and myself believe that he was involved."

"But behind the scenes," Kenson added.

"Always behind the scenes," Wyan added. "He has a very uncanny way of popping up at the most inopportune times. Not only does he appear to have unlimited wealth, but he seems to have a very powerful energy about him."

"He's not connected to us, so his 'power' must come from the one that Lucius will overthrow," Kenson added.

"Has anyone attempted to contact him?" the German asked.

"Certain members of our organization have tried," Wyan began, "in recent times. All our attempts, however, have failed, and two of our agents who managed to contact him were so shattered by the experience that both went insane."

"How?" Skin Cancer asked.

"One committed suicide; the other died in a sanitarium."

"What caused this?" the Japanese man asked.

"We're not certain. Both of our agents were trained adepts, and of course were dedicated to Lucius," Wyan said.

"So how do we stop him?" the German demanded.

Wyan proceeded, for this was the part of the presentation he had waited for. "We have set in motion a trap to bring him to us. The tomb is the bait, and we believe he will take it."

"What if something goes wrong?" Skin Cancer asked.

"Always a possibility," Wyan admitted. "But we believe the deck is well stacked in our favor."

"Well, when do you expect him?" the German asked.

"Soon. The wheels are already in motion. We believe he will have several other people with him who should be eliminated also."

"It is always important to dispose of those who would oppose Lucius," the German said.

"Is the sacrifice being readied?" Skin Cancer asked.

"Yes, it is. I'm seeing to it personally," Wyan said.

"Well, I'm sure you will keep us informed," the Japanese man offered.

"Yes, the time for the reemergence of the Bethlehem star grows closer, and with it the manifestation of the New Christ," Wyan said. "As you know, most of the nations are sending representatives for our presentation here in Rome. When the star emerges during the full lunar eclipse, along with the exhumation of the body of Jesus, those who are in attendance won't be disappointed."

A murmur of approval spread in the room.

"We've also added a new dimension." He paused for effect. "We're going to use teleportation technology, which will create the appearance of a life-sized three-dimensional person, in this case Mr. Kenson"—and Wyan gestured toward his associate—"as he communicates from inside the tomb. The teleportation technology will also give Mr. Kenson the ability to achieve two-way eye contact for real-time, two-way interaction between himself and the assembled delegates."

"Like a holograph?" the German asked.

"Similar but more realistic," Wyan said. "The viewers will be able to see Mr. Kenson in three dimensions just as if he was standing in front of them, instead of thousands of miles away."

The lights were turned on, and the men began to exit the room.

On the way out, Skin Cancer stopped and took Mr. Wyan aside. "Do you think you can kill him?" he asked.

Wyan smiled and replied, "Johanen? Aren't all things possible with Lucius?"

They left the room and joined the others.

20

✦ ⬤ ✦

Qumran, Israel

The huddled figure had remained throughout the night with his cloak gathered around him, its hood pulled over his head. At the coming of dawn, he rose and surveyed the barren terrain that surrounded him. It looked familiar, unchanged from the last time he had visited this desolate spot.

His eyes searched the rocky cliffs, and he noticed there were openings he did not remember. But he was certain this was the place. He remembered a particular grouping of rocks, although worn by time, which still looked like the head of a lion. He began to make his way toward the base of the cliffs, underneath the lion's head, and started his ascent on the faintest of paths.

An hour later he stopped. In front was an overhanging rock that blocked his path. The sun was growing hotter, and he threw the hood of his cloak back to reveal a bearded face with long unruly hair. He began to climb, looking for hand-holds in the rock. He worked his way upward until at one point he was hanging almost upside down. He was sweating now, and his hands, although calloused, were cut in several places. He struggled to find a handhold, and searched the face of the rock with one free hand . . . there it was. The handhold he himself had chiseled into the face of the rock—worn, and filled with a residue of pebbles, but still there. He slipped his hand into it and pulled himself upward, then reached out and found the next indentation in the rock. He finished the ascent, and when he came to the top of the outcropping he sat and rested.

Far below him the desert stretched in all directions, bleak and foreboding. He slipped a pebble into his mouth and sucked on it, which brought a flow of saliva that helped to quench his thirst. He got up, rubbed his hands together, and continued upward. The going was treacherous, for now he climbed a face that was almost vertical. His eyes searched above him, and he spotted a small indentation. He climbed faster now, and reached the spot. There was a small ledge just large enough to accommodate him, and he crouched on it. Then he began to remove the rocks that were fitted together and sealed with pitch to conceal the mouth of a small cave. He set them next to him in a neat pile until he had opened the entrance.

He crept into the cave, relieved to be out of the heat of the sun. The interior was dark and cool. He crawled forward and after ten feet or so reached the back of the cave. His hands rested on the clay jar, whose dark wax seal was still in place around the lid. He brushed the dust off the jar, pried the seal off, and reached in and took out the contents. An animal skin was wound around a scroll, and he loosened the outer wrapping that held it together and began to unroll it. Finding it somewhat brittle, he decided to roll it back up. He placed it back in the jar and fastened the lid.

Chiseled into the rear wall of the cave was a ledge, and on it rested a long narrow bundle. He touched the skins that once had served as an outer wrapping, and they disintegrated. He ran his hand down the length of the bundle, brushing the decomposed skin away, and revealed a long wooden staff. He took it from the ledge and felt the weight of it in his hands. He ran his fingers down the length of it and rubbed it. Then he rested it on his shoulder while he loosened part of the belt that was wound around his waist, and fashioned a sling, which he attached to the jar. He placed the sling around his shoulder so that the jar rested on his back. Then he grabbed the staff, headed out of the cave, and began his descent.

21

Near the Swiss Alps

Mac looked out the jet's window and asked himself for the umpteenth time, *Why is it always an airplane? Why not a train, or a car or a bicycle, for crying out loud?*

Only a few hours before, Johanen had docked his boat in a small port on the coast of France. Johanen had hired a local taxi, and the three bedraggled-looking men made their way to a private airport where Johanen's Lear jet awaited them.

As if on cue, the plane hit a bit of turbulence, causing Mac to grab the armrests of his chair. *My stomach feels like it's about to come out of my throat*, he thought.

Mac yelled toward the cockpit where Johanen was seated at the controls. "Can I ask you something?"

Johanen looked back over his shoulder. "What is it, MacKenzie?"

"You navigate the ocean, and you fly. Is there anything you can't do?"

The man laughed good-naturedly. "I suppose not, MacKenzie. It just takes training and time, and at my age I have a lot of both. You know, Mac," he added, "I am sure you will enjoy the section of the Alps we will be flying over. They are quite spectacular."

Mac looked out his window at the quiltlike pattern of French farms growing smaller as the jet ascended. "You still haven't told us how you knew where to find us," Mac said.

Johanen checked his altimeter. Satisfied that all was well, he set the plane on autopilot and moved aft to where Mac and Austin sat.

"General Nathan or 'Roswell,' as you prefer to call him, Mac, sent me a coded communiqué, through our website. Ever since I decoded it, the contents have been on my mind."

"Was this the week he died?" Austin asked.

"Several days before," Johanen answered.

"Were you able to answer the communiqué?" Mac asked.

Johanen frowned. "No, and that is what troubles me. Roswell slipped faster than any of us expected, partly, I think, due to his false healing. At any rate, the information, as I said, is very troubling. As to how I managed to find you." He looked at Mac. "The general informed me that you and Colonel Austin might be going to Peru. I followed this lead, and from there, I was able to trace you to Cornwall with the help of my organization, which, by the way, was aware of your father's crop circle appearance."

What could possibly be more troubling than what we just went through? Mac thought, and felt a chill run down his backbone as he remembered his father claiming to be the harbinger of the New Christ as he floated in the air beneath a UFO.

Johanen continued, "It appears that certain people who have yielded themselves to the Mystery of Lawlessness, details of which I explained to you both earlier, claim to have discovered—*invented* would be a more appropriate term—the tomb of Jesus."

"*The* Jesus?" Mac asked, his eyebrows arching.

"You have to be kidding," Austin added.

Johanen nodded. "Yes, supposedly one and the same. Of course, *we* know that this is not the real body. It is part of a clever ruse. But there is more, and the particulars are most troubling. It appears that along with the body there are what Roswell called alien artifacts. Both are preserved, according to General Nathan, in a container, a sarcophagus-like structure, the construction of which resembles glass."

"Alien artifacts?" Mac repeated. "Why would that matter?"

"Those who are on the side of the Evil One will link the body of Jesus to an alien civilization, and the idea that the aliens were our progenitors, and because of that, they have supremacy over us. Of course, we know that the alien agenda is, in fact, Luciferic in nature, and I believe, will be *the* Great Deception in these last days. But most people are not aware of this. The aliens will claim that it was through their direct intervention that Jesus became the Christ. They will claim that the miracles attributed to him were something they devised. Most troubling is their version of the Crucifixion. Jesus never died, he just became unconscious and was later resuscitated. Then afterward, he married Mary Magdalene and sired children."

"Who's going to believe that? And where is this tomb located?" Mac asked.

"As to the tomb, we don't know. General Nathan didn't have that information then. He did, however, acquire it, but just days before he died. Laura, his daughter, informed me that his dying wish was to have her hand me the disk, containing the information that will give us the precise location. As to who will believe the supposed union between Jesus and Mary Magdalene, there are many living in Europe who claim to be of the royal bloodline."

"The royal bloodline?" Colonel Austin asked.

"They claim to be descendants of Jesus, and therefore lay claim to the throne of David in Jerusalem."

Mac saw that Austin appeared as baffled as himself. "That's one of the strangest things I've ever heard of. So, where's Green Eyes? Is she meeting us with the disk?" he asked, a smile escaping as he thought of her.

"Green Eyes?" Johanen asked.

"Sorry. It's a nickname. She sometimes wears green contacts."

Johanen let the explanation pass. "Laura is on her way here. In fact, I would expect her arrival at the castle within twenty-four hours, but I must return to my duties in the cockpit."

Mac was left with his head full of unanswered questions. He was exhausted and emotionally fried, but he gained some comfort in the fact that he was with Johanen, and that since he had been with him he had felt a peace that seemed to emanate from the man like an aura.

22

✦ ⊙ ✦

New York State

Helen looked at the map that had been in the safe-deposit box and traced the highlighted route again with her finger. *I must have missed it,* she thought. *It's probably a few miles back down the road.* She pulled the Honda back onto the two-lane highway and made a U-turn.

It's beautiful in this part of the country, she mused, as she admired the dense foliage of the forest which bordered both sides of the road.

A few miles went by, and still the sign that she was looking for hadn't appeared. *I'm so stupid.* She steered the Honda off the road and looked at the map again. She took a deep breath. "Okay, I'm lost," she said aloud.

She got out of the car, stretching her legs. She noticed a sweet, pungent smell and wondered what it was.

The car was still running. She reached through the window and turned the motor off.

The engine stopped. *It's so quiet. I can't believe how still it is,* she thought. She laughed as she thought of her old Bug coughing for half a minute before it finally died.

She looked around again, and for a moment entertained the idea of going into the woods. Her hand rested on the warm hood of her car. Something underneath the hood ticked like a clock for a few moments, and then all was still again. She reached into the car, pulled the map out, and set it on the hood. *What did the sign say? What was the name of the last town I drove through?* She racked her brain, trying to remember.

She looked at the map. *It's just one stupid little turn-off,* she thought. *How could I possibly get so turned around?*

She looked into the forest at a grove of birch trees that had white bark with dark black circles that looked like eyes. Shuddering for a moment, she gathered her arms in front of her. She began to feel uneasy, although she wasn't sure why. She looked back at the trees. *It reminds me of them . . . of their eyes,* she thought, growing frightened. She grabbed the map off the hood and backed her way into the car, afraid that she would see something she didn't want to see. She started the engine and was relieved when she heard the door-locks click shut. She steered the car back onto the road. *Don't be silly, Helen,* she scolded herself. *They're just a bunch of stupid trees that have nothing to do with them.*

For some reason she was afraid to look in her rearview mirror, but she forced herself to do so.

See . . . nothing there. She looked again and thought for a moment that her eyes were playing tricks on her. She looked out her side-view mirror, and then she saw it clearly.

Her breath came in desperate little pants. *Not here . . . No, it can't be . . . Not now, I'm so close.*

She looked again in the mirror and saw the familiar shape of a UFO and from it coming a deep pulsating orange glow. Her upper lip began to quiver. "No!" she screamed. She slammed the pedal down, and the car shot forward. "No! Not here!" And she gripped the wheel harder as she began to cry.

She thought of the black markings on the birch trees. *Oh, I hate their eyes,* she thought, and tried to clear her mind and control the fear that welled up in her. The car began to lose control around a bend in the road.

"Calm down, Helen," she said, and took a couple of long deep breaths. She realized that she was perspiring. *Where is another car, a house, anything? Don't people live here?* She felt the rear tires slip around another bend in the road.

"You're not going to get me. I don't care anymore. I'm not letting you touch me again, never! I'll kill myself before I let you. Do you hear me?" she screamed.

She was startled as the car began to sputter as if the engine wasn't getting enough gas, the way her old beat-up VW had run most of the time.

"Come on . . . come on," she coaxed. She glanced in the mirror again and bit her lower lip, making it bleed. *I can't out-run it,* she thought, and shook the wheel with both hands as if she could somehow will the car to keep going.

The car sputtered again.

She pumped the gas pedal up and down. She was going too fast around a left turn, and the car almost went off the road. She fought to keep control of it. *What's that? A store?* she thought, as a building loomed in the distance. *No, it looks like a church. What is a church doing out in the middle of nowhere?*

The engine stopped altogether and the steering wheel locked up. Somehow she had the presence of mind to throw the car into neutral. The car coasted. She looked in her mirror and saw a series of bright orange pulsing lights that were getting closer. Because the wheel was locked, she had no control over where the car was headed. The road began to curve again, and she realized that the car was going to hit a tree further down its path. Much to her amazement, she saw a small gravel parking lot and a car parked beside the building. She waited until the last possible second before the car hit the tree, then slammed on her brakes. The car skidded sideways to a stop. She threw open the door and ran toward the church. She glimpsed a historical marker sign; as she ran the words flashed by.

First Church of Christ
Established 1782

The ground around her became illuminated so brightly she had to shield her eyes. Her legs felt very heavy. She willed herself to move them. "You creeps!" she yelled. Her hair flew around her face, and then she lost her shoe. The light grew in intensity, and still she forced herself forward. *I'll reach the door. I'll get inside*, she told herself, then yelled, "I'm not going with you. Never!"

The rugged wooden door of the church opened, and an old man stood in the doorway.

"Help me!" Helen yelled. "Don't let them take me," she cried. Helen saw the man's face change from bewilderment to fear.

"No, don't shut the door," she sobbed. She was only a few yards away.

The door slammed shut just as she reached it, and she heard the frantic closing of the lock.

"Open up!" she screamed, pounding on it with her fists. "Open up!" Then she collapsed on the ancient stone step and curled herself in a little ball, waiting for *them* to take her.

23

Spiral of Life Headquarters, the Alps

Here we are, MacKenzie, Colonel Austin," Johanen announced as their van pulled up in front of an ancient stone castle.

Finally, Mac thought. He mentally calculated the difference between the Alps and California. *I can call Maggie,* he decided.

As the van stopped, Mac looked through the front window. Even with his restricted view, he saw jagged, snow-capped mountain crags towering over verdant valleys.

"Incredible," Mac exclaimed, as he got out of the van and filled his lungs with crisp mountain air.

"A man could retire in a place like this," Colonel Austin added, climbing out of the rear of the van.

They were interrupted as a stout woman ran out through the two iron and wood doors that were the entrance to the castle. "Johanen, Johanen," she cried. "So you got them out safely? That's good, we never stopped praying for you." She gave Mac and Austin a quick nod of recognition. "But something terrible has happened. Laura Nathan's plane . . ." She burst into tears.

"What? What about Laura's plane?" Mac said.

"Tell me, Hilda," Johanen said.

The woman took a deep breath. "The plane exploded after taking off."

Mac felt as if someone had slugged him in the stomach. "No. Is she dead?" He moved closer to Hilda. "Are you sure it was her plane?"

"Not here," Johanen instructed. "Let us continue this inside." Taking Hilda's hand, he led the way into the castle.

Mac followed, feeling sick to his stomach. He stepped inside, then Johanen closed the doors and fastened the locks.

Mac found himself in a large hall with tapestries hanging on the walls and thick oriental carpets on the stone floors. A large living room with a walk-in fireplace opened directly off the hall. Several groupings of chairs and couches with reading lights and end tables graced the room, forming a semi-circle around the fireplace. A prodigious library on the far wall went up two stories, and rustic, hand-hewn beams spanned the width of the room.

Mac saw two men descend from the staircase that circled down from the second story to the great hall. One of them, a small man with broad shoulders and the body of a weight lifter, wore a headset that was attached to a receiver on his belt. The other, a tall, lanky man with a thick mane of almost-white hair and a large hooked nose, called Johanen's name in an anxious voice.

"Knud," Johanen answered, "is it true?"

"Ya, is true," Knud said in a thick Danish accent.

Mac was stunned and barely heard Johanen introducing Stephan, the man with the headset, and his companion, Knud.

"When was her last communication with us?" Johanen asked, rubbing his beard.

"Last week, just after her father passed away," Stephan answered. Mac detected a slight French accent.

"And there was nothing since? Not on the website?" Johanen asked.

Stephan shook his head. "No . . . Nothing."

Johanen looked annoyed. "She sent us no word concerning her arrival, or the disk from her late father?" Johanen asked.

Stephan shook his head. "Nothing."

"What about the satellite link?" Johanen asked.

"Not here. I just checked it," Knud replied.

"Where did the bombing happen? " Mac asked.

"In Rome. The media is labeling it a drug cartel-related incident," Stephan replied.

Mac looked at Johanen. "She had the disk with her?"

"Yes, I assume so," Johanen replied. "Is there word from Elisha and Uri?"

"Ya, Elisha says he's fine, and wants to join us here," Knud answered.

Mac saw that this news brought a faint smile to Johanen's lips.

There was an awkward silence as everyone waited for Johanen to speak. Mac realized that the other side had deliberately killed someone he knew, and it was no accident. The thought sobered him, and he recalled Johanen's discussion of the Mystery of Iniquity. It scared him.

"We are all very hungry and tired," Johanen announced. "Stephan, can you show our guests their quarters where they can shower? Knud, will you bring some clothes for Colonel Austin and MacKenzie? They may not fit you exactly, but will certainly make do until your own clothes are washed and dried. Hilda, can you fix something? We'll meet at the round table, let us say in about an hour, and discuss this tragedy further."

"Johanen," Mac said as the group began to disperse, "I need to contact Maggie."

"Yes, MacKenzie, follow me." Johanen started down the long hallway.

Mac soon found himself in the communication room of the castle. An array of computer terminals was linked to a mainframe computer set up in a temperature-controlled glass booth at the far corner of the room. Bookshelves bordered the room, and on a large flat screen was a satellite view of the Middle East, with Israel at the center.

Mac motioned toward the map. "Why just the Middle East?" he asked.

"I believe that this area of the world is the most important. You see Jerusalem? How I have highlighted it?"

Mac nodded.

"Well, Jerusalem has been controlled for almost two thousand years by the Gentiles, but that time has now come to an end."

"What's the importance of that?" Mac asked.

"In 1965 the Jews took control of the Old City and regained the area of the Temple Mount for a short while."

Mac shrugged. "So?"

"I believe that this starts the prophetic clock ticking. And you should be aware that everything hinges on Jerusalem and the Jewish people. I believe we are about to enter the last seven-year period that Daniel speaks of."

"Daniel?" Mac asked.

"Daniel the prophet. I see that there is much for you to study, MacKenzie," Johanen remarked. He smiled good-naturedly. "Here is a secured phone you can use. It has a satellite hookup. You might experience a slight echo because of the voice scrambler on it, but it will connect you with your wife. If you like, I can dial the number for you."

Mac gave him Maggie's number. Johanen punched it in and handed the phone to Mac. He walked to a computer terminal at the other end of the room, giving Mac his privacy.

Mac put the phone up to his ear and heard the first ring. Two more rings. "Hello?" Maggie's voice echoed in his ear.

"Maggie, it's me, Mac."

"I've been so worried, Mac. Are you okay?"

"I'm fine, I guess. I'm in the Italian Alps with Colonel Austin."

"I thought you were in Peru to help with Cranston!"

Mac whistled between his teeth. "So did I. They found the body . . . of my father in England. So Austin and I flew there for me to make a positive ID on it."

"That's horrible."

"Then things got out of hand," Mac added.

"Out of hand?" Mac heard the worry in her voice.

"I don't want to get into all of it now, but one thing led to another, and so here I am, but Maggie . . ." He lowered his voice. "I just want to come home and be with you and Jeremy and Sarah, and watch the grapes grow, like your dad used to say."

"We miss *you*. Did you know that Austin left four men here to look after things while you were gone?"

"Yeah, he told me that. Do you feel safe?"

"They've been great, even helped with the harvest."

"Listen, Maggie, I'm doing everything I know how to do to get back there." He paused.

"I know."

"Something else . . . Remember Laura, General Nathan's daughter?"

"After what she went through here, how could I forget?" Maggie replied.

"We just received news that the plane she was on had a bomb on it and it exploded."

"Oh, Mac . . . that's terrible."

"No official word yet, though. We're all hoping that she wasn't on it."

"I'm afraid for you."

"I'm afraid for me too, Maggie."

"Mac . . . Mac, I can't hear . . ."

"I think we're losing the connection. Maggie? Can you hear me?"

"Mac . . ."

"Maggie?" He heard nothing but static. "Gone," he said, walking to where Johanen sat at a computer terminal.

"How is she faring, MacKenzie?" Johanen asked.

Mac shrugged. "She's being a real trooper, but I can tell she's worried."

Johanen looked at Mac with concern as he rose from the terminal. "We will pray for her, MacKenzie, and for your children." He put his hand on Mac's shoulder. "Let me escort you to your room, and after you have settled in, you can call her again."

Mac nodded and followed Johanen up the spiral staircase to a long corridor on the second floor.

"You will be comfortable here," Johanen said, as he opened the door to one of the bedrooms.

"I'm sure I will," Mac answered. Then he thought of Laura. "Did you know her?"

Johanen let out a sigh. "Not personally, but I communicated with her several times when she accessed the Web site. But do not give up hope, MacKenzie, there is still the possibility that she was not on the plane. We will have to wait and see how things play out." Johanen once again placed his hand on Mac's shoulder.

Mac patted Johanen's hand with his own and went into his room, closing the door behind him. He went to the bathroom to take a shower, letting the hot water pour over his body. These last few days had become a blurred nightmare. Mac reflected about the fragile condition of Cranston, then his father's ranting, coupled with the ever-menacing demonic UFO activity, and now, the possibility of Laura's death. Tears spilled from his eyes as he was overcome with fear for the safety of his own family. He leaned his head against the tiled wall and prayed in earnest.

24

New York State

Helen screamed and struggled, as she felt someone grab her arm. She opened her eyes, expecting to see what she feared the most, an alien. Instead, the man who had slammed the door of the church in her face was dragging her into the building. He looked terrified.

The UFO was hovering over the small church, flooding it in a beam of blinding white light. Nearby, trees swayed in every direction, as if they were in a windstorm, and bits of litter, dust, and dead leaves swirled like snowflakes in a blizzard.

Helen's hair flew in all directions and her clothes flapped on her body. "Oh, thank you . . . thank you so much," she sobbed, as the man slammed the door and fumbled with the lock. He pulled Helen, now on her feet, toward the interior of the church and stopped when they reached the hand-carved wooden pulpit.

He managed to speak. "What is that . . . out there?"

"What does it look like to you?" Helen blurted back at him.

"A flying saucer," he said. "I never believed in them."

Helen looked at his shaking hands, then pointed to a row of stained-glass windows, lit up as if they had spotlights set behind them. She screamed, "Look, they're going to come in."

"Oh, my," the man exhaled.

Helen's body trembled, "They're after me . . ."

"What are they?" he asked.

Helen shook her head, wrapped her arms around herself, and began to cry.

Two of the stained-glass windows exploded inward, spraying the floor with shards of colored glass.

Helen screamed and dived under the pew next to her.

The man stepped back from the broken window as a shaft of brilliant light poured into the opening, illuminating the interior of the church. The entire building trembled, as if it were in the epicenter of an earthquake.

"What's happening?" the man shouted.

"Make it go away," Helen screamed. She crawled further under the pew.

The old man dropped to his knees, shouting, "This building is over two hundred years old; it can't take this. We've got to get out of here before it falls on us." He reached out to her.

"No," she cried, moving away from him.

A horrible, groaning sound came from the front doors. "The doors sound like they're breaking apart!" the old man shouted. He fell to the floor and covered his head with his hands.

The groaning grew louder, and Helen heard the tearing of wood. The doors came apart, and panels, styles, and rails flew into the church, crashing against the pulpit, knocking it over. It went end over end, splitting in two as it crashed against the back wall.

"Do something," she moaned.

Then she noticed that something had changed in him. He seemed to no longer be afraid. Where moments before there had been only fear and uncertainty, now he looked determined.

Helen watched as he straightened himself to his full height and turned toward the front door.

"What are you doing?" Helen screamed at him.

"Fighting what I've fought before," he said. In a loud voice, he cried out, "His faithfulness will be your shield and rampart. You will not fear the terror of the night, nor the arrow that flies by day, nor the pestilence that stalks in the darkness, nor the plague that destroys at midday."

He paused for a moment, then lifted his hands defiantly and began again, even more boldly than before. "Then no harm will befall you, no disaster will come near your tent. For he will command his angels concerning you to guard you in all your ways. 'Because he loves me,' says the Lord, 'I will rescue him; I will protect him, for he acknowledges my name. He will call upon me. And I will answer him; I will be with him in trouble.'"

Helen strained to hear what he said. In spite of the turmoil and deafening wind, she caught snatches of what the old man said. "Help your servant now . . . the forces of darkness . . . angels about us . . . break the hand of the enemy . . . Help us, Lord Jesus."

Helen moved closer to the old man from under the pew. *Isn't that what the man claimed on TV—that Jesus' name kept them away?* she thought.

The wind began to die down, and the shaking of the building subsided. Helen crawled out. "Is it leaving?" she asked.

Then, as if someone had pulled the plug, the blinding light pouring in from the empty window frames and doorway was extinguished.

Her body trembled as she listened for any sound that would indicate their return.

She got to her feet. "They're gone," she whispered, amazed. "They're really gone."

The old man took a deep breath and collapsed on the pew she had been hiding under. He raised a finger and pointed at the remains of a cross that still hung from the ceiling over where the pulpit had been. Her eyes followed, and it dawned on her that a force greater than that of the aliens had been called upon, and it had responded.

She wiped a tear that streaked down her cheek, then muttered, "Whoever you are . . . thank you."

25

✶ ⬤ ✶

Spiral of Life Headquarters, The Alps

Mac walked out of his room into the wide hallway that ran the length of the upper level. There were six bedroom doors set opposite each other in the hall. He found his way to the stone spiral staircase leading to the main hall of the castle, and, as he reached the bottom, he heard voices coming from a room down a corridor. He followed the sound to find Johanen, Knud, and Stephan seated at a large round table.

Johanen looked up as Mac entered and said with a wan smile, "Come and join us, MacKenzie. Hilda, as always, has prepared something delicious for us."

Mac took a seat next to Johanen and eyed the hot meal.

Moments later Colonel Austin entered and sat down. Now that all were present, Johanen raised his hands and blessed the food. Hilda dished out the hot stew, first to Mac, then Austin, then to everyone else, serving Johanen last.

Mac couldn't remember a more somber meal. He finally broke the silence as he turned to Hilda. "Wonderful stew," he said as he tore off a piece of dark rye bread and spread a generous amount of butter on it.

Hilda nodded in recognition, and silence once again settled over the table.

After the meal, Stephan and Knud helped Hilda clear the table and then found their places again. Hilda, the last to return, placed a single red rose in a crystal vase at the center of the table.

I wonder what the significance of the rose is, Mac thought, as Johanen began to pray first for Laura, and afterward for wisdom as to what the assembled group should do in her absence.

"Everything said here is *sub rosa*, meaning under the rose, and is regarded as confidential." He gestured to the rose. He took a deep breath. "Laura's plane has exploded and has killed all who were on board, but we must not abandon hope. There still might be a chance that she was not on it, but if that is not the case, then we also must face the fact that we may never know all of what General Nathan had intended for us." Johanen looked at each person before continuing.

"I think that in light of Laura's disappearance and possible death, I should inform you that General Nathan worked both sides of the fence. He was, in fact, a double agent, but his loyalties lay with us. He had almost unbearable pressure brought upon him, involving members of his family. He went to great lengths to find out about the tomb and the plans of our adversary. Whatever information General Nathan encrypted on the disk provoked someone to insure its destruction and Laura's. Other lives are dependent on what we do here, so we must continue."

Mac brushed a lock of hair from his forehead. "You mentioned earlier that the disk contained the location of the tomb."

"Yes, the tomb of 'Jesus,'" Johanen said. "In General Nathan's communiqué, he asserted that the tomb and the alien artifacts with the body were soon to be revealed to the world's governments. He also indicated that he would provide documentation, indicating a deliberate coverup by NASA concerning the ancient civilization on Mars."

"I thought those photos—what was it, the face on Mars?—weren't they disproved a while ago?" Mac asked.

Austin cleared his throat. "Some of us connected with black operations knew that story was released as disinformation for the public. All, of course, part of the coverup, so as not to initiate panic."

"The face on Mars is located in a region that our astronomers have named Cydonia. Aligned with the face are pyramids and other ancient structures that some say correspond with the complex of pyramids at Giza. In fact, these may be the ancient remains of the civilization that once was on Mars," Johanen began, "but not built by an alien race. The 'stones of fire,' as certain passages of Scripture refer to the planets in our solar system, are the planets that were given to Lucifer, the 'Son of the Morning,' to rule. One possible scenario might be that when he led a third of the angels in rebellion, his home planet, which now makes up the asteroid belt, was destroyed. That, along with the destruction of the civilization on Mars, may have been the first great war in heaven. Of course, you all must realize that this is conjecture."

"The first war?" Mac asked.

"The final war will be after Armageddon. Lucifer or Satan will be bound for one thousand years, then released for a short while. He will gather his forces and attack Jerusalem one last time. He will be defeated by the Meshiach Nagev, Messiah the King, who will then rule over the earth from Jerusalem."

"So from what you just said, you believe that the artifacts on Mars exist?" Mac asked.

"Yes," Johanen stated, "but they are the remains of the cities that the angels built *before* their rebellion. This deception—the supposed existence of an ancient alien civilization—will be used to ensnare the peoples of the earth. It will lead people away from the truth, which is the deity of Christ and his ransom for us by his death on the cross. Many inhabitants of the earth will believe the lie. Part of that lie will be to blend the religions of earth into one system. That system will be used to exalt the Son of Perdition, and the people of earth will worship him as God. And what better way to do it than to say that the aliens were responsible for all the great religions in the first place. By exhuming the body of Jesus, along with the supposed alien artifacts, they are well on their way to establishing their connection."

Knud looked at his watch and then excused himself.

"He has to check the computers and see what new information is on the Web site," Johanen explained as Knud left the room.

"The location of the tomb," Johanen continued, "could be anywhere on the planet, but I have a feeling that it is located somewhere in the Middle East."

"Why the Middle East?" Mac asked.

"Some believe that the Middle East is the cradle of civilization. With the abundance of undiscovered and ancient sites in the area, it would make sense to have the tomb located in Iraq or maybe Lebanon or even Egypt."

"The disk that Laura was carrying would have provided the location?" Hilda asked.

"That is what General Nathan led me to believe," Johanen replied.

"Is there any other way of finding the location?" Mac asked.

"My intelligence has informed me that soon they will reveal its location to a select group of people and connect it with extraterrestrial contact. They have specified a 'sign in the heavens' during the full lunar eclipse."

"And what will this sign be?" Mac asked.

"I do not have the answer to that, MacKenzie, but I have a feeling your father's crop circle might have something to do with it. His ranting about the New Christ would substantiate this line of thinking."

Knud rushed back into the room. "She's alive!" he exclaimed.

Johanen stood up. "Laura?" he asked.

Knud nodded. "Ya, Laura, alive, she contacted the website. I just now unscrambled the message. She's staying at a hotel in Rome. I answered her and said we would pick her up there."

"Good news," Johanen cried out.

"What happened? How did she know not to get on the plane?" Mac asked.

"She knew she was followed, ya? So she never got on it," Knud explained.

"Very resourceful woman," Johanen remarked. "We need to give thanks, right now, that she is alive."

Before Mac bowed his head and closed his eyes he saw Johanen's face broaden into a smile, as the man lifted his hands high into the air and gave thanks for Laura's safety. The little group congratulated each other after the prayer was finished, and Mac knew that a weight had been lifted from them all.

"I will leave to get her, unless you want me to do something different," Knud offered.

"No, what you have planned will work well. How is the media spinning the plane explosion?" Johanen asked.

"Still with the drugs, the smuggling of heroin," Knud answered.

Johanen thought for a moment. "Be on your guard. The Evil One is aware of us, and he seeks to destroy all that we do."

Then something happened that Mac had never seen before. Johanen, Hilda, and Stephan gathered around Knud and laid their hands on him.

"What are you doing?" Mac asked, confused by what he was seeing.

"It is something that was practiced in the early church," Johanen explained. "The laying on of hands. It will not hurt, I promise." He smiled at Mac.

Mac found a place between Johanen and Stephan and reached out with his right hand, and rested it on Knud's shoulder.

Mac listened while Johanen spoke words of encouragement to Knud and asked for the protection of both him and Laura. Afterward, he embraced the man.

They all ushered Knud to the massive front door and bade him Godspeed.

"He will be back in the morning," Johanen remarked.

If all goes well, Mac added to himself.

"MacKenzie, I would like to discuss something with you in private, before you retire," Johanen said.

Mac followed him back into the room with the round table. Johanen closed the door and took his customary seat.

Mac sat across from him.

"Sub rosa," Johanen reminded him as he pointed to the rose. "MacKenzie, you have been called to service."

Mac frowned. "Called by whom?"

Johanen folded his hands on the table. "By the Ancient of Days."

"You mean Jesus?" Mac asked.

"Yes, it is he, Jesus, in the Greek, Yeshua in Hebrew, or as I prefer to call him, Ancient of Days. I believe he is calling you from out of this world and its system into his service, but, of course, you have a choice."

Mac grimaced. "A choice like Colonel Austin gave me when he told me about my father's body and that we had to go to England?" Mac stated. "Not much of a choice there."

"No, not like that at all," Johanen countered. "If you choose not to serve, he will find another who is willing. You are not someone special, MacKenzie. Indeed, none of us are. But he has called you, and if you do not choose to serve, he will find another to accomplish his will."

Mac fidgeted in his chair. "Can I be honest?"

"Of course," Johanen replied.

"Johanen . . . I'm terrified of them, the aliens. If I stop and think about what I saw . . . at the base . . . if I start to dwell on it . . . it just shuts everything down. I feel I'm a prisoner of my own fear." He looked at the ceiling.

"You must learn to control your thought life, to take every one of your thoughts captive. You will find that if you do this, the enemy will not be able to gain a foothold in your mind. Remember that is where the battle lies."

Mac ran his hand through his hair a couple of times. "You know what else? I'm devastated by what has happened to my father. How do I know that something like that won't happen to me?"

"It will not, MacKenzie. Your father made a choice long ago to allow a satanic spirit to enter him, but you have the spirit of the living God in you. There is a world of difference."

"It's almost too much to think about," Mac said.

Johanen leaned forward at the edge of his seat. "MacKenzie, you must realize that forces are at work. What happened to Elisha, which manifested in his stroke, was no accident. Your interrogation, your father in England waiting for you, Laura's plane exploding just after takeoff . . ."

"But who's behind all of it?"

"MacKenzie," Johanen began, "what I am about to tell you will tie into our earlier discussion when we were on my boat. Do you remember?"

Mac nodded. "The Mystery of Iniquity?"

"Yes, those who serve the Evil One have many names attributed to them. Indeed, there is no one single entity, but many. The men and women who belong are diverse in power and geographical positioning. They share the commonality of money and power. They are like the tentacles of an octopus, but they are not limited to only eight arms. There are many more. They are not connected in the formal sense. There is no roster or membership roll, and yet they have been a driving force for centuries. It is they who are preparing the way for the

Man of Perdition, or, as many call him, Antichrist. Remember when I told you about him on the boat?"

Mac nodded.

"It is he who will take power and control the earth."

"Won't anyone stop him?" Mac asked.

"He is unstoppable in human terms. Only by God's direct intervention will he be put to an end."

"But what will happen to those on the earth?"

"It depends. Some hold to the position that those who believe in Yeshua will not go through what is called the time of Jacob's trouble. Others think that we will experience the rise of this person."

"You mean we will see the Antichrist?"

"It is a possibility. The early church was not spared persecution. But, MacKenzie, all of this is to help you understand that which you and I and others are to fight. You must know that you are a target. The enemy knows you and will try to destroy you."

Mac nodded.

"MacKenzie, I want you to rest tonight with what we have talked about. Turn it over in your heart, and pray that you will face your fear and yield to your calling. When the Ancient of Days was in the garden before his crucifixion, he prayed that the cup that was before him would be taken away."

Mac thought for a moment. "The cup? You're referring to his death? The Crucifixion?"

"Yes," Johanen said. "But in the end he uttered the words that changed the course of human history: 'Not *my* will but *yours* be done.' You see, MacKenzie; you also are faced with a decision. Will it be your will? What you want? Or will you choose to serve and let *his* will be worked through you?" Johanen paused a moment. "Pray for strength, MacKenzie, and I will add my prayers to yours. The hour is late, and we should sleep, for Laura will be here in the morning and with her the disk from her late father, General Nathan."

"I'll pray," Mac stated, "but I wish there was another way."

26

❖

New York State

W hat did you do?" Helen wanted to know. "Why did they go away? I'd give *anything* to be able to do that." She tried to smooth her hair back into place with her fingers.

The old man looked exhausted as he slouched in the front pew next to Helen. "I'm a retired missionary," he began. "I spent most of my tenure in Africa and then India. At first I was startled by it—the UFO."

"Who wouldn't be," Helen agreed.

"I'm the custodian of this old church," he went on. "I'm sort of a history buff, and this church is one of the oldest in this part of the state. I don't live far from here, so I volunteered to help look after it, and here I am."

"Lucky for me," Helen said.

"Oh, I don't think it was luck," the old man said.

"What do you mean?" Helen asked.

He chuckled. "I'm too tired to give you the explanation your question deserves, but God put me here today to help you."

"To help me?" Helen asked, confused by his statement.

The old man nodded. "The Lord knew of your need. He knew that I could help you, and that's why I'm here."

"I don't understand."

"Like I started to explain to you, my wife and I were missionaries. We experienced some very unusual supernatural occurrences while we were in Africa and India."

"Like what?" Helen asked.

"Exorcisms," the old man stated.

She gave him a puzzled look. "Like the movie?"

"I've never seen the movie, but while in India we were involved in several. One went on for several hours before we rid the person of the demon."

"But what does that have to do with UFOs and what just happened here?" She pointed at the debris scattered over the church.

"Everything," he said without hesitation. "I heard you screaming, so I went to the door and there you were, running toward me. I looked overhead and had the scare of my life. I reacted in fear. I must apologize for slamming the door in your face."

Helen nodded.

"After I shut the door, I realized the terrible mistake I made, and so here we are." He smiled. "Sometimes during an exorcism some very bizarre things occurred. The air would have this strangeness about it, almost like it was electrically charged, very much like what we felt today. I don't mean the wind bursting through doors. No, there's a feeling that starts way down in your gut and makes you very uneasy, something unseen, the presence of wickedness, of evil. I felt that here today." He shook his head at the disarray.

"Satan has many names. One of them is the Prince of the Power of the Air. Did you know that?" he asked.

Helen shook her head. "I've never been much on religion."

"What I'm talking about is not religion. It has to do with the truth that has been handed down to us through the centuries.

When I saw the UFO, I dropped my spiritual guard. I was terrified. But as the experience continued, I rallied and began to sense that what we were dealing with was in fact demonic . . . a manifestation from the Prince of the Power of the Air."

"But how can you be so sure?" Helen asked. "I've had to deal with these creeps since my early childhood."

"That's an interesting word for them, *creeps*." A tired smile spread across his face. "Look at what happened. I took authority over them. I commanded them to leave, and they were not able to stand against that."

"Why?" Helen asked.

"Because of my relationship with the only power that is *greater* than the Prince of the Power of the Air."

"God?"

"Yes, God, and his Son, Jesus. You know about Jesus?"

"Some. But what does that have to do with anything?"

"Jesus showed his authority over nature when he walked on water. He demonstrated his authority over the elements when he fed the five thousand with just a few loaves and fishes. He revealed his authority over the supernatural when he cast many demons out of a man."

"I've never heard those stories. But I still don't see any connection. Jesus wasn't here."

The old man shook his head. "No, you're wrong there. He was here. The psalm I recited just before I prayed, remember?"

Helen nodded.

"'He will call upon me and I will rescue him,'" the old man quoted.

"You called on 'him,' and they went away. I've never been able to do anything like that," Helen said.

"Because all of this takes place in a different realm. You are fighting powers that you can't imagine. Powers that are ancient and very real."

"I spent the night in a hotel in Philadelphia, and there was this talk show on about aliens. There was a panel of people. One guy didn't think aliens existed. Another believed in them, but thought they were ETs here to help mankind evolve. They also had a woman who, like me, claimed to be abducted. Anyway, the last person was this man who said, like you do, that Jesus could stop abductions. He even had names of several former abductees to back up his story."

"That's very interesting. It's like you were shown ahead of time what was going to happen."

"I don't get it."

The old man leaned forward in the pew. "Isn't that what happened here?"

Helen thought for a moment. "Yeah, I suppose."

"Weren't they trying to abduct you?" he asked.

"Yes, they were." Helen gave him a brief explanation of what her life had been like since her early childhood, then explained the letter her father had given her at his death.

When she finished there was a long silence between them, which the old man broke. "So you're trying to get to Ithaca to find the pilot that your father told you about, who will take you to this man, Johanen?" he asked.

She nodded and twirled a strand of hair in her fingers, managed not to nibble at the ends of it, but instead, chewed one of her nails. She picked the piece of fingernail out of her mouth and admitted, "Right now it's the only thing that makes sense in my crazy life."

"You're welcome to stay with me and my wife for a while," the old man offered.

Helen sat up so that she faced him. "No one has ever done anything like that for me," she said, "except my mom."

The old man chuckled. "We'd love to have you."

Helen folded her arms as she thought the offer over. "I can't. I want to, but I can't. I have to see this thing through to the end. I want to be free from them."

The old man sat up and stretched. "You do what you have to, but you hold the key in your hand to your own prison."

"Huh?"

"The key is to ask Jesus in your heart. Then his authority becomes your authority."

She nodded, but she didn't fully understand what he was saying.

Car tires crunched on the gravel outside and interrupted the moment.

"Looks like we have some company," the old man said.

They got up and walked down the aisle to what had been the front door.

"Oh, boy, how are we going to explain this?" the old man said.

"You two okay?" a state trooper called, as he got out of his patrol car and donned a big Smokey-the-Bear hat.

"We're fine," the old man called back.

The trooper reached them and whistled through his teeth as he saw the damage. "What happened here, bear get inside or something?"

The old man caught Helen's eye. "No, Officer, I'm the caretaker of this church, and I'm afraid we had some unexpected visitors." He winked at Helen.

"Have you filled out a report?"

"No, I haven't done that yet," he replied.

Helen looked at her car, which was off the road with the door wide open, and tried to think of a good excuse as to why she had left it in that condition.

"Are you two related?" the trooper asked.

Helen looked at the old man, and they both burst out laughing.

"Is that your car? The one with the door open?" the trooper asked.

Helen put on her best smile. "Yes, it's a bad habit of mine; sometimes I forget to close the door."

"Oh," the trooper replied.

Helen knew that he didn't buy it. *He must have seen the skid marks*, she thought.

"I'll get my book, and you can fill out a report. And I'd like to see some ID from you, miss," the trooper said.

"Sure." Helen went to her car, slipped her lost shoe back on, got her purse, and came back. "Here it is," she said, handing it to him.

The trooper looked at the ID. "Changed your hair color, huh?"

Helen smiled. "You like it?"

The trooper didn't answer as he handed her the wallet.

"So tell me what happened," the trooper said. He pulled out his pen and listened to the old man begin a lecture on the attributes of the Prince of the Power of the Air.

Half an hour later, a nervous and confused state trooper pulled away.

"I thought he'd never leave," Helen said.

"I hope I didn't scare him," the old man chuckled. "I just told him the truth, from a biblical perspective."

Helen managed a laugh.

"Well, what are you going to do?" he asked, picking up the thread of their former conversation.

Helen played with a strand of hair and almost put it in her mouth. She said, "I have to go. But I know you understand."

"I do, but what I offered still stands."

"About staying with you?" Helen asked.

"Yes, but more importantly, that you have the key," he said.

"I'll think about that," she said. "Like I told you, I'm trying to get to Ithaca. Will you help me get back on the right road?"

He chuckled again. "You did get turned around, didn't you?"

"Will you? Take me to the right road?" she asked again.

He smiled and nodded okay.

* ο *

A while later the old man pulled off to the side of the road near an intersection and got out of his car. "Make a right up there at the light, and that will take you to Route 72, and from there follow the signs to Ithaca," he said.

Helen grabbed her purse and took a wad of bills out. "I can never thank you enough for how you helped me. This is something for the church, to repair it."

"I can't accept that," the old man began.

Helen took a step away from him and held out her hand. "I won't take no for an answer, and that's final," she said.

The old man shook his head. "Okay," he said as he took the money. "You know, I don't even know your name."

Helen smiled. "Helen," she replied.

"I'm Robert Sorenson," he said.

Without another word they embraced. He held her, as a father would a daughter, and she nestled her head against him.

27

✦ ◉ ✦

Israeli Desert

The robed man leaned on his staff and paused between two large boulders. He had walked the remainder of the morning, his sandaled feet picking their way through the rugged terrain, and the path he had traveled wound its way over and across a wadi, a dry stream, for several miles. He stopped, for his eyes had spotted a slight movement in the desert before him. He moved closer, always with his staff in front of him. The thing moved, and he knew it was an asp, a very poisonous snake lying in front of him.

"One bite from you, my friend, will leave a man dead in less than a minute," he said out loud. He moved closer, and the asp coiled itself and flicked its tongue out of its mouth several times, testing to see what was approaching.

The asp coiled itself, and then without warning shot forward toward the intruder. The man had anticipated this, and remained a safe distance away where he knew the snake could not reach.

He placed his staff on the ground in front of him. He watched as it began to move, to change its appearance, and become a living thing. A few moments later the staff had transformed into a very large asp that wiggled in front of him. He watched as it approached the smaller snake, and then, without warning, began to devour it, in several jerking motions. The tail of the snake being eaten wiggled from its mouth, and then it too disappeared. The man reached down and grabbed the large asp by the tail, and the form began to change again. It grew rigid, and once again became the staff. He paused at the spot where the snake had been eaten, and glanced at landmarks in the distance that he had memorized long ago. He got his bearings, then continued on his journey.

28

Rome, Italy

Good to hear your voice, Bernstein," Mr. Wyan called out to his speaker phone. "Mr. Kenson is here, so you'll be talking to us both."

"Very well. Greetings to both of you," Bernstein's voice responded. There was no mistaking the excitement in it.

"How are things at the tel?" Wyan asked.

"More fantastic by the minute. We have cleared most of the sand from around the megaliths, and at the base of each there is writing that corresponds to what we found on the sarcophagus in the tomb."

"Splendid," Wyan said. "I assume you have found the area where the altar is. Is it where we thought it would be?"

"Yes, my associate Mr. Haney is supervising it personally. Gleason will be sending the photos of it over the Internet soon," Bernstein responded. "No later than mid-day."

"I want the area around the altar tented and roped off. Also make sure that you place a few of your security men around it. Which brings me to my next point. Are they earning their pay?" Wyan asked.

Bernstein chuckled. "The laser fence is in place and working. Last night they caught a shepherd boy and some sheep hiding in a small cave at the perimeter of the tel. One of the sheep must have triggered the fence."

"And how did you handle it?" Wyan asked.

"Oh, the boy was scared witless. Security drove him out of the area. We won't be seeing him anymore," Bernstein stated.

"Good work, Doctor. Did you discover any peculiarities about the altar?" Wyan asked.

"Yes, sir, it is buried deeper than I anticipated. We have, however, cleared much of the rubble and sand from around it, and something else. We found artifacts . . . Haney believes they may date to the Crusades. We found spearheads, and portions of a shield, and quite a few bones. All fairly well preserved."

"Interesting, Doctor," Wyan said.

"Puzzling, though, much too far south to have been Crusaders. There appear to be signs of a battle that took place near the actual tomb itself."

"Grave robbers?" Wyan suggested.

"A possibility, but it's of little importance in light of our real discovery."

"Yes, Doctor, you're right," Wyan replied. "Of course you will be able to meet our broadcast date? We have added another dozen nations to our growing list favoring the disclosure of the alien presence. They are eagerly anticipating the sign in the heavens."

"We're on task," Bernstein said. "I'll be running a test of the teleportation technology equipment personally."

"I look forward to seeing it so I'll leave you to your work, but before I do, I want to remind you again to provide an enclosure around the area of the altar. It is very important to me that you do this."

"As you wish, Mr. Wyan. I want you to know that everyone participating in the tel is very excited. Several have asked when . . ." He cleared his throat. "When the Watchers are going to make a visit."

"The Watchers will arrive at the appointed time. After all, it is they who are responsible for the tomb in the first place."

"Of course, we're all just very anxious, or perhaps apprehensive is a better word."

"Nothing to be apprehensive about, Doctor. After all, *you* have had contact before, and most of the others in your group have had similar encounters, which is one reason why they were recruited and groomed for what we are engaged in at present."

"Yes, you're right, of course, Mr. Wyan. I suppose it's the enormity of knowing that we will bring the truth to the world when the extraterrestrials reveal themselves."

"Understood, Doctor. Well, I'll be waiting for your photographs and your testing of the equipment."

"You'll be seeing both shortly."

"Great, keep up the good work. Mr. Kenson sends his regards. Goodbye, Doctor." He hung up the phone. "Well, Mr. Kenson, there you have it. All proceeding just as we hoped."

Kenson nodded, but remained focused on the levitation of three silver balls that spun around each other in concentric circles above the six fingers of his hand.

29

Spiral of Life Headquarters, the Alps

Mac was awakened by a loud knock on his door.

"Good morning, Mr. MacKenzie," Hilda called out. "I have some fresh coffee, and more importantly, Laura has arrived safely. She is with us now."

Mac sat up and looked around; the room was still dark. He climbed out of bed and opened the heavy curtains, which had blocked almost all of the daylight from the room. *No wonder I slept in,* he thought, then answered Hilda. "Come in, Hilda, I'm decent."

Hilda entered with a large steaming cup of coffee. "Here you are, Mr. MacKenzie." She handed him the mug.

"Thanks. So Laura's here . . . that's great. What time is it?"

Hilda glanced at her watch. "Almost nine-thirty. What a miracle that she lives."

Mac nodded. "Yes, Hilda, a miracle." He took a sip from the mug. "What's in it that tastes so good?" he asked.

Hilda grinned. "Cinnamon and chocolate."

"Tell Johanen I'll be down in a minute. Let me just get a quick shower," Mac said, taking a long sip of his excellent coffee.

∗ ○ ∗

Mac found his way to the round table room, as he had begun to call it, and found everyone else huddled around Laura, asking her questions. Unnoticed by the group, he stared at Laura for a moment, and was taken aback by how beautiful she was. For a moment he let his mind go to what might have happened if he had not gotten back together with Maggie . . . but only for a moment. He checked the thought with a quick prayer and realized that he was beginning to get control over his thought life, as Johanen had admonished him to do.

Laura's eyes met his and she smiled. The group parted and Mac walked toward her.

"You're lucky to be alive," he said as he hugged her.

"It was much too close," she admitted. "I see the colonel accomplished another mission," she said, referring to Mac's rescue from Scrimmer.

"Thanks to your father," Mac admitted. "I'm sorry about his death."

"I still can't believe he's gone." She looked away for a moment.

"It's ready to go, sir," Stephan's voice interrupted.

"Good, then let us put it up on the big screen," Johanen answered.

Stephan took out a remote control, and the screen came down on the far side of the room.

"You will have to adjust some of your seats to get a good view," Johanen said.

Mac found a chair between Laura and Colonel Austin. The lights were dimmed, and the first of the decoded documents appeared on the screen.

"It looks like some sort of genealogy," Mac offered.

"Yes, that is, in fact, what I believe it is. Those who claim lineage to Jesus and Mary Magdalene," Johanen stated. "But we know that this union between them never took place. It is, of course, heretical, and in spite of all that has been done to refute it, the heresy remains very much alive today."

"But it appears to be so complete," Laura stated.

"Only if you believe that Jesus didn't ascend to heaven but remained on earth, siring children," Johanen stated.

Stephan scrolled down to the next page.

"This appears to be a very old map of the Middle East. I believe this map shows Jerusalem under the rule of Mohammed," Johanen said.

"The countries are drawn out of proportion," Laura added.

"They don't sync with anything modern," Colonel Austin confirmed.

"Look at the cross at the bottom of the page," Johanen pointed. "I would venture to say we are looking at a map from one of the Crusades. This cross is one used exclusively by the Knights Templar."

"Who were they?" Mac asked, wondering what new information he would become privy to.

"Perhaps they are one of the reasons why we're having this meeting," Johanen said. "It is that group of men, the Knights Templar, who, when they regained control of Jerusalem from the Mohammedans, carried out primitive archaeological digs. Their most noteworthy find was the Shroud of Turin."

"The burial cloth of Jesus—at least that's what some believe," Knud added.

"But what does this have to do with the tomb of Jesus?" Mac asked.

"I'm sure General Nathan will tell us," Johanen said. "Scroll down to the next page."

"What are we looking at now?" Mac asked.

"It appears to be a photograph of a very old document," Stephan suggested.

"Yes, but what does it say? What language is it?" Austin asked.

Mac saw Johanen stare at the document. "It has been written on parchment, and I am certain that it is very ancient Hebrew."

Mac turned to Laura. "Your father didn't expect us to read this, did he?"

"He must have provided a translation. Scroll down further," Laura suggested.

Johanen chuckled. "I am very familiar with the language. But see if your father provided a translation."

"Bingo," Mac said under his breath, as Stephan scrolled down showing the translation of the document. "English, my first and only language," Mac quipped.

Laura elbowed him and flashed Mac a smile, enjoying his levity.

"This is what we have been waiting for," Johanen said. "Read at your own pace, and when all have finished we will go to the next page."

There were three pages, and when he reached the end, Mac found himself in a state of confusion.

"Well, here are some of the roots of the present-day deception," Johanen announced.

"It sounds so believable though, doesn't it?" Laura said.

"I agree," Mac added.

"There is a body, and there is a tomb, of that there can be no doubt," Johanen said. "But we know that this goes against the account of those who were present at the time of the Lord's ascension." He flashed the group a broad smile.

"The Knights Templar record the tomb on the map," Knud said, using a laser pointer to show the tomb's location, "but they are not responsible for its construction."

"So where does the location of the tomb correspond in modern times?" Mac asked.

"I'll get a map," Stephan offered, and left the room. He returned with a large, rolled-up map of the world. He spread it on top of the round table, setting the vase containing the rose over North America as he did so.

Knud examined the ancient map. "Here." He circled the area of the map with his forefinger. "Present day Yemen."

Johanen pointed to the map on the screen with the laser pointer. "According to this, the tomb is located south of the Red Sea, here." He circled the area with his pointer. "Yes, Knud, I agree, this is the modern country of Yemen."

"But if the Knights Templar knew of the tomb why didn't they exhume it themselves?" Mac asked.

"Good point," Laura agreed.

"Let's see what else your father's disk has to offer us," Johanen suggested. "He may provide the answer to your question."

Stephan continued to scroll down, and on the following pages were descriptions of a flying disk along with a rendering of the site in Yemen.

"What are those? Giant stones?" Mac asked.

"They are megaliths," Knud said.

"Megaliths," Mac repeated. "Like at Stonehenge?"

"Very similar," Johanen said. "In fact, the same intelligence that is responsible for Stonehenge might also be responsible for the megaliths found here."

"Who put them there?" Laura asked.

"How much do they weigh?" Mac added.

"Hundreds of tons each," Knud said. "This site in Yemen must predate Islam by thousands of years."

"It all may go back to the Sons of God, or what I would call the 'Fallen Angels,'" Johanen said. "These sites scattered in different locations on earth may be the remains of the civilization that existed before the flood of Noah, built by the fallen angels. Have you ever heard of Baalbek?" he asked the group.

Mac shook his head in bewilderment along with Laura and Austin, but he noticed that Stephan, Knud, and Hilda seemed to be on familiar ground.

"Well, the site of Baalbek is truly one of the unsung wonders of the ancient world."

"How so?" Mac asked.

"There are columns that are erected at Baalbek that we, in the modern world, would be hard pressed to move today, and yet they have been quarried and placed with precision at the base of the Temple at Baalbek. Local legend has it that the 'giants' built it just after the flood."

"By giants, do you mean the Nephilim?" Mac asked.

"Yes, Mac, the Nephilim," Johanen replied.

"Are you aware that certain ancient Hindu manuscripts describe flying disks and a great battle in the skies?" Knud asked.

"I've heard that story," Laura replied.

"All part of the legends that have come down through history describing some of the mischief of the Fallen Ones," Johanen said.

"They would have the technology to place the megaliths, from what we've seen," Stephan added.

"Yes, precisely," Johanen agreed, "and according to General Nathan, when this is discovered, it will link directly to the monuments on Mars."

"So it will tie the two civilizations together," Knud added.

"And more diabolically, establish that it was alien intervention that allowed Jesus to do the miracles," Johanen said.

"But why didn't the Knights Templar try to get it?" Laura pressed. "Wouldn't this be *the* Holy Grail?"

"Who knows, maybe they attempted to do that very thing, but were stopped by this." Johanen used the laser to point to the picture of a flying disk that was drawn on the parchment. "Because the time for the tomb to be revealed did not jibe with Satan's timetable."

"So what do we do now that we know of the tomb's location?" Mac asked.

"Destroy it," Johanen said without hesitation.

"Destroy it?" Mac repeated. "How?"

"Before I reveal what I have in mind, there is more we need to discuss. Laura, I need to prepare you for what I am about to disclose to you. This was the last communiqué from your father, and as I understand it, not even you were aware of this." Johanen handed a picture of a young woman to Stephan and asked all of them to examine it closely. "The person you are looking at is Helen Mintzer. Laura, she is your half sister."

Mac turned in time to see Laura's face twist in confusion. He reached out and grabbed her hand.

"I am sorry to be so direct, Laura, but it is precisely what your father, General Nathan, instructed me to do before he succumbed to his illness."

"But I had no idea," Laura managed to exclaim.

"He kept it secret until he was sure he was going to die, then he sent me this." Johanen held up a disk. "It is how the picture was reproduced. According to his disclosure, Helen Mintzer, his illegitimate daughter, haunted him all the years of his life. Here is an overview of what transpired. In the years after the Roswell crash, General Nathan was told that the aliens wanted one of his children, specifically you, Laura, for genetic testing. You were just a baby at the time. Remember it was an era when the United States government was desperate for the alien technology, and because of that we allowed them a certain degree of access to our population. All of this was to be under government supervision. Initially, the aliens seemed to be cooperative, but then a disk went down at Kecksberg, Pennsylvania, and human body parts were found on board. This, of course, outraged your government. Your father began to realize that they couldn't be trusted, that there was a hidden agenda, and that the aliens were compulsive liars. But they continued to insist on one of his children. Your father was put in a horrible position, and in the end he compromised by allowing the aliens to pick out the woman he was to have an affair with, the sole purpose being to sire a child. She was a nurse who was stationed near Roswell. Unknown to her, the child, Helen, was taken periodically for what appeared to be genetic testing by the aliens. Your father informed me that Helen bore a child when she was just thirteen. What makes this especially troubling is that he believes the father of the child was someone very important in the alien hierarchy. He lived his entire life regretting his decision, and since reading the letter I have wondered why he didn't seek my help long before this. But I did not meet your father until several years ago, and by then the damage was done. He informed me that he left her money and the means of contacting me here at Spiral of Life. She has been abducted all her life, and your father's one last wish was to set her free from them."

Mac looked at Laura, who remained in a state of shock. He glanced around the table and saw that all eyes were on her. He saw her straighten and lean forward so that her elbows rested on the table. "It makes sense . . . ," she began, and rubbed the tears that were streaming down her face. "It's the one thing he was trying to tell me about, at the end. He tried several times but never could cross the line. It must have tortured him."

"It did, Laura," Johanen replied. "The choice he made to save you put another life in your place."

Laura stifled a sob. "So where is she?"

"I am not certain, but I do believe she is on her way here. According to your father's letter she is making her way to someone I helped a few years ago, a pilot by the name of John Crawford."

Laura nodded, then rose from the table. "I need a few minutes," she said. Johanen took her in his arms. Hilda rose from her seat also and together they led her out of the room. Mac heard her unrestrained sobs echo through the halls of the castle.

When Johanen returned without Hilda, Mac thought he looked very tired.

Johanen pulled the map closer to him. "Now that we have the precise location, I can finalize my thoughts. I will send a copy of this to Dr. Elisha and Uri in Israel, so they will be up to speed on this when we arrive. Now look here . . ." Johanen reached for the vase containing the rose and set it in front of him as he began to outline his idea. But all Mac could think about was Laura and the sacrifice that had been made for her.

30

* ◉ *

Ithaca, New York

Helen pulled her car into the small airport just outside the city of Ithaca. She grabbed her purse, dug out the letter from her father, and looked for the hangar number.

"Hangar 11," she read out loud. She looked past the chainlink fence that separated the parking lot from the hangars.

She grabbed her purse, got out of her car, and walked to the open gate in the fence. She went by several hangars until she came to one that was open.

"Listen, Charlie," she heard one man say, "the part needs to be replaced; it's showing signs of metal fatigue."

"It's good for another few . . ." and his voice trailed off as she moved past the entrance.

She reached number 11 and found it, too, was closed.

Now what? she thought, staring at the closed corrugated door.

A cold breeze blew, and she folded her arms in front of her. She walked back to the open hangar, the one where the two mechanics were arguing.

"Excuse me," she called out, at the entrance. *It really is getting cold,* she thought as she waited for an answer. *I wonder if I should go back to the car for a sweater.*

"Just a minute, okay?" a voice bellowed. "I'm telling you, Charlie, the part has to be replaced." The mechanic crawled out from the rear of a small private jet.

He looked Helen over as he stood up and smiled. "Can I help you?"

"I'm looking for a Jack Crawford . . . in hangar number 11. Do you know where I can find him? Is he here on weekdays?"

"Crawford?" the man repeated. "Think he's at lunch . . . should be back in a few minutes." He looked outside at the sky. "Something comin' in . . . looks bad too."

Helen glanced over her shoulder and saw the dark line of an incoming storm.

"You can wait for him here, if you like," the mechanic offered, pointing to a plastic chair with some lewd magazines stacked on it.

Helen glanced at the chair. "No, thanks, I'll just wait in my car." She turned to leave.

The mechanic grinned once more at Helen and headed back to his work.

* ○ *

Helen waited almost half an hour, and the storm broke. The rain came in sheets so intense she couldn't see more than ten feet in front of her rain-soaked windshield.

A jeep pulled up in front of hangar 11. She saw a man bolt out of it and fumble with the lock on the hangar door. The key wouldn't spring the lock. She watched as the man finally resigned himself to getting soaked while he opened the hangar door. The lock finally sprang, and he rolled the door up and disappeared inside.

Helen saw the door roll back down, half closed. "I guess it's my turn," she said out loud, as she wished for an umbrella. She waited another minute, hoping the storm would ease up.

Finally admitting that it wouldn't, she opened the door, clutched her bag like a running back, and made a dash toward hangar 11.

She arrived at the hangar, ducked under the door, and almost crashed into the man who happened to be standing just on the other side with his back toward her.

"I'm sorry," Helen said as she wiped her face.

He turned around, and she got her first glimpse of him. He was about the same age as she, well over six feet, with sandy blond hair cut close to his scalp. His eyes, besides being set too close, also had a black spot near one of the pupils. He looked at her with a mixture of surprise and interest.

"Are you Jack Crawford?" she asked, moving the wet tangles of hair from her face.

"Yeah, that's me," he said, wiping his wet palm on his jeans and offering his hand to her.

"I'm Helen," she said, taking his hand. As their hands touched she felt a tingle course through her which she tried to ignore.

"Just Helen?" Crawford asked, and he smiled at her.

She nodded. "It's a long story, but Helen will do ... for now."

"Hold up a minute, I'll get us a towel." Crawford hustled back in the hangar and returned with a roll of paper towels.

Helen wiped her face, then used another and patted her hair. "Thanks," she said. She searched her purse, found a comb, and began to comb out the tangles.

"What can I do for you?" Crawford asked.

Helen pulled out the letter her father had given her and handed it to him.

Crawford took it and turned to the last page to see who had written it.

She saw the lightheartedness disappear from his face. "General Nathan wrote this? Why don't we go back into my office?" He closed the hangar door and locked it. "I have a portable heater there. We can get warmed up and dried off."

She followed him to the rear of the hangar.

"What kind of plane is that?" she asked as she passed a plane that was undergoing an overhaul.

"It's a German fighter plane from World War II, a Messerschmidt 109," he answered. "I restore them . . . it's a part of what I do, other than run my charter business. It's something that I really enjoy."

They entered the office, and Helen's eye went to the wooden airplane propellers that hung from the walls and ceiling.

"You collect these things?" she asked.

He looked at her and smiled. "A couple of these are pretty famous, like this one here." He touched one that hung closest to his desk. "Amelia Earhardt," he said.

"Really?" Helen asked.

"Yep, this one once made her airborne." He ran his finger over it. He motioned toward one of the chairs in front of his desk.

Helen smoothed her wet skirt several times, then sat down.

Crawford spread the letter out on the desk and began to read. Afterward, he folded it and handed it back to Helen.

"Well?" she asked.

"Oh, boy," he said. He kept his eyes lowered. "And you've lived with this for how long?"

"Since I was a little girl."

"So he's your father?"

She nodded. She gathered her hair with both hands behind her head and ran her fingers down its length, causing drips of water to fall on her neck and shoulders.

"What's your connection?" Helen asked. "Why didn't he just tell me where this Johanen guy lived and let me go there? Why are you so special?"

Crawford put his hands on the folder. "I think maybe he did this for two reasons . . . brought me into this, that is," he began. "The first is that I'm a lot like you. I've had similar experiences with them. The second is that I know Johanen and lived with him for almost a year. He freed me from what was going on."

"The abductions?" Helen asked. She leaned forward on the desk so that her wet hair began to drip on it. "Oh, sorry." She wiped it off with the back of her hand.

"Yes, he stopped them cold. They've never returned."

"So how did you know my father?"

"At one time I was a test pilot for the Air Force. I flew a lot of experimental aircraft, and that's how your father came into the picture."

"In the Air Force?" Helen repeated.

"Yep, and I still rue the day I met him."

"What do you mean?"

"He approached me with a top-secret assignment, but it was on a volunteer basis. After I heard what was required, if I found it too risky I didn't have to volunteer for the duty."

"It was UFO stuff, wasn't it?" Helen asked, anticipating where he was headed.

"Yeah, two other guys signed up for it also, and out of the three of us, I was the only one who made it through."

"What happened to the others?"

"Both of them cracked up."

"You mean they crashed?"

"No, I mean they went mental. The testing involved dealing with alternative life forms, as we were told to call them. We were taught a technique called remote viewing. We would 'go' to a prearranged place in our thoughts and use the technique to establish contact with the alternative life form."

Helen looked confused. "I don't understand what you're talking about," she said.

"You project your thoughts or consciousness to wherever you are told to go, and then report what you see. But what your father neglected to tell us is that the technique was a springboard into the occult. It opened a door into a terrifying world, and in my case only Johanen was able to close it."

"So how does that tie into the UFO thing?"

"Your father asked me to project myself to Roswell, New Mexico, in the summer of 1947. I did, and made contact with an alien being."

"And what happened?"

"It wouldn't leave me alone. I couldn't turn it off anymore. It had control of my thought life. The other two guys, like I said, couldn't handle it. They went over the deep end."

"And what did my father do to help?"

"That's where Johanen came in. The other two had cracked up. Your father realized that whatever it was we had contacted was evil. He pulled the plug on the project and introduced me to Johanen. I stayed with him a year, and learned a lot."

"Like what?" Helen asked.

"Like what I was experiencing from the remote viewing was what people for thousands of years have called 'having a familiar spirit' or demon possession."

"You believe in that?" Helen asked.

"After what I've been through, yes."

"But how can you make a connection between UFOs, aliens, and demons?"

"You know from your own experiences what they're like. How they lie and manipulate, how they try to control everything you do. The way they take you whenever they want to."

Helen shuddered, as she thought of her very recent encounter at the church.

"I hate him," she stated.

"Your father?" Crawford asked.

"He's not my father," she raised her voice. "Maybe he sired me in some one-night stand with my mother, so I guess you could say that he was biologically responsible for his share of the chromosomes, but in no way was he ever a father. Like I said, I hate him, and how he's ruined my life."

"I hated him too. I felt used, and cheated out of what I loved, being a test pilot."

"He just uses people," Helen continued. "Part of me is scared that this whole thing, the money, and the mystery man Johanen, is just some ploy that he's using from beyond the grave to get me to do something that he wants. I don't trust him, and yet what other choice is there? Not to go?"

Crawford said, "I don't think your father had any other motive except that he felt guilty as all get out, and he was trying to make amends."

"Maybe you're right, but it still doesn't change the way I feel about him. To think he set me up to be abused by the aliens. Do you realize that while most kids were thinking about Santa Claus, I was being abducted and probed, and I thought this was normal! I thought that everybody went through this. I thought . . ." And she started to cry.

Crawford got up, came around the desk, knelt down on one knee, and held her. "You're not alone," he said. "I'm here, and I'll help you."

He too began to cry, and they clung to each other.

31

＊◉＊

Tel Aviv, Israel

Mac watched Johanen and Austin leave the cockpit of Johanen's private jet and move aft, where he and Laura were seated.

"Auto pilot?" Laura asked.

Johanen nodded. "And good weather for flying too," he remarked, as he swiveled in his seat so that he faced Mac and Laura, while Austin chose to remain standing.

"From what Dr. Elisha told me, both of you had a very dangerous encounter," Johanen said.

"Yes, it nearly killed me," Laura said, shuddering. "I'll never forget the rage, the hatred that came from it."

"Overwhelming hatred," Mac agreed.

"And so it is with those who serve the Evil One," Johanen began. "Hatred is what possesses them. They become more twisted and malevolent as time passes. They seek only to enslave and destroy as many souls as they can."

Mac thought about his father cursing as he hovered above the field in England. "My father is an example of that, isn't he?" he asked Johanen.

"I am afraid he is, MacKenzie. But there is always hope, until one passes from this life; still a chance, however remote it may be, that your father will turn his heart to the one who holds the keys to life and death." Johanen changed the subject. "When we arrive in Israel we will rendezvous with Dr. Elisha and Uri at the prison where the Nazi guard is being held."

"Isn't that what caused Dr. Elisha to have the stroke in the first place?" Mac asked.

"Yes, and it is why we are meeting him at the prison. It is for Elisha; he will forgive the guard."

"Forgive the guard who killed his brother?" Mac asked.

"Isn't that a little much to ask?" Laura said.

"If he chooses not to forgive, then the guard will always have power over him. The root of bitterness will override all else until it consumes him," Johanen answered.

"Why can't he just telephone the guard and be done with it, or write a letter?" Mac asked.

"The guard doesn't deserve as much," Laura added. Mac noticed that she did little to hide the contempt on her face.

"It is the main reason why we are taking this little detour from our present objective," Johanen answered. "There is something for all of us to learn by this."

"All of us?" Mac asked, unsure what Johanen meant.

"Yes, MacKenzie, we are all going to be there," Johanen announced. "We will be present during the confrontation."

"Confrontation?" Laura echoed.

"I say shoot the jerk, he doesn't deserve it," Austin interjected. Mac suppressed a chuckle.

Johanen paused a moment. "The Nazi guard has spent a lifetime in service to the Evil One. When Elisha was asked to confirm the guard's identity, the meeting opened up a deep wound in him, and who can blame him for feeling angry and bitter?"

"I don't understand," Laura said.

"He went into that meeting remembering the most desperate time in his life, and when he saw the guard who was responsible for his brother's death, it was too much for him. What he did not realize, and what I have come to believe, is that this guard may have been placed there by those who seek to destroy Elisha and the rest of us."

"You mean this is all connected in some way?" Mac asked. "I find that incredible."

Johanen nodded. "Yes, what happened to Elisha is bound up in the many threads of the Mystery of Iniquity, as I have labored to instruct you. This is the power of the Evil One. The guard has given himself over to lawlessness, to evil, and much like your father, Mac, there is only the shell of the man that was. He was used like the pawn he is."

"And Elisha is up for this?" Mac asked.

"He is strong now, and he realizes who it is he will confront. But that is why we will be present with him. The power of the Ancient of Days is stronger. Indeed, he that resides in you, MacKenzie, is stronger than he that is in the world. As I said earlier, this Nazi guard has a chance to reverse his eternal destiny, even at what may seem to be this late hour. Heaven or hell is before him, and Elisha has a very poignant opportunity to shake this man to his core by choosing to forgive him, and in doing so perhaps save the man's soul."

I wonder if my father has that chance, Mac thought. He felt an unwanted shiver run down the length of his spine.

* ○ *

Mac watched with admiration as Laura landed the jet on the tarmac of the Tel Aviv airport.

"Very nice," Johanen praised her, while Austin nodded his approval.

"A little different than the BlackBird, hey, Mac?" Austin teased.

"Just a little." Mac added to the chatter but felt left out, as he was the only nonpilot among the four of them.

"Oh, I've always wanted to fly in that plane," Laura said, the envy rising in her voice.

"We'll see if we can get you up in one when all this is over," Colonel Austin promised.

Is it ever going to be over? Mac thought.

Laura taxied the jet where the control tower indicated.

Johanen depressurized the cabin and then opened the door. Israeli soldiers positioned a boarding ladder in place, and an officer boarded the plane. "Shalom, and welcome to Israel," he said. "I'm Lieutenant Cohen, and from Dr. Ben-Hassen's description, you must be Johanen."

Mac watched the two men greet each other.

"Dr. BenHassen has arranged everything," Cohen said. "If you will all follow me, we'll transport you to the meeting place."

Mac was the last to exit the jet. He and Johanen climbed into one of the two waiting vans while Laura and Austin found seats in the other. Soldiers moved their baggage to the vans, and they were on their way to meet Elisha and Uri.

Cohen turned around from the front passenger seat and asked Mac, "Is this your first time in Israel?"

"No, actually I was here fairly recently," he answered.

"And you?" Cohen directed his query to Johanen.

"I have been here more times than I can count," Johanen answered. "This country is in my bones, and in fact my heart resides here." He laughed.

"Dr. BenHassen is feeling much better," Cohen began. "We were afraid we were going to lose him. From what I hear, he had a miraculous recovery."

Mac saw Johanen's face brighten as he declared, "I am delighted that the elder BenHassen is doing better."

"He is very anxious to see you," Cohen added. "The Nitzan prison is in Ramleh, about twenty minutes from here."

* ○ *

"Here we are," Cohen remarked as the van pulled over to the curb. "The Nitzan prison."

"It doesn't look like a prison," Mac replied.

"No," Cohen replied, "the building has been deliberately designed to blend in to the surrounding structures." He called Mac's attention to several of the adjacent buildings. "I can assure you, however, Mr. MacKenzie, that the interior of the building has the most sophisticated means of detention."

The van transporting Austin and Laura arrived, and they joined Mac and Johanen.

"This way, please," Cohen instructed.

Mac and the others entered the prison through a solid six-inch metal doorway.

"As I was saying," Cohen continued, "we have very sophisticated equipment monitoring our every movement." He pointed to an array of cameras that moved in conjunction with them.

Mac felt Laura tug on his shirt. "This place gives me the creeps," she said.

Mac nodded as they entered the first of a series of guarded doors leading into the interior of the prison.

"The bars as well as the main entrance door you entered are made of a titanium alloy," Cohen remarked.

Mac was patted down and then went through a metal detector.

"It's procedure," Cohen apologized. They moved down a long hallway which led to the administration area of the prison. Mac saw Elisha and Uri seated on chairs at the end of the room.

"They've arrived safely," Cohen called to Elisha, who was already on his feet.

Mac greeted Elisha and Uri, and quick introductions were made to the others. It was clear to all that any lengthy conversation was going to have to wait until later.

Cohen called for everyone's attention. "Dr. Elisha has arranged this meeting, and while it is a very unusual request and normally wouldn't be granted, an exception has been made. There are, however, some stringent rules that you all must follow."

Mac looked at Elisha. *His hands don't appear arthritic anymore,* Mac thought. He noticed the octogenarian's nimble fingers adjust his trifocals and brush an unwanted wisp of gray hair from his temples. *He looks younger, not so frail and hunched as I remember.*

"You will be led into an interview room," Cohen continued. "It's what we use for our parole hearings. I can assure you that it is very safe and none of you will be in any danger. The prisoner is well advanced in years and poses little physical threat. He has been in isolation since his internment here. Only Dr. BenHassen may address the prisoner. The rest of you may take notes if you wish, but there is to be no direct communication between any of you and the prisoner. You are to remain in your seats at all times. The prisoner will be brought into the room after you are seated. He will be shackled and will be under constant guard by two of our finest men. After the interview you will remain seated while the prisoner is escorted out of the room. For your information, the prisoner has been under a suicide watch since his arrival. I will apologize ahead of time, but the prisoner's language at times is very abusive and vulgar." Mac saw Cohen single out Laura. "I trust you won't let it affect you. If you are all ready, then we can begin."

There was a solemn chorus of agreement, and Cohen led the way down a well-lit hall. They came to a room which had metal detectors and two sets of barred doors. Mac waited for Uri to come alongside of him. "How's he doing?' he whispered, nodding toward Elisha.

Uri brushed his black mustache with his index finger. "Good to be seeing you, Mac." Uri motioned to his grandfather. "Look at him, he's looking so much younger, thanks to Johanen, but I'm thinking it would be a good thing if he wouldn't be doing this."

Mac gave a nod of agreement. "Have you seen the Nazi?"

"Only his picture when he was a soldier years ago," Uri whispered.

"If you'll sit here," Cohen announced, pointing to a long table behind which were a dozen very comfortable-looking chairs. In front of the table, less than ten feet away, was a seat with bullet-proof glass in front and behind it. Mac assumed that this was where the prisoner sat.

Elisha sat so that he faced the booth, flanked by Johanen on one side and his grandson Uri on the other. Mac sat next to Johanen while Laura sat next to Uri, and Austin next to her.

Another guard entered with two pitchers of water and set them on the table.

There was a phone on the end of the table, and Cohen picked it up. "Bring in the prisoner," he said.

A few moments passed, and Mac looked at the guarded door at the end of the room, and realized that this was where the prisoner would enter.

Mac heard the metallic echo of a door closing, followed by someone muttering in German, and the sound of footsteps accented by the jingling of chains.

"He'll be here shortly," Cohen informed them.

Mac saw Johanen lean forward, set his hand atop of Elisha's folded hands, and utter a few words of encouragement. Mac shot a glance at Uri, whose eyes were riveted on the door where the prisoner would pass through.

This is it, Mac thought. Following Johanen's example, he offered a quick prayer for strength for Elisha and Uri.

Mac heard the door lock spring at the end of the room, followed once again by the sound of chains and shuffling feet as the prisoner and two very large guards entered the room.

They escorted the prisoner to the glass booth and he took a seat.

Mac looked at the Nazi. *He's harmless looking,* he thought, as he noticed how thin and frail the man looked next to the muscular guards, who towered above him.

The Nazi looked dazed, and turning to one of the guards, muttered something that Mac couldn't hear.

In the corner of Mac's eye he saw Cohen take a seat at the end of the table.

"Herr Schneider," Elisha called to the guard.

So the Nazi has a name, Mac thought.

Schneider looked up with dark circles under his eyes and squinted at Elisha without responding.

"Herr Schneider," Elisha began again. "I have asked to see you one last time."

A thin, crooked smile appeared on his sunken face, and he moistened his lips with his tongue. In a quivering voice he hissed, "Dirty Jew."

Mac was shocked. He felt like rising out of his chair and demanding an apology. He saw Elisha glance at Johanen. Mac saw that the man remained stoic and unmoved.

"Herr Schneider," Elisha began again, but was cut off.

Schneider tried to rise from his seat but was restrained by the guards, who placed their hands on his shoulders from both sides of him.

"So the dirty Jew is back!" he shouted, and his voice was shrill. "I thought I killed you ... too bad, too bad, too bad." A miserable, grating chuckle escaped from the man.

Mac turned to Elisha and waited, his breath held, to see what he would do.

"Herr Schneider, as you can see, I am alive and well. I'm sorry I disappoint you," Elisha said.

Schneider mumbled something that Mac couldn't hear. "You are nothing to me, *Juden,*" he said, reverting to the German word for Jew. "You're vermin ... and so was your brother!"

"My brother was a gifted man," Elisha said softly. "If he had lived, he would have been a caring doctor."

"He was nothing, like you are nothing," Schneider shot back. "Why have you come back to bother me ... an old man?" To Mac's amazement he smiled and almost looked like a kindly grandfather, in contrast to the overt hatred that a few moments ago had possessed his face.

"I have come to forgive you," Elisha said, "for killing my brother."

Mac saw Schneider look at Elisha, trying to figure out if this was some sort of a clever trick.

Finally he mumbled, "I've told them everything already. So they hang me ... so what. I did what I did, and I don't regret ... I don't care about your forgiveness, I spit on it."

Mac heard a gasp from Laura, and saw Uri whisper something in Elisha's ear. Elisha shook his head at Uri. "Nevertheless, in spite of what you have become, you are still made in the image and likeness of your Creator, and so I forgive you."

There was a moment of silence as all eyes were on Schneider. Mac saw the old Nazi breathe deeply and rest his chin on his chest as if he had fallen asleep. Then suddenly the man leaped from the chair, turned sideways, and slammed his cuffed hands into the guard's groin, then darted by him, out of the booth. He jumped toward Elisha, screaming, "Dirty Jew, I'll kill you."

Mac and Uri sprang out of their chairs and started over the table to block the Nazi guard's advance.

Schneider reached the edge of the table and started to climb over it. He spat at Elisha, but before he could do anything more he was yanked off his feet by the other guard, who grabbed the man around his neck and began to drag him away. The guard who had been hit in the groin had drawn his gun, and now aimed it at Schneider's head as the three of them headed for the exit.

Elisha remained seated with the man's spittle dripping down the side of his face.

"Dirty Jew!" Schneider shrieked a last time, before the door closed behind him.

"Are you all right, Dr. Elisha?" Mac asked, as he and Uri collected themselves.

Mac saw that tears had collected in the corners of the old man's eyes.

"I'm fine, MacKenzie," he said, and wiped the spittle off his face with a Kleenex that Laura handed him. "But what of him?" he asked, nodding toward where Schneider had left the room. "The man is consumed with hate. He is hopelessly bound up in it."

Mac saw Johanen stir for the first time. He rose to his feet and made eye contact with all who were present. Then he turned to Elisha. "You have the heart and mind of Christ. You have forgiven, and you have turned the other cheek, and for most men this would have been impossible. The burden now is on the guard, and he will reap what he has sown." He paused a moment. "You have all learned something very important. You have seen one of the many faces of evil. How it dwells alongside the human form it inhabits. How cunning and full of hate it is. This is what we fight against, although what awaits us is much more powerful. Now, there is much to do before this day ends." He led the way out of the room.

Mac started to follow, but noticed that Uri was hanging back, waiting for him. "Thank you for being here with us, Mac."

"I didn't expect him to be so . . . crazy," he replied.

Mac saw Uri glance over his shoulder toward Johanen and the others. "Yeah, crazy like the fox," Uri added. "Did Johanen tell you about Grandfather? How he healed him?"

"What are you talking about?"

"He told you nothing of what he did?"

"No."

"Look, you know I'm not believing in these miracles. But you know what? He came in the room where Grandfather was dying."

"Austin told me it didn't look good," Mac admitted.

"He was going," Uri said. "It was matter of time." Uri stopped, and Mac sensed the man was on very unfamiliar ground.

"He comes in room, and says prayer over Grandfather, then poof! Grandfather sits up in the bed, and everything is being okay."

"Johanen healed him?" Mac asked.

"He healed him, and you know what?"

"What?"

"I'm thinking this is too much for me to be believing, but I was seeing it with my own eyes."

At that very moment Johanen turned and looked at Mac almost as if he could hear what Uri had just said.

He smiled and made the sign of the cross with a slight movement of his hand as if to turn the attention away from himself and herald something far greater.

32

Ithaca, New York

It's a hole in the wall, but they have great Italian food," Crawford said, as he pulled his jeep into the parking lot of the restaurant.

"I'm starved," Helen replied.

Crawford killed the engine and went around the rear of the jeep to open the door for Helen.

She took his hand. "This was a great idea. I'm glad we're doing this."

"Me too," he replied. There was an awkward silence between them as they made their way into the restaurant.

A teenaged girl took them to their table, which was covered with a faded red and white checkerboard cloth. A single candle in the center of the table cast a faint circle of light around them, adding a touch of ambiance.

"Not bad?" Crawford asked.

"It's wonderful." She smiled back in spite of the fact that she felt the color rising in her cheeks. "Have you eaten here before?"

"Every Wednesday. They have a special—spaghetti and meatballs, a salad, plus a drink for five bucks. I'm a regular."

The waiter came, and Crawford ordered ravioli, along with two glasses of red wine. The entrees were written in Italian with dreadfully misspelled English subtitles underneath. Helen and Crawford tried to outdo the other in finding the more outlandish errors.

The waiter dropped a basket of hot bread on the table and returned later with the entree. They devoured the ravioli, then splurged on tiramisu for dessert with piping hot cappuccino.

"I can't eat another bite," Helen exclaimed, holding her cup in both hands with her elbows on the table.

"So should we ruin this by talking about tomorrow?" Crawford asked.

Helen nodded. "Things do end, don't they?"

"Maybe it's just the beginning," Crawford said. The double meaning wasn't lost on her.

She played with a strand of hair. "I wish this wouldn't. I feel . . ." She stopped midsentence and looked down at the tablecloth to avoid his eyes. "I feel safe with you. I know we've only known each other for a few hours . . . but I do."

Crawford toyed with the spoon on his saucer and replied, "We share many of the same experiences."

She nodded.

Crawford took a gulp of coffee. "There is a way out, trust me. I've been through it."

He seems so certain, she thought, then leaned forward and whispered, "It seems so hopeless. They do whatever they want to. It's *always* been that way."

Crawford scooted his chair closer to the table. "I've been there. I know what you're feeling . . . the hopeless part especially . . . but there is a way out, and Johanen showed me. If it wasn't for him, I'd have cracked up too, like the other pilots."

She grabbed her napkin and twisted it like she was wringing out a wet towel. "I don't know how much more I can take. What I told you about what happened at the church? I'm so afraid they're going to come back."

Crawford reached across the table and grabbed her hands. "Helen, there is a way to stop them . . . really." The look on his face demanded that she take notice of what he said.

"You made it . . . got rid of them . . . stopped the abductions with his help," she said, referring to Johanen.

She watched his eyes search her face, and it felt almost as if they were touching her. She blushed and looked down at the tablecloth.

"What your father didn't understand was the nature of these entities," Crawford began. She watched him look over at the couple sitting two tables away from them. After he satisfied himself that they couldn't be overheard, he continued, "General Nathan believed that they were extraterrestrials."

"Aren't they?" she asked.

"No, like the missionary who saved you, I believe that they are only masquerading as aliens."

"A disguise?"

He nodded. "They are able to alter their appearance into almost anything. Johanen told me that they can assume the form of an angel if they choose to do so."

"I think I know what you mean," Helen said. "Sometimes during my abductions I would see what appeared to be a lizard-man . . . that's my name for him. He seemed to be the one in charge. I got the feeling the small grays were afraid of him."

"Johanen referred to these as reptilians," Crawford replied. "He thinks that this may be what the fallen angels look like in their true form."

Helen nodded. "Reptilian is a good name for it. It was hideous, and when it looked at me I felt that even death wouldn't be able to hide me from it."

Crawford was silent for a moment. Then he asked, "Have they ever told you the truth about anything, ever?"

Helen thought for a moment. "No, not once," she admitted.

"They violate you in every possible way. I hated the way they used me. I've had my share of probing." Helen saw him grit his teeth. Then he asked, "What, if anything, do you know about demons?"

"Nothing, why?"

"It's the key to understanding them," Crawford whispered.

"How is it the key?"

"This is going to take a while to explain, and we don't have all night. Actually, I suppose we do." He corrected himself and smiled at her.

"Speaking of that, I was going to ask if I could spend the night on your couch because . . ."

"Because you don't want to be alone?" he finished her sentence.

Helen nodded.

"No problem, then we can talk all night if you want. I can show you passages of Scripture that relate to all of this."

"Scripture?"

"Letters, documents that were handed down to us thousands of years ago by forty authors who compiled sixty-six books. The Bible."

"That will help?"

"Yes, and after what I've been through, it has become my lifeline. Let's go back to my house and we'll talk there. Okay?"

I can't be alone, she thought. "I'll listen to everything you have to say, I promise."

Crawford paid the bill. They left the restaurant and drove back to the hangar, where Helen picked up her car and followed him to his house.

* ○ *

This is nice, Helen thought, as she followed the jeep up a driveway that led to an old two-story brick house. It was surrounded by a small forest of trees.

She turned off her motor and got out of her car. "Secluded," she said.

"The nearest neighbor's half a mile away," Crawford answered. "Here, let me help you with your things."

She opened the trunk and Crawford got her suitcase. They headed for the front door.

"The house was built just after the Civil War," he said. "It's a cozy cottage."

Helen found herself in a spacious living room with wainscot walls, and roughhewn, pine plank floors. Over the fieldstone fireplace were four propellers stacked horizontally, one atop the other.

"You really have a thing for those," she said, nodding toward the propellers.

"Sure do." He motioned to a comfortable-looking couch in front of the fireplace. "Have a seat."

Helen watched him build a small fire using the wood that was stored in a large wicker basket next to the hearth. Crawford balled up some newspaper and lit it with a long wooden match, and soon the fire was crackling. He dimmed the lights and pulled a worn leather chair closer to the fire, across from where Helen sat.

"Well?" she said. "You start."

"In the letter from your father, he admits allowing the aliens to abduct you. In fact, he set it up."

"Can you imagine anyone doing that?" Helen said. "I hate him for that."

"But he also asks for your forgiveness and at least tries to make amends."

"He's just trying to buy forgiveness with the money. Why didn't he do this sooner?" she countered.

"I don't know . . . but he's dead now, and he can't change what he did."

"And I'm stuck with the consequences."

"But he led you to me," Crawford reminded her.

Helen slipped off her shoes, brought her legs underneath her, and allowed herself a hint of a smile. "That's true."

"Back to what I started to say at the restaurant," Crawford began, and Helen saw the earnestness on his face. "Simply put, in the Bible there is a book called Genesis, and in one of the chapters it talks about the Sons of God coming down to earth and taking women for wives. From that union a race of hybrids called Nephilim were formed."

"But who are the Sons of God?" Helen asked.

"I'm no biblical scholar. Johanen can give you a much more detailed explanation than I can. But my understanding of it is that the Sons of God were the fallen angels."

"Fallen angels?" Helen asked. "Like what you said in the restaurant?"

"Yes, and as I said, their offspring with human women were called the Nephilim. When the Nephilim were destroyed in the Flood, their spirits may have become what are referred to as demons."

"Demons?" she asked.

"You really have never been to church, have you?"

Helen shook her head. "All of this is new to me."

"These demonic entities seek to inhabit bodies because they're spirit beings and want to interact with the physical dimension. Johanen believes that the small gray aliens might be manufactured biological 'suits' that allow the demons to possess some kind of physical body. Haven't you noticed that they all look almost exactly like each other?"

"Yes, they're almost like robots," Helen replied.

"You said you saw a television show where one of the guests claimed that he knew of people who had stopped alien abductions by using the name of Jesus, right?"

"That's what he said, and some of the audience laughed at him," Helen replied.

"But what he said was the truth, Helen, and I know because I'm one of those people that he was referring to."

"Mr. Sorenson, the retired missionary at the church, said pretty much the same thing."

"From what you told me about the encounter there, he stopped it when he began to call upon the name of Jesus."

"He did, but it sounds so silly, like it's a trick or something. Say 'Jesus,' and you can control flying saucers. It's too crazy. I don't believe it."

"What don't you believe?" Crawford asked.

"I don't believe in God. I think it's just all made up by people for whatever reason they need to get through life. It's a crutch."

"Helen, the missionary stopped what was happening. How do you figure that?"

Helen folded her arms in front of her and stared at the fire for a moment. "I don't know, it happened so fast."

"Yeah, but you told me that he took a stand against it. Helen, I was powerless to stop them when I worked for your father. The other test pilots also. We thought they were here to help us, to show us their technology. We were wrong, and it almost cost me my life."

"If there is a God, then why did he allow this to happen to me?" she challenged.

"I don't have that answer," Crawford admitted.

"There are no answers. It's hopeless. Things happen, and no one can change them. The aliens are here, and they're here to stay. They're going to do whatever they want to, and even your God can't stop them."

"Helen, you're wrong. He will stop them at some point."

"How can you be so sure? You don't know that. You're just guessing."

She saw Crawford grope for an answer and felt sadly pleased that she was able to stump him.

He looked into the fire for a moment. "Let me ask you this. Everywhere you turn, the TV, the missionary, and now me, all are pointing you to the same thing. If you don't believe any of it, why do you want to go to Johanen?"

He's right, she thought, *what's so special about Johanen, and why am I trying to see him?* "I don't know," she whispered.

"Anything is better than what I've been through. I guess maybe I'm trying to run from all this. Trying to find the father I never had, and the money is allowing me to do whatever I want for the first time in my life." She stared into the fire. "Also because way down inside me, there's a little bit of hope that maybe this will stop. My father knew Johanen, right?" she asked.

Crawford nodded.

"Well, he's a connection to someone I never knew, and even though I hate him, I find myself taking his picture out and staring at it." She looked at him. "You're a connection too, you know."

He smiled at her, and they sat in silence for a moment. "Well, we leave in the morning—if you still want to go."

"I want to. I have to see him. I have to see where this takes me."

Crawford rose from his chair. "It's late. I'll show you the guest room; you can sleep there."

Crawford got her bag and led her upstairs to the guest room.

"It's got its own shower and bath, clean towels, too. I'm right down the hall if you need anything."

"This is perfect, thank you so much," she said.

She looked at him as he stood in the doorway and felt another moment of awkwardness between them.

Crawford took a step backward and pointed to his room. "In there, if you want anything."

"Thanks," Helen said, and closed the door to her room.

She undressed and took a hot shower, shampooing her hair three times, then dried herself, combed out her hair, and slipped into a new pair of flannel pajamas.

She turned the light off, then slid underneath the covers. As she drifted off to sleep, she thought only of Jack Crawford and how much she liked being with him.

33

The Tel in Yemen

Bernstein was on his hands and knees scrutinizing the base of one of the giant megaliths that made up part of the tel. He ran his fingers across the ancient inscription that had been concealed for centuries underneath the desert sands.

"Remarkable," he mumbled to an assistant. "Look here." He pointed to a disk-shaped object on the stone. "There is no mistaking this."

The assistant, a graduate student from the university where Bernstein taught, nodded his agreement.

"Even then they were visiting us, watching, observing, testing, and of course"—he rested his hand on the megalith—"building a monument for themselves in stone."

"Yes, Doctor, like in Peru?" he asked.

"Yes, I have always believed that Machu Picchu could not have been built by natives. The stones are precisely fitted, and the city's location so high in the Andes mountains. How did they get the stones there? And why was the methodology they used forgotten?" He chuckled. "So many mysteries are solved when one realizes that we are not alone." He rubbed his hand on the disk again. "Has Gleason photographed this yet?" he asked.

"Yes, sir, early this morning as soon as it was discovered."

"Very good. Find Gleason and tell him to send those photos to Mr. Wyan and his colleagues immediately."

Bernstein got up and turned to leave.

The assistant stopped him. "Dr. Bernstein, I was wondering if I could ask you a question, sir, before I go?"

Bernstein loved the way some of these people sucked up to him, thought him important. "Yes, what is it?" He rested his hands on his enormous belly.

"Well, sir, I was wondering, sir, the armor and skeletons that we found . . . some of us have been talking, and we were wondering, sir, did the uh . . . extraterrestrials kill them?"

"What makes you arrive at that?" Bernstein replied.

"Well, sir, like I said. Several of us examined the bones, and they have an abnormal amount of radioactivity in them. Also several of the skulls appear to have holes bored in them by something resembling a laser. Do you think that this was extraterrestrial intervention?"

Bernstein rocked on the balls of his feet. *How much should I tell him? The man is smart and has managed to piece together some of the puzzle.*

Bernstein cleared his throat. "Well, some of this is conjecture on my part, but you, and the others who are participating in this tel, have signed papers to insure secrecy." Bernstein gave the man the sort of look that one gives another who is privy to an inside secret. "The discovery of this tomb, and the body of Jesus, will shake certain institutions off their foundations. Part of what we are piecing together is that this tomb has been here for almost two millennia. And the builders of it, for reasons that are just coming to light now, have guarded it until just the right time. My theory is that at the time of the Crusades, when Jerusalem was freed from the Mohammedans, a certain group of knights encamped on what is now the Temple Mount in Jerusalem and explored many areas underneath. They were looking for treasure. Perhaps they made off with relics and some booty, who knows?"

"Didn't the Dead Sea scrolls mention something like that?" the man asked.

"I believe you are referring to the copper scroll. It is a list of treasure recorded on a scroll of copper. It offers the location of many of the artifacts that the Jews used to make their ritual sacrifices at the temple in Jerusalem."

"So are these skeletons the remains of these knights?"

"It appears this group of knights came to explore the ruins here and stumbled upon the tomb itself. In their attempt to gain entrance to the tomb they were met by the Watchers, who desired at all cost to keep it secret. Now what I am about to tell you has been told to me by Mr. Kenson himself. And I need not remind you that it is he who is financing this expedition."

The man nodded.

"Mr. Kenson has informed me that the location of this tomb has been handed down through the centuries by members of his family who can trace their lineage to the union of Jesus and Mary Magdalene. They are in fact the royal heirs to the house of David, but they also boast of a direct union with the extraterrestrials. I'm sure you've heard about Mr. Kenson's abnormality? The six fingers on each of his hands?"

"Yes, sir, some of us here have discussed it."

"Mr. Kenson is a hybrid, part alien, part human. The aliens have determined that this is the time to unite the many different religions of earth. It's the key to them forming a world government. You can't have these ongoing religious wars now, can you?"

"No, sir."

"So you see, this is the time they have chosen, based on their superior knowledge and learning. A thousand years ago, mankind was not yet ready spiritually or technologically to handle such information. Now, of course, we are, and that is the reason for all of this." He gestured to the tel around them.

"It is time to reveal the truth about their presence to mankind. As I said earlier, they have always been here, watching, helping. I believe they are our creators." Bernstein was pleased with his discourse and noticed to his delight that the man had hung on every word.

"Thank you, sir. I can't thank you enough for taking the time to explain this."

"Very good. Now please convey my request to Mr. Gleason. There is much to do before the broadcast. We must insure that it coincides with the lunar eclipse and the reemergence of the Bethlehem star."

Bernstein waddled away from the megalith and climbed into the golf cart that he was using for transportation around the tel. *Splendid,* he thought, as he saw two large trucks unloading their equipment under the direction of his assistant, Bob Haney.

Bernstein drove his cart over. "When do you think you'll be operational?" he asked Haney.

"Less than twenty-four hours," Haney responded, opening the back door of the truck and surveying the equipment, as a handful of men under his direction began to unload.

"Mr. Wyan informed me that most of the world's countries will be present for the private viewing. I know he's *very* anxious to test the teleportation equipment."

Haney nodded. "Shouldn't be a problem. I'll let you know when we're ready."

Bernstein watched for a few minutes more, then, satisfied that all was proceeding as it should, left the area and headed for the large tent that was used for the dining room. He braked the cart and then sniffed the air. *Lunch will be served soon,* he thought, and hurried as fast as he could toward the entrance.

34

✦•◉•✦

Tel Aviv, Israel

Mac stood just outside the prison, hanging back from the group as more formal introductions were made among those who had not met before.

"And this, as you know by now, is Laura Nathan." He heard Johanen introduce Laura to Elisha.

"I'm charmed," Dr. Elisha said as he took her hand.

"You really held yourself in there. I don't know that I could have done what you did," Laura complimented the older man.

"I relied on a strength much greater than my own," Elisha replied, pushing his trifocals up on the bridge of his nose.

Mac moved a little closer as Uri began to introduce Colonel Austin. "Grandfather, this is Colonel Austin. He is the one who I'm almost shooting in the helicopter." Austin came forward and shook Elisha's hand.

"If it had been me instead of you in there, I would have rearranged his face so that his mother wouldn't have known him . . . if, in fact, he had a mother to begin with."

"One does wonder how the child that he once was became the monster that he now is," Elisha replied.

Mac worked his way over to Uri and pulled him aside. Two vans pulled up, and everyone else turned their attention to the seating arrangements. "What were you trying to say in there, about Johanen?"

"Elisha is in hospital almost dead. I'm thinking about making funeral for him. Johanen had some power"—and he nodded toward the man—"that . . . I don't know, filled the whole room. It made me feel like first time I kissed Rebecca. I know I'm to be sounding nuts, but I felt I was being loved by something that I couldn't be seeing."

"You felt God, Uri," Mac replied.

Uri nodded, then shook his head. "But I still can't be believing it."

Mac reached over and put his hand on Uri's shoulder. "You know what, Uri? I needed to hear this."

"What do you mean, Mac?"

"It shores me up, Uri, makes me feel like somehow we just might get through this."

The two men stared at each other for a moment.

"MacKenzie, Uri," Johanen called.

Mac gave Johanen a quick thumbs-up, as he noticed everyone else had boarded.

"You are going to the tomb, right?" he asked Uri, as they walked over to the van.

"Elisha and I were told some things, but we don't know all details yet," Uri answered.

"You will," Mac said, as he and Uri climbed into the rear of the van.

"Where are we going now?" Mac asked Johanen, who sat in the passenger seat in the front.

Johanen turned to face Mac and Uri. "Elisha has arranged for us to use a conference room in Mossad headquarters. Like the roundtable room at the castle, it is a secure room and will suit our purpose well." He paused a moment. "Any comments on the interview with the guard?"

"I thought Elisha exercised almost supernatural restraint," Mac answered, throwing a glance at Uri. "What will happen to the guard?"

"Most likely he will be executed," Johanen answered. "In another decade or so, there will be no one left who survived the camps," he added.

"You know what? Even now, everything is passing into history," Uri stated.

"And in a generation or two the memory of it, the atrocities that were committed, will grow dim," Johanen replied.

"There are certain groups back in the States who swear the Holocaust never happened," Mac added.

"They should be talking to Grandfather about this," Uri huffed. "Have them look at the tattoo, the faded numbers still on his arm."

"All part of the curse we, the human race, labor under," Johanen replied.

"What do you mean?" Mac asked.

"Each generation so easily forgets the mistakes of its predecessor. Men live for what, eighty or so years? Just when a man begins to sort things out, to learn, to know himself, he falls asleep . . . he experiences the sting of death. The struggles and victories are forgotten. It seems that the human race is doomed to repeat the same mistakes."

"So, you are saying, what? This goes around and around?" Uri asked.

"On one level, yes, but as I told MacKenzie previously, one day history as we know it will come to an end—when the Meshiach Nagev, Messiah the King, returns. At that time there will be no death, no pain or suffering, no sickness, no tears. People will live forever, and the curse will be removed. It is mankind's only true hope." He paused for a moment, then added, "And I know, Uri, that this is difficult for you to accept."

Uri looked out the window and remained silent.

"I could use some of that right now," Mac added. "The no pain, sickness, tears part."

"I understand how you can feel this way, MacKenzie," Johanen began. "You are a journalist used to a certain lifestyle. But now you find yourself surrounded by situations that are unfamiliar. You see that the secure boundaries you once lived in have vanished. The rules that governed your life no longer seem to apply, and reality as you knew it has disappeared. In its place are things so extraordinary that you fear for your own sanity."

Mac glanced at Uri, who seemed to mirror what he was feeling. "You've articulated what's been brewing inside me for weeks, but have been too afraid to put into words."

"That is going for me too," Uri added.

Johanen's face shed the faintest smile. "There is a calling on both your lives. You have been called out, but you must make a choice to serve or not. Uri, you must recognize and accept the one who has called you. And you, MacKenzie, must face your fear. You can both leave now, if you wish," Johanen continued. "The door is always open. But in order to remain and serve, you must die to yourselves, to your own desires, and that is the pain you both feel. And yet, in dying to yourselves, you will both find that life is more full than you could ever have imagined it. You may look to Elisha as an example of this. It is one of the main reasons that all of us were present when he forgave the guard. He faced his fear and died to the anger that he felt. He became dead to the bitterness, to his own hate, however justified. The Scriptures say that perfect love casts out all fear. You both must search your hearts," Johanen concluded, turning around in his seat.

* ○ *

Mac sat opposite Johanen at the other end of a conference table deep inside the protective walls of Mossad headquarters. From his position he could see everyone else that was present. He nodded at the newest addition to the group, a man he knew from his last visit as the Major. Then he mentally accounted for each person seated with him.

He looked first at Johanen, and marked the man's indefatigable energy and assuredness in almost every situation. His mind flashed back to the nightmarish scene in the wheat field with his father, and afterward, when Johanen had appeared from nowhere and led him to safety. Mac realized he was very glad he and Johanen were on the same side.

Next, he looked at Elisha and recalled that if what Uri had told him was true, then Elisha should have been dead, and yet here he was laughing as if nothing had happened.

Then Uri. He wondered how the Israeli, or for that matter he himself, would hold up under this next adventure. *What if we do encounter another one of the Nephilim?* Mac shuddered at the thought.

He turned to Green Eyes, his nickname for Laura, and wondered what it must have been like growing up with General Nathan as a father, and how she would react if she did meet her sister, realizing that her father had been forced to make a choice between the two of them.

Last was Colonel Austin. Tough and battle hardened, a true warrior. He smiled as he thought of Austin's boyish enthusiasm when he talked about the BlackBird.

Johanen cleared his throat, which brought Mac out of his reflections. "So Elisha and Austin will return to the castle and monitor our progress from there, with Stephan, Knud, and Hilda to assist them. The Major will assist them in monitoring our progress from his headquarters here in Tel Aviv. I have instructed Knud and Stephan to examine anything from the international press that might be pertinent to our expedition. Which brings me to this." He handed out an article that he had received a few minutes ago from Stephan via the Spiral of Life website. "As you can see," Johanen continued, "This sign in the heavens, or reemergence of the Bethlehem star, is already getting some attention from the press, and it is only a matter of time before the whole story comes out. All of this is orchestrated to coincide with the lunar eclipse. We also know that many countries have opted to send representatives to witness this sign via closed-circuit television."

"Our intelligence indicates they're gathering together in Rome for this," the Major offered. "And security is tight. They're using DNA tests to verify the delegates. Look at this." He passed around a folder. "It is a copy of what was sent to the Israeli government concerning the sign in the heavens. You should know that Israel has declined to send a representative to the gathering based on the work of Johanen and Elisha, which exposed the alien agenda as one of lies and deception. And our government agrees with the United States that we do not want to disclose the alien presence to the world at large."

The folder reached Mac and he scanned the material.

"As you can see from the document, the sign will coincide with the revealing of the tomb, and the alien artifacts . . . and of course the landing of a UFO at the site," the Major stated.

"It is a first step toward full disclosure," Johanen added. "Many people will wonder at what they are seeing as the Moon eclipses and the sign manifests, but those in Rome, at the closed-circuit broadcast, will have live footage of the landing and the exhuming of the body from the tomb and so have all the pieces of the puzzle."

"How much time before all this happens?" MacKenzie asked.

"Two days from now, which is why we are leaving tonight," Johanen replied. "We will board a barge that has been altered for our use, and sail down the Red Sea until we reach the drop-off point here." He pointed to a small map he had placed in the center of the table. "From there we take the jeeps, travel inland, and if all goes well, destroy the site."

The Major nodded. "Thanks to the disk provided by General Nathan, we were able to pinpoint the site, and my government has supplied us with recent satellite photographs of the area, so you will have good intelligence as far as the precise location of the tel. Also, in the event of trouble, we have at our disposal a new top-secret weapon. It is a laser cannon that we hope will be able to damage the alien craft. Until now they have been able to elude any offensive posturing on our part. This new weapon, however, may be our high card. In recent field tests it knocked out two Scud missiles with one blast."

Colonel Austin cleared his throat. "From my understanding it's going to be rough going once you land," he added. "The roads are in poor condition, and sections of them disappear altogether."

"Not to mention patrolling army details in the area," Uri offered. "It is a Moslem country."

"That may be your biggest threat," Austin said.

"All valid points, which we must consider," Johanen agreed. "It is now time for me to elaborate on what we expect to encounter at the site."

Mac glanced at Uri with an oh-boy-here-it-comes look, then focused back on Johanen.

"As you know, there is a group of men and women—I refer to them as the Cadre—who are interested in bringing about the advent of the Man of Perdition."

"The Antichrist?" Laura asked.

"Yes," Johanen replied. "It is this same group who are using the contents of the tomb to further their own aims."

"And what are they?" Mac asked.

"You must understand that there are forces at work that have continued for centuries, forces with evil intent. These men and women who have joined this dark fraternity are links in a chain that goes back to man's earliest beginnings. It is they who will help to set up an unholy deception that may, if it is allowed to succeed, shake the Christian world to its very foundations."

"So they want to do what?" Laura asked.

"When the Ancient of Days walked on the earth, he was asked a very specific question by his disciples: What would be the sign of the end? Listen very carefully, please, for I quote now from Matthew. 'Take heed that no one deceives you. For many will come in my name, saying "I am the Messiah," and will deceive many . . .'

"If the tomb containing the body of 'Jesus' is exposed to the public, along with the alien artifacts that are allegedly with it, this could be the beginning of what I refer to as the Great Deception," Johanen said.

"But won't people see through it?" Laura asked.

"And what will the church say?" Mac added. "Won't they argue against it?"

"My guess is that the church's response will be swept away by the force of the media storm that will be generated with both the body and the artifacts being exhumed, and the disclosure of ETs to a select group from many nations around the globe. The manipulated evidence will deceive many. In conjunction with this, according to the briefing that General Nathan has given us, it also appears that certain nations have broken ranks with the United States' official position of denial of the alien presence and are now favoring full disclosure, which is why they're sending their delegates to Rome. Remember, what is particularly pernicious about this is that the alien artifacts will link the body to extraterrestrial intervention, and once that is done the lie that will appear as revelation will cause hearts to grow cold, and many to stumble in their faith. This, I believe, is part of the *deception* that will begin to bring about a one-world religious system. Remember the ancient writings in the book of Daniel the prophet? They tell us, and I quote: 'He shall regard neither the God of his fathers nor the desire of woman, nor regard any god; for he shall magnify himself above them all. But in their place he shall honor a god of fortresses; and a god which his fathers did not know he shall honor with gold and silver, with precious stones and pleasant things.'

"This passage speaks of the Son of Perdition, who will regard a new god, a god of fortresses. It is my belief that he will embrace the alien god, and in doing so will lead multitudes in a lie."

"But if we destroy the tomb along with the artifacts, then the scenario that you just outlined becomes moot," Dr. Elisha suggested.

"At least that particular tentacle of it," Johanen agreed. "Which is why it is imperative to destroy it at all costs."

"But if the artifacts are genuine, why destroy them? Aren't they a kind of a missing link?" Laura countered.

"Yes, it is a missing link to another time," Johanen admitted, "but it is not what you suppose. We have several hours before we rendezvous and head to the barge. I suggest those of you who are not familiar with it read the Book of Enoch during that time." He passed out copies to everyone present.

Elisha explained, "This book was found in the Dead Sea scrolls, and it pertains to what we may encounter as we approach the tel. In the book, the fallen angels are referred to as Watchers."

"I want to expand on what Elisha has just told us," Johanen said. "*Watchers* is a term used exclusively in the Book of Enoch to refer to the fallen angels. But I must warn you that I have discovered that they can appear in many different forms. For instance, it is known to us that fallen angels are once again seeking to cohabit with the women of earth. We know that they have a very rigorous breeding program, the offspring of which are called the Nephilim. You must realize that this breeding program has resulted in many types of Nephilim. But overall the goal seems to be the breeding of a perfect hybrid. Different from the giant that you encountered at the base, MacKenzie," and Johanen threw Mac a look. "One that has much of the obvious distinctions bred out, so that the hybrids can pass for humans. I have come to believe that there are various stages of hybrid development, but they may differ in appearance from one another. For instance, I have received a very interesting series of photographs from a contact and dear friend in Rome. I have a set of duplicates here." He held them up and then passed them around. "You will notice that the photos are somewhat grainy and the subject passes out of view before the transformation is complete; nevertheless we can see that his physical form is being altered. I have had this particular photograph enhanced." Johanen circulated the photo. "You will notice that the human form is in the process of being changed. I refer to this as shape-shifting. In other words, what we first see as human, is in the process of shape-shifting or changing into what the creature's true form is."

"And what is that?" MacKenzie asked.

"I would refer to it as a Reptilian, and this may be what its true form is."

"You mentioned a breeding program," Laura said. "Isn't this precisely what forced my father into having my sister against his wishes?"

Johanen nodded gravely. "Yes, and the breeding program has been going on for at least two generations, so there is a good chance they have succeeded in developing the perfect hybrid.

"But getting back to the Book of Enoch. Give yourselves a good overview of the material. You will find that the Watchers or fallen angels were capable of some very diabolical deeds."

"And of course there is a possibility of encountering a Watcher," Elisha added.

"So what do we do then?" Mac interjected, doing little to hide his consternation.

"I am glad you asked that, MacKenzie, for we must brace ourselves for just such an encounter. And I warn you that although we use the term *alien* freely among us, let there be no mistaking who it is we mean when we use that term. For as you know, MacKenzie, and you too, Laura, these are *not* extraterrestrial beings from other planets, they are a remnant of what remains of the fallen angels, and they are completely demonic in nature. We must guard ourselves with the power that is greater than us . . . and them."

A silence settled over the group, as each person was lost in his own private thoughts. Mac's eyes darted from one person to the other as he tried to read the expression on each face.

Johanen began again. "Let us ask now for protection, wisdom, strength, and courage. We will leave here and head to our point of departure in two hours. In the meantime, I have ordered us a meal, which should arrive shortly."

Mac slumped in his chair, and soon after, the meal arrived. He was eating a rice dish and talking to Elisha when Laura came over and sat next to him.

She turned to Elisha. "Mind if I have a private word with Mac, Doctor?"

Elisha smiled, rose from his seat, and hailed the Major. Mac took another bite of his food and turned his attention back to Laura. "What do you think of all this?"

"Well," she said, "I'm at a point where I want to believe what Johanen is saying, but I just don't know how to do it."

Mac took another bite, feeling unsure as to what to say. He blurted, "You just believe, that's all. Ask Jesus in your heart. Ask him to forgive you."

Laura nodded, but Mac could see that she was unable to make a decision. "You could talk to Johanen about this," he suggested.

"I know, but I want to talk to you. My father died a broken man. It was horrible, Mac. He was really bothered by something, and now I know it was my half sister. Do you know what his dying word was?"

Mac shook his head.

"He said, 'Believe.' He breathed a few more times, and the horrible death rattle happened, and then moments later he passed away." She wiped a tear away from her face.

"What do you think he was telling you to believe in?" Mac asked.

"I'm not sure, except that after what I saw at the farmhouse with your wife and mother-in-law, and everything else that's happened . . . I want to believe in what Johanen and you believe in. But I . . ." She leaned forward, put her head in her hands, and began to cry.

Mac felt awkward but forced himself to put his arm around her. She cried for a while, and then straightened up in her chair. "I'm sorry, Mac," she laughed.

"Laura," Mac said, "you ask . . . just ask."

She nodded and bit her lower lip. She got up as if changing her mind. Mac saw the inner conflict mirrored in her face.

"Not now," she mumbled and then walked out of the room.

35

✦ ◉ ✦

Ithaca, New York

Helen awakened and wondered where she was. Then everything fell into place. *Crawford's guest bedroom,* she reminded herself.

Oh, that smells good, she thought, as the aroma of fresh ground coffee quickened her senses.

She looked out the window at the fiery red hue of a maple tree. *It's beautiful here.* She pulled the covers up to her chin, content to linger.

There was a knock at her door, followed by Crawford's voice. "Are you awake yet?"

She found herself smiling at the sound of his voice. *This is silly,* she told herself, *I don't even really know him.* But another part of her argued that she knew much about him because of the mutual abduction experiences that they had shared.

She sat up in bed and answered, "I'm awake . . . what smells so good? Coffee?"

"Freshly brewed," Crawford answered, peeking around the door. He stepped into the room and handed her the mug. "You sleep okay?"

She nodded as she took a sip. "No bad dreams. It was wonderful."

"I'm fixing some breakfast for us. How do you like your eggs?" he asked.

She forced herself not to smile. To pretend that all of this was normal, as if good-looking men made breakfast for her every day. "Oh, I don't know . . . surprise me?"

"You asked for it," he said. "I better get back downstairs. See you in a few minutes."

She watched him close the door as he left, but then he stuck his head in again and gave her one last smile.

She shooed him away, suddenly conscious of the fact that her hair was a mess, and she didn't have her makeup on.

She sipped her coffee and looked again out the window. *I wonder what it would be like to live like this every day,* she thought. *What serenity there is here, at least now.*

Forcing herself to get out of bed, she headed for the bathroom, where she took a quick shower. Then she dressed for comfort, thinking about the plane ride, and opted for a pair of jeans and a sweater. She did, however, spend more time than usual fixing her hair and applying her makeup.

When she finished, she checked herself one last time and tried not to notice the butterflies building in her stomach as she found her way downstairs.

Crawford was pouring orange juice as she entered the breakfast nook. It overlooked a yard that sloped down to a running creek, which was visible from the bay window by the table.

The sun was coming up behind the trees, setting the fall colors blazing, as shafts of light streaked through the forest like golden beacons.

"This is beautiful," Helen said, leaning against the doorjamb.

Crawford played with the bacon that sizzled in the pan. "My favorite time of year," he confessed.

"How do you make yourself leave this?" she asked.

He chuckled, then looked at her for the first time since she entered the room. She noticed that he stopped playing with the bacon, and before he turned his attention back to the pan, she caught him trying to hide an embarrassed smile.

"Simple," he stated. "I love to fly, more than anything."

"If I lived here . . ." She stopped herself short, and apologized, "Oh, I didn't mean that . . . I meant . . ."

"I know what you meant," he reassured her.

"I meant to say if I lived in a place like this . . . well, I know, *I* wouldn't want to leave."

"I feel the same way. I have a shop out in the garage, and on the weekends I build furniture."

"What kind?" she asked.

Crawford pointed toward the table and chairs. "That's one of my pieces. And the grandfather clock in the hall is another."

Helen ran her hand on the pitted tabletop. "What kind of wood is this? Does it grow like this with all the holes in it?"

"Wormy chestnut. I salvaged it from an old barn a couple of miles from here. The planks that make up the table are over one hundred years old."

"Is that where all the holes come from . . . worms?" she asked.

"Yep."

"Icky, but it's still beautiful," she added, not wanting to hurt his feelings.

"No argument there. Eggs are done, hope you like them." She watched him fumble with a spatula as he panned the omelet onto two plates. "Take a seat." He placed a plate on the table and then added another for himself.

Helen leaned forward and inhaled the aroma. "This smells delicious. What kind of omelet is this?"

"It's my own concoction, but you take a bite first and see if you can guess. But first, can I ask you something?"

Helen reached for her fork. "Okay, ask away."

"I'd like us to say grace together. We didn't last night, and that's okay, but this is where I live and it's something that's really important to me. To give thanks, because I don't take any of this, my being free from 'them,' for instance, for granted."

"It's fine with me," she said. "What do I do?" Crawford gave her an are-you-kidding-me look. "I haven't said grace since I was a little girl. I've forgotten what you're supposed to do."

"How about you just listen, and if you agree maybe you can give a little nod or something. Okay?"

Helen listened as Crawford began. "We thank you, Lord, for your provisions this day. We're grateful for all that you have given us and ask your blessing on this food. In your Son's name we pray, amen."

Helen nodded her assent.

"Okay, now take a bite, and guess what kind of omelet it is," Crawford prodded.

Helen cut into the omelet and took a bite. "Tomato sauce . . . sausage . . . peppers . . . oh, and the cheese . . . what is that, Parmesan?"

"So what's your guess, French omelet?" he kidded.

She giggled and put her hand to her mouth as she chewed. "Don't make me laugh, not while I eat. That's not fair."

Crawford forked in a huge mouthful and began to chew. "What? Like this?" he mumbled through the food in his mouth.

"No, I mean it . . . stop . . ." Helen managed to swallow. "Italian, right?"

She watched him throw his hand in the air in a mock gesture of surprise. "Right you are. But do you really like it?"

She rested her elbows on the table, hiding a smile behind her hands. "Honestly, I love it, but it's guy food."

"What?"

She started to laugh. "Guy food. I can't explain it, but if there was another girl here, she'd back me up."

"How conveniently sexist," he teased.

"She would."

"Then give me an example of girl food," he challenged.

"Okay, I will." She slipped another bite into her mouth and looked up at the ceiling. "Chocolate mousse."

"That's not food, that's a dessert."

"My point exactly," she said.

"I like chocolate mousse," Crawford said.

"So when was the last time you had it?"

"I don't know."

"See, girl food," she said.

She saw him arch his eyebrows and shake his head. "Okay, you win," he said.

They finished the omelets, and Helen cleared the table, then insisted on doing the dishes.

"Where do these go?" she asked as she began to dry them.

"It's okay, I'll put them away when I get back."

Helen stopped wiping a dish, as his words reminded her that, indeed, only he would be returning.

"What's wrong?" Crawford asked.

"Oh nothing . . ." she replied, then thought, *He's right, Helen, once he gets you to Johanen, he's coming back here, and you are going to stay there. Don't kid yourself into making more of this than what it is.*

"We should be going to the airport soon," Crawford stated.

"Yep, I'll go get my things. It will only take a minute."

"Call me, and I'll help with your bag."

"No, I can manage," she said, forcing herself to begin withdrawing from him. *There's no use fooling yourself. He's just being friendly . . . nothing more. You've hired him to fly you to Europe, and that's what he's doing.*

Helen left the kitchen and trotted up the stairs.

A few minutes passed, and she struggled with the bag as she started downstairs.

"You sure you don't need any help?" Crawford called from the hallway, where he waited for her, holding a small overnight bag in one hand.

"I can manage, thanks," she said, and she knew it was a cold response. *But what should it matter, in a few hours he'll be out of my life. I won't let him hurt me . . . I won't,* she told herself.

She put her bag in the trunk of her car, then backed out of the driveway and followed his jeep to the airport. She parked the car in front of his hangar and got out.

"There's room in the hangar," Crawford offered. "Why not park it in here until you return?"

"I suppose you're right. Are you sure it's okay?"

He smiled. "I'm sure."

She reparked the car in the hangar. "We haven't discussed how much you're going to charge me."

"Nothing," Crawford replied.

"I don't understand."

"This is payback for me, a way I can help someone else get free of . . . them."

"Are you sure? I want to pay you. You've done so much for me already."

He shook his head adamantly. "No."

"Okay . . . so when do we leave?" She smiled at him.

"As soon as you want to. I have to do a preflight checklist, and afterward, send a message to Johanen's Web site letting him know we're on the way. Then we can take off."

"He has a Web site?" she asked.

"Yes. Before I left he told me that the door was always open, so even with the last-minute notice he'll be happy to receive us. I'm going to tell him about you, and what we have in common."

"You mean my father?"

Crawford nodded.

"Well, why don't you go and do that, and I'll wait in the office," she said. Without waiting for an answer, she headed toward the office.

She could feel Crawford's eyes follow her as she left him. *Keep going, and don't look back.*

She went into the office, closed the door, but then opened it again, cracking it just enough so she could see out. Crawford was nowhere to be seen. She closed the door and sat down at his desk, found a piece of paper, and wrote a quick note. Then she pulled out two thousand dollars from her purse. She found an envelope and put the note and the money in it, then she opened the top desk drawer and put the envelope there.

"Helen?" she heard him call.

She got up and went to the chair opposite the desk and sat down.

"Helen?" he called again as he entered.

"What?" She gave one last glance at the drawer and smiled to herself.

"This will only take a minute," Crawford said, as he slipped into his chair and turned on the computer.

"You're going to send the message to Johanen?"

He nodded as the computer booted up. "Take a look." He turned the monitor so Helen could see it, as he began to punch in the web address. The Spiral of Life logo appeared on the screen. Crawford punched in a command, and a picture of Jesus ascending into heaven replaced the image. Crawford explained the importance of the Resurrection to her as he typed in another command. Then he typed a short message detailing their flight path and subsequent arrival in Rome as well as connecting train times. That finished, Crawford shut down the computer. "Are you ready to leave?"

"What did you type? It all looked in code of some sort," she asked.

"It was a code; the computer scrambles everything so that only those with the appropriate software are able to send or receive messages from Johanen."

"I'm impressed," she said as she followed Crawford out of the office.

"Get your bags, and we'll load them into the cart, then drive to the jet," Crawford said.

Helen loaded her bag, and soon found herself speeding across vast expanses of tarmac toward a jet that she presumed to be Crawford's.

"Is that your plane? It's big." She gathered her hair and held it in one hand behind her head to keep it from blowing in her face.

He nodded yes. "I reworked the engines on her. It's an old 707. Great plane. I do some charter flights for private groups. Hunters, fishermen, business execs."

"Oh."

"Between the repair work and the charters, I make a decent living."

They rode the rest of the way in silence.

Crawford swung the cart to where a worn aluminum stepladder was set up to access the plane's door. He climbed the ladder and opened the door.

"You'll have to climb up, sorry."

"No problem," she said, glad that she wore her jeans. "What about the bag?" she asked.

"I'll stow it below with mine."

Helen boarded the plane, then looked back at Crawford. She watched him stow the bags, then ascend the ladder. After he boarded, he pushed it away with his foot and closed the hatch.

"You want to sit up front?" he asked. "You can be the copilot."

"How about after takeoff?" She saw the hurt look in his face. "Really, after takeoff. Okay?" She chose one of the comfortable oversized seats.

"Had them built custom; everybody rides first class," he said, as he headed to the cockpit.

Helen reclined in her seat, then heard the turbines start up. She moved a little, trying to get a look at the cockpit.

"This is your captain speaking," Crawford's voice came over the loudspeaker. Helen giggled.

"Prepare for takeoff, and please fasten your seatbelts."

Helen buckled up, then looked out the window as the plane taxied to the runway.

Here we go, she thought. She grabbed the handrails of the chair, looked out her window, and saw the tarmac begin to streak by.

36

＊ ● ＊

Rome, Italy

"This will be fine, Antonio, thank you," Cardinal Fiorre said, as the car pulled up to a small two-story house just outside Vatican City.

"Do you need any help with your things, Your Eminence?" Antonio asked as he put the car in park.

"No, Antonio, I'm fine. Only my briefcase tonight." He waited for Antonio to open the door, then stepped out and retrieved his briefcase.

"The usual time tomorrow, Eminence?" Antonio asked.

Cardinal Fiorre thought a moment. "No, Antonio, I'm going to allow myself the luxury of sleeping in. All of this has made me weary." He gestured to his briefcase.

"Goodnight then, Eminence." Antonio got back into the car and disappeared into the brisk Italian night.

Cardinal Fiorre opened the brass gate that was set back in an ancient stone wall. After locking it behind him, he made his way over the stone path that led through a well-kept rose garden. He stopped for a moment, set his briefcase down, gathered one of the late-blooming roses in his hand, and inhaled the aroma. He muttered a prayer of thanks that he had been blessed with the use of this house.

He picked up his briefcase and ambled to the front door. The knocker had an old bronze head of a gargoyle. *I must find something more suitable,* he told himself for the thousandth time. It was one of those things that held his attention when it was right in front of him, but after a few steps inside his house the knocker would be forgotten until the next time he entered.

He turned on the light and made his way into the kitchen. There was a note from his housekeeper. He read it, then went over to the stove and lifted the cover off a pot of freshly made soup. He turned the stove's burner on and stirred the soup with a wooden spoon.

He tasted it. *Needs a little more oregano,* he thought, and added a few pinches, stirring it into the soup. He tried it again. *Much better.* He fetched his briefcase from the hall and set it down on the table in the dining room just off the kitchen. Opening it, he found the thick file he was looking for. His hand went absentmindedly to the cross that hung around his neck. He unfastened its chain and set it on top of the papers. He went back into the kitchen, found a ladle, dished himself a bowl of the soup, and retired to the table.

He began to read the report that he was going to send to the pope. The information collected had taken him the better part of four years, and thousands of man-hours. It was an alarming document, detailing a vast conspiracy that in Fiorre's mind seemed to pave the way for the Apocalypse. He crossed himself several times as he read the last few pages. "I have enough; it's time to act," he said aloud. He spooned another mouthful of soup and his eyes strayed to the collection of photographs on a sideboard near the table. He smiled as he saw a picture of his favorite nephew and himself. He was looking forward to the lad's birthday party on the weekend. *I must bring him something special,* he thought, and made a mental note to get something in the morning.

He turned his attention back to the document and looked at several of the photographs accompanying the file. *Who is this Mr. Kenson?* He reached for a small magnifying glass on the sideboard next to the table, and examined the photographs more carefully. He set the glass down and spooned more soup into his mouth now that it had cooled to his liking.

What if this is the dreadful man that prophecy has predicted? he thought. He shuddered.

There was a knock on his door.

Strange, he thought as he rose from the table. *I thought I locked the gate.* He went into the vestibule. "Who is it?" he asked.

The voice was muffled. "I'm sorry, sir, it's Antonio."

What does he want at this hour? Fiorre asked himself as he unbolted the door.

It was not Antonio, but two very tall men who wore dark sunglasses. Before he had time to react, they rushed through the open door. One man grabbed him and pinned his arm behind his back so far that Fiorre was sure it was going to break. The other closed the door and locked it.

"Where is it?" one of them asked, taking off his glasses.

Fiorre gave a cry of alarm, for the eyes were not human. They were twice as large as humans' and were black as the eyes of a shark.

"God have mercy . . . on you," Fiorre stammered.

The one without the glasses stepped toward Fiorre so that his horrible eyes were only inches from Fiorre's own. His mind exploded with horrible images that poured into it. He cried out and wanted to grab hold of his head, but the other man wouldn't allow it.

"Where is it . . . the papers, your report?" the man hissed at Fiorre.

"Stop . . . Stop. In there . . . all in there." Fiorre trembled with fear.

The one holding Fiorre pushed him into the dining room, pulled out a chair, and forced him into it.

The other, who had asked the questions, went to the end of the table where Fiorre's files were. He looked at the crucifix that Fiorre had set there, and swept it aside with such a force that it flew off the table and embedded itself in the wall at the far side of the room. He sat in the chair and looked things over. Then he gathered them back into the file.

"Is this all of it?" he asked.

Fiorre had turned ashen, and his hands trembled. He nodded yes. "What are you?" he stammered.

The intruder looked at Fiorre. "You wrote about us in your report."

If it were possible, Fiorre grew more terrified and managed to answer his own question. "Nephilim. You're both hybrids, aren't you?"

Fiorre saw the hybrid nod and then grotesque images exploded in his mind. He began to feel pressure in his forehead as if the blood vessels were about to burst.

The hybrid's stare grew more intense.

Fiorre's body began to shake. He felt a stab of pain over his heart.

"I . . . I . . ." he stammered as the pain grew, traveling down his left arm.

He grabbed the arm. His breath came in short, desperate, little gasps.

Another jolt hit him, and he felt his head crash to the table.

"Oh, God," he cried out, groping on the tablecloth in front of him, spilling the soup as he tried to steady himself. He realized that he was dying. His head turned sideways, and his eyes rested on the photograph of his nephew. Tears formed in his eyes. "May God protect him," he stammered, just before his whole body convulsed, continuing for a full minute before it grew still.

"I was hoping for more of a fight," said one hybrid.

"Weakling, wasn't he?" the other said, looking at Fiorre's lifeless form.

"Yes, he went quickly. You should have toyed with him more."

"I wanted to, but he must have had a weak heart."

"He didn't call on his God. I wonder why," the hybrid sneered.

"They never do until it's too late, which is why Lucius will be the victor and ascend to his rightful throne." He motioned to the other hybrid to leave.

The two men put their glasses on and left the house. One of them opened the gate and peered around the wall, to see if the street was clear. "Let's go," he said.

They slipped out onto the street and were lost in the darkness of the night.

37

An Oasis: Formerly the Land of Moab

The robed man was sweating in the heat of the sun. He pulled his hood to shield his face and looked at the expanse of desert before him. *So much has changed,* he thought, as he tried to find some familiar landmark. He knew he had traveled beyond the borders of Israel and was now in the land of Moab. He drew a rough map in the sand, using his staff, and looked at the sun. In the distance far off to his left appeared the beginnings of barren, windswept mountain ranges. *Here is something I recognize,* he thought, as he shielded his eyes with his hands. He made a mark with his staff corresponding to the mountains, then put another where he thought his position was. Satisfied, he began his journey again.

After several miles he stopped. *Ah, what good fortune is this,* he thought, for just before him was a small oasis. There were hoofprints in the sand, which he recognized as camels. He set his hand into one of them. *Over several days old,* he thought, tracing the outline with his finger. He went over to the small spring, which had a cluster of palm trees around it. He got down on his knees, cupped his hands, and began to drink.

The water was cool and sweet. *Another blessing*, he thought, looking at the palms. He saw that they were date palms, and that there were a few ripe dates left on the tree, overlooked by others who had no need of their sustenance. He reached overhead and knocked several of the dates off with his staff. He popped one into his mouth and savored the fruit, then ate a few more. He took another drink from the spring and pulled his robe around him. He settled beneath the date palm, using the trunk of the tree to support his back, and fell asleep.

Several hours later he awakened. It was nightfall, and the first stars twinkled in the heavens. Refreshed by his rest, he was eager to proceed on his journey. He took one long drink from the spring, then knocked off a few more dates, which he put into the fold of his robe for later. He then proceeded on his way.

Hours passed and he reached the base of the mountain chain he had seen earlier that day. The moon was high in the sky, and almost full. *This is a good place for it to start*, he decided, and he loosened his hood so that his long graying hair fell about his shoulders. He set his staff before him and leaned on it, driving the point of it into the desert floor. He stepped back from it a few paces. Lifting his hands above his head, he began to sing in an ancient tongue, faintly at first, then louder. He sang to the one whom he knew dwelt in the third heaven, the one true God of the universe.

Soon he began to notice the change he was looking for. The wind gathered at his back. At first it was gentle, a welcome refreshment from the still desert air. But it grew in intensity, so that strong gusts began to whip the man's robes, making them flutter against his sturdy legs. He continued to sing and kept his hands raised above him. Soon his voice was drowned out by the sound of the wind. He let his hands down and looked before him. Something was happening in the desert. For miles in all directions, a black wall of sand began to swirl and lift itself toward the sky, so that in minutes it blocked the light of the moon. He took his staff out of the sand and continued his journey, and the black swirling sand went before him.

38

✦ ◉ ✦

The Red Sea, Middle East

Mac sat on the bow of a large barge, his legs dangling over the side, and watched the calm water of the Red Sea sparkle in the moonlight as it slipped underneath the battered hull. Uri came up and sat beside him, and for a while both men were content to stare at the water as it slid hypnotically beneath them.

"You think we're close?" Mac asked, breaking the silence.

"I was asking the skipper . . . we should be landing soon," Uri replied.

Mac gestured to the camouflaged tarps that covered the two jeeps, their supplies, and the new clothes he had been provided. "You think those tarps will hide us?"

"Yeah, we look like just another ship," Uri said.

"You nervous?" Mac asked.

Uri looked up at the stars. "Yes," he admitted.

A while later, Mac saw the faint outline of a wooden pier on the shoreline, and the barge began to head for it.

"Looks like we're here," he said, and gave Uri a nudge.

Uri got up and stretched his legs.

Mac watched the barge maneuver toward the pier and heard the engines whine in protest as the captain reversed them. It drifted sideways to the pier. When it was close, several crewmembers jumped onto it, holding thick ropes which they wrapped around weather-beaten poles to secure the barge.

"It will be morning in maybe eight hours," Uri stated. "We will be moving quick to get unloaded."

"I'm glad the crew is Israeli Mossad," Mac said.

"The Major is making everything all in the family, right?" Uri replied.

Mac watched as a flurry of activity began. The tarps were thrown off the jeeps, and then the vehicles were driven off the barge and onto the pier.

"We'll take the lead one," Johanen said as he and Laura came up alongside them.

"Very chic," Mac whispered as he checked out Laura in her desert gear which, like his own, consisted of a loose khaki-colored shirt, heavy cotton pants with several deep pockets sewn into the legs, and a safari hat.

"We're supposed to be an American oil surveying team. At least that's what our phony passports say," she replied, her voice lowered. "I think we look the part."

"Let's hope we don't have to find out," Mac replied.

One of the crew hurried over. "You're unloaded and ready to go."

"Good. All ready then?" Johanen asked everyone.

Mac nodded, and they followed Johanen off the boat.

Mac was the last onto the pier. As soon as both his feet were planted on the wooden deck, the crew of the barge unwrapped the ropes, gunned the engines, and headed back into the Red Sea.

The group huddled around Johanen. "You drive our jeep, MacKenzie, and I will navigate." Mac nodded as Johanen continued. "As discussed in our briefing, the jeeps have been outfitted with satellite global positioning and other communications equipment, while Uri and Laura's jeep has, among other things, a hidden compartment concealing the explosives and incendiary devices that we will use to blow up the tomb." Johanen looked everyone in the eye and then, with a nod, headed toward the lead jeep.

Mac followed, climbed in, and fired the engine and put the jeep in gear. "Which way?" he asked.

Johanen looked at the global positioning monitor display, which was linked to satellites pinpointing their exact location, and compared it to the map, transferred now to a digital representation that Elisha had provided for him. "For now, follow the road that heads due east," he replied.

Mac put the high beams on and began to drive. After a few hundred yards the road became more distinct, although it still had sections that were without asphalt. They passed a cluster of single-story whitewashed houses, and further on, several abandoned cars.

The walkie-talkie that hung from the dashboard crackled to life. "Are you sure you're on the right road?" Laura asked.

"Well, are we?" Mac asked, throwing a sidelong glance at Johanen, who picked up the walkie-talkie. "Unless the global positioning satellite is feeding us wrong information, this is it."

A moment went by, and then Laura returned, sounding doubtful. "Okay, we're right behind you."

"This reminds me of Nevada," Mac said, "remote and desolate."

"Good place to bury something for a millennium or two," Johanen quipped.

"Should we contact Elisha and Colonel Austin?" Mac asked.

"Yes, I am sure that they have reached the castle by now. Thank you for reminding me," Johanen answered.

Mac saw him open the glove box and pull out a laptop computer that had been wired into it.

"You going to access the website?" Mac asked.

"Yes, I will send a coded message that we arrived safely and are pursuing our goal."

Johanen booted the computer and then typed in a long password.

"This is a new feature, MacKenzie," he began. "Are you familiar with how the American government used the Navajo Indian language as code during World War II?"

"Not really," Mac replied.

"The American army had a series of cryptographic failures. The master cryptographers in Tokyo were able to decipher all of your country's coded messages. A former Marine, the son of missionaries, grew up among the Navajo. It was his idea to have a Navajo Indian at every radio. All shortwave and walkie-talkie messages between troops were sent in the Navajo language. It sounded incomprehensible to the Japanese, and this was important in the Allied victory in the Pacific."

"Why couldn't the Japanese find someone to learn the language?" Mac asked.

"Because the language was restricted to Navajos alone, so it was untranslatable without the direct help of a Navajo Indian."

"Are you using Navajo now . . . in your communication?"

"Yes. My message will be converted to an audio file using Navajo words, which will then be sent to Spiral of Life on a special frequency. They must then download it and decode it. But Stephan has added another element to it." Johanen smiled cryptically. "In case someone intercepts the message, in order to have any of it make sense, they must be receiving the audio file at a precise frequency. The principle is much like that of a cell phone in that each individual owner uses his own frequency. Since there are almost an infinite number of frequencies, this added feature further complicates detection."

"Impressive," Mac said, as Johanen finished typing the message.

Mac was driving with the window down and the warm, arid air billowed through the jeep. Several strong gusts of wind rocked the jeep.

"Looks like the weather is changing," he remarked to Johanen as another gust hit them.

"Yes, and I do not like what it may indicate," Johanen replied, as he rolled up his window.

"What?" Mac was interrupted by Uri's voice on the walkie-talkie.

"I'm not liking this weather," the Israeli said, almost as if he had been listening to their conversation.

Johanen answered, "No, Uri, I do not like the looks of it, either. Your grandfather showed me a satellite printout before we left, and everything was clear. Even the projected three-day forecast hinted nothing like this."

"We should have a plan in case something happens," Uri said.

"I agree, Uri," Johanen answered.

"Will one of you kindly tell me what you're talking about?" Mac asked.

"It is too early to be certain, but we might have the beginnings of a sandstorm," Johanen answered.

"A sandstorm?" Mac asked.

"It is a real possibility. They are very unpredictable."

"So what do we do?" Mac asked.

"Pray it doesn't happen," Johanen answered.

39

Over the Mediterranean Sea

Helen giggled again as the loudspeaker boomed with Crawford's voice. "This is your captain speaking. We are now on the final leg of our journey, to our destination of Rome, Italy."

"You're silly," she shouted toward the cockpit where Crawford had left the door open.

The loudspeakers crackled again. "Why don't you come up and check the pilot's-eye view?" Crawford offered.

She got out of her seat and walked toward the cockpit. "You sure you want me up here? Won't it be too much of a distraction?" She began to bite her nail.

She saw him look at her and took her finger out of her mouth.

"Take a seat. You can be the unofficial copilot," he offered, patting the seat next to him.

"Are you sure it's all right?" she asked. "Don't they have laws that keep people out of the cockpit?"

"Only on commercial airlines. Buckle your seatbelt, though."

Helen slid into the copilot's seat. "It's really different up here," she said, buckling her belt.

"Almost like being a bird," he commented. "Remember the propellers hanging in the office? In the old days the pilots were sitting outside with the wind and rain and everything else literally in their hair. They were the real birds."

She nodded. "Where are we exactly?"

"Just over the Balearics near the coast of Spain."

"The Balearics?" Helen peered out the front window to get a better view.

"Islands in the Mediterranean Sea, incredible climate, lots of tourism, although it's getting late in the season for that."

"So how soon do we . . ." She never finished her sentence, for the plane pitched downward, as if a giant hand had pushed it from overhead.

"What's happening?" she screamed, gripping her armrests with both hands to keep from falling forward.

Crawford was fighting with the controls. "I'm not sure!" he yelled.

Then the plane leveled off and flew as if nothing had happened.

"What's going on?" Helen asked. She tightened her seatbelt.

She saw Crawford check and recheck his gauges. "I don't know," he mumbled.

The plane shuddered and then began to lose altitude.

"What's that?" Helen screamed. "They're here! They're back! Look!" She grabbed Crawford's arm, as she pointed out the window on her side of the cockpit at a bright disklike object that was keeping pace with them.

Crawford leaned forward. "Oh, no . . ."

"It's starting to glow orange . . . it's going to do something . . . I know it!"

"Oh, Lord, in your name . . ." Crawford started to pray in earnest, but broke off as he concentrated on banking the plane, pushing the aircraft to its limits.

"It's coming closer, I can see it . . . it's coming right at us!" she yelled.

The plane shuddered as the UFO passed overhead. Frantic, Crawford grabbed the stick with both hands, trying to regain control.

"It's done something to the electrical system!" Crawford yelled.

Helen heard the engines sputter as if they were running out of fuel.

"I don't think we're going to make it." Crawford grabbed the radio and yelled, "Mayday, mayday." He turned to her. "It's no use, the radio isn't working."

The plane dropped in altitude as the engines died and then sputtered back on again.

"I'm going to bellyflop her into the ocean," Crawford yelled. "It's our only hope."

Helen brought her legs up, grabbed them, and began to cry. *They're not going to get me,* she said to herself. *I don't care if I die, but they're not going to get me.*

"I can't hold it level much longer," Crawford yelled again. "We're going down, Helen!"

Helen closed her eyes and wrapped her arms around her knees. Then she heard the front of the plane slap the surface of the ocean, followed by the sound of water streaking by the body of the plane. Then a horrible tearing noise came from behind her as one of the wings caught the water. The plane spun in a whirling whiteout of spray. Helen screamed. Something struck her head, and she tried to fight against the blackness that began to overtake her. She cried out Crawford's name before everything blacked out.

40

＊◉＊

Rome, Italy

Mr. Wyan entered the private spa where Kenson lay face-down on a table, a masseuse rubbing a pungent balm into his shoulder muscles.

"It's all right. He doesn't understand a word of English," Kenson said. "But I'll dismiss him." Kenson snapped his fingers and pointed toward the door. The masseuse threw a towel over Kenson's shoulders and hurried out.

"The phone call I just received confirmed the unfortunate demise of Cardinal Fiorre," Wyan stated.

"And his papers?" Kenson asked.

"In my possession."

"Good," Kenson replied. "I'm very anxious to see the information they contain. Did Fiorre make copies of them?"

"Not as far as I know. I believe we have everything."

"The woman?" Kenson asked.

"On her way across the Atlantic."

"And will she be intercepted?"

"Yes, Abaris is taking care of it personally."

"What about Johanen?" Kenson asked.

"Elusive as always, but we're ready to strike at his main residence."

"And where is that?"

"In the Italian Alps, not far from the Swiss border," Wyan replied. "We have set a plan in motion that should cause grave consequences for him and his associates."

"But no sign of his present whereabouts?"

"He was in Jerusalem as recently as yesterday. He seems to have made contact with one of our older associates," Wyan answered.

"Who?"

"The Nazi concentration camp guard that we sacrificed for the cause."

"The one who struck at the old Jew . . . BenHassen . . . and killed him?" Kenson queried.

"Not exactly . . . the Jew didn't die. In fact, when he left the hospital a few days ago, he was accompanied by Johanen."

"Then our plan is failing?"

"A minor setback. Overall it's proceeding very nicely. The American journalist MacKenzie was present also, along with the Jew's grandson and the Nathan woman. The American faction didn't want the Nathan woman to get the disk to Johanen, so they destroyed the plane that she somehow managed not to board."

"So Johanen has the disk?"

"It appears that he does, so he's taken the bait," Wyan replied.

"Wonderful," Kenson answered.

"We tested the teleportation technology in the auditorium this morning. I had Bernstein do a dry run from the tomb."

"How did it look?"

"The transmission worked exceptionally well . . . it was like he was standing right there on the podium. By the way, most of the delegates have arrived."

"Is everything ready for the banquet this evening?"

"Yes. Are you prepared to give some interviews in private?" Wyan asked.

Kenson paused a moment. "Of course. Select the delegates from the countries that are somewhat committed to our agenda and have them meet in one of the anterooms before the banquet. I'll give them half an hour."

"Your time is fast approaching . . . I've waited a long time to see this," Wyan said. Suddenly his tongue flicked ten inches out from his mouth, grabbed a fly that was buzzing near his face, and then recoiled.

"I'm going to get dressed now," Kenson said, sliding off the table.

"I'll send a car for you in an hour," Wyan offered.

"Very good," Kenson replied and left the room.

41

The Mediterranean Sea

Pain exploded in Helen's head as she regained consciousness. She touched her forehead and felt a large bump.
Then it all came back. "Crawford!" she yelled, as she struggled
to free herself from the seat that was now partially under
water.

"Crawford! Are you all right?" She saw that he was
slumped over the controls.

What if he's dead? she thought. Fear gripped her. *What if
THEY come back?* "Crawford, answer me. Are you okay?" As
she began to get out of her seat she cried out in pain. Her
ankle was either badly sprained or broken.

She looked toward the rear of the plane, and where the
wing had once been was now a jagged ruin of twisted metal.
Colored ends of frayed wire dangled in midair. In the faint
light she could see the expanse of the sea. She heard the water
lap at the plane, felt the rocking motion, and smelled the pungent salt air.

She steadied herself on the seat in front of her. "Crawford?"
She began to cry, then bit her lower lip in determination. *I'm*

not going to lose it here, she told herself, and turned to Crawford.

She reached out and touched his bleeding forehead, then put her hand on his chest to feel if he was breathing.

"Thank God," she said out loud as she realized that he was alive.

She brushed his sandy hair away from the gash on his forehead, and washed it with a handful of seawater from the floor of the plane.

"Ohhh," he moaned.

"Crawford, are you all right?" she sobbed. "What should we do?"

She saw him force open an eye and search for her. She watched his mouth attempt to form words.

She leaned forward again so that her ear was next to his mouth. "I'm listening, Jack. Try to say something. What do you want me to do?"

The plane shuddered and tilted further down.

"It's sinking, Jack," she said, holding back some of the panic in her voice.

"Get . . . Get to the . . . .emergency . . . exit," he muttered. "Red handle . . . red handle."

"I'm not leaving you, Jack." She clutched him.

He moved his arm, trying to push her away. "Red handle. Pull the red handle, then get me."

"Okay, Jack . . . red handle." She forced herself to move back into the main cabin of the plane. The water was deeper, halfway up her calves now. She found the emergency door and located the red handle that was covered by glass. She took her shoe off and pounded on the glass, which shattered. She slipped her shoe back on, then grabbed the red handle and yanked it up. She heard a small explosion, the door blew off, and then a slide inflated. She looked down and saw that the water was perilously close to the bottom of the door.

She tumbled back into the cockpit. "I did it."

"Help . . . me . . . up," he groaned.

She hopped around the back of the pilot's chair, put both arms around his chest, and leaned back. She pulled and strained every muscle in her, and finally succeeded in getting him in an upright position.

"Oh, no . . . hold it," she gasped, as she hurried around to the side of the chair and blocked him from falling.

"Did you do it?" he asked.

"Yes. Let's get you out of here," she replied.

"My head . . . And I think . . . I've got broken ribs," he groaned.

"Oh, no, and I just grabbed you around your chest like that," she cried. She stroked his hair, pulling his head close to her body.

"Give me a minute, okay?" he said. A crooked smile emerged through his blood-stained face. "Is the raft . . . floating?"

"I don't know," Helen answered. "You mean the slide thing?"

Crawford nodded. "Get us . . . lifejackets . . . put them on . . . then out of here."

"Where are they?" Helen asked. "Are you going to be all right if I leave you?"

There was another groaning sound, and the plane rocked a little, the nose tilting further into the ocean.

"By the . . . emergency . . . exit," he said.

Helen hobbled out of the cockpit, wincing every time her weight came down on her sprained ankle. She got to the open door, and to her horror saw that the water had started lapping over the edge of the doorway. She opened the cabinet door labeled "emergency only" and saw the life jackets. She also spied a handful of flares and a flare gun, and reminded herself to get them on her way out . . . after she got Crawford. *How am I going to get him from where he is to here?* she wondered.

She slipped her life jacket on, fumbled with the straps, then made her way back into the cockpit, clenching her teeth to fight off the pain. "I got them, Jack."

Crawford's head hung over the back of the seat. He opened one eye; the other was now completely swollen shut. "Good . . . let's do it."

She watched him take a couple of shallow breaths, and then he grabbed the control stick in front of him. Using it to steady himself, he leaned forward.

Helen slipped the life jacket over him, cinching it tight.

"Get close . . . here." He motioned to her with one finger. She bent down.

"Take my arm . . . around your . . . neck."

Helen took his arm and wrapped it around her neck. *It feels so heavy,* she thought, and wondered how she'd find the strength to lift him.

"Ready?" Crawford asked.

"Ready."

"On three, okay? One . . . two . . . three." Helen lifted for all she was worth, and tried to ignore the pain that erupted in her ankle. She saw Crawford grit his teeth. "Oh," he moaned, as he swayed on his feet. Helen felt as if she would buckle under his weight at any moment.

"Let's go," he said.

Helen tried to take a step, but the moment she did they both tumbled forward into the cold seawater gathering on the floor of the plane. "Oh, no! Crawford?" she screamed, as he went face-down into the water. She pulled him back up, and he collapsed against her, his head like a dead weight on her shoulder.

"Oh, Jack," Helen sobbed. "Are you all right? I'm sorry I fell."

"Okay . . . we'll try again . . . My head . . . I feel dizzy," Crawford mumbled.

"Okay, Jack, let me stand first." Slowly she got up, putting all her weight on her good leg while steadying Crawford so that he wouldn't fall over.

"Ready?" he said, tilting his head back and looking up at her.

"Ready," she replied. She put her hands underneath his armpits and heaved. "Come on, Jack," she commanded. "Use your legs."

She somehow managed to get him to his feet, and the two of them leaned against the cockpit door for support.

Helen was breathing heavily from the strain. "We've got to try now," she said between gasps.

"I feel like I'm going to pass out," Crawford said.

"Hold on to me," Helen instructed. "One step at a time, okay?"

"Yes," Crawford groaned.

"Ready? Here we go." Helen took one small step forward. "Hang on," she said, then added, "We made it," as they completed the first step.

The plane slid a little deeper into the water. Helen glanced back at the pilot's chair and noticed that the water was beginning to rise.

"We've got to get out of here," she said. There was no hiding the fear in her voice. "Ready, another step . . . one, two, three." She ground her teeth together as the pain shot up from her ankle. But they made it another step.

Crawford motioned to the wall. "Get me there . . . it'll be easier."

Helen looked at the wall that separated the cockpit from the main body of the plane. Even though it was only a few feet away it seemed impossible to reach. "Okay, let's try," she said, and readied herself for the pain.

Three grueling steps later they reached the wall. Crawford leaned against it, taking most of the weight off Helen. The going was easier, and they arrived at the "emergency only" cabinet.

"Flares . . . get flares and the Berry gun . . . waterproof," Crawford said. He rolled his one open eye toward the cabinet. Helen hobbled around him and retrieved the flares and the flare gun.

"Put 'em in the vest," Crawford said, nodding at the front of Helen's vest.

Helen stuffed them into a watertight compartment in the front of her vest, then thought of the money in her purse. She hobbled over to where she had left her bag and found it floating near her seat. She grabbed it, took out her wallet, stuffed it and the money inside one of the vest pockets, then went back to Crawford.

They moved closer to the door.

"We don't have any more time," Helen said, as the water started to pour into the open emergency door.

"Go down the slide . . . .hold onto the end . . . of it," Crawford said.

"I'm not going first. Why can't we go together?" she protested.

"Go . . . now," Crawford said.

Helen looked at him for a second. She wanted to stay with him, to make sure he got out too. "You sure?" she asked.

"Go . . . now!" Crawford commanded.

Helen felt the plane pitch violently forward. She dove for the slide and landed in the cold water. She struggled to hold onto the end of the slide, but it eluded her grasp. She tried to swim back to the slide, and then to her horror she saw the nose of the plane sink beneath the ocean.

"Crawford!" she screamed, but there was no answer as the rest of the plane plunged into the sea, dragging the life raft with it.

42

✽ ◉ ✽

Yemen

It's getting worse," Mac yelled over the growing turbulence of wind that made him grip the wheel with both hands. "I can barely see the road."

Johanen grabbed the walkie-talkie. "Uri, I think we had better find somewhere to ride the storm out." Johanen looked at the digital map superimposed on the laptop.

"Anyplace on there?" Mac asked as he glanced over at Johanen.

Johanen looked troubled. "There is not much here, and I am not sure that we could find it even without the sand-storm."

"So it's a sandstorm?" Mac asked.

Johanen checked their GPS. "Yes, MacKenzie, it is a sand-storm, and because of it our GPS is not working properly."

"I can't see two feet in front of me!" Mac slapped the edge of the wheel with the palm of his hand.

"We haven't hit the worst of it yet," Johanen replied, then spoke into his walkie-talkie. "Uri, I think it would be good to pull over soon before we get separated."

Mac waited for the Israeli's response, but it never came.

"Uri, can you read me?" Johanen repeated.

"What's wrong?" Mac asked.

"Our walkie-talkie does not seem to be working," Johanen answered.

"Try it again. Hit the side of it, maybe the batteries are loose," Mac suggested.

Johanen slapped the side of the walkie-talkie and tried hailing Uri again.

Mac held his breath and also slowed the jeep. "Nothing?" he asked.

A surge of wind and sand hit them broadside with such force that Mac almost lost control of the vehicle. He turned the wheel into the direction of the wind and tried to see the road. "I can't see a thing," he yelled above the howling wind.

"We have lost them," Johanen replied.

"What do you want me to do?" Mac asked.

"We have not traveled that far since our last contact with them, so there is a chance of finding them after the storm blows over. Stop the jeep, and we will ride it out here," Johanen said.

Mac stopped the jeep, turned off the engine, and yanked back on the emergency brake. Now that the noise from the engine was silenced, he could hear the grains of sand tearing into the metal of the jeep. Another blast of wind and sand rocked it.

"How long could a man last out there?" he asked.

"Without protection, not long." Johanen gestured out the front window to the dark clouds of whirling sand. "Not more than a few minutes."

Mac looked at the storm that raged around him. He slumped down in his seat and flicked the keys that dangled from the ignition. "Uri told me that you healed his grandfather, Elisha, when he was in the hospital."

Mac watched Johanen's face carefully, trying to read his body language.

"That is not entirely true." Johanen ran both his hands through his beard, brushing it vigorously downward. "I did as I was instructed to do, which was to pray. The Ancient of Days chose to heal Elisha; I was just the instrument by which his power went through. A conduit, if you will."

"Have you always been the recipient of this gift?" Mac pressed, fascinated by what he was hearing.

"I began to notice it in my early twenties." Mac noticed the faintest hint of a smile.

"So for the last forty or so years you've had this gift . . . to heal?" Mac asked. "I'm assuming that you're around sixty years old, right?"

Johanen's smile broadened, and Mac saw that his blue eyes looked almost mischievous. "Your estimate of my age is off . . . considerably."

Mac adjusted his position so that his back pressed against the window. He could feel the sand vibrating the glass. "Hope the glass holds." Then he returned to Johanen's last statement. "By the way, you look great for your age." It was a genuine compliment.

Johanen settled down in his seat.

"How much older are you then?" Mac asked, wondering how the man maintained such physical vigor.

"MacKenzie, I was hoping that this conversation would have taken place some other time, if at all," Johanen stated.

Mac looked out the front of the window and gestured to the storm. "Why not now? It's not like we're going somewhere in this."

"True, but I am not sure this is the best time, considering that we are, for the present, confined here." He gestured to the inside of the jeep.

Mac regrouped his thoughts. "Then can I ask you about the healing?"

Johanen nodded.

"Why did you heal Elisha, and not other people in the same hospital? I mean, if you have this gift, then why not use it?"

"It is not for me to decide who is healed and who is not. The Ancient of Days sent me to Elisha in much the same way that I was told to go to you. I obeyed the calling. I am, you see, his servant."

"How long have you had this gift?"

"For a considerable time."

"How long is that?" Mac pressed.

Johanen turned his head away from Mac and looked out the front window. He said something but it was almost lost in the noise of the storm.

Mac froze in his seat, thinking that the wind must have played tricks with his ears. He cleared his throat and forced himself to repeat Johanen's last words, assuring himself that what he'd heard was obviously impossible. "Did I hear you correctly? Did you say almost two thousand years?" He laughed nervously as he waited for an answer.

43

✳ ◉ ✳

The Mediterranean Sea

Helen flailed her arms as she treaded water, turning herself around and around, looking for any signs of Crawford in the fading daylight.

She felt something slide beneath her. She screamed, thinking it was a shark, but then she realized that it was the wing of the plane sliding past her as it began to sink. She felt it begin to suck her down, so she kicked with her legs and propelled herself upward and away from the sinking plane. "Crawford?" she yelled again, as her eyes darted from place to place on the water.

What's that? she thought, and began to swim toward an object that had just surfaced. She stopped when she realized that it was part of the wreckage.

Something else popped up to her left. She kicked with her feet to get higher in the ocean. *More junk,* she thought. "Crawford!" she yelled, on the verge of tears, for she was afraid he had drowned. "Crawford!"

Then something caught her eye. She saw an orange life vest and his plaid shirt floating on the surface of the ocean.

What if he's dead? she thought. The thought panicked her as she kicked and paddled for all she was worth, never taking her eyes off of him.

She maneuvered herself in front of him. His head was tilted so that his chin rested on the life jacket, keeping his nose and mouth less than an inch above the water. She held his head and lifted it so that it rested on the collar of the life jacket. "Crawford, are you all right?" she asked as she combed his wet hair back from his forehead. She lifted one of his eyelids, and noticed that the pupil was rolled upward. Then she remembered the flare gun.

She reached into her vest, pulled the gun out, then grabbed one of the flares and inserted it into the chamber. She had never shot a gun before, and as she fumbled with the safety, the flare gun went off.

"Oh, no!" she screamed, and almost dropped the gun.

The flare missed Crawford's head by mere inches, and she watched it speed a few feet above the surface of the water before it hit a small wave and disappeared.

She fished in the pocket of the life jacket, brought out another flare, and reloaded the gun. This time she held it above her head with both hands as her feet kicked beneath her. She closed her eyes, pulled the trigger, and screamed as the flare exploded from the mouth of the gun. She watched as it streaked upward, leaving a trail of smoke. It finished its arc, and then seemed to float down, a sparkling orb of bright orange before it was extinguished in the sea.

She reloaded and fired again, this time clamping her teeth together and bracing herself for the recoil of the gun. She watched as it made another arc in the sky.

She kicked with her feet, still holding onto Crawford, and turned him around to see if any boat had responded to the flares.

There was nothing on the horizon but endless water.

She loaded another flare and was about to fire it. *I'm panicking,* she thought, *I've got to remain calm.* She counted how many she had left. *Seven.* She made sure they were snug inside her vest. *Make them count . . . wait till you see something before you go firing another one,* she told herself.

She looked back at Crawford, saw his head was out of the water and that he was breathing.

Parts of the wreckage began to surface around her. Seat cushions, a ragged section of the damaged wing, pieces of carpet, and even a few bits of clothing. She thought the wing might serve as a life raft, and decided to swim for it. She put the flare gun back in her jacket, then faced Crawford. She spread her legs around him, held onto the front of his life jacket, leaned back in the water, and began to frog kick her way toward the wing. The going was slow.

At times it seemed like the wing was moving away from her.

Crawford moaned, and she stopped kicking. "Crawford, are you all right? Say something, anything," she pleaded, but she saw he was out again.

She resumed her frog kicking.

The waves were small, but still large enough to hide the wing from her when she was in their trough. At those times she would worry about losing sight of it, and she'd kick all the harder to reach the peak of the wave, get her bearings on the wing, and start kicking again as she rode the back of the wave down into the next trough. She continued like this for an hour, and then thinking she would never reach it, startled herself as she hit the back of her head against the edge of the wing.

"Finally," she moaned as she rested one arm on the surface, relieved that she no longer had to frog kick to keep afloat. She held onto Crawford, and wondered how she was ever going to get him on top of the broken section of wing.

She kicked her way around her new life raft looking for a low spot to drag Crawford on to it. Part of the wing dipped down so that its tattered edge was a few feet below the water. She maneuvered Crawford so that he floated on his back. Then she grabbed the collar of his life jacket and floated him over the low spot of the life raft. The back of her hand struck the metal, and she cut herself on an exposed rivet. But Crawford was now almost halfway out of the water. She rested a moment, and then hauled herself up onto the raft.

She collapsed next to Crawford and began to cry. "I was so close . . . so close, and they ruined it. Like they do everything," she said, thinking of how the UFO made them crash.

She glanced at Crawford, and realized that his face was exposed to the sun. She tried to move him further up onto the raft but he was too heavy now that his body was out of the water. She picked up one of his arms and rested it over his forehead. *Now if it will only stay there,* she thought.

But the motion of the raft on the waves jostled it from its position, and the arm slid away.

She noticed part of a seat cushion floating about thirty feet away. She forced herself back into the water and swam over to it. Without Crawford, the going was much easier. She climbed back on the raft, loosened Crawford's life jacket, and tied the cushion so that it blocked out most of the sun. She brought her legs up underneath her and looked around for any sign of a boat. In the distance she saw several. *But they're probably too far away to see the flare,* she thought.

She decided to try anyway. So she slipped a flare into the chamber, fired the gun overhead, and waited. She squinted her eyes and watched for any sign of course alteration from either of the ships. *They didn't see it,* she lamented.

She fired one more and waited, hoping that somebody on board would notice, but again nothing happened, and after another few minutes the ships had vanished altogether.

She lay down next to Crawford and looked at him. She let her eyes follow the contours of his face, looked at the stubble of his beard, at where he had missed a few hairs underneath his nose shaving, at his blood-soaked hair matted to his forehead. She touched the gash. *At least the bleeding's stopped,* she thought. And then she saw something that chilled her. His blood, although just a few drops now, fell onto the life jacket, lapped away by the seawater as the pitch and roll of the ocean moved the raft. She had read about sharks, and she knew that they could smell blood in the water over a mile away.

She slipped off her life jacket and wrapped it around her leg. Then she took off her sweater and ripped one of its sleeves so she could fasten a bandage for his head.

She succeeded, and was pleased to see that it covered the wound. She put her life jacket back on and scanned the horizon. Still nothing. No ship in sight.

She loaded another flare in the gun and counted them again, realizing that there were only five remaining.

The sun was getting lower on the horizon and she wondered how much daylight was left. The thought of spending the night on the ocean terrified her. She also realized that all her exertion had made her ravenously hungry, and there was nothing to eat or drink.

She sat up again and checked for boats. *Surely someone must have heard the Mayday he sent,* she thought, but then remembered that Crawford had said that the radio was dead. *The radio and all the rest of the electrical went dead because of the UFO,* she reminded herself, *so that means that no one knows we're here.*

The realization made her start to cry again. She lay back down and pressed her body close to Crawford, wishing he would wake up and save them. *But he might not, and you're the one who's going to have to save the both of you,* she scolded herself.

She sat up again, drew her knees close to her body, and chewed on her nails. *Crawford's so sure that there is a God, and look what happens,* she thought bitterly. *We were so close, and look where we wind up. Proof that God doesn't exist,* she told herself, folding her arms in front of her. *He can't even get me to where I'm supposed to go to get help.*

She looked out over the expanse of ocean, hoping to see a ship. Instead she saw something that made her heart sink, and she began to shiver. She looked again and grew even more fearful because there was no mistaking the two fins, side by side, knifing their way through the ocean. Sometimes they vanished in the trough of a wave, but then always reappeared . . . and they were headed directly toward her.

44

The Tel in Yemen

"Throw some rope around that tent," Bernstein yelled from the base of a huge megalith, as he watched a supply tent flap in the growing dust and wind. He clamped his hand down on his hat as he went over to the pit. He climbed down the ladder, then lumbered down the stone steps that led to the hidden tomb. He welcomed the silence and the constant temperature of the tomb's interior.

"Where is my cell phone?" he bellowed to an intern.

"I have it here, sir," an intern replied.

He grabbed the cell phone and stabbed at the numbers with his fleshy fingers, then shouted into it, "It's growing much worse by the minute. I'm starting to be concerned for the safety of the tomb itself."

"The tomb has been through two millennia of weather, so I can assure you, Dr. Bernstein, that it will remain as it has for centuries ... safe from the forces of nature," Mr. Wyan answered.

"I know that," Bernstein shot back impatiently. "What I'm referring to is that this storm might throw off our timetable.

You and Mr. Kenson are still planning on arriving for the broadcast, and unless the storm subsides I don't see how you're going to make it."

"We've been monitoring it on our end, Doctor. I'm assured that it will dissipate in time."

"Let's hope so. By the way, how did the teleportation look?" Bernstein asked.

"You looked more real than you can imagine, Doctor," Wyan answered, referring to the testing of the equipment. "Of course Mr. Kenson's teleportation from inside the tomb to the delegates here in Rome, will be . . . of . . . evening."

"You're starting to break up," Bernstein shouted into the receiver, as if by raising his voice he could make Wyan hear him better. Then just static, and the red light on the phone flashed, indicating no service.

"Just great," Bernstein yelled, looking at the dead cell phone.

"What's going on?" the aide asked.

"Have you looked outside lately?" Bernstein replied.

The intern, a young woman in her early twenties who was helping route the endless lengths of television cables, shook her head.

"It's a sandstorm, and a nasty one at that. There's no telling how long it will last," he snorted. "In the meantime, everything that isn't nailed down is being blown away." He waved his hand in dismissal and watched as the young woman hurried from the tunnel and vanished up the steps. He walked toward the room holding the sarcophagus. Stopping, he leaned against the side of the tunnel clutching one hand over his chest as he fought to catch his breath. He wiggled his toes in his shoes, and much to his consternation realized that his feet had swollen again. *I must sit down and rest*, he admonished himself as he pushed off the wall of the tunnel and resumed his hike, ignoring his own advice.

A profusion of television cables lay along the edge of the tunnel, along with an eclectic cluster of equipment at the entrance to the chamber. Powerful studio lights had been erected at the four corners of the room, and had been positioned so their light beamed toward the center. Two television cameras were on, their monitors showing the sarcophagus from different angles.

Bernstein was alone. He huffed his way to the sarcophagus and ran his fleshy hands over the glasslike box which contained the body of Jesus of Nazareth. "Old friend," he muttered as he tapped the surface of the box with his forefinger. He couldn't wait to open the lid and collect the tissue samples for the DNA testing. "And the artifacts," he mused, "what did they do?" He squatted so that his face came alongside one of the alien artifacts. *This will be the lever that moves the world into a new paradigm, and you, Bernstein, you're the man who will help present it.*

He straightened and walked back down the corridor. At the long staircase, he placed one foot then the other on the same step, making a slow ascent. By the time he reached the top, he had broken into a light sweat. He noticed that the heavy tarp that had been in position over the entrance was now shredded in several pieces and was flapping wildly. Several members of his team, along with a few security guards, were erecting a makeshift barrier so that the sand wouldn't re-cover the hole. Bernstein held on to his hat with one hand as he climbed into the reinforced pit. Several streams of sand fell into the pit, much like sand in an hourglass, collecting in piles at the bottom. *If this continues,* he thought, *in a few hours the pit will be filled.* A sudden gust of wind tore his hat from his head, but he was able to grasp it.

One of his team, whom he couldn't identify because of the towel wrapped around the man's head, spotted him and yelled in a muffled voice, "We haven't much time, sir. It's getting worse."

"Lower the lid and seal the tomb," Bernstein shouted.

The man shook his covered head. "It won't work because of the cables."

Bernstein had forgotten them. As he looked back to see the cables, he forgot to hold his hat, and this time it was blown away by another gust of wind. "Then disconnect the cables," he shouted.

The man shrugged and hurried away to get more help.

Bernstein held his hand in front of his eyes as another surge of wind blew grains of sand in his face. He became annoyed as the sand bit at him.

"Sir, several of our Yemeni guides have indicated that this is the worst storm they've seen in more than a decade," someone yelled.

Bernstein began to climb the ladder out of the pit. He recognized the voice as belonging to the captain in charge of the tel's security.

He reached the top and was almost blown back into the pit as the wind and sand hit him full force for the first time.

Two security people reached out and grabbed him.

"Get me to my trailer," Bernstein ordered.

The two men, both with wrapped towels over their heads, struggled against the wind and sand to where Bernstein had left his cart.

"Good . . . good," Bernstein said as he moved his bulky frame into the seat.

One of the men climbed in next to him, and the cart moved forward. When they arrived at Bernstein's trailer, which he had positioned against the base of one of the megaliths nearest the tomb, the huge rock offered some protection from the wind.

Bernstein climbed out, holding his hand in front of his eyes. He peeked out at the black swirling wall of dust that was less than a mile away.

Without acknowledging his driver, he hurried as fast as he could up the metal steps to his trailer and slammed the door behind him.

45

❖

The Mediterranean Sea

Helen loaded the flare gun and pointed it at the incoming sharks.

"Two fins," she said out loud to Crawford, even though he was still unconscious. "Two fins. I can't shoot both of them." She thought maybe if she wounded one of the sharks then the other might go for its injured comrade. She took some hope in that.

They were coming closer, always side by side. Sometimes one would disappear, but then it would resurface and resume its position next to the other.

Helen closed her fingers around the flare gun. "This is it, Crawford," she said aloud. "Less than a minute and they'll be here." She kept the nose of the gun pointed at the incoming pair of fins. *Wait till you have a shot,* she told herself. *Don't panic.*

She reached into her life vest pocket, took out another flare, and then put it in her mouth sideways. She clamped her teeth down on it and followed the fins as they began their last approach. It was less than fifty yards now. She was amazed to see how they were eating up the distance, and then they vanished. She saw them dive in tandem when they were only a short distance from the raft. Adding to her dread, it appeared that they had separated.

She looked to her left and then snapped her head back again. Nothing.

Her hands were sweating.

Then she heard something surface behind her. She spun around, ready to kill, and to her utter amazement there was a dolphin with its head out of the water.

"What?" she whispered in astonishment.

Another head surfaced next to it, and the two dolphins greeted each other with excited squeaks. It sounded like two children giggling.

She lowered her flare gun and just stared at the two mammals.

"They're dolphins," she said with a mixture of relief and excitement to Crawford, even though she knew he couldn't hear her. "Two friendly dolphins."

One of them flipped its tail and swam backward, then submerged, resurfacing a moment later next to its mate.

Helen watched them play for a while. One would circle the raft while the other would dive and try to intercept it. It was, in the midst of her ordeal, very humorous and wonderful to watch, taking her mind off her predicament and Crawford's injuries.

This continued for fifteen minutes while Helen sat next to Crawford, wishing he'd open his eyes and see the dolphins playing.

Then they did something that astounded her. One of them came over to the edge of the raft, gave it a little push with its nose. Helen felt the raft move a little in the water. The other dolphin took notice, and with a flick of its tail, came alongside the other.

More talking ensued between them, and then the other dolphin pushed its nose against the raft. Sometimes they would push the raft together, synchronized as if they had been trained to perform this in a show, and other times only one would push while its mate swam around the raft.

Helen looked at the sun, the lower edge of it just touching the ocean as it began to set, and figured from its position that the dolphins were heading north to what she hoped would be land.

The dolphins continued pushing the raft. Crawford was still out, although he moaned from time to time.

Helen tried not to panic as the last of the sun extinguished itself as it sank into the sea. She curled up next to Crawford, and hearing the reassuring chirps and squeaks of the dolphins, drifted off into an uneasy sleep.

46

Yemeni Desert

Mac felt the hair on his arms stand up, and he whispered, "You said almost . . . two thousand years . . . old?"

"You heard correctly," Johanen remarked. His piercing blue eyes never wavered from Mac's.

Mac saw Johanen begin to grin, and for a moment, much to his relief, thought that it all might be a joke.

"I want you to read something, MacKenzie," Johanen said, as he reached into the back of the jeep. "Here it is." He produced a worn black leather Bible.

He flipped through the pages, found the passage that he was looking for, and handed the book to Mac. "Read, starting here." And he pointed to the place with his index finger.

Mac read the passage, looked uncertainly at Johanen, and then read it again. "Okay, so what are you trying to tell me here?" he asked, as he waved his hand over the open book.

Johanen smiled and recited the verses from memory: "Peter turned and saw that the disciple whom Jesus loved was following them. (This was the one who leaned back against Jesus at the supper and had said, 'Lord, who is going to betray you?') When Peter saw him, he asked, 'Lord, what about him?' Jesus answered, 'If I want him to remain alive until I return, what is that to you? You must follow me.'"

Mac shifted in his seat, glanced down at the passage that Johanen had just recited, then looked back at the old man. "Are you trying to say that this is you?" he managed.

Johanen nodded and smiled.

"Then you're the disciple John?"

Again Johanen nodded.

Mac turned away, pressed his cheek against the glass of the window, and felt it shudder as the sandstorm raged on outside.

"You're *really* two thousand years old?" he asked, keeping his face turned away. "How does . . ." And his voice trailed off.

"How does what?" Johanen coaxed.

Mac sat up, brushed the hair off his forehead, and looked at Johanen. He opened his mouth, started to say something, then shut it again. He covered his face with his hands and groaned.

"Really, MacKenzie, with God all things are possible. Surely you remember Methuselah?"

Mac groaned again, this time a little louder.

"He lived almost a thousand years," Johanen informed him.

Mac let his hands fall on his lap and shifted in his seat so that his body faced Johanen. "I don't believe this. You're joking, right?"

He watched as Johanen's head moved in the opposite direction that he had hoped to see.

"Who else knows? Does Elisha know?" Mac asked.

"No, Elisha does not know."

"He doesn't know?" Mac stammered in disbelief.

"He doesn't need to, at least not yet."

"What about Knud and Stephan?"

"No, but Hilda does."

"Why . . . " Mac began, but his voice trailed off.

"I have been left here to keep an eye on things until he returns," Johanen stated. "You might say I am his caretaker . . . of sorts."

"An eye on things?" Mac repeated, the anxiety rising in his voice.

"When he feels that a certain situation needs some special handling, he sometimes sends me."

"A certain situation? Okay, give me an example, something he got you involved in that needed special handling," Mac challenged.

"From what century?" Johanen quipped.

"I don't know, for crying out loud, the last century," Mac answered, well past exasperation.

Johanen grew serious. "Ulysses S. Grant at Appomattox."

"You were at . . ." Mac's journalistic training got the better of him, and for a moment he thought that he had the beginnings of a great story. He dismissed the thought, realizing that no one would believe him. "What about Appomattox?"

"There was a plot to assassinate Grant that day. I helped deter it."

"John Wilkes Booth?" Mac asked.

"I'm not permitted to give you specifics," Johanen replied.

"Really, no specifics?"

"Much too risky."

"You stopped an assassination," Mac repeated.

"If you know where to look, I'm in one of the pictures taken that day."

"Oh, come on."

"When we get back to the castle, I'll show you."

"Really?" Mac's curiosity grew. "Why did you tell *me*?" Mac asked.

Johanen's face grew serious again. "The Evil One's time is approaching. A period that the Bible calls 'The Time of Jacob's Trouble.'"

"You mean Armageddon?" Mac asked.

"That is part of it, the ending, but the time leading up to that dreadful day is more of what I had in mind. It is a time when the powers of darkness rule the earth, when the Evil One will incarnate and reveal himself in the flesh. A period when the nations are deceived by the miracles, signs, and wonders that he is able to produce; a period of a great falling away of believers, when hearts grow cold and people's love of God grows dim."

Mac felt dazed, overwhelmed by what Johanen was telling him.

"And you, MacKenzie, are but one person whom the Ancient of Days has elected to warn others of these troublesome times we are about to enter."

"Why me?" Mac asked

"Certainly not because you're anyone special, or that you have some great spiritual gift. But you know of the deception that the Evil One is using, that being, of course, the alien UFO phenomena. You are tied to it because when you were just a boy your father showed you the artifacts from Roswell. But more importantly, he sees your heart, into your innermost thoughts, and he knows that you have a heart like King David of the Bible."

Mac nodded, not knowing what to say.

"You must face your fear, MacKenzie. You must know that he that is in you is much more powerful than anything you could ever encounter. You must learn to use your authority in *him*."

Mac looked at the old man, then at the Bible, which was opened on his lap. His mind had been taken to the brink of what it could handle. He managed to say, "I'll give it a shot, Johanen . . . I'll give it a shot."

47

✳ ◉ ✳

The Mediterranean Sea

Helen was awakened by Crawford's moaning. It was still dark and she had no idea of how long she had slept. She was cold, hungry, and wet, as the seawater had lapped over the wing continually. She sat up and saw to her amazement that the dolphins were still pushing the raft.

Crawford moaned louder.

"Are you all right, Jack? Can you hear me? Jack?"

In the dim starlight, Helen saw Crawford work his mouth slowly to speak. "You . . . okay?" he whispered.

"I'm fine. The plane crashed. Do you remember?"

"Yeah," Crawford moaned.

"We're being pushed by dolphins. At first I thought they were sharks. But then they surfaced. I wish you could see them, Jack, they're incredible. The sun was setting, and you were bleeding, and I was so afraid," she blurted, not wanting him to go out again before she brought him up to date with all that had happened.

Crawford managed to grin, and gestured with his hand to slow down. "Any ships? Rescue?" he asked.

"No, not yet, and I've fired off some flares. We still have five left, I think. It's going to be all right, isn't it?"

"Fire a flare," Crawford said. "It's dark . . . someone might see it."

"Okay." She pulled the gun from her vest and fitted a flare into it. She pointed it toward the stars overhead and fired. The flare shot up into the sky and exploded.

"It's beautiful," she said, as it burst high overhead, glowing deep red as it floated back toward the water. "Should I fire another?"

Crawford took a deep breath. "No, wait a while."

"I think it's almost morning," Helen said, noticing a faint glow in the horizon to her right.

"Wait . . . until . . . a ship," Crawford instructed her, and then he slipped under again.

"Don't go," she moaned. "Don't leave me alone." But then she noticed the dolphins, and she laughed through her tears and rubbed her eyes. "You guys haven't given up on us, have you?" she said to the dolphins.

She brought her knees up to her chest, wrapped her arms around them, and began to shiver. She waited for the sun to crest the horizon. It seemed like hours before it happened, and during that time she thought of the food she would eat when they were rescued, the hot coffee that she would hold with both her hands, the bath she would languish in. She was determined they were going to get out of this, that with the coming of the sun there would be a ship and they would be rescued.

She watched the dolphins as it grew lighter. Only one was pushing now, and the raft continued to inch its way through the water. She wanted to reach down and pet its nose, but thought better of it.

"There it is," she shouted, as the first part of the sun glimmered above the horizon line and soon became a dull orange ball of flame that pulled itself up from the endless blue expanse of sea.

Still shivering and holding herself, she turned her head in both directions looking for a ship, any ship, and to her dismay saw nothing but a perfect circle of blue around her.

Hours passed, and the sun climbed higher. It became warmer and she stopped shivering. As the day began to heat up, she realized just how thirsty she had become. Her lips were swollen, and her bare arms became sunburned. She checked to make sure Crawford's face was covered. Although he groaned from time to time, he still remained unconscious.

The water shimmered in the sunlight, and she had trouble seeing because of its glare. She held her hand like a visor over her eyes and surveyed the sea again, and then she saw it . . . or at least she thought she did.

She rubbed her eyes and looked again.

"A ship! Crawford . . . there's a ship," she shouted. She fumbled for the gun, and realized her hands were shaking. *From fear? From hunger?* she wondered, as she slipped another flare into the chamber. She held it above her head with both hands and squeezed the trigger. The report of the gun startled her, but she watched with growing satisfaction as the flare sped skyward and then exploded in a burst of red. She loaded her gun again and looked at the ship. There was no doubt it was headed right across their path.

She waited another minute, then fired one of the three flares left. "Oh, no," she said as this flare fizzled out and dropped into the ocean after a short, erratic flight. She loaded the gun again, and looked where she had last seen the ship. To her dismay, it seemed to be turning away from them. She pointed the gun over her head and yanked on the trigger. This time the flare shot upward and exploded. Her eyes darted from the glowing flare to the ship, and back again. She bit her swollen lower lip, and it began to bleed. "Come on!" she yelled. She started to stand up on the raft, which made it tip at a dangerous angle. Crawford started to slip off. She sat back down, grabbed Crawford, and yanked him a few inches toward her, all without taking her eyes off the ship. She had one flare left, and she held onto it with her trembling hand as the ends of her fingers turned white from her grip. She slipped the flare into the gun and looked at the ship that had crossed their path and was now heading away from them. She fired it, and this time ignored the flare as it streaked upward overhead. Her eyes were married to the ship.

"Come on . . . look . . . look at us," she coaxed.

Still the ship kept its course. The flare came down so that it seemed to hover for a moment between the ship and her raft.

"Look at it," she yelled, just before it vanished into the sea.

Tears began to form. In her frustration she threw the now useless flare gun into the sea, but the ship didn't turn.

She fell on Crawford and began to sob, her entire body convulsing. She felt bile rise up in her throat and then she vomited, managing to get her head to the side of the raft just in time.

Then she heard the dolphins squeaking and giggling again.

"It's no use," she muttered.

But they kept it up. One surfaced near, splashing water on her head with its flipper.

"Stop it, it's no use, can't you see . . . " Her voice trailed off as the sound of a horn reached her ears. It was distant but clear. She tensed and listened but was still too afraid to look. Then it came again. She forced her head in the direction of the sound. Through her tears, she saw that the ship had turned and was headed for them.

"Crawford, they see us!" she cried.

She looked one more time and waved her hand overhead, which brought the welcome response of the ship's horn, a little louder now.

"We're safe, Crawford," she said. She leaned forward and kissed his cheek.

48

Jordan

The Palestinian truck driver slammed his fist against the steering wheel of his truck and cursed.

He threw the gears into reverse and pushed the worn gas pedal as hard as he could down to the floor, as if the added exertion on his part would somehow make the tires turn faster. He heard them spinning, and glanced in his rearview mirror at a cloud of sand spraying back from the tires. The unexpected sandstorm had caused him to pull over and wait for it to pass. Now hours later, the sand had buried his truck, making it impossible to move.

He tried to push the pedal further down, and cursed again as he realized that it had reached its limits.

He took his foot off the gas and stomped it down on the brake pedal. He threw the truck into low gear and repeated the process, this time watching the sand fly in back of the truck.

To his surprise his eye caught a figure that remained just outside the miniature sandstorm that his tires were creating. He took the cuff of his worn muslin shirt and wiped the dirt off the side mirror.

"What does he want?" he muttered, as he glanced at the robed figure.

He turned his attention back to the truck, and began to jam the gears, alternating from forward to reverse, all the while holding his foot to the gas pedal. He felt the truck inch forward, then jerk backward, metal and rubber responding to his will. For a moment he began to hope that the old trick would work. He looked again, and saw to his dismay that the truck had dug itself deeper, now almost up to its axles in sand. He spit out his window and looked again at the robed figure that remained motionless on the shoulder of the road.

Where did he come from? the driver wondered. He pounded the wheel again with his fist and turned off the engine. It was hot, and although the air conditioner in the cab kept things somewhat cool, he had worked himself into a sweat with his antics in trying to get the truck out of the sand.

He had deliveries to make, and if he wasn't on time his boss would be angry and maybe dock his pay. He had traveled the route before, from the Jordanian border south through Saudi Arabia close to the Yemeni border. His truck carried used irrigation pipes and sprinklers from Israeli farming kibbutzim.

He thought there might be a phone several miles back down the road from where he had just come, but he wasn't sure. It was beginning to get dark, and he had to do something. He also remembered that the clasp on the roll-up door was broken, and to leave the truck abandoned, even for a few hours, would risk his cargo being ransacked by local thieves who were always eager to capitalize on another's misfortune.

He spit out the window again, and was startled as he realized that his spittle had landed at the feet of the robed figure who now stood almost next to his window. He looked down at the man, saw his long tangled hair and beard and his coarse one-piece hooded robe reaching to the leather sandals on his feet.

"Go on, take your dirty carcass away," he called out in a gruff voice.

The robed figure leaned on his staff with both hands, and to the driver's amazement, said in perfect Arabic, "Would you like me to help you?"

"What?" the startled driver managed to ask, thinking, *How can this fool of a man help me?*

"Are you going south?"

The driver nodded.

"But your wheels are in the sand, yes?"

"Very observant of you," the driver scoffed. As he waved his hand to dismiss the man, he noticed the eyes. He had seen such eyes before in the faces of some of his own countrymen who sought to liberate the holy city of Jerusalem from the Jews. He had seen his cousin strap dynamite to himself and drive his car into a Jewish settlement where he became a living bomb, all because of the promise of paradise, to be with Allah. These were the same eyes he saw now, and they scared him. He sat up in his seat, glanced at the man again, and fought the urge to roll up the window. He kept an old pistol in the glove compartment, and thought about reaching for it as he glanced at the robed man again, this time avoiding his eyes.

"Let me try? Will you?" the old man called.

The driver laughed. "Sure, old man, whatever you want to do . . . don't hurt yourself, that's all, yeah?"

The old man strode to the rear of the truck and disappeared from both side-view mirrors.

"Crazy old camel," the driver muttered.

"Make it go." He heard a muffled voice call out.

"Make it go yourself," he said under his breath, but to humor the old man, he turned the key and the engine roared to life. He thought about throwing the truck in gear and spraying the old crazy, and was about to do so when he felt the rear of the truck shudder and lift itself up out of the sand.

He grabbed the wheel with both hands and stared wide-eyed in his rearview mirror at the rear of his truck, which was moving out of the sand toward the black asphalt.

The truck suddenly dropped, and both wheels bounced on the solid surface of the road.

"How . . ." the driver began to say to himself, and he saw the robed man in his side mirror.

"Can you go back?" the man called.

The driver put the truck in reverse and backed out so that the entire vehicle sat with all four of its tires on the asphalt.

"How did you . . ." His voice trailed off again. He looked out his window, but the robed man had disappeared. The driver was about to get out of his truck when a knock on the passenger side window startled him.

He turned and saw the robed man.

"You are going . . . south?" he asked.

The driver nodded with his mouth open.

"And you will take a sojourner?" the old man asked.

Again the driver nodded, trying to remember what a sojourner was.

"Then open the door so that I may get in," the old man instructed.

The driver wanted to push his foot on the accelerator and leave the old man, but he didn't. Instead he leaned over and unlocked the passenger side door, and tried not to think about how the old man had gotten his truck out of the sand.

49

Yemeni Desert

In his dream Mac was back in the interrogation room, but instead of Scrimmer interrogating him it was an alien who forced Mac to look into its merciless black eyes. Mac found that he was paralyzed, unable to speak. He gathered all of his strength and tried to call on the name of Jesus, but was choked further by the alien, who bore down on him as if it would rip his soul from his body.

"MacKenzie, wake up."

Mac jerked upright in his seat.

"You were having a bad dream, Mac," Johanen stated, his hand still on Mac's shoulder.

"Are they ever going to stop?" Mac moaned, wiping the sweat from his forehead.

"It is one of the ways the enemy tries to scare you," Johanen stated. "He plays upon your fear, your weakness, and will attack again and again in those areas, for he seeks to destroy you."

"This happens almost every night now, Johanen," Mac said. "I'm growing very weary of it."

"You need to cover yourself in prayer, read the psalms, and ask for protection, MacKenzie. As I said earlier, you can never let your guard down. You are in the front lines of a war, and although much of the time the enemy is unseen, he will attack your weakest point."

"There's so much I don't understand, Johanen. I'm new at this and feel inadequate."

"Then learn from my example, MacKenzie . . . draw close to God, and he will draw close to you. Resist the enemy, and he will flee from you."

Mac nodded. "How do I resist the enemy?" he asked.

"Through prayer. By taking your thoughts captive. By making your mind a fortress where no thought can enter unless you allow it."

"But that's just it. The fear. It gets me thinking about my children being abducted again. Or Maggie. I don't have control over any of this."

"None of us have control over anything, which is why you must rely on God. Rest in him. Ask for his strength, his wisdom, his power. He will give these to you, but you must ask for them."

Mac looked at Johanen and nodded, pondering what had been said. Johanen smiled and rapped his knuckles on the window next to him.

"Looks like it is dying down, yes?"

"What?" Mac felt the abrupt non sequitor. He glanced out the window. "Yeah, it seems to be subsiding." His lower back ached from slumping down in the seat, and he stretched as best he could, still confined to a sitting position. His mouth was dry and he licked his lips, realizing they were swollen and chapped. He reached into the back of the jeep for a water bottle, put it to his lips, and guzzled.

"Much better," he said, looking out the window at the yellow haze of swirling sand. Mac held out the water bottle to Johanen.

Johanen took it and drank. He looked at the GPS monitor. "It appears it is working again. I wonder if we can hail Uri?" He gestured at the walkie-talkie as he took another long sip.

Mac picked up the walkie-talkie and pressed the talk button. "Uri, can you read me? Uri, come in if you read me?" They waited for a response, but none came.

"Now what?" Mac asked. "Can we go outside yet?"

Johanen rolled the window down enough so he could put his hand outside. "Yes, it seems that the worst is over. But we must not lose eye contact with the jeep. It might start up again."

Mac turned around in his seat. "I'm starved," he muttered, as he reached into the backseat and fished out a couple of Israeli army rations. He handed one to Johanen and unwrapped his own. He took a bite. "What is this stuff?" he asked, as he worked his mouth on the tasteless mass.

"A concentrated source of protein." Johanen unwrapped his own ration.

"Disgusting," Mac said.

Johanen took another bite. "I will grant you . . . it is not too palatable."

"An understatement," Mac replied.

Mac washed it down with several gulps of water. He had to admit that the rations had at least appeased the growling in his stomach.

"What now?" he asked.

Johanen surveyed the area around the jeep. "We must get the jeep out. There is a winch located in front. If we find something to attach the cable to, we can pull the jeep out."

Mac looked out the front windshield at a fresh swirling of sand that pelted the jeep, rocking it. "Time is drawing down on us, and if we're going to get to the tomb . . ." He gestured outside at the storm.

Johanen rolled his window down the rest of the way, extended his arm. "I really think that the worst is over." He pushed open his door.

"So what does it feel like to be another day older?" Mac asked, as he watched Johanen push sand out of his way.

"What?" Johanen shielded his eyes and waded through the sand to Mac's side of the jeep. "Almost like walking in the aftermath of a snowstorm," Johanen remarked, as his feet sank several inches in the loose sand.

"You know, another day ... in an endless life. Don't you grow tired of living?" Mac asked as he, too, pushed open his door.

Johanen shielded his eyes from a sudden gust of wind. "There have been times when I have grown weary, but that is only because I long to be in his presence, to see him face-to-face."

"So you don't see him anymore?"

"No, that is not what I mean ... I do see him, when it suits his purpose."

Mac stepped out into a pile of sand. He stood for a moment scanning the bleak countryside, which seemed to be growing more visible by the minute. He pressed the question. "What is it like to see him? Give me some details."

Johanen brushed the sand from his beard and eyed Mac. "Mere words cannot describe it. For it is the most intense, overwhelming feeling that a human being can have ... to stand in the presence of both his Maker *and* his Redeemer. To feel his unbridled love fill the spaces between the atoms in one's mind, body, and soul. For he is holy, and when I stand in the midst of that holiness, it ignites a fire within, and makes every cell in me dance with joy."

Mac nodded, having lost any frame of reference with which to gauge Johanen's words.

"And now the winch," Johanen said, getting back to the problem at hand as he made his way to the front of the jeep.

"What?" Mac cried. "How can you go from the sublime to the ridiculous? One minute you're giving me a description of God that is unlike anything I've ever heard, and then, almost in the same breath, you talk about the winch? I don't get it."

Johanen chuckled. "MacKenzie, we have a task at hand that is very important, wouldn't you agree? You asked me a question and I answered it, but at the same time I know that the present task, what is set before me, is of great importance, therefore . . ." Johanen gestured toward the winch.

Mac shook his head and watched the old man unhook the winch, pulling a few feet of cable from the reel below the jeep's bumper.

"Take this and see if you can find anything to hook it on," he instructed, handing the cable with a large hook on the end of it to Mac. "Most likely, it will be in the crevice of a large rock."

Mac put the cable over his shoulder and plodded his way across the sand. His body leaned forward as he put some distance between himself and the jeep. He noticed that in some places the sandstorm had swept areas of the desert clean, while next to anything that rose above the desert floor, sand drifts formed. At fifty yards the cable jerked tight, and he stopped. He turned and saw Johanen motion for him to walk to either side.

Mac walked to his right, keeping the cable taut, and searched the ground for someplace to set the hook. To his relief, only an occasional gust of wind and sand hit him, but when it did, it made him stop and lean against the cable for support.

He walked so that he was almost beside the jeep, and still hadn't found anything he could set the end of the winch into. Johanen pointed in the other direction. Mac retraced his steps, searching for anything that might aid in fastening the cable. He reached the spot where he had first stopped when the cable had reached its end. Frustrated, he threw it to the ground and made his way back to the jeep.

"Is something wrong?" Johanen called.

"There's nothing out there to hook it up to, for crying out loud," Mac yelled.

"There has to be something."

Mac clamped his jaws together to keep himself from saying something he'd regret later.

"We will do it together then," Johanen offered, walking toward Mac.

"There's nothing out there that's going to work," Mac repeated.

"Something will turn up," Johanen said, with confidence.

The two men walked to the end of the cable.

"You know something, Mac," Johanen began, "in some ways your life can be compared to this jeep." He reached down and took the end of the cable in his hands.

"The jeep? What do you mean?"

Johanen slung the cable over his shoulder and motioned for Mac to follow as he began to search for someplace to hook the end. "You are the jeep, and the sand piled against it, keeping it immobile, are your fears that keep you from moving into where God desires you to be," Johanen said.

"Huh?"

"I find it fascinating that we are in this predicament . . . You know, there are no coincidences," Johanen stated.

Mac threw the old man a glance, shook his head, and mumbled, "Just cut to the chase and stop being so cryptic, for crying out loud."

Johanen stopped and faced Mac. "As I said, MacKenzie, you are the jeep; the sand is your fear. The cable, your free will, is your way to victory, providing that you connect it to the rock—God. But as you can see, the cable is useless, at least at the present moment." Johanen jiggled the cable.

"Let me see if I get this," Mac asked rhetorically. "Let's recap this for just a moment, okay? My father, or what's left of him, is possessed by some malevolent satanic being, his most recent accomplishment being flying around in a UFO making crop circles. Then there's the bizarre adventure we're on, racing against the mysterious 'sign in the heavens' coinciding with the lunar eclipse, and trying to destroy the bogus tomb of Jesus . . . very original. And now, to top it all off, I'm stranded in this godforsaken wilderness with a man who informs me that he's two thousand years old. But all of these are common, everyday occurrences that I really shouldn't give a second thought to, right? And of course there's nothing *fearful* in all of this." He raised his voice and jabbed his hands above his head. "I didn't sign up to be Paul the apostle, for crying out loud."

"Are you finished yet?" Johanen asked.

"No, I'm not finished, and thank you for asking." Mac launched into another bout of grievances, with his voice getting louder all the time. "I'm tired of all of this. Tired of never knowing what the plan really is, but always going out on some shaky limb, and for what? What do I get in return for this? I'll tell you what I get." He was yelling now. "Separation from my wife and kids, loss of my job, and nightmares every night, a new one custom-designed just for me. That's what I get, and I'm tired! Do you hear me, old man? I'm tired!"

Johanen nodded, but Mac saw a slight smile on his face, which infuriated him all the more.

"Wait." He threw his hands in front of him. "I've understated the situation again. Tired is the wrong word. More like fed up, peeved, even abandoned would go well here. I'm tired of the game. You tell him to take his ball and go home, because I don't want to play his stupid game anymore. Go ahead, tell him." Mac pointed to the sky as he waited for Johanen to say something.

"Never mind, I will," Mac said. He threw his head back and yelled with all his might. "I don't want to play anymore. Do you hear me up there?" Mac's breath came rapidly, and his nostrils flared as he waited for the answer that he knew would never come. He started to pace in front of Johanen, cupping his hands around his mouth and yelling, "I . . . won't . . . play . . . any . . . more."

He glanced at Johanen, threw his arms up in the air, and headed back for the jeep with no clear idea of what he was going to do when he got there.

"MacKenzie," Johanen called. To Mac's annoyance he detected the old man's stifled laughter. "Really, Mac, you have to see this."

Mac stopped but didn't turn around. "See what, old man?" he said in his best taunting voice.

Johanen was laughing openly now. "No really, Mac, please come back and see what you've done."

Mac turned around, setting a scowl on his face, and walked over to Johanen. "What?"

Johanen just pointed toward the ground. "There."

To Mac's amazement, in the very place where he had been pacing in frustration, the sand had been moved back just a little. There was no mistaking the good-sized fissure in a rock formation.

"Perfect place for the hook to rest, yes?" Johanen said, and started laughing again.

50

✳ ◉ ✳

Yemeni Desert

Uri BenHassen rubbed his eyes and glanced over at Laura who was still asleep, curled up in a ball on the seat next to him. *Women seem to be able to adapt to almost anything,* he thought, running his finger around the steering wheel and gazing out the jeep's front window at the yellow haze of swirling sand.

He looked at his watch and clicked the walkie-talkie button a few times, trying to hail MacKenzie and Johanen. "MacKenzie, can you read me ... over? MacKenzie? Johanen?"

He set the walkie-talkie back in its holder on the dashboard and shifted in his seat. He heard a disturbing noise, faint at first, but there was no mistaking the sound of a very large diesel engine. He had spent too many years as a commando in the Israeli Air Force not to know the sound. He reached over and shook Laura's shoulder.

"Has it stopped yet?" she asked, as she unwound her limbs and sat up.

"Not yet, the storm is wearing down, but more important is, I'm hearing something ... maybe army halftrack or tank."

Laura gathered her long hair and put it up in a bun, slipping her safari hat over it.

"I think I hear it too," she agreed. "What now?"

Uri ran the back of his hand against the dark stubble of beard on his face and shrugged. "We hope that they don't find us."

"And what if they do?"

"We have our surveyors IDs . . . we hope that they believe."

Laura nodded. "And hope they don't look in the trunk and find the false bottom."

Uri gave her a stoic nod.

"It's getting closer . . . don't you think?" she said.

Uri tapped his hand on the steering wheel. "Closer . . . yes."

"We could try to run from them in the jeep," Laura suggested.

"The road is gone, where?" Uri motioned with his hand out the front window. "Besides all of this, we don't know where we are. I'm thinking we count our luck on the IDs."

"Maybe they won't see us?"

"If they have infrared and sonar . . . they see."

A large shape appeared in front of the jeep. Even in the subsiding swirling of sand and wind, there was no mistaking the outline of the long barrel and turret of a tank.

"I think it sees us," Laura said, as the tank bore down on them.

Uri felt his stomach muscles tightening, as he went over his fake identity. He could hear the clanging of the iron treads, felt their vibration as they advanced on the desert floor.

The tank jerked to a stop, looming menacingly through the haze of swirling sand. Uri saw the hatch open, and a helmeted soldier appeared.

"This is it," Uri said. "Get your passport ready, and the ID card."

Laura unbuttoned her shirt pocket and got her passport.

Uri saw the soldier pull a rifle from the hatch and climb out to the small platform next to the turret. Another soldier followed. They fitted their protective goggles and headgear into place, jumped off the tank, and headed toward the jeep.

Uri gave Laura's shoulder a pat for encouragement.

The soldiers made their way toward the jeep, and one of them pounded on Uri's window. Uri rolled down the window, shielding his eyes against the sand billowing into the jeep. The soldier yelled something, but it was muffled by the breathing filter he wore around his nose and mouth. He yelled again, making it very clear that Uri was to get out of the jeep.

Uri opened his door and got out, holding his ID and passport with the letter explaining that they were part of a survey team looking for oil.

The soldier poked his head in and saw Laura. He yelled something to his partner, who pointed his gun at Uri and motioned for him to step away from the vehicle. The other gestured for Laura to get out. Laura's door opened and her head appeared above the jeep's canopy. Her hat blew off her head, and although she made an attempt to grab it, it vanished in the haze of sand. Her hair began to unravel in the wind, and soon long strands of it were blowing behind her head. Uri could see that the soldier was fascinated by her, knowing full well that the country of Yemen adhered to strict Moslem law which never allowed a woman to show any skin, much less her hair. He watched the man caress the ends of her hair with the muzzle of his rifle. The soldier laughed, and motioned her to join Uri.

A fresh gust of wind blew sand into Uri's eyes; he had to close them for a few moments until the wind subsided.

The soldier yelled something in Arabic.

Uri shrugged and pointed to his passport. "Americans!"

The soldier glared at him. "Area no limits."

Uri rubbed his eyes and held his papers in front of him.

The soldier waved them away and gave a command, which was made clear by the prodding end of a rifle, motioning toward the tank. Uri looked at Laura who was shielding her eyes and trying to gather her loose hair. He nodded and, leaning into the wind, began to march.

They reached the tank and the soldiers made Laura climb down through the turret, then Uri. It took a moment for his eyes to adjust to the light. There were two more men inside, a driver, and another who manned a machine gun.

The two soldiers entered and closed the hatch. The interior of the tank was hot and smelly, and Uri loosened the collar on his shirt.

There was a flurry of chatter directed at Laura. Then one soldier reached out and grabbed the papers in Uri's hand.

Uri looked at his uniform and noted that the man was an officer. He scanned the document, then motioned for Laura's papers as well.

"You American?" he asked in a very thick accent.

Laura answered, "Yes, American oil pioneers."

"What is py-o-near?" the soldier asked. "Bad English me."

"We . . . look for oil," Laura offered.

"You no look USA," the soldier said, directing his attention back to Uri.

"I'm an American citizen," Uri answered, trying to hide his accent.

"You marry her? She pretty," the soldier said with a wicked grin.

Uri shook his head. "We work for the same company."

"Too bad you . . . she too pretty."

"We're Americans who are searching for oil and have the appropriate papers from your government," Laura said.

"You shut up, I talk." The soldier smacked the end of his rifle butt on Laura's boot.

She cried out and Uri lurched forward, but checked himself as the barrel of a gun snapped in his direction.

"American woman . . . pretty," the soldier said again. "Oil for USA Satan. You take everything USA. Big pig."

Uri glanced at Laura, who gave him a look that said she was okay.

"You spy USA! Maybe you USA Jew," the soldier said.

He snapped a command that Uri recognized as Arabic and the engines revved. The tank lurched forward. The noise was deafening, and silenced for the moment the inquisition by the soldier.

"Where are you taking us?" Uri yelled.

"No matter now . . . you spy in no-limit area," the soldier said.

"We're not spies," Laura said. "We're searching for oil."

The man shrugged. "We see."

"What about our jeep? It has valuable equipment," Uri added.

"What about? Not going away." the soldier answered. "Wait, check papers, then"—and the soldier's lower lip protruded from his face—"all is okay, then okay."

"How do we get back to our jeep?" Uri asked.

"No more." He snapped another order to the tank's driver.

Uri heard the engines accelerate. He saw where the men were positioned. He knew he could take out the guy next to him before he ever knew what hit him. He mentally practiced the snap of his forearm with his fist smashing the bridge of the other man's nose, taking his gun, and shooting the commander. By that time the driver and gunner would start to react, but he would have the upper hand. It would work, and if he were alone he would have risked it. He would have waited for the right moment when the soldiers let down their guard, and then all his years of training would come into play and he would strike. He might even be wounded in the process, but he would be the victor. He would have tried it too, except for Laura. She was the factor that made it impossible for him to act, because Uri knew that her reaction to his movements could endanger them both. So it was too risky.

Uri folded his hands on his lap, averted his eyes from everyone, and resigned himself to wait.

51

* ◉ *

The Mediterranean Sea

Helen sipped the hot soup that she held in both hands. "This tastes so good," she exclaimed to Captain Bolton, an expatriated Englishman with a thin face, cropped hair, and a very long nose.

"Drink slowly, miss," Captain Bolton said in a crisp English accent.

"How is Crawford?" she asked, shivering in spite of the two blankets that were wrapped around her shoulders.

"So-so. The ship's doctor is looking after him. We've called the Coast Guard. He'll be fine until then."

She took another sip of the soup and looked at the stack of color-faded buoys in the corner. "What kind of boat is this?"

"Fishing trawler out of Naples, Italy," Bolton replied. "She's an old bucket, but still seaworthy. How long did the dolphins stay with you?" he asked in turn.

"They were there after our plane went down . . . I thought they were sharks at first."

"In all my years on the sea I've never seen anything like that. I've heard stories from other captains. Do you know that they followed our ship for a few miles before they left?"

Helen smiled. "I didn't even get a chance to thank them."

"Where did your plane go down?"

"Somewhere over the Balearic Islands . . . I'm not certain."

"What happened, engine failure?"

Helen looked into her cup and her body shivered as the unwanted memory of the UFO flooded her mind. "Yes, engine trouble."

"Didn't you send a Mayday?"

"I think Crawford tried, but the radio went dead . . . I'm not sure. It all happened so fast."

"And this was yesterday?"

She nodded and sipped some more of the soup. "Late in the afternoon. I was so excited about seeing Rome, and now all of this."

"Do you want me to notify anyone back in America?"

Helen thought for a moment. "No, I'll do all that when we get to land. Is there a place to take a shower?"

The captain let a smile spread over his gaunt face. "Can't let you take one in the crew's quarters, though the men would enjoy it," he chuckled. "I'll let you use my personal cabin."

Helen finished the soup and set the cup down next to her.

"More?" he asked.

"Please."

Captain Bolton got up from a battered stool that had one leg wrapped with fishing line to hold it together. "I'll be right back," he said, grabbing the cup from the floor next to Helen.

He returned in a few moments with another cup of soup.

"Thanks," she said, taking the cup. "I'm sure glad you saw the flare."

The captain shook his head. "That's what I've wanted to ask you about. We didn't see the flare at first."

"What do you mean?" Helen asked.

"One of my men saw something in the sky."

"What do you mean?" she asked, fearing the worst.

"Giuseppi was working on deck, fixing some nets. You know sailors, always looking at the sky. Watching the weather, looking at every cloud, and then he saw it, the shining light."

"Shining light?" Helen repeated, feigning ignorance.

"A UFO."

"I don't understand what you are talking about."

"He saw the UFO first. That's what got his attention, and then, right after, he saw your flare."

A horrible feeling crept over Helen. "What do you think it was?" she asked.

The captain shrugged. "I don't know. Out here you see a lot of strange things. But it was terribly good he saw it. Because of it you've been rescued."

Helen stared into space. *I don't feel safe. They've manipulated circumstances. They're in control . . . as always.*

"You look tired. You can use my bunk if you like. I'll show you where the shower is, and then you can lie down for a while and get some rest. Everything is going to be all right now." The captain helped her up, and she allowed herself to lean on him, because of her ankle, as he escorted her to his cabin in the stern of the ship.

"It's small, but the water is nice and hot," he said, shoving the shower curtain out of the way. "The bunk's over there." He gestured over his shoulder. "I'll get you a clean towel, and you can change into some of my clothes until yours are dry." He went over to a small closet that lacked a door and produced a worn pair of trousers and a heavy cotton shirt. "This will keep you warm, all right."

"Thank you," Helen said. After he left the cabin, she let the damp blankets fall from her shoulders and peeled off her wet clothes. She reached into the small plastic shower stall, adjusted the water, and stepped in. She let the hot water fall on her head and cascade down her body, but in spite of it she couldn't stop shaking, and she knew the reason for it. "I hate them." She spat the words out, then cried the tears she had held back from Bolton.

52

❋ ◉ ❋

Wheat Field, Italy

Mr. Kenson parked his car on the shoulder of a narrow country road and looked across a flourishing wheat field in the Italian countryside. At the farthest edge of the field, a large UFO was hovering a few feet above the wheat, reflecting the sunlight off its polished surface.

Kenson opened a crude gate made of sticks and started to walk through the wheat. As he did so, a strange thing happened. The wheat bent out of his way, creating a pathway to the saucer that hovered on the other side of the field. He saw that a door had opened, and two small, gray, humanoid creatures had descended from a ramp protruding from the craft.

His thoughts went out to them, and in return he received a telepathic greeting from the two grays.

Kenson reached them and was led up the ramp to the inside of the craft. A much larger being was there. Kenson recognized him as Semjaza, a captain of the host of the one whom they both served. Scmjaza was over seven feet tall and looked insectlike, having long arms and a face that resembled a praying mantis. But Kenson knew that this was the form the being had chosen for this meeting . . . it was not Semjaza's true form.

"The time is nearing," Semjaza said, although he did not move his mouth. "The time when he will reveal himself and take his rightful place as prince of this world."

Kenson affirmed this announcement saying, "Hail to the Prince of the Air."

"To the Prince of the Power of the Air," Semjaza replied. His voice was thin and high, almost like that of a female.

"And the woman?" Kenson asked.

"She has been located," Semjaza replied. In his mind Kenson saw pictures showing a fishing vessel rescuing two people from a makeshift raft.

"We have never left her, although we have been hindered by a man who is accompanying her. He is protected, at least for now, but we will sift him like the wheat of this field, and he will be of no consequence to you."

"I look forward to meeting her," Kenson said. "Where is the woman's ship headed?"

"Naples." Semjaza raised a long arm and pointed to the roof of the ship. "The lunar eclipse will take place soon. Is all ready?"

Kenson nodded. "Everything is in place . . . the peoples of earth have taken centuries to arrive at the point where their technology is sufficient to provide their half of our equation . . . those we have assembled will see the sign and believe." Kenson stared into the dark eyes of Semjaza and looked away. His head had begun to ache, and for a moment it seemed like the walls were pressing in on him, about to crush him.

A crooked smile spread across the being's face.

"It is time for me to go," Kenson managed to say. "Did you bring it?"

"Yes, I have it here." Semjaza gestured that Kenson should follow.

Kenson was led further into the interior of the ship. A young woman was lying on a table being examined by a group of grays.

"I'm doing some egg-taking. Would you care to watch?" Semjaza asked.

Kenson heard the woman moan and cry out. He looked at her again, and saw that the woman had picked her head up so she could see who was talking. For a moment their eyes met, and then one of the smaller grays forced her head back down on the table.

Semjaza floated past Kenson to the table, where he leaned and looked into the woman's eyes. Kenson watched as the woman struggled to look away, then grew calm again.

Semjaza moved toward an open compartment where he took up a long black box. He returned and held it out to Kenson. "Here it is. It was made before the time of the Great Flood."

Kenson received the box and stared at the ornately inlaid lid of black onyx in the shape of a dragon.

"See that he uses it well." Semjaza then turned and floated back to where the woman lay on the table.

Kenson tucked the box under his arm, walked down the ramp, and left the ship. He stepped back from it, watched the ramp retract into the belly of the ship, and saw it tilt as it rose into the air. It hovered above him for a moment, then blinked out of sight as if it had jumped somehow into another dimension.

Kenson retraced his steps through the field and played with the shafts of wheat that bent away from him as he reached out to touch them.

53

✳ ◉ ✳

Yemeni Desert

Mac stared at the fissure in the rock large enough to accommodate the hook at the end of the cable. He avoided Johanen's eyes and put his hands in his pants pockets. He felt like a fool in one respect, but mixed with that feeling was another emotion, the stronger of the two.

His fear was justified.

Johanen broke the silence. "There is a passage from Scripture that pertains to what you are feeling. Would you like to hear it?"

MacKenzie picked his head up.

"'There is no fear in love but perfect love drives out fear,'" Johanen recited. "Answer me this, MacKenzie. A short while ago you described what you were afraid of."

Mac nodded.

"If you are honest with yourself, you can see that the hand of God delivered you from them all: the abduction of your children, your failed marriage with Maggie, the evil of your father, and, of course, the giant hybrid at the base. At every

327

turn he has been there or provided one of his agents to assist you." Johanen let his hand rest above his heart and smiled.

Mac shook his head. "You've had two thousand years to get used to the way he does business. I'm new at this, and don't think I'm cut from the same cloth as you and Elisha."

"Maybe, MacKenzie, but you are a man like us."

Mac picked up the cable and fiddled with the hook on the end of it, as he eyed the fissure in the rock.

"I don't know what to say, except that I lost my eldest son, ruined my marriage, and became a drunk. And just at the point in my life where I feel that there's a new beginning, in getting back with Maggie and the kids, I'm afraid I'll lose it again, or worse, that I'll wind up like Cranston or my father."

"MacKenzie," Johanen began, "you and I have discussed how God delivered you at the base in Nevada, and from what Elisha tells me, also from the bitterness in your heart at the death of your son. As I said, you have seen his hand in many things in such a short time. Isn't that evidence of his love toward you? How can you then fear?"

Mac stared at Johanen. His mind was numb, and in many ways what was happening reminded him of what had transpired on the shores of the Sea of Galilee with Elisha, where he had come to grips with the death of his son and reconciled his faith. He looked away from the piercing blue eyes of Johanen, and took a couple of steps away from the man, still holding the hook in his hand. He gazed at the wilderness where he was, for all practical purposes, stranded. He saw the jeep half buried in the sand, stuck, and remembered that Johanen had told him he was stuck in his fear just as the jeep was stuck in the sand. He took a deep breath, ran his hand through his hair, amused as tiny grains of sand fell onto his shirt. He smoothed the sand at his feet with his boot and looked up at the haze of dust that filtered the sun.

And then something changed in him. There was no great revelation. No tears or emotional scene. No voice of God resounding in his head, not even a whisper. There was no supernatural reassurance or sign. But it became very clear that Johanen's words were true. That indeed God had been there, had delivered him and was continuing to do so . . . because God loved him. And all he had to do, his part of the bargain, was to stand and trust and face his fear. He realized that what he was engaged in, this quest, his relationship to everyone inside Johanen's circle, was the most important thing he could do with the remainder of his life. All that had happened to him, everything that he had seen and been instructed in, was part of a greater truth. For if the Second Coming of Christ was imminent, then what in the world could be more important than his involvement in that?

He turned back to Johanen. "I've let my fear dominate me," he said with resolve, "but no more." He reached down and slipped the hook into the crevice of the rock.

54

A Road in Saudi Arabia

The Palestinian driver glanced at his unwanted passenger, who had fallen asleep. *At least he doesn't smell,* he thought, as he looked again at the clay jar that the old man had hidden in the folds of his robe. *It's like the ones I have seen in the museum,* he thought. *I wonder if it is valuable.* For a moment he contemplated trying to find a way to steal it.

The old man's staff rested on the seat between them. Because of the poorly maintained road and all the potholes, the staff had inched its way closer to him with every unwanted jolt.

The driver wondered again how the old man had managed to get his truck out of the sand. *Did he lift it? No, that is impossible . . . but how then?*

He eyed the staff and reached out to touch it. "Ah," he stifled a yell, so as not to wake up the old man. He could have sworn that the end of the staff had begun to turn into the head of a snake. *Must be a trick of the light,* he told himself, and he decided to turn his headlights on because of the fading sunlight. The old man stirred in his sleep and muttered something in a language he had never heard before.

The driver gripped the wheel with both hands and muttered a prayer to Allah. *Maybe I have a jinn with me. Eeeee, I'm a dead man . . . but how else did he get the truck out? He's going where? To Yemen, he said. What's in Yemen? I'm a dead man for taking a jinn with me,* he lamented.

"Where are we?" the old man asked, and at the sound of his voice the driver almost jumped out of his seat.

"Close to the border . . . near Yemen, but I'm not going that far."

The old man reached into his robe, and the driver held his breath.

"Would you like a date?" the old man asked, holding the fruit up so the driver could see.

The driver panicked. *If I say no, he will be insulted and curse me . . . but if I take it, it may have some magic in it . . . Oh, Allah protect me.* "Are you sure you have enough? I don't want to eat your supper." He held his breath as he waited for an answer.

The old man tossed the fruit in the air and caught it with his mouth. "Good," he said as he chewed.

The driver nodded and laughed. To his relief he saw the road sign he was looking for. "This is where I turn off and make my delivery," he said, indicating the trailer.

The robed man continued to chew. "You said we are near Yemen?"

"Close to the border, yes. I have a map I can show you when I stop."

The driver eased off the accelerator and turned off the road. "I should let you off here so you can get a ride the rest of the way," he said as he stopped his truck.

The old man gathered his robe around him and, taking his staff, climbed out of the truck and slammed the door. The driver put his truck in park, fetched the worn, sun-yellowed map that he kept on his dashboard, and got out. He went around the front of the truck, unfolding the map, but to his astonishment, the old man was gone.

I knew he was jinn, the driver thought, as he retraced his steps. "Allah protect me . . . ," he moaned. He flung the map into the air as he fumbled with the latch on the handle of the door. The door opened, and he dove into his cab, slammed the truck in gear, floored the gas pedal, and sped off into the night without once looking in his rearview mirror, all the while saying prayers to Allah for protection.

55

Yemeni Desert

Uri watched every move that his interrogator made in the tent where he was being held. He had been separated from Laura as soon as they arrived, at what he assumed was the base camp. He stared at the canvas floor of the tent and tried not to think about what might be happening to Laura.

His hands had been tied with wire behind him, wire that he now knew was connected to a car battery and then to an ignition coil of an automobile, which amplified a common twelve-volt battery with upwards of thirty thousand volts of electricity. He had seen these crude torture devices before, and even been trained in how to deal with the pain. He had already felt the shock course through his body, and it had knocked him off the stool he sat on.

The interrogator, a fat little man with a pock-marked face, picked up Uri's fake ID card and went over to him, slapping it in the palm of his hand. He spoke very little English, and his breath reeked of garlic.

"What . . . here you . . . in Yemen?"

Uri nodded toward the ID. "Oil. American oil."

"You spy . . . girl spy . . . nobody know truth." He leaned over so that his head was in front of Uri's.

Uri eyed the man and tried not to inhale to deeply. "Oil for America," he said, sticking to his cover story.

Uri saw the man look over his head at the soldier who held the coil at Uri's back and braced for another shock, but this time he extended his leg so that it touched his inquisitor just as he felt the arch of electricity hit his body. Uri cried out as the coil arched and the current slammed through him. His voice, however, was drowned out by the screams of the other man, who was more than surprised, as the current jolted him.

The man holding the coil withdrew it while the interrogator glared at Uri, rubbing his leg.

"Have to kill you," he swore at Uri through his teeth. He stomped out of the tent, and Uri could hear the man letting go a string of cursing in Arabic as he left.

He was gone for several minutes, and when he returned, to Uri's dismay, he brought Laura with him. She was blindfolded.

The interrogator shouted an order to several other soldiers, who unbound Uri's wrists and hoisted him off the stool.

The interrogator motioned to Laura, and the soldier who had held her pushed her down on the stool.

Oh no, what have I done? Uri watched as they bound her wrists with the same wire that they had used to bind him. He noticed that her hair was loose and disheveled, and some of the buttons on her shirt were missing as if they had been ripped off.

"No, wait," he said, turning to the interrogator.

The interrogator signaled the man holding the coil, and to Uri's horror the man brought it near Laura's back, where a ragged arch of electricity jumped from it. She screamed and fell to the floor, her legs kicking.

Uri forced himself to remain calm. He knew from all his training that the time would come to act. He thought about the ride in the tank and cursed himself for not trying then, when the odds were better.

Laura curled herself in a ball on the floor, crying. The interrogator seized a handful of her hair and picked her head up only inches from his own.

"More?" He shook her head in his hand as he looked at Uri. "More . . ." He let go and signaled so that the man holding the coil brought it near her leg.

Laura screamed in agony as once again the electricity jumped from the coil. She banged her head against the floor of the tent.

All of Uri's training kicked in as he rushed the interrogator and managed to hit him with his shoulders, knocking him into the coil man. Then he felt a rifle butt smash against his head, and he lost consciousness before he hit the floor.

56

✳ ◼ ✳

The Mediterranean Sea

Crawford? How are you feeling, Jack?" Helen whispered, looking down at the bunk in the small room that served as a makeshift sickbay and storage area for the fishing boat.

The man attending him pointed at himself. "No English," then gestured to Crawford's head and put a bad expression on his face.

"I know," Helen said, acknowledging the man's sign language, "he's been going in and out of consciousness since all of this happened." She didn't care whether he understood her or not. "We've got to get him to a doctor." She reached down, took his hand, and held it.

The shower had refreshed her, and she had taken more of the soup before seeking out Crawford. Her main desire was that he would just come to.

The man disappeared for a moment, returning with a rickety folding deck chair, which he set up and motioned for Helen to sit in.

Helen thanked him and he left, but before doing so he pointed at his watch indicating that he would return in an hour to check on her.

Helen thanked him and managed to smile. She brought her feet up under her and pulled the captain's shirt over her knees. *I'm thankful to have been rescued,* she thought, but mixed with that was a feeling in the pit of her stomach that wouldn't go away. *They did it, they're manipulating as always, trying to get me to do something. And now my one hope, my link to Johanen, has been severed. But I'll never go back living like that again. They can kill my body, but they won't take my spirit.*

Here was a new thought for her. She realized that there was something *more* than just her body and mind; she had a feeling somehow that when she died, she would continue. *Where would I have gone, if I had died in the plane crash?* she wondered.

Her mind was filled with questions. She looked at Crawford and wished that he would awaken so that he could help her sort through some of this. Without knowing why, she whispered, "Thank you," not sure *whom* she was thanking, but feeling that it was something she had to do.

✳ ◦ ✳

The captain of the fishing boat poked his head into the room where Helen was keeping her vigil on Crawford.

"The Italian Coast Guard just radioed us. They are flying a rescue helicopter out, so your friend can get the proper medical treatment."

"I'm getting worried about him," Helen replied. "He doesn't seem to be getting any better."

"They should rendezvous with us in a little over an hour," the captain said.

"How are they going to get us?" Helen asked.

"They lower a cage from a cable. The sea is calm right now so it should be an easy thing for them to do."

"I've lost all my clothes . . . everything except my ID, and some of the money I had in my wallet."

"You can replace them when you reach the mainland," the captain assured her. "Just relax; everything is going to be okay."

*　○　*

An hour later the rescue helicopter arrived and made a slow pass over the ship. The captain and several crewmen waved their hands overhead, signaling it. It moved to the bow of the ship, where some of the men had cleared the fishing nets away, exposing part of the otherwise cluttered deck. A cage large enough to accommodate four people was attached to a boom that swung out from the belly of the chopper. A man and woman entered the cage and began their descent toward the ship. When the cage landed on the deck, the cable was detached and the chopper moved away from the boat, hovering just off its bow. The two occupants opened the cage door and Captain Bolton introduced himself and Helen in fluent Italian. They made their way to the cabin where Crawford lay and began their examination.

Helen stood just behind them, waiting for their assessment. The woman doctor spoke only Italian so Captain Bolton translated.

"She says it looks like a very bad concussion . . . but he'll be all right," Bolton said.

The doctor checked Crawford's vitals and then rattled off something to Bolton.

"She wants to get him X-rayed immediately," he added.

Helen began to chew a fingernail as the doctor and Captain Bolton conversed again.

"She wants to move him first, and then you," he informed her.

The woman doctor took a walkie-talkie from her pocket, clicked it on, and spoke into it.

"She's asked for a portable stretcher," Bolton translated.

"Ask her if he's going to be all right," Helen said to Bolton, who translated the question.

The woman doctor nodded and smiled reassuringly at her.

A few minutes later two men from the medical chopper entered with a portable stretcher and lifted Crawford onto it, taking special care to fit his head and neck with a special brace that immobilized it. They also started an IV drip and began a blood transfusion.

They made their way to the deck of the boat and signaled to the chopper hovering several hundred feet off its bow. The chopper maneuvered itself over the deck. It lowered the cable, which was reattached to the cage, and the two men placed Crawford into it, positioned themselves on either side of him, and signaled that they were ready.

Helen saw the cage rise into the air until it came alongside the bay doors of the chopper and disappeared inside.

The woman doctor pointed toward the chopper.

Helen nodded. "I'm ready," she replied, slipping on a life preserver.

The cage landed with a metallic clank on the deck as a sudden swell of the ocean lifted the boat. The cable dangled for a moment, and then grew taut again as the operator in the chopper above caught up the slack.

The woman doctor opened the door of the cage and helped Helen get in. She followed. Closing the door behind her, she spoke in her walkie-talkie. The cage rose into the air.

Helen yelled to Captain Bolton, "Thank you . . . to everybody," and waved good-bye to the crew.

She saw several of the crew wave their hats in the air, and Bolton smiled, holding up two fingers in a victory sign.

The cage clanked against the arm of the winch that held it just outside the bay doors of the chopper. Two men moved the arm of the hoist inside and closed the bay door. Helen climbed out and settled as close to Crawford as she could get.

"When will we get to Naples?" she asked.

The woman doctor shrugged, but she smiled at Helen, then pointed to Crawford and gave her a thumbs-up.

57

* ◉ *

Yemeni Desert

Uri felt the throbbing in his head as he became conscious, but he remained still, keeping his eyes closed and his breathing steady. He listened to the sounds around him, the shuffle of booted feet in the distance, the subdued talk of the Yemeni soldiers, a jeep accelerating and pulling away.

"Uri," someone whispered, and he knew it was Laura.

He still didn't move but waited for her to say something else.

"Uri, can you hear me? We're alone. Except for the guard just outside the tent."

Uri groaned, then moved his head so that he could see Laura. "What are you saying?" he whispered back.

"After they hit you, everything got crazy. I thought they were going to kill us both. By the way, thank you for what you did."

"Not to worry about it," Uri said. He sat up and touched the swollen gash on the back of his head. "This is hurting bad," he grimaced.

"You were out cold, and then this other man entered the tent. He seemed to be in charge of everyone, and he was angry at what was happening. He yelled at the guy with the scars on his face, and for a moment it looked like someone was going to get shot."

"I'm thinking it could have been us," Uri mumbled.

Laura nodded. "The guy with the pockmarks backed down, and stormed out of the tent. The other guy checked our ID, then gave instructions, and we were moved here."

A European-looking man came into the tent. He stood at the entrance with his hands folded behind his back and looked at Uri. "There has been an unfortunate mistake. I'm sorry for the way you have been treated. Here are your passports and IDs."

Uri stood up and took his papers. "So we are free to go back to our jeep?"

The man shook his head. "No. We are, however, going to move you to a new location, where I can assure you that you both will be more comfortable."

Uri stared at the man, trying to size him up. Sticking to the oil exploration story he said, "We're just looking for oil. You see the letters from the Yemeni government. Why not let us get back to looking for the oil?"

"After we have confirmation about your citizenship and status here, I promise you will be released. Now if you'll follow me." He held the tent flap opened and gestured outside.

Uri and Laura followed, but behind them were two soldiers with their weapons trained on their backs.

58

* ○ *

Naples, Italy

Standing alone on the hospital's helicopter landing pad, Helen was frantic because she couldn't find anyone who spoke English. The doctor who had been with her in the helicopter had left as soon as she and Crawford were unloaded. She was also vexed because hospital personnel who no doubt meant well had tried to separate her from Crawford, something she wasn't going to allow to happen at any cost. Now she was in the midst of a flurry of activity. Several doctors gathered around Crawford examining him. Two nurses fastened the IV drips to the upright poles on Crawford's stretcher.

"I'm all right . . . really," Helen stammered, as an orderly tried to get her into a wheelchair.

The man motioned for her to sit.

Her hand was clenched around the rails of Crawford's gurney, and she wasn't about to let go of it.

"No, I'm all right. I'm staying right here," she said again.

The orderly followed her as the gurney bearing Crawford moved from the small asphalt helicopter pad into the main wing of the hospital.

The cluster of doctors, nurses, orderlies, and Helen hurried down the hallway and through the double doors of an emergency room.

Helen spied a woman who seemed to be waiting for her.

"I'm Dr. Terri Blanchard. I'm an American doing my residency here." The woman hurried over to Helen and extended her hand.

"Finally, someone who speaks English." Helen breathed a sigh of relief.

"I heard about your plane wreck. You've become quite a celebrity here."

"What?" Helen looked confused.

"How long were you at sea, in the open?" Blanchard asked.

Helen pulled at her hair. "The better part of twenty-four hours, but it seemed a lot longer."

Blanchard took her hand. "You've had quite an ordeal. I've been assigned to check your vitals. Although from what the doctors radioed to us, except for your ankle, you seem to be fine."

"I am, but he's not." Helen nodded in Crawford's direction.

"He's going to have a CAT scan," Blanchard said, pointing to what to Helen looked like the inside of a submarine.

"I don't want to leave him."

"You might feel better if you changed into some other clothes and had something to eat," Blanchard suggested. "Besides, you can return when the test is over."

Helen shook her head, "No, I'm not leaving him."

"Well, it's against hospital rules for you to stay here. You're not married to him, are you?"

"No . . . but," she began, but Blanchard cut her off.

"Relative?"

Helen shook her head.

Blanchard reached out, tried to take Helen's arm.

Helen pulled away. "Listen, I don't care about the rules. Do you understand that? I'm not leaving his side."

"I'm sorry, I was only trying to help," Blanchard said.

Helen was distracted as a commotion came from the doors followed by several camera flashes.

"What's going on?" she asked.

"You've become a celebrity, at least for the moment. It's the paparazzi. They want pictures," Blanchard explained.

Helen moved behind Blanchard. "This is crazy," she said, trying to hide.

One of the double doors opened, and the reporters pressed their way into the room. Several more camera flashes followed. Two hospital orderlies shoved the reporters back, as all the participants yelled at each other in Italian.

"Can't you get them to shut up?" Helen asked.

"We didn't expect this," Blanchard replied.

"How are we going to get out of this room?" Helen asked.

"We'll go through here." Blanchard pointed to elevator doors at the far end of the room.

✳ ◦ ✳

An hour later Helen was seated next to Crawford in the private room they now shared. She had filled out so many forms that her hand began to ache from all the writing. To her relief, the elevator had allowed them to give the reporters the slip, at least for the moment.

The CAT scan showed that Crawford had had a severe concussion that had produced a slight swelling of the brain.

Helen had asked if it were dangerous, and had been reassured that after a few days of rest he would be fine.

Terri Blanchard had slipped an ace bandage around Helen's ankle and told her that because she had been in the water and hadn't put any weight on it the sprain had almost healed.

Just as she was beginning to settle in, there was a knock on her door.

"Who is it?" she asked.

A nurse entered. "I'm sorry, my English not so good, yeah? You have a visitor. Understand?"

Helen frowned. "What visitor? I don't know anyone here," she protested.

"No, no . . . he's a visitor for you." She nodded her head and smiled. "He right downstairs, yeah?"

Helen chewed her nail, looked at the door, then back at the nurse. Not knowing what to do, or who it could possibly be, she shrugged in resignation.

The nurse smiled. "He give you this." She held out a small brown envelope.

Helen got up and took the envelope. She looked at the signature and caught her breath. It was signed *Johanen*.

* ◯ *

Helen glanced at the card again, as she pressed the elevator button for the lobby. *I wonder how he knew I was here,* she thought, then realized that the press coverage and the radio contact between the rescue vessel and the mainland were responsible for alerting him. *But why do I feel so uneasy? I wish Crawford was with me,* she thought.

The elevator doors opened into the lobby, and she looked around before getting out. Still clutching the card in her hand, she started out of the elevator. A very tall man was smiling and walking toward her.

I wonder why Crawford never mentioned Johanen's unusual height, she thought. She saw a prominent scar above his left eye. Something inside her recoiled at the sight of it, and she wondered again why Crawford had never mentioned yet another obvious oddity. A thought that was trying to free itself from the back of her mind exploded in her head.

"Oh, no!" she said, as she stepped back into the elevator and slammed her fist against the row of buttons. The doors began to close. She scurried to the rear of the elevator and pressed her back against the wall. The doors were almost closed when a hand thrust itself between them.

To her horror she saw the man's skin change into something that resembled the hide of an alligator. For a moment she hoped that the doors would close all the way. But then they jerked back, and she saw the man who pretended to be Johanen. She screamed.

She collapsed to the floor of the elevator in a little ball as the man entered. She heard the doors close behind him, and then felt his hand reach down and grab her behind her neck.

"No!" she screamed, hoping that someone would hear as the elevator started its ascent.

The man lifted her so that she was dangling in front of him like a helpless doll.

"You've been very bad, Helen," he hissed at her. She saw his face change. Where the scar had been there was now a mass of knotted scaly tissue that throbbed over the slanted lidless red eye.

She struggled to get free, but his hand tightened around her throat so she couldn't breathe.

"Stop it or I'll crush the life out of you now, you little worm," he hissed, his breath horrible.

Helen stopped struggling, terrified to move. She was paralyzed with fear by the way the man's face had changed into a reptilian monster, something she had seen before while aboard a UFO. It had always terrified her.

"I'm surprised at you, Helen. Did you think you were going to be free of us? Did you think your stupid friend or his puny god could save you? You've been ours from the beginning, and you will be ours at your death, when we take your soul from you."

Helen began to shake so much it felt as if all the bones in her body were being jarred loose. The elevator slowed down and the doors opened. Helen looked past her captor and saw the look of terror on an orderly's face. Still holding her, the reptilian looked at the orderly, who backed away.

The doors closed, and the reptilian scanned the buttons on the control panel, pushing the one corresponding to the underground parking garages. The elevator began its descent. Helen didn't move, but hoped that it would stop at another floor. To her dismay, it didn't. The elevator jolted to a stop, and the doors opened. Her captor had reverted to a human-looking form. He set her down, and with his arm grasped around her waist, escorted her out of the elevator.

They walked to a parked Mercedes. He pushed the remote button to release the locks while he was still several yards away. He opened the trunk, picked Helen up, and stuffed her into it. But before closing it, he once again changed into a reptile. With his head only inches from hers, he said, "You'll want to relax and think how nice it will be to see your friends again." Then he slammed the trunk down, and Helen was immersed in total darkness.

✳ ○ ✳

Helen curled herself in a tight little ball and chewed on her fingernails as the hours passed in the back of the car. Again and again she visualized the hideous face of the reptilian. The image immobilized her and drained her of the will to do anything but chew on her nails and whimper.

Hours passed and then the car stopped. She heard the reptilian get out and walk away.

At the sound of voices, she covered her head with her hands and shut her eyes so she wouldn't see the horrible face again. She felt hands grab her and lift her out of the car, standing her upright.

"Take her to the plane," the reptilian said.

Helen forced herself to open her eyes and saw two men with ski masks carrying out the reptilian's order.

"Yes, Mr. Wyan," one of them answered. They moved her to a small golf cart, and headed toward a jet that was refueling on a private runway.

"Where are you taking me?" she asked.

To her dismay they ignored her. They reached the jet, the man next to her got out, and motioned that she should follow.

She looked around, and saw that at the end of the runway were several fields that had just been harvested. She began to walk toward the metal gangway that led to the door of the jet, and then she thought of Crawford. *If only he were here . . .* With that thought, and the realization that the reptilian wasn't nearby, she grew bold, and began to run as fast as she could toward the end of the runway. She heard the men cursing as they pursued her. She knew one of them was closing in on her. She pumped her legs as fast as she could, and put everything she had into her sprint, ignoring the growing pain in her ankle.

He's gaining, she thought, and her breath came in great pants. Then she felt him hit her from behind, and she tumbled forward. She heard something snap in her wrist as she held her arm out to break her fall, and then her head hit the tarmac and she lost consciousness.

* ○ *

Helen awakened to find that her wrists had been tied and a crude splint had been fastened to one of them. "Oh," she moaned, as she tried to move it. She realized that she was in the jet, and it was in flight. *Where are they taking me?* she wondered. Looking out the window next to her, she saw nothing but the stars above, and what appeared to be water below.

The two men wearing the ski masks were in the seats in front of her so that they faced her. The reptilian, or Mr. Wyan as her other captors had called him, was not to be seen. She heard his voice call from the cockpit. "We'll be landing soon. Is the woman awake?"

"Yes, Mr. Wyan," one of the men said. " She's been conscious for a few minutes now."

Helen looked toward the front of the jet, and saw that Mr. Wyan, the reptilian who had abducted her, was sitting in the copilot's seat, and for the moment was choosing to appear in his human form.

Helen stared out the window. She had resolved that no matter what, every chance she got she would put up a fight. If they killed her it didn't matter, but she wasn't going to go down easy.

The plane was nosing down, getting ready to land. *It's not water—it's the desert,* she thought, as the terrain grew more visible. The jet banked to her left, and her view was lost. It leveled out, and she felt it rock from side to side as the pilot wiggled his wings. The plane slowed, and then she felt the wheels hit the tarmac.

She saw Wyan step out of the cockpit. "You won't try anything so stupid, will you?" he asked her.

She didn't answer him, and stared at her feet.

Wyan moved closer to her. "Give her this," and he passed a vial of liquid, a syringe, and several needles to one of the men wearing the ski masks.

Helen pressed her back against the seat and stared at the syringe. She hated needles—and who knew what was in this one?

One of the men took the set of works from Wyan, filled the syringe with fluid from the bottle, and moved to Helen.

"Hold her," he said to his companion, who grabbed Helen by her fastened wrists and yanked them so she shrieked from the pain.

She tried to move away, but the man with the syringe immobilized her further by pinning her leg with his knee.

"Here's a nice one," the man holding the syringe said. He tapped one of Helen's veins in her arm, bringing it to the surface of her flesh. She turned away and pressed her eyes shut as she felt the man jab the needle through her skin. She felt the drug push its way into her vein and almost immediately felt dizzy. Her limbs felt like dead weights. The men moved her out of her seat to a helicopter that was waiting for them. Everything was out of focus, and though she tried she couldn't make sense of the blurred images.

"How is she doing?" she heard Wyan ask.

One of the men who carried her in his arms began to laugh. "She won't give us any more trouble," he said, squeezing her waist.

Helen found herself laughing. She realized that whatever they had given her was powerful enough to scramble her emotions and thoughts. She focused her mind with all the will she had, and managed to turn her head so that her chin rested on the man who carried her. Although her head felt as if it weighed a ton, she opened her mouth and clamped her teeth on the guy's shoulder.

"Ow!" the man howled as he let go of Helen. "She bit me . . . the little minx bit me," he yelled.

Helen tumbled to the ground and lay there, content to watch everything spin around her.

The other man reached down and smacked her across the face, but she didn't feel it, only heard the smack of his hand on her cheek.

"Get her now." It was Wyan's voice, and he was angry.

The men picked her up by the ankles. This time they dragged her on her back the rest of the way. When they reached the helicopter, they picked her up and threw her into the belly of the craft. She heard the helicopter's engines rev, and it rose into the air.

59

❖

Spiral of Life Headquarters, the Alps

Any word yet?" Dr. Elisha BenHassen asked Colonel Austin as he entered the war room at Johanen's castle.

Stephan, who was at the helm of one of the computer terminals, looked dismayed. "Nothing. The sandstorm has knocked out communications in the region."

"Lousy luck for us," Austin growled, as he sipped from a mug of coffee.

"Look here." Stephan pointed to a large screen. "A satellite view of the area." He clicked a few keys, and the area just below Jordan was enlarged. "It started here hours ago, and spread south, encompassing the entire area."

"I'm sure it has affected the tel," Austin offered.

"It certainly will delay them, maybe even throw off the timing of the broadcast," Stephan suggested.

"Nothing will stop them from that," Elisha responded.

"I think we should proceed with the backup plan," Austin suggested.

"That would give them no chance to reach the tomb," Elisha responded.

"But it might save their lives," Austin replied.

Elisha took off his trifocals and rubbed the bridge of his nose. "What do you think, Stephan?"

Stephan swiveled his chair so he faced Elisha. "I think we should give them time to destroy the tomb," he said.

"Where are Knud and Hilda?" Elisha asked.

"Knud has been monitoring the plane incident. The media is playing up the drug angle. They've even managed to find a picture of Laura, and they are alleging that she is trafficking heroin between the U.S. and here."

Knud's voice was heard from the hallway. "We've got to get out now!"

"Why?" Elisha asked, as Knud burst into the room.

"We've got to leave . . . now. They're planning a drug raid. I was tipped off, but they'll be here soon . . . less than five minutes."

Elisha frowned. "Who's planning a drug raid?"

"I'm not sure, but there is no time, we must leave. Hilda is already at the tunnel waiting."

"Do we have time to send a message to Israel . . . the one requesting the backup plan?" Elisha asked.

"It's set to go, but it will still take a few minutes," Stephan answered. "You three go ahead, and I'll stay until the message is sent."

All eyes looked at Elisha. "It will have to do for now." He turned to Knud. "Take us to the tunnel."

"I'll stay here with Stephan, help hold the fort down," Austin offered.

Stephan interrupted. "No, Colonel, you should go with the others. There is nothing you can do here."

Austin glanced at Elisha then back at Stephan. He puffed his cheeks and huffed, "I suppose you're right. Let's go, Doctor." He headed toward Elisha and Knud.

"We'll wait as long as we can," Elisha said, then he followed Knud toward the tunnel.

60

✳ ◉ ✳

The Yemeni Desert

A re you sure you want to leave the jeep here?" Mac asked. "Yes," Johanen answered, "the camouflaged tarp will offer good concealment, and as long as the jeep is in the wadi it should remain undetected."

"Wadi? Is that what this dried-up stream is called?" Mac asked.

Johanen nodded. "Help me here?" he asked as he tugged at a buried palm branch.

Mac finished fastening the tarp, then helped Johanen pull the branch out of the bottom of the dry creek bed. Johanen placed it along the length of the jeep.

The digital map had been accurate and the wadi had appeared where it was supposed to. Mac had followed it until he found an opening that allowed him to drive the jeep down into it. He maneuvered along the dry bed, once using the winch to move several large boulders out of the way.

They had found a spot where the current had carved a cavelike opening in the bank during the rainy season. Mac had parked the jeep so that most of it was hidden in this fissure, and to their good fortune, even the roof was below the desert floor.

"As long as they aren't searching for us, I don't think they'll find it," Mac said.

"The map indicates that this wadi intersects the south-ernmost part of the tel," Johanen stated. "It may allow us to pass undetected through the laser security boundary that the Major's satellite picture revealed to us. We will wait for dark and then make our move."

"What about contacting Elisha again?" Mac asked.

"There has been no reply, and that worries me. Something is not as it should be. True, the sandstorm knocked out our communications, but that does not explain the silence now."

"And nothing from Uri and Laura," Mac added. "I think they were discovered."

Johanen peered over the side of the wadi and looked in all directions. "I hope you're wrong, MacKenzie. In the meantime we should eat a meal and rest here until nightfall, then see what lies ahead at the tel."

"What if we don't hook up with Uri? His jeep was carry-ing the incendiary grenades, so how do you plan to destroy the tomb?" Mac asked.

"I have done a mental inventory of what we have . . . our packs, rations, shovels, night vision goggles, and one set of infrared binoculars and a dozen or so flares. I am praying that Uri will show up with the grenades. If he does not, then we will weigh our options at that time and make a decision. In the meantime, take several of these and put them in your pock-ets for safekeeping." Johanen handed Mac several flares. Mac put them into one of the pockets of his heavy cotton pants.

* ❍ *

"I'd give anything for a hot cup of coffee," Mac said, as he followed Johanen. Both men shouldered lightweight packs as they made their way in the dark along the bottom of the wadi.

"Coffee would be nice." Johanen stopped. "Look there, just off to our left." He pointed.

Mac let out a slight whistle between his teeth. "Incredible," he said as he got his first view of the tel.

Over a dozen megaliths rose above the desert floor forming a semicircle of silent sentinels. In front of the standing stones was an array of lighting equipment, scaffolding, and a small stage. The entire area was well lit, and Mac could see a variety of personnel moving around. A row of sleek metal trailers were parked at the foot of a large hill a hundred yards away from the megaliths. But what drew his attention was the ancient stone that towered above the others that flanked it on either side. At the base of it, the entrance led to the tomb.

"Notice the red beams of light at the outer perimeter?" Johanen said.

"Yea, the laser fence the Major briefed us about . . . but there seem to be breaches in it."

"Look at the area to our right at the extreme edge of the tel." Johanen directed Mac's attention to the area.

"Seems as if the sandstorm knocked the relays out."

Headlights from a jeep shone over their heads.

"They're patrolling the perimeter until they get the laser fence fixed," Mac stated as they ducked back down in the wadi. "Now's the time to get in."

"We will make for the southernmost extreme," Johanen said. "By the looks of it, they haven't gotten to that area yet . . . hurry now."

Mac followed Johanen, quickening his pace as they followed the wadi.

* ○ *

A while later, Mac eased his head up and peered over the edge of the wadi using his night vision binoculars. "Bingo," he whispered to Johanen.

Johanen pulled on his sleeve and Mac dropped back down next to him.

"They have the place lit up and it's crawling with security," Mac added. "It's going to be tough getting in there."

"Pray that something will open up to us. We must be patient."

"There's a convoy of army trucks headed toward the tel." Mac handed Johanen the binoculars.

"If the Major's briefing is correct, they belong to the Yemeni Army."

"But what are they doing? Delivering supplies?" Mac asked.

Johanen kept looking through the glasses. "They have stopped near a satellite dish by one of the trailers," he reported. "There's a lot of activity around the rear of one of the trucks. MacKenzie, look here, will you, and tell me what you see?" Johanen handed Mac the glasses.

Mac adjusted the lenses and the images came into focus. "It looks as if security apprehended someone, but there's too much activity . . . Oh no . . . I think it might be Uri."

"Are you certain?" Johanen asked.

"I just got a glimpse, but the build looked the same. Should we abort?" Mac asked, as he handed Johanen the glasses.

"No, we don't know for certain whether it was Uri, so let us wait and see what happens. Besides, *they* are running out of time. The lunar eclipse that is pivotal to their timetable is fast approaching, and by the looks of things, the sandstorm has hit them very hard. There appears to be a lot of frantic activity to put things in order," Johanen said, as he scanned the area of the tel.

"It looks like several of their trailers got blown over," Mac stated. Then something high in the sky caught his eye. "Johanen, something else is coming in very fast." Mac yanked on Johanen's sleeve and pointed toward the glowing object that grew nearer to the tel.

The old man put down the glasses. "I was wondering when they would show themselves."

Mac moved closer to Johanen, and the two men gazed at the night sky. Two UFOs with pulsating orange lights descended over the tel.

"This might be a good time to move *into* the tel," Johanen suggested. "MacKenzie?"

Mac was transfixed by the pulsating UFOs. He gave a start as Johanen touched his shoulder. "Remember, Mac, he that is in you is greater than he that is in the world."

"They're so hypnotic," Mac replied as they lowered themselves to the bottom of the wadi.

"According to our map the wadi should get very narrow as it intersects the point where they employ the laser fence. Hopefully this is how we will gain our entrance," Johanen said.

"Let's get to it then," Mac said, regaining a measure of self-control as he scrambled after Johanen.

* ◊ *

Fifteen minutes later the wadi was so narrow they had to move in single file. In some places Mac wedged his body between large boulders. They spent several minutes clearing a tangle of dried vegetation that made them come to a halt.

"There's a lot of loose sand in this section," Mac whispered, as he wiggled on his belly over a large boulder.

"Yes," Johanen whispered, "I think I know what is happening . . . they filled the wadi in so that the laser fence would not have a weak spot."

"I think you're right," Mac replied.

Johanen crawled back to MacKenzie and the two men scrambled up the side of the wadi. "Look, the fence isn't working right," Johanen said.

Mac looked at the flicker of four parallel red lights that streaked above the sand. They would blink out, only to reappear a few seconds later. "How are we going to get through?"

"We will have to trust to providence," Johanen said.

"We don't have much time. Look . . . here they come." Mac gestured to the two patrol jeeps that had stopped several hundred yards away.

"They are adjusting one of the relays," Johanen remarked. "We have got to do it now."

Mac nodded. The two men slid up out of the wadi and crawled on their bellies toward the laser fence.

"Get into a low crouch, MacKenzie," Johanen whispered as they stopped several feet away from the flickering lights.

Mac watched as the lights went on and off again at random intervals.

"We can't sync with this," he said. "It's random."

"We have got to try," Johanen said. "I will go first."

Johanen waited for the laser to go out again. Then he leaped up and dived over the area that the laser had just marked.

A few moments went by and the lights came on again.

Mac waited as a full minute passed. "What if they don't go off again?" Mac whispered.

Johanen didn't answer. He looked toward the jeep that was less than a hundred yards away. "I think they are finished and coming this way."

Mac heard the engine start and the jeep put in gear. "Now what?" he called from the other side of the laser fence that separated them. Still the red beams remained on.

The jeep's searchlight began to play over the sand as it moved closer.

Mac saw that even now with the jeep bearing down on them, Johanen remained calm. Mac checked himself, following the older man's example.

Then the lasers flickered, but only for a second before they came on again.

The jeep was now fifty yards away.

"I'm going for it," Mac called, diving forward through the laser fence. He held his hands out in front of him to break his fall as a shower of sand kicked up in his face.

"Don't move, MacKenzie," Johanen whispered.

From the corner of Mac's eye he saw the searchlight of the jeep lighting up the area a few feet away from him. The laser fence flickered again. Sand had caught in one of Mac's eyes and he fought the urge to wipe it. He hoped that the light wouldn't reveal his presence.

The spotlight inched its way toward him. He knew that if it landed on him they would be discovered. He remained still. The light moved away toward Johanen but then bounced back toward him. *Please, Lord, blind their eyes,* he prayed. He could hear the jeep getting closer, and then the searchlight moved away.

"Quick, MacKenzie," Johanen whispered. Mac reached him and the two men crawled behind a small sand dune which hid them from the approaching jeep.

The jeep pulled up next to the flickering laser fence and Mac heard muted voices as the technicians began their work.

Mac felt Johanen's hand on his shoulder and the older man pulled himself close to Mac so that he could whisper in his ear. "To the last of the megaliths," Johanen said, pointing to the giant rocks.

They crawled between several sand dunes and reached the last of the megaliths. They moved to the side that hid them from the technicians fixing the fence but at the same time offered a good view of the tel.

"Wow, look at that, will you?" Mac said, as one of the disks hovered over the megalith that towered over the tomb.

"Remember whose service they are in," Johanen admonished. "It is best not to look at them."

Mac crawled up alongside Johanen. "If we only had the explosives in Uri's jeep," Mac said. Then he saw two large diesel generators on a flatbed truck on the opposite side of the tel. "What about the generators? We might be able to get to them and knock out all the power."

Johanen nodded. "Yes, a good option, but let us wait and see."

Mac reached out to touch the surface of the giant stone that they hid behind. "It's one thing to see pictures of these, but to be next to one and realize how immense they are . . . somehow the theory of ropes and pulleys and a couple of hundred thousand half-naked, sweaty slaves doesn't add up."

Johanen chuckled. "You have an interesting way of putting things, MacKenzie. Like Baalbek, these were erected by the same power that makes those disks fly." He glanced at the disk that still hovered nearby. "One thing I failed to mention in our briefing with the Major was that this spot was an ancient temple site and was used for human sacrifice to the demon god, Molech."

"Thanks for letting me know," Mac said, inching away from the megalith and burying his body in the loose sand.

"This would be a good time to enter the tomb."

"With everyone around it? That's crazy," Mac replied.

"Not at all, MacKenzie. We have the diversion we need. You see those cables by one of the trailers there." Johanen motioned toward them. "Our clothing matches theirs, at least reasonably so; the Major and his satellite pictures saw to that. So, we pick the cables up and move toward the tomb, blending in as two technicians. Their camp is in a state of disarray from the sandstorm . . . we may go unnoticed."

Mac nodded. "I agree . . . let's do it."

The spotlights were focused on the megalith that loomed over the tomb, but most of the outlying areas were dimly lit. Mac and Johanen walked in the shadows as long as possible, and then they engaged in conversation and walked across a good deal of open space to the trailers. To the casual observer, they looked like two technicians helping to ready the site for the broadcast.

"Take one end of this," Johanen said, handing Mac a large coil of cable, which he had divided in two, so that each man would carry part of it. "Ready?" he asked.

Mac shouldered the cable. "It's heavy," he commented, as he adjusted it on his shoulder. "I'll follow you."

Johanen rested his cheek against the cable, which concealed a portion of his face. The test came quickly, as a man and woman who were part of the operation walked past them. Mac held his breath and turned his head toward the cable. He heard a snatch of their conversation as they walked by.

"The sandstorm has ruined everything," the woman said.

"Yes, but I talked to Dr. Bernstein and he assured me that the broadcast . . ." The man's voice trailed off.

We passed, Mac thought. He began to think that they might have half a chance. He noticed that the area around him was growing brighter. He stole a glance over Johanen's head and saw the giant megalith and the pulsating orange disk that hovered over it.

"We are almost there," Johanen said, turning his head in Mac's direction.

"I know," Mac whispered back.

Moments later Johanen stopped. They were at the base of the megalith. Directly in front of them was the excavated entrance to the tomb. There were several security guards around it, but their attention was on the disk.

They started forward again and Mac felt his hands grow sweaty around the cable.

"Television crew?" a guard asked.

"Yes, satellite linkup," Johanen replied. To Mac's amazement, he never stopped for a moment, but kept walking.

"Even with all the briefings I've had from Dr. Bernstein it's hard to believe, isn't it?" the guard asked, and nodded toward the disk. "Say hello to the big 'J' for me," he laughed, as they began their descent into the tomb.

The two men descended the stairs. When they were about halfway down, Mac exclaimed, "Will you look at all of this equipment?" He pointed to an array of cables to his right.

"No expense has been spared," Johanen responded.

They reached the bottom, and Johanen stopped for a moment. "Look at this, MacKenzie," he said, pointing to the change of materials that constructed the wall of the tunnel.

"It looks extraterrestrial, like what I saw at Area Fifty-One," Mac answered. He looked at the smooth, round surface of the shaft that led away from the staircase. "What now?"

"This way." Johanen started down the passageway.

"Incredible," Mac whispered as they neared the end of the corridor.

"We will set this down here." Johanen let go of his end of the cable.

Mac set his end down, and the two men moved into the dimly lit room in front of them.

"Look at that, will you?" Mac whispered.

In front of them was a glass sarcophagus emanating a faint glow.

"There it is." Mac moved closer. "Oh, I didn't expect this," he said, as he got his first view of the body. "It looks just like him . . . Sorry, I mean, you know, with all the paintings and pictures over the years . . . Well, does it look like him?" he asked Johanen.

"There is a certain likeness, but no, it doesn't *look* like him," Johanen replied.

"Are you certain?" Mac asked.

Johanen looked at him.

"All right, for crying out loud, I was just asking. This place gives me the creeps."

"Let us take the lid off," Johanen said.

"Huh?"

"Take the lid off, MacKenzie, and lay to rest the poor soul whose body this is." He moved closer to the sarcophogus and began to try to pry the lid off.

"Johanen," Mac said, his voice urgent.

"What?"

"I think those cameras are on."

Johanen stopped, eyed Mac, then looked at the cameras. They heard the sound of footsteps hurrying toward them.

"Grab the cable again," Johanen said, as he rushed toward the entrance.

Mac grabbed the cable, pretending to connect it to a junction box on the floor.

"Oh, really, gentlemen," a voice called out to them, "Johanen, MacKenzie, you don't have to pretend."

Mac froze and looked at Johanen. "They know! How did they know?" he stammered.

To his amazement, he saw that Johanen somehow remained calm as he shook his head. "I don't know, MacKenzie." He rose to his feet.

Mac stood next to Johanen and saw that the men were almost upon them. There were three, two security goons with guns drawn, and another who was a good deal taller than they. It was he who now addressed Mac and Johanen.

"We've waited a long time for this," the one in the middle said to Johanen.

"I've got them covered, Mr. Kenson," one of the guards stated, aiming his gun toward Mac and Johanen.

Mac noticed the six fingers on his hand. His mind raced back to the secret room under the Temple Mount in Jerusalem where he had first seen the remains of an ancient giant, the offspring of an unholy union between the daughters of men and the fallen angels, the Nephilim. It too had six fingers.

"We knew you'd come . . . someone in your organization made sure of that," Kenson said.

Johanen started to speak, but before a word could leave his lips, Kenson had moved his hand in front of his body. Somehow, a gun flew from the hand of one of the security guards and landed in Kenson's, with a sudden slap of metal against skin. Without hesitation he fired into Johanen.

Only when the report began to echo in his ears and he could smell the gunpowder did Mac finally come to his senses. "No!" he yelled, and he rushed the man who had shot Johanen. But before he reached him, he was met with a kick in the stomach by one of the security guards. He fell to his knees holding his solar plexus, gasping for air. Then he felt a blow to the back of his neck, and before his body hit the floor he was unconscious.

61

Spiral of Life Headquarters, the Alps

Elisha peered out an arched window and saw a line of police cars approaching on the road that led to the castle. "They're driving without their lights," he said.

"I count ten vehicles," Hilda replied.

"Make that eleven," Austin corrected her.

"They'll be here soon. We've got to get into the tunnel," Knud admonished.

"Where does this go?" Elisha asked.

"To the village a few miles away," Knud answered.

"Clever the way the entrance is concealed," Austin commented.

"Very much so." Elisha looked at the entrance to the tunnel that had been concealed by the interior of the linen closet. Knud had found a hidden release button which had allowed him to roll it out into the hallway, shelves, linen, and all.

"What about Stephan?" Elisha asked.

"He's weighed the risks and knows his options. Ya, we should go now . . . please." Knud gestured for Elisha to go inside.

Elisha stepped through the closet, into the cool interior of a stone tunnel. "Who built this?" he asked as Austin entered.

"It looks ancient," Austin replied.

Knud followed Hilda and then rolled the shelves of the linen cabinet back in place. "Further down it becomes a labyrinth of passageways. Unless you know the way you would be lost in a matter of minutes. Here, take a lantern." He handed each one a battery-powered flashlight.

"And you, of course, know the way, but how?" Elisha asked.

"*Ya, Ya*, in a while, I'll show you," Knud said, as they began to walk down the tunnel. As they came to the first intersection of passageways, Knud shined his flashlight on the wall. "See here?" he said.

"Yes, the sign of the fish, like Christians used in the first century. I remember seeing these in the catacombs in Rome," Elisha said.

"They mark the way at every intersection, always on the right side of the tunnel, and the head of the fish points you in the right direction."

They continued on and at some points there were as many as five intersecting tunnels going off in all directions. Elisha realized that without the aid of the markers or a detailed map of some kind, a person would be lost very quickly.

The tunnel was cold, and at some points there were stalactites of ice hanging from the ceiling. Elisha could see his breath in front of him as he followed Knud. He wished he had had a chance to get a coat, as he walked with his hands in his pockets.

After a while he noticed that the tunnel began to angle upward. He felt his leg muscles tighten, and his breath became more labored as he began to climb an ascending passage.

A short time later the tunnel widened into a room. "This is it. We're at the end." Knud stopped in front of a narrow wooden door.

Elisha came up next to him. "Where does it lead?"

"You'll see, in a minute, Doctor." Knud reached overhead on a wooden cross beam and produced a set of keys. He went over to the door and fitted a key into one of the locks. "It's rusted," he said, as he struggled with the key. Finally the lock sprang, the bolts were undone, and the door flew open with a sudden burst of light that flooded the tunnel.

"Halt!" a loud voice commanded.

Elisha froze and raised his hands.

"Halt!" the voice rang out again.

Elisha heard something moving away from him, and he realized it was Austin. A heartbeat later uniformed police surrounded Knud, Hilda, and Elisha. But what added to Elisha's terror were two German shepherd dogs, which lunged toward him. The policemen who controlled the snarling beasts strained to hold them back as they barked ferociously, the sound echoing down the tunnel, rebounding off the walls. This reminded Elisha of the camps, how the Nazis would let a dog go at one of the prisoners until the unfortunate soul was mauled beyond recognition.

Two policemen grabbed Elisha, and his hands were cuffed behind his back. He heard Hilda cry out as one of the dogs lunged at her, almost biting her face. Knud began to talk to the policemen in Swiss. But from what Elisha could gather he was told to shut up. The three of them were hurried out of the tunnel into the cellar of a warehouse. To Elisha's dismay, members of the press were there, and cameras flashed as he came out of the tunnel. He kept his head down as he was ushered out to a waiting police van. He looked back as he stepped into the van and caught a glimpse of Knud and Hilda behind him.

How did they know? he wondered, but what gave him hope was that Austin had managed to slip away.

There were several more pictures taken as the vans pulled away from the sidewalk. Elisha stared ahead, ignoring his captors, as the siren wailed and the van sped through the streets of the village.

✳ ◯ ✳

Elisha sat alone in a small windowless room that was empty except for a battered old table and several wooden chairs. A single light in the ceiling was covered with a protective grid of metal. It had been several hours since Elisha's arrest. In that time he had been fingerprinted, searched, photographed, and hustled from one closed room to another. He had demanded to call the Israeli consulate, but his request had been ignored.

He heard the locks turning in the heavy metal door and an official entered the room.

"Dr. Elisha BenHassen?" the man began. "Let me introduce myself. I am Inspector Simone of the Swiss police. Do you have anything to say for yourself?"

"What am I being arrested for?" Elisha demanded.

Simone lit a cigarette and sat on the edge of the table. "An accomplice to the smuggling of heroin."

"What are you talking about?" Elisha responded, rising from his chair. "That's preposterous, if I may . . ." He stopped mid-sentence as it began to dawn on him to what degree they had been set up. He took a deep breath, sat back down, and said, "What evidence do you have?"

Simone reached into the file next to him on the table and produced several glossy photos. "We just got these back, but I'm sure you'll recognize the interior of the castle."

Elisha took the photos and began to look through them when he stopped and his hands began to tremble. He stared at the photo in his hand. "You shot him . . . you shot Stephan."

"He resisted arrest," Simone said, puffing on his cigarette.

Elisha held the picture. "You shot an innocent man."

Simone blew a cloud of smoke toward the ceiling but didn't respond.

Elisha raised his voice and demanded, "What proof do you have of anyone trafficking in heroin?"

Simone took another drag, then ignoring Elisha's question, asked one of his own. "What do you know about the explosion of a small jet at the Rome airport this week?" he inquired.

Elisha frowned. "What does that have to do with this?"

"Everything," Simone said. "We know about Laura Nathan so there's no reason to hide her from us."

"She has done nothing," Elisha said.

Simone ignored him. "We found traces of heroin in the wreckage."

"But you haven't established a link with the explosion and Ms. Nathan, or us, for that matter."

"So why, then, were you fleeing via a secret tunnel?"

Elisha sat silent.

"We are making a thorough search of the castle, and I'm sure we will find the evidence that has eluded us so far. Ms. Nathan was supposed to be on that plane."

"But that does not prove that she smuggled heroin," Elisha shot back.

Simone ignored him again. "For the sake of diplomatic relations with your country, I'm going to allow you to make a call to the Israeli consulate. If you'll follow me . . ."

Elisha followed Simone out of the room.

"You can call from here," Simone said, pointing to a phone on a cluttered desk in a small office.

Elisha went in and sat down, leaving Simone leaning against the doorjamb of the office.

"I don't have the number," he said, holding the receiver toward Simone.

The inspector shrugged. "Call the operator."

Elisha dialed, and as he listened to the ringing, his thoughts were on Colonel Austin and whether he had managed to escape.

* ○ *

Colonel Austin had felt uneasy as Knud had groped for the key to the wooden door. Something just didn't feel right. He had turned his light off and taken several steps backward, unbuttoning the leather strap in his sidearm holster that held the nine millimeter Walther P99 in place. As he waited for the door to open, he saw a flash of light in the slight crack under the door. But before he could sound a warning, the door had opened and the police had rushed in. In that brief second or two before the door opened he had slipped back down the tunnel. He curled himself into a tight ball, pressing his body close to the wall, and waited until the police finished leading everyone out. When he was sure they were gone, he started to work his way back up the tunnel, always searching with his lantern for the sign of the fish.

He reached the false back of the laundry closet and pressed his ear to it, listening for any sound. Drawing his Walther P99 from its holster, he pushed the false back out of the way and stepped into the hall. Once again he listened. The castle seemed empty. He walked the length of the hallway and stopped when he reached the conference room. It was empty. He made his way to the war room, as he thought of it, the room with the computers and large digital map of the Middle East. To his amazement, things were much as he had left them an hour ago. There were no signs of a search or struggle, and the main frame was still on and running. Stephan's chair was tucked into the workstation, and the monitor was showing its screen saver. Austin went to Stephan's workstation, laid the Walther on the table, and poked a key with his index finger. The screen saver vanished, and in its place was a detailed statement of a bank account.

He scrolled down and then realized that he was looking at the considerable personal wealth of Johanen. He also noticed that an online transfer of funds was scheduled to take place.

He froze, for in the reflection of the screen he saw someone moving toward him from the doorway of the room. He waited and controlled his breathing, preparing himself.

The reflection grew larger in the screen. Incredible. It was Stephan.

Austin began to type a command on the keyboard, keeping his eye on the growing reflection.

Stephan raised a knife.

Austin whirled around on the balls of his feet. He thrust his leg straight out, so that the bottom of his shoe smashed into Stephan's solar plexus. The kick landed true, forcing Stephan back, crashing into a table, as the knife flew from his hand and slid across the floor.

Austin bore down on Stephan but the man surprised him, rising quickly from the floor. Austin closed the distance and when he was no more than three feet away he spun his body like a top, at the last instant letting his fist fly out from his torso toward Stephan's face. To his surprise it was blocked by Stephan's raised arm and then countered, as Stephan responded by throwing a kick of his own, which Austin in turn blocked. *He's been trained in the martial arts,* Austin thought, as he let two punches fly toward Stephan's face, which pushed him backward to avoid being hit.

The fighting was furious, a blur of arms, fists, and legs that probed each other's defenses. Austin blocked a wild kick to his face and countered with a forward kick aimed at Stephan's groin. Stephan sidestepped the kick and tried to flick his fingers in Austin's eyes to blind him. *Careful, he almost got you,* Austin thought, as he kept himself between Stephan and the Walther that he had left on the table.

Stephan pressed toward Austin, throwing another shot at his face, driving him backward and off balance, and then swung his leg up from behind him, a blinding arc aimed at Austin's temple. Austin saw it just in time to duck under it, but felt the man's shoe brush his scalp. The kick had given him the opening he wanted and he rushed Stephan, throwing a feint to the man's face, then slammed his other fist into his rib cage. To his satisfaction he heard a loud crack. Before Stephan could counter, Austin jumped back and grabbed the Walther from the table.

"Hold it or I'll blow you into the next world, you stinking little traitor." He aimed the barrel at Stephan's chest.

Stephan held his ribs and glared back at Austin.

Austin kicked the chair that had been at the workstation toward Stephan. "I think you should sit your rear end down and start telling me what I want to know," Austin growled.

Stephan grimaced as he eased onto the chair.

"If they hurt Elisha in any way, you'll pay for it. Now let's begin, shall we?" Austin said, and his gun barrel never strayed from Stephan's torso.

62

✦ ◉ ✦

The Tel, Yemen

Mac tried to focus on the voice that called him, tried to come out of the black fog he was in, almost made it, then slipped away.

"Art, can you hear me? It's Laura . . . Laura Nathan. Uri's here with me."

Mac felt a hand on his shoulder. He groaned and opened his eyes and looked around, trying to get his bearings. He saw that he was inside a storage trailer with Uri and Laura.

Then the horrible realization that Johanen had been shot, that he had died, washed over him. He felt sick to his stomach as his mind kept repeating the scene of Johanen crumbling to the ground while the blood spurted from his wound. "They shot him . . . Johanen." The words tumbled out of his mouth. His chest heaved as the first sobs rose from his throat. He felt hopeless and confused as he wondered why God would allow this to happen.

"Who, Mac?" Uri asked.

Mac looked at Uri as if he didn't know him. He shook his head several times as if by doing so he could shake the image of Johanen's last moments on earth from him, but it did no good. "I can't believe it," Mac gasped. He brought his knees up to his chest and wrapped his arms around them, cradling himself. He wondered if the same fate awaited Maggie, his children . . . and himself. "Oh, God . . . why?" he cried out. "Why?"

Laura bit her lip as she knelt and wrapped her arms around him. Mac felt Uri's hand on his shoulder.

"What happened, Mac?" Uri asked.

"One of the Nephilim . . . he just shot him . . . blew him away . . . then . . . I rushed them, and I was knocked out, that's all I remember. I can't believe it . . . it doesn't make sense." His body shuddered as once again his mind replayed the scene.

"The Nephilim? Here?" Mac heard the fear in Laura's voice.

"Six fingers . . . and he was well over seven feet." Mac wiped his face with the back of his hand.

"Grandfather warned we should be seeing some of this," Uri said.

"At least you two are safe," Mac said, giving Laura a hug and grabbing Uri's hand. "Johanen and I thought we saw you being moved from a convoy, but we weren't sure."

"Are you sure he's dead?" Laura asked.

Mac nodded. "Yeah. The whole thing keeps going in my head like a horror movie . . . but the hybrid shot him at almost point-blank range. He's dead."

"MacKenzie, we maybe can be doing something," Mac noted the determination in Uri's face.

"Like what, Uri? Didn't you hear me? Johanen's dead, and there are hybrids, Nephilim, here." Mac felt the back of his neck. "Boy, that smarts . . . how long was I out?"

"A couple of hours, but that won't stop us from trying to blow the place up, huh?" Uri countered.

"We've got to try, Mac. We owe that much to Johanen," Laura added, rallying with Uri.

"You're both right . . . it happened so fast . . . the stinking freak blasted a hole in him. Not a moment's hesitation, just bam!" Mac slammed his fist on the floor.

"Did you get near the tomb?" Laura asked.

Mac nodded. "Yeah, we were inside it when Johanen was shot." Mac rubbed his eyes, then sighed. "Did you guys see the disk come in?" he asked.

"We see nothing from here," Uri answered. "No windows."

"There was a disk hovering over the megalith. It provided the cover we needed to get into the tomb."

"So you saw the body?" Laura asked.

Mac nodded. "It was strange. It looked like the real goods to me. It had the marks of crucifixion, and the face is very similar to pictures I've seen over the years. But it's not him. Johanen assured me of that." Mac realized that he almost let slip the true identity of Johanen, but then thought it would make no difference if he did, because the man was dead.

"How could he be so sure of that?" Laura asked.

Mac shrugged. "He was certain. But there's more. The Nephilim hybrid who shot Johanen called us by name. Like he was expecting us. As if he knew we were going to be there."

"So there *is* a leak in our circle," Laura said. "That explains why I was followed in Rome."

Mac nodded. "Yeah, and somehow they knew we were coming. They knew who we were when they apprehended us in the tomb."

"I'm trusting both of you." Uri said, "I'm thinking Elisha is going to be sending backup soon."

"You're right, Uri, Elisha must have notified the Major, and he in turn would have put the rescue operation in motion by now, at least let's hope so."

"But what if he didn't? What if something went wrong on his end?" Laura challenged.

"We first must get out of here," Uri added.

"They have guards stationed in front," Mac said. "I saw them posted after you arrived. I'm sure they're standing outside the door now. Any way out of this thing?"

Uri shook his head. "Not unless you have some tools. I've been looking but nothing is here."

"What do we do?" Laura asked.

Mac looked at both of them and said one word, "Pray."

63

✳ ◻ ✳

Yemeni Desert

The robed figure strode over the desert floor, his sandaled feet avoiding large rocks as he planted his staff ahead of him, then pulled his body after it, always the free arm swinging in time, helping to propel him forward.

He was sweating, for it had been several hours since he had left the driver of the truck. His spirit was troubled, and the cause of it made him hurry all the more. He glanced up at the stars and marked his bearings, all the while keeping the same rhythmic gait with his staff, legs, and arms. The jar that was fastened around his neck rubbed his side, adding to his rhythm as he hurried along.

Hours passed, and then, in the distance, he saw what he was looking for, a glow of light on the horizon. He saw a jeep cross the desert in front of him, and he stopped and reduced himself to a huddle on the desert floor. The jeep passed, and he resumed his pace. He was close, and there was much work to do, and an old score to settle. He set his staff into the earth, then tied his robe up so that his legs were bare. He let his hood fall down, and taking his staff in his hand, he set off at a run in the direction of the lights.

64

Department of Defense,
Tel Aviv, Israel

"Sir, I have just decoded a message. It's a level three, sir." An aide poked his head into the office.

The Major looked up from his desk, paused, then gave his aide permission to enter. The man handed him a sheet of paper and then was excused.

The Major read it, set it before him on the blotter of his desk, and dialed a number on a secure phone line. "I'm going to need special forces for an Entebbe-type raid, with plausible deniability," he said into the receiver.

"For what we talked about earlier?" the man on the other end asked.

"Retrieval of personnel . . . with a possibility of extraterrestrial exposure."

"How certain are you of an alien encounter?"

The Major leaned forward and set his elbows on his desk. "Very certain."

"We aren't prepared to handle a major exposure to our personnel."

"So you'll notify the Americans?" the Major asked.

"They're better equipped if things get messy, but we'll do the initial strike."

"I have IDs on those you're going to pick up. There's four of them. One is a woman."

"I understand. As soon as you send over what we need, we'll launch."

The Major looked at his watch. "You'll have it in less than half an hour. Notify me when you're ready."

"Understood, Major."

The phone went dead and the Major set it back on its base. He opened the top drawer in his desk and thumbed through the file, stopping to look at the photo of his friend Elisha BenHassen. "We'll get them home safe, old friend," he whispered, as he rose from his chair and left the room.

65

＊○＊

The Tel

Helen hovered on the verge of consciousness, fighting to stay awake. After her biting episode, they had injected her again. She was so drugged that breathing seemed like a great effort. She tried to focus her gaze out the window to see if she could tell where she was, but the window moved in and out of focus. She realized, however, that it was night, and that the chopper was doing something different. She felt it tilt back and she heard muffled radio contact coming from the cabin. Saliva dribbled from the corner of her mouth, and she wanted to wipe it away, but she couldn't move her arms.

The chopper landed, and she heard its whirling blades slow down. Then they came for her. She was picked up as if she were no more than a doll and carried out of the chopper. She felt a warm breeze surround her, and it tingled every inch of her skin. She looked around, but before she could see anything, someone had thrown a black sackcloth over her head. She tried to struggle against it but found it impossible to do so. She felt herself bump on the shoulder of the man who carried her and realized that she was going down stairs.

Then she heard his voice, the reptilian, and it sent a shiver through her.

"Bring her and secure her."

She felt herself being placed on something hard and cold.

Then the voice again. "How much time do we have before the eclipse?"

"Seventy-two minutes, Mr. Wyan," someone answered.

"Where is Mr. Kenson?" she heard Wyan ask.

"In the tomb, sir, helping Dr. Bernstein with last-minute preparations. He asked me to deliver this box and letter to you."

There was a pause as Helen heard the tearing of an envelope.

"Wonderful news," he began. "Tell Mr. Kenson that he has found the victory where others have failed, and that I have the woman with me."

"Yes, sir," she heard the man answer.

"Make sure she stays comfortable. I'll return soon," Wyan said.

She tried to move her head, but someone's hands forced it back down.

"Oh, Helen," she heard Wyan call out to her, "I think you might be interested in knowing that the real Johanen lies buried in the sand a short distance from here, where no one will ever find him."

In spite of the drugs, which gave her a false sense of euphoria, at hearing of the death of Johanen, Helen abandoned any hope of escaping whatever it was they had prepared for her.

66

✳ ◼ ✳

Swiss Alps

It had been a few hours since Elisha BenHassen had made a call to the Israeli embassy. Because of the late hour it had been difficult to talk to anyone of importance. The operator at the switchboard had managed to connect to a secretary. She, in turn, had promised to relay his message to higher-ups.

He was now sitting in the same room where Simone had interrogated him earlier. Simone threw the newspaper on the table so that it slid to a stop in front of Elisha. "You made the front page." He sat on the table and pulled out a pack of cigarettes.

Elisha grabbed the paper and saw, to his dismay, pictures of himself, Knud, and Hilda being led out of the secret tunnel and then placed in the police vans.

"This is libel, you know." Elisha pushed the paper away from him. "You have no evidence."

Simone raised his eyebrows and puffed away on his cigarette, remaining silent.

Elisha heard a knock on the door, and a police official entered. He glanced at Elisha with a nervous expression and indicated to Simone that he had something to show him.

Simone blew a cloud of smoke in Elisha's direction, then left the room.

Elisha picked up the paper. Although he was unable to read the entire article, for it was in Italian, he was able to pick out enough words to get the gist of the story. His mind went back to the picture of Stephan, and he muttered a prayer for the dead man.

Simone came back into the room, and Elisha noticed that the man seemed agitated. He pulled another cigarette from his crumpled pack and lit it using the one that he was still smoking.

"It seems we have been used as pawns, Dr. BenHassen," he said, as he handed a telexed message to Elisha.

Elisha glanced at the signature, then a smile spread across his face. It was obvious that Colonel Austin had contacted the Major. He continued to read, and learned that it had been Stephan who had manipulated the police into believing that he was exposing an international drug cartel to them. But more important was the realization that Stephan had betrayed Johanen and the group. Elisha was stunned by the news, and he wondered about the fate of Uri and the others, as the Major also indicated with a few code words that a rescue mission had commenced. The telex concluded by saying that he was to be driven to the airport where, along with Austin, they would be flown to Tel Aviv. Elisha rose from his seat.

"I am very sorry for this, Doctor," Simone began in earnest. "It seems we were duped by this man and whoever it is he was working for. This, of course, is a great embarrassment to us, and I would ask your forgiveness. Somehow we will make amends for the inconvenience we have caused. We have this man in our custody, and I can assure you that he will be prosecuted to the full extent of the law."

67

Yemeni Desert

The robed figure ran without breaking his stride, his muscular legs flying over the desert terrain, propelling him closer to his destination. He felt he was getting near to what he was looking for. His eyes searched the area ahead of him, looking for the sign. He ran up a small hill, and as he crested it, saw a soft green light emanating from the ground no more than a quarter mile away. He hurried to it, and as he reached the spot the light began to fade away.

He untied his robe and raised his staff over the sand in front of him, passing it back and forth several times. As he moved the staff, the sand vibrated and rolled away like a wave on the ocean, to his left and to his right, following the direction of the staff. Soon a hole was formed in the sand, and as he moved the staff, it grew deeper. His eyes never wavered from the area in front of him. As he passed his staff yet another time over the area, there appeared small patches of red, which expanded as he went deeper, until the patches of sand were wet with the color.

The robed man gazed at the crumpled figure of a man lying on his side at the bottom of the hole. He walked around the body several times looking at it from all different angles, seeing the wound from where the blood had seeped, noticing the pale skin and blue lips. He set his staff in the sand above the figure's head, and climbed down into the hole. He gently rolled the man over so that he was on his back and set his legs straight in front of him. Then he placed himself on top of the man so that he was arm to arm, face to face, chest to chest. He breathed in the man's face, once, twice, three times. Then he got up and unloosened the man's shirt so that the ugly wound was exposed. He stood at the dead man's feet, singing softly an ancient song to the Holy One, the God of the Universe.

The dead man's chest jerked upward as the lungs filled with air. His eyes began to flutter, and his fingers twitched a few times. The robed man watched with satisfaction as the breathing became more relaxed and the wound began to disappear.

The man opened his eyes and sat up. He felt his side with his hand, looked at the robed figure, and whispered, "While I was separated from my body . . . the Ancient of Days showed me in a vision that you would come."

"I am he who walked with the Holy One and then was taken. I am Enoch." The robed man extended his hand to help Johanen to his feet. "The one who is fallen will be here?" Enoch asked.

"That I cannot answer," Johanen replied, "but you must know that there are many men, and they have weapons, the likes of which you have never set eyes on." Johanen put his finger into the bullet hole in his blood-stained shirt as he buttoned it.

"So have we." Enoch walked to where he had left his staff in the sand and offered it to Johanen.

Johanen balanced it in his hands a moment, then handed it back to Enoch. "What will you do?"

"The power to call down fire from heaven, to produce the plagues that the Holy One sent to Pharaoh and Egypt, is given to me. For I am one of the two who will witness of him who made the heavens and earth, for the time of the end is at hand."

Johanen nodded. "Then do what you think is best."

* ○ *

"I've gone almost twenty-four hours without a break," a man who was part of the tel's security complained, as he took a drag on his cigarette. He looked behind him at the trailer that held Mac, Uri, and Laura. "Two guys got through the lasers?" he asked. He waited for an answer from a heavyset woman with short cropped hair, who sucked on her cigarette.

"Yeah. Bernstein chewed me up one side and down the other for not reporting when the alarm sounded."

"It wasn't your fault, the laser fence was down. How were you supposed to know the alarm was real?" the man offered.

"Still, it happened on my watch," the woman stated.

"We got them anyway." He motioned toward the trailer and lowered his voice. "I helped dispose of the body."

"The one that Kenson shot?" the woman asked.

He nodded, feeling important.

"The guy had no business being here in the first place." She exhaled a stream of smoke toward him.

He moved closer to the woman and looked around for a moment. "Can I ask you something?"

The woman nodded.

"Is Kenson part of their . . ." He paused and motioned toward the saucer that hovered over the megalith. ". . . breeding program?"

He watched her pick some nicotine from her teeth as he waited for an answer. "Uh huh. By the looks of him he's what Bernstein refers to as an advanced hybrid. The end product of the breeding program between us and them."

"Creepy." He shivered.

"For sure," she agreed.

"How about the woman who arrived in the chopper a little while ago?" he asked.

"I was on the radio with the pilot just before they landed with her."

"We helped move her to where the altar was located," the man offered. "Have you seen what they've done there?"

"Yeah, Bernstein was nuts to find that thing, wasn't he?"

"I've got another few minutes before I'm back on duty, I'm going to get . . . Ow. Something just bit me." He slapped his neck. "Ow. Got me again."

She took a step away from him, "Hey . . . they're all over you," she said, fear rising in her voice.

He looked down and yelled as he saw a black cloud of mosquitoes swirling around him. He swatted at them as the woman backed away. She turned and ran toward the main section of the tel, yelling a warning as she went.

"Get them off me," he yelled. As he ran after her, he glanced behind him. To his horror, he saw a black wave of insects that swarmed across the floor of the desert, spreading over the tel.

* o *

Helen lay on the cold slab of stone, her thoughts coming in distorted, dreamlike images. She heard her name being called and felt someone pick her up by the shoulders to a sitting position. She still had the black cloth sack over her head and strained to hear what was going on around her.

Someone began to untie the cord around her neck that held the sack on. They yanked it off and her hair flew upward and fell across her face in a disheveled mess. Someone gathered her hair and held it behind her head.

"Have you opened the box?" she heard a new voice say. She tried to focus on the speaker.

"Yes, did you notice that the dragon on the lid is replicated on the handle of the blade?" She recognized the voice of Wyan, and tried to move away from him, only to feel her hair being tugged, making her cry out in pain.

"The tooling is exquisite," she heard the new person answer.

She tried to get her eyes to focus, but all she could see was the bright glare of torchlight around her.

"Is this her?" the new person asked.

"I think there's a strong resemblance, don't you?" She heard Wyan's grating laugh, and then the new voice replied, "You think so?"

"Oh, yes," Wyan's voice again. "Look, you have her eyes."

Helen managed to hold her focus steady. She saw a man who appeared to be in his early twenties.

"Please don't hurt me," she whimpered as they came toward her.

Wyan's face transformed into the reptilian monster and his tongue forked out at her.

"Please . . . leave me alone . . . don't hurt me," she sobbed. Her eyes focused for a moment and she saw the large stone altar on which she was held prisoner. It was placed in the bottom of what looked like an ancient amphitheater. Above her appeared a huge tent with the silhouette of a large crimson dragon. It billowed in the slight breeze and appeared more diabolical as the light from a circle of torches lit it from below.

"Maybe she needs another shot?" The man who held her yanked her head back once again, causing her to shriek from the pain.

"Yes, another shot, but not just yet," Wyan said. "Helen, I told you earlier that I had someone very special I wanted you to meet."

"Go away . . . please," she pleaded.

Helen hung her head and sobbed. She was aware enough to know that there was to be no escape. She felt the stone beneath her and wondered how many other helpless victims had met their doom before her on that cold slab. Tears streaked down her face. She cursed her life and the god that didn't care about her, despite what Crawford had said. Her desire to live was ebbing from her and now all she wanted was to die without too much pain and lose herself in the nothingness that she knew awaited her.

"Helen?" Wyan called to her in a soothing voice. When she didn't respond, he hissed in anger, "Hold her head up so she looks at me."

The man behind her grabbed her jaw and steadied her head.

"Helen, do you see who is standing next to me?" He didn't wait for her to respond. "He's special, Helen. Do you remember when you had your baby on board my ship? Long ago, when you were still a little girl?"

"No . . ." Helen moaned.

"All these years you've tried to forget that, haven't you? But you knew that this day would come. You didn't think I would forget, did you?"

She tried to move her head away but it was yanked back in place.

"Helen . . . this is your child, your son. Mr. Kenson, this is your mother."

Helen stared at the man who stood before her. Her limbs trembled, and it seemed she would lose her mind as she threw her head back and screamed.

⁎ ⊙ ⁎

"Listen . . . something's up," Mac said, pressing his ear on the door of the trailer.

"I'm thinking so too," Uri agreed.

"I thought I heard a woman screaming," Laura added.

"Yeah," Mac agreed. "How much time do we have left before the eclipse?" he asked.

"They took my watch when they searched us but it must have started by now," Laura replied.

"Listen," Uri said, as he pressed his ear to the door. "I hear it again . . . screaming."

"What now?" Laura asked.

"Break the door down?" Mac suggested.

"I don't think so, Mac. It opens in," Laura said, pointing to the hinges.

"Can we take them off?" Mac asked.

Uri wrapped two fingers around the top hinge and tried to free the hinge-pin. "No use. They're welded in."

"Somebody's coming up the steps," Mac said.

"I'll get behind the door," Uri answered.

Mac looked around the floor, trying to find anything he could use as a weapon. "The boxes . . . Laura and I will throw boxes, and you slam the door in their face and we'll rush them," Mac suggested.

Uri nodded and pressed his body next to the door.

Without warning the door exploded inward, bouncing off Uri. He recovered and started to come around the door, ready to strike a blow with his fist.

"Wait!" Mac yelled, "Wait!"

Uri held up. His face grew pale, "I thought you said he was dead?" he said.

Mac rushed for the doorway, "Johanen!" he called, and he embraced the man whom he had seen shot to death just hours ago.

"Yes, but we have no time for explanations," Johanen stated.

"Who is this?" Mac asked, getting his first glance at the mysterious figure who had remained at the bottom of the trailer's steps.

"Not now, MacKenzie, but all of you come now," Johanen instructed. "We must hurry."

Mac, Laura, and Uri ran out of the trailer and stopped at the bottom of the metal stairs. Mac let out a gasp of astonishment. "What's happening?" he asked as he turned to Johanen for an explanation of the millions of flying insects that swarmed over the tel.

Johanen motioned toward the robed figure. "This man is from another time. He is the one responsible for my resurrection and for the insects you see before you. But he has a greater purpose, one that has been set down long ago. He has returned to this time, because his day of witness is at hand."

Laura interrupted, "What are those?"

Mac looked over Johanen's shoulder to the undulating mass of insects so thick that the trailer they swarmed over was hidden from sight.

"A plague of mosquitoes," Johanen answered. "One of the ten that befell Egypt. I see they have thrown the tel into disarray, as we had hoped it would, but they will not harm us."

Mac looked at the robed figure, then back to Johanen, then once again at the mass of insects that made his skin crawl. "He's responsible for this?"

Johanen nodded, "Yes, MacKenzie, and look there," Johanen said, pointing behind him. To Mac's amazement the disk which had been hovering over the tomb wasn't there anymore.

"It's gone!" Mac exclaimed.

"At least for now, but listen, we must not waste a minute, for the eclipse has started. This is what we will do." He began to outline the details of his plan.

As Mac and the others listened, shrieks and screams echoed through the tel as the insects found their way into the eyes, ears, and noses of those to whom they were sent.

* ○ *

Four helicopters flew in tight formation south over the Red Sea. They were so low that the turbulence from their blades fanned the otherwise calm water into a momentary frenzy.

Their commander, a career soldier who sported an eye patch and was sitting next to the pilot in the lead chopper, checked his watch and adjusted his headset. "Remember that the Yemeni government has no knowledge of our mission, so no mistakes. I want to fly as low as possible. Scrape the shingles off the roofs of the houses, is that clear?" he barked.

The four pilots' voices chorused a definitive, "Yes, sir."

He had been briefed a few hours ago by the Major. He had been shown the route he was to take and had been given pictures of the people he was to rescue. He opened his briefing packet and looked again at the photos, memorizing each face. He took the photo of a UFO taken over the Negev in broad daylight. He had been briefed that there was going to be a very high probability of encountering this kind of craft. If at all possible, he was to use the new top-secret weapon . . . one that supposedly did not exist. He glanced to the rear of the chopper at a high-powered laser cannon. He had seen reports of the tests that the laser had knocked out two Scud missiles simultaneously. It was an incredible feat, the laser sending out two bursts of light that upon impact blew the Scuds out of the sky. He had been briefed that it would be his only offensive weapon against the UFO he was expected to encounter. He slipped the pictures back into the mission packet. He checked the chopper's position with the on-board GPS. *It won't be long now,* he thought. He adjusted himself in his seat, then slipped on a pair of night vision goggles that hung around his neck.

* ○ *

"It's starting, look." Mac directed Uri and Laura's attention to the beginning of the lunar eclipse as they ran toward the megalith that towered over the tomb. On the way they saw a confusion of technicians, security, and other personnel running toward the shelter of the trailers as clouds of mosquitoes swarmed over them.

Mac stopped at the communications trailer, positioned in front of the tomb, and hid behind it.

"They're everywhere," Laura said, pointing to the mosquitoes. She made a face at Mac.

"Yeah, but they don't seem to be bothering us," Mac answered. He watched Uri set down the gas can he was carrying, and then edge around the side of the trailer.

"Nobody," Uri called out as he came back to retrieve the can.

They went to the trailer and saw that the door was open, and that the personnel who were manning it had fled before the plague of mosquitoes.

"The cables prevented them from closing the door." Mac pointed to a thick bundle of cables that led from the trailer to the tomb. "It's all yours, Laura," Mac said, pointing to the television monitors, satellite links, and controls that were inside.

Laura bolted up the metal steps into the trailer. "Everything is up and running," she called out, "and by the looks of things, they're ready to broadcast. Mac, I can see the interior of the tomb and the sarcophagus . . . there's people down there."

Mac turned to Uri. "Any ideas?"

"We could be torching this trailer," Uri said.

"Yeah, but that's not going to get rid of the body," Mac reminded him.

"Okay, so we go down then," Uri agreed and pointed toward the tomb.

Mac and Uri made for the entrance.

"Look, Mac," Uri exclaimed, "I'm thinking too close." A wave of mosquitoes appeared over the tomb's entrance.

"Yeah, but Johanen said they wouldn't bother us." Mac bolted toward the pit.

"They're all over," Uri said as they reached the top of the pit.

"I know, but what choice do we have?" Mac began to inch his way down the aluminum ladder into the pit. He was immersed in a cloud of mosquitoes that hovered over the entrance.

"MacKenzie, be careful," Uri called from above.

"They're not touching me, Uri . . . not even in my eyes . . . this is weird," he called, as the cloud parted, allowing him to enter the stairway to the tomb. He began to descend the stairs to the tomb itself, two at a time. He reached the bottom. "Hurry up, will you?"

"I'm the one who carries gas," Uri said, as he shifted the large gas can from one hand to the other. He looked back at the entrance that was still clouded with mosquitoes. "This is crazy. They didn't bite."

"Look at this." Mac pointed to the smooth round corridor.

"Extraterrestrial, yeah?" Uri came alongside Mac.

"How much time left?" Mac asked.

"I don't know, but I'm thinking we're going to make it," Uri replied. "Get your flares."

Mac took one of the flares from his pocket and held it in front of him as they quickened their pace. They reached the end of the corridor and came to an abrupt halt.

Thirty feet away there were four men taking the lid off the sarcophagus. Mac gasped as he recognized Johanen's murderer. "He's a Nephilim, the same one who shot Johanen," Mac whispered.

The Nephilim who had shot Johanen jerked his head up, as if he sensed another presence in the room. Still holding the lid, he bared his teeth, and to Mac's astonishment emitted a horrible, growling noise.

Mac took a step backward while Uri unscrewed the cap of the gas can.

"You will not stop this," the hybrid called. He let his end of the lid go which caused the other men to almost drop it. He took a step toward Mac and Uri and held out his hand.

Mac saw the concentration on his face, the merciless eyes, the sneering lips, the six fingers on the hand, and was shocked when the can of gas jerked out of Uri's hand and fell to the floor, spilling gas everywhere.

Another gesture from the hybrid, and the flare jumped from Mac's hand and ignited midair. It landed in the spilled gas and a whooshing sound filled the cavern as the fuel ignited. "Kenson, stop it, you'll ruin everything," a heavyset man holding the lid yelled.

For a moment Mac thought he would be engulfed in the flames, but he felt Uri's hand on his shoulder, pulling him back up the corridor.

"Mac . . . quick," Uri yelled, and the two men ran as fast as they could away from the fire. Mac glanced behind him, and to his horror saw a large ball of fire rolling toward them, engulfing the entire tunnel. He reached the stairs and followed Uri upward, running for all he was worth, taking two steps at a time, feeling his muscles ache at the effort. He reached the top, scrambled up the ladder, and threw himself on the sand next to Uri just as the fireball exploded out of the opening and shot up into the air.

"I'm on fire!" Mac slapped at his clothes while Uri scooped up sand and threw it on Mac's pants, putting out the flames. Uri extended a hand to Mac and he got to his feet. "Did you see that?" Mac yelled. "The way he controlled the flames . . . he made the fireball!"

"He's coming after you," Laura yelled as she flew out of the trailer. "I saw the whole thing. There was no way to warn you, but he's on his way. We've got to get out of here."

"Let's find Johanen," Mac yelled as he and Uri ran up to her and the three of them headed off toward the tented area just outside the ring of megaliths.

"Wait . . . I'm hearing something," Uri said as they neared the tent.

"Yeah, what is that?" Mac asked, "Helicopters?" But what drew his attention was a dark shadow that fell over them. "Uri, Laura . . ."

Then a bright orange light from a UFO exploded around them.

"Get to the tent . . . to Johanen," Mac yelled, as he ran toward it.

They hurried inside the tent but froze in their tracks, for what they saw below shocked them.

"Into the fire," Mac whispered, for there was a woman lying on an ancient stone altar. A ring of torches encircled it, but what terrified him was a creature with alligatorlike skin that Mac estimated to be well over seven feet tall. Its head resembled a lizard, and over one of the red lidless eyes was a hideous blob of scar tissue. Its clawed hands held an ornate dagger to the throat of the unconscious woman. Johanen and Enoch were perhaps ten feet away. Mac realized that it was a standoff.

"What is that?" Laura stammered.

"What Johanen warned us about at Mossad headquarters," Mac blurted out. "A reptilian."

A burst of light hit just outside the tent, crystallizing the sand and turning it a greenish color. The tent shot up into the air, as if a giant hand had pulled the top of it and then cast it aside. In its place Mac saw the pulsing underside of the UFO overhead. Another burst of light, and Mac saw it had come from one of the helicopters.

"Get down!" Uri yelled, pulling Laura to the ground.

Mac stood transfixed as the saucer begin to wobble. Then a red beam shot out from it, and one of the helicopters exploded.

Mac was jolted back as he heard the reptilian's shrill voice cry out, "She will die." He looked down at the altar, and to his horror saw that the reptilian was about to draw the knife across the woman's throat. He saw Johanen and Enoch, their faces grim with determination, close the distance between themselves and the reptilian, trying to gain some advantage.

The chopper fired again and a brilliant beam of light exploded on the side of the UFO. In that instant when the reptilian was distracted, Mac saw Enoch run forward, wielding his staff over his head, bringing it crashing down on the altar. A shower of green sparks flew into the air. The slab of rock shuddered a moment, then split in two, sending a spray of dust and rock into the air. The woman rolled onto the sand while the reptilian jumped out of the way of the falling slab. The reptilian threw the dagger at the woman, and Mac saw the blade slice through her hand, pinning it to the sand. To

Mac's astonishment, the reptilian leaped into the air over Johanen and Enoch and ran up the almost vertical sides of the excavated pit, heading toward the tomb.

The saucer blacked out its lights, tilted on its side, and flew away. Mac heard the chopper follow it, and as he stared at the sky he saw that the eclipse was almost total.

Then he saw it.

"Look at the sign," Mac called as he pointed overhead to the strange star in the shape of a cross that had appeared in front of the eclipsed moon.

"Where did it come from?" Laura asked.

"MacKenzie?" Johanen called from below. "Help us here."

Mac, Uri, and Laura ran down the stone ramp to the altar. On the way they passed Enoch, who held his staff in front of him, looking like a prophet of doom as he hurried past them.

"Is this her?" Mac asked Johanen.

He nodded gravely.

Laura dropped to her knees and cradled the woman's head in her lap. "It's my sister, Helen," Laura said, crying as she stroked the woman's hair.

"What about her hand?" Mac asked, looking at Johanen.

Johanen knelt next to Helen and extracted the blade from her palm. Helen's blood poured out of the wound. Johanen took her hand. Mac heard him praying softly as he pressed Helen's hand, then he slowly let go of it, and Mac saw that the bleeding had stopped. What was more incredible, the wound began to close. Moments later it had closed completely, and where jagged skin had been, Helen's skin appeared like new, without even a trace of a scar.

Mac glanced at Uri and Laura, whose faces mirrored his own astonishment.

"We must leave this place now," Johanen said. "What about the tomb? Did you destroy it?"

"No, the Nephilim that shot you was there, and he made the gas explode into a fireball. We ran for our lives," Mac said. He saw Johanen look up at the eclipse and the cross.

"There is the false sign . . . we haven't much time. Laura and Uri, move Helen to a safe place. Mac, come with me." He began to ascend the ramp.

Mac followed Johanen. As they reached the last of the giant stones in the semicircle, he saw another saucer land behind the megalith that towered over the tomb. Fingers of light streaked through the megaliths for a brief instant, then all was dark again. But what riveted his attention was the figure of Enoch standing in front of the ancient megalith . . . alone. He leaned on his staff as if he had been expecting this and was waiting for it.

"What's he going to do?" Mac whispered.

"This is one of the reasons Enoch was sent here to us, to confront them," Johanen answered.

"Look, two of the guys that were down in the tomb," Mac said, as he saw the men emerge from the tomb and hurry into the communications trailer. His attention reverted back to Enoch as the man cried out in a loud voice, "Come out, fallen one, watcher of old, defiled creature who has left his first estate."

"What's he doing?" Mac asked Johanen.

"He is calling out one of the watchers, a fallen angel," Johanen answered.

The lights on a scaffold in front of the giant megalith were switched on, illuminating the area in front of the tomb, and then Mac saw the same heavyset man that had held the sarcophagus lid hurry out of the trailer and disappear into the entrance to the tomb.

"They're going to try to do the broadcast," Mac exclaimed.

A brilliant light escaped from inside the UFO as a landing ramp touched the ground between the megaliths.

"What is that?" Mac whispered, as he saw a silhouette emerge from the craft.

"It is what Enoch has called. One of the fallen ones that he has a score to settle with . . . watch and pray, MacKenzie," Johanen instructed.

Mac saw Enoch grab his staff in both hands and raise it high above his head. The fallen angel passed between the giant stones and Mac got his first look at the creature.

"It's hideous," he whispered, as he gazed at the tall, wraithlike creature with spindly arms and legs and scaly, lizardlike skin. "It looks like a . . ."

"Yes, MacKenzie, another one of them. A reptilian. Steady yourself," Johanen replied.

The being faced Enoch, and then half a dozen smaller gray "aliens" who had followed close behind gathered around the fallen one.

"Semjaza," Enoch bellowed, "you have grown drunk with your own iniquities, judgment is upon you, and the Holy One has sent me to proclaim to you that you shall have no peace, and that for all eternity you are doomed!"

"He called it by name. How did he . . ." Mac asked, but was interrupted.

"Pray, MacKenzie," Johanen urged. "Add your prayers to mine, for that is our most powerful weapon."

Semjaza stood his ground. "You are nothing but a decrepit old man in the service of a weak god," he taunted. "You see the Bethlehem star!" He pointed overhead to the radiant crosslike star that had appeared in front of the eclipsed moon. The small gray beings began to walk toward Enoch.

"Mac, look there," Johanen said, "something else approaches." He pointed to a light that was streaking toward them.

* ○ *

Inside the tomb a feverish Bernstein and Gleason positioned the cameras and made some last-minute adjustments. They had linked to the satellite and were ready to begin the teleportation.

"We don't have much time," Kenson warned, remaining calm in spite of the debacle on the surface. "No more interruptions, Bernstein. Begin the broadcast."

Bernstein talked into his microphone. "Haney, are you getting a picture?"

"We're up and running," Haney's voice responded over the monitor. "but it's really crazy up here."

Bernstein cleared his throat and looked into the camera. "Never mind that . . . let's begin."

He waited a few seconds and then began. "Those of you who are gathered in Rome, representing your countries, are about to share in an incredible mystery, one that has been carefully guarded for almost two millennia. Now, as we witness the lunar eclipse and the reemergence of the Bethlehem star, join with me as we present to you extraordinary archaeological evidence revealing the true identity of the one called Jesus of Nazareth, and the missing link of humanity—the extraterrestrial."

Bernstein gestured toward the sarcophagus, and Gleason, who was operating the camera, panned toward the body lying there.

Bernstein walked over to the open container and rested his hands on the side of it. "You see here in a state of perfect preservation the remains of the man who was called Jesus. But consider, if you will, these artifacts that are alongside the body." Bernstein reached in and took a long glasslike object that began to glow as soon as he held it in his hand. "Incredible, isn't it?" he asked as he looked into the eye of the camera. "This is just one of the artifacts that the extraterrestrials left for us, as proof of their intervention. Here is the lid that until a few hours ago had remained fastened over the body. You will notice that its pictographs show a migration between the planet Mars and that of Earth. It speaks of a time in which the inhabitants of that planet came here and were responsible for the evolution of our species. It was also by their direct intervention that the sages and wise men of the past were able to perform such astounding miracles . . . even raising someone from the dead. But as the lid of the sarcophagus shows us by way of the pictographs, the resurrection of Jesus was a direct result of extraterrestrial intervention. It was they who led the wise men to Bethlehem with the mysterious light that was *misunderstood* as the Bethlehem star, which as we will see soon, was in fact produced by the technology from an alien craft. It was they who infused this preserved body with the Christ consciousness that . . ." Bernstein stopped. Something made a terrible noise above him and several fractures appeared in the ceiling above him as the room shook.

"What's going on?" Bernstein asked.

"Don't stop . . . keep the broadcast going," Kenson ordered, but Bernstein and Gleason looked at the ceiling.

* ◦ *

In Rome two elderly men sat in the back of a large private auditorium. They had entered after the delegates, representing many nations, had been seated. Both were wealthy industrialists. One man's nose was bandaged due to an ongoing battle with skin cancer. The other, his German counterpart, had been an ardent Hitler youth. Both had made fortunes during World War II. And both were part of an organization known as the Cadre.

"Look, it's beginning," Skin Cancer said, nudging the German sitting next to him.

"Ah, yes . . . Finally." The German checked his watch. "And the lunar eclipse has started."

"Look at that. Incredible," Skin Cancer exclaimed, as the image of a man suddenly appeared on the stage.

The German nodded. "Dr. Bernstein appears more real than if he was actually present in the flesh."

They listened as the three-dimensional teleported figure of Dr. Bernstein, who was actually thousands of miles away, began his discourse. On the platform behind the image of Bernstein, on a large split screen, were two live digital video feeds, one showing the interior of the hidden tomb of Jesus, the other a UFO hovering over a giant megalith. The delegates gasped and murmured amongst themselves as they gazed at the images on the screen.

One of the images changed, showing the eclipse of the Moon, then directly in front of it appeared the sign that they all were promised would be revealed. The audience gave a collective gasp.

"Ah, there it is at last," the German said with satisfaction. "The reappearance of what was erroneously called the Star of Bethlehem."

"Something's wrong," Skin Cancer said, sitting up in his seat and grabbing the arm of the German.

Both men watched with a mixture of anger and frustration as the teleported image of Dr. Bernstein began to flicker, then disappeared entirely.

* ○ *

The Watcher, Semjaza, pointed overhead at the Bethlehem star. "This is the sign of our prince! Run and hide yourself, old man." He took several steps forward, but Mac saw that Enoch remained defiant with the staff over his head.

Johanen nudged him. "Look MacKenzie . . . there."

Mac saw what he thought was an incoming UFO, moving very fast, and almost upon them. "Enoch's in danger," he said.

"No, MacKenzie, look." Johanen pointed to the descending light. "This is something altogether different."

Mac saw, to his astonishment, a glowing, fiery red ball of light. Its sides were made of what looked like crystal, and it reminded Mac of a fiery chariot. From the bottom of it came what looked like a whirlwind of fire that made a sound like a tornado. It descended upon Semjaza and the group of grays near him, covering them in a mantel of light so bright that Mac shielded his eyes from the intensity of it.

Semjaza's face distorted in rage. His body began to writhe in pain, as the whirlwind covered him. Streaks of light began to course through the creature's body so that parts of it began to vanish, as if being stretched and pulled into nothingness.

"What's happening?" Mac asked Johanen.

"Semjaza is being translated," Johanen answered, "taken into another dimension against his will. He will no longer be able to move between the realm of the spirit and here."

"You shall have no peace!" Enoch bellowed again, raising his staff over his head and shaking it at Semjaza. As his final words of judgment fell from his lips, the whirlwind began to rise in the air. Mac could see Semjaza clawing at the sides of it, trying to find a way out.

"I curse you and your god!" Semjaza screamed, and Mac saw the lizardlike skin begin to disintegrate on Semjaza's face, saw his hate-filled eyes bulge out of their sockets. Then the whirlwind began to vanish, as if it were passing into another dimension. When it was gone the fiery red chariot streaked skyward.

Then two choppers roared overhead followed by a UFO. A blast of light streaked from the UFO and hit one of the choppers and the rotors disintegrated.

"It's going down," Mac yelled as he saw the chopper nose-dive into the hill and explode in an orange fireball of flames that mushroomed skyward. Mac and Johanen dove to the ground and covered their heads as burning debris from the chopper rained down on them.

"There's two of them now," Mac yelled. "Two UFOs." He scrambled on his hands and knees looking for shelter.

The remaining chopper banked hard and dived behind the ring of megaliths. It streaked overhead, circling behind the UFO. Mac glanced up and saw the laser cannon in the open cargo door. A streak of light like a lightning bolt left the cannon and smashed into the UFO.

"They hit it," Mac yelled, as the beam of light burned into the ship, making it wobble.

"Look, MacKenzie," Johanen said, pointing toward the megaliths.

Mac saw the reptilian being that he had last seen scrambling up the sides of the pit. It leaped out from behind one of the megaliths and streaked toward Enoch, sending trails of sand flying into the air as its clawed feet flew across the desert floor.

"Look out!" Mac yelled, and he started toward Enoch running for all he was worth.

The reptilian reached Enoch first and smashed his extended arm into the man's back, sending him sprawling to the ground. Without breaking his stride he ran between the megaliths into the belly of Semjaza's UFO, which still remained on the ground.

Mac reached Enoch and helped him up.

"It's taking off," Mac shouted as the ramp of the UFO went back into the belly of the craft. A moment later the ground around the UFO exploded in a burst of brilliant orange light as it hovered for a moment, then shot upward and vanished in the sky.

A burst of laser fire crystallized the sand near Mac. He leaped away, then saw the chopper fire another burst at the remaining saucer. The laser burned into the UFO, creating a gaping black hole. The craft tilted on its side and began to wobble as it moved toward Mac and Enoch.

"It's going to crash!" Mac yelled.

The edge of the UFO slowly tilted forward and hit the ground, plowing into it, sending a torrential shower of sand before it that covered Mac and Enoch. The two men ran for their lives.

Mac glanced behind him and realized that he was running too slow, that the UFO was going to smash into him and sweep him away with it. At the last moment he dove headfirst and the UFO skidded past him, missing him by inches, its rim furrowing into the earth like a giant plow.

Then the UFO crashed into the base of one of the megaliths. The giant stone swayed for a moment, teetering to the right and then back the other way. Then it buckled in two, the larger half falling into the stone next to it, which in turn toppled into the one next to it. Like dominoes, the giant megaliths thundered to the ground, raising a thick cloud of dust as the UFO buried itself deeper in the earth.

* ○ *

"It's caving in," Bernstein yelled as he dropped his microphone and took a step toward Kenson, who was backing out of the chamber.

"We've got to get out of here!" Gleason yelled.

"Not without something to show for this," Bernstein answered, and he grabbed one of the artifacts in the sarcophagus.

"Hurry up, Doctor . . . I don't think it can last much longer," Gleason cried.

Bernstein ran toward the opening, but his shoe caught on one of the cables. He tripped and fell, and the alien artifact slid across the stone floor. Part of the ceiling buckled and several large stones crashed to the floor, sending a torrent of dust through the chamber.

The lights flickered once and then went out.

"Gleason? Where are you?" he yelled as he crawled on the floor looking for the artifact.

Several of the lights came on again. He saw the artifact, grabbed it, got to his feet, and hurried toward the exit. He heard a groan above him and froze with fear. A large stone glanced off his shoulder; sudden pain sent him tumbling to the ground. "It's broken . . . Gleason . . . my shoulder."

The lights flickered out again.

"Doctor, where are you?" Gleason yelled.

"Over here . . . Gleason, don't leave me." Bernstein whined as pain exploded in his shoulder.

The lights sputtered and came on again.

Gleason coughed from the dust. "I see you, Doctor . . . hold on," he said, and Bernstein saw him coming toward him.

"Come on . . . I'll help you." Gleason moved several large pieces of stone that had landed on Bernstein.

The ceiling groaned and then another large block collapsed and landed on Bernstein's legs, pulverizing the flesh and bones. His last scream of agony never left his throat as the rest of the ceiling collapsed on him and Gleason, entombing them.

* ○ *

The megalith that had towered over the tomb lay broken, and several large pieces lay across the pit that led to the tomb's entrance. Through the swirling dust from the crashed UFO, Mac saw a figure emerge from the rubble.

The dust thinned and he recognized the Nephilim that had shot Johanen, the one whom he had heard called Kenson. "Look, it's him!" he yelled.

Kenson glared at Mac, then hurried toward the communication trailer but stopped when he realized that it was a complete ruin. The electrical cables had been severed and were now twisting like frenzied snakes, shooting a shower of sparks from their ends.

Kenson spun around and sneered at Mac, baring his teeth like an enraged animal. Then he thrust his arm out, stretching all six fingers of his hand. One of the abandoned jeeps began to vibrate and then buck violently from the front tires, then back to the rear ones, like a crazed metallic bronco. Suddenly it flew into the air, twisting end over end right at Mac.

Mac felt every nerve in his body jolt, as he dived for all he was worth out of the way.

The jeep slammed into the ground where he had been standing moments before and exploded in flames. Mac rolled several times on the ground and then got to a kneeling position. He realized that he was alone. To his horror he saw a ring of fire begin to encircle him, trapping him in a wall of flames. As the circle of fire began to close, the last thing he saw was Kenson directing the flames, willing the ring of fire to grow in intensity, until several of the trailers spontaneously combusted. Mac heard the terrified screams of men and women who had fled into the trailers for protection from the mosquitoes.

"MacKenzie!" Johanen yelled from somewhere on the other side of the flames.

Mac was blinded by smoke and flames and his clothes were beginning to smolder. The realization that he was about to burn terrified him.

* o *

Uri held Helen in his arms, protecting her as best he could as he ran toward the rear of the tel. Laura was next to him. He had only one goal, to reach the place where he had seen one of the choppers put down with its men. The ring of fire, growing in intensity, cast a nightmarish glow over the area, turning it into a living hell. Uri was almost to the chopper when he saw it and lost all hope. Another UFO crested the hill, just behind the back of the tel. It hovered there a moment and then headed toward Uri.

"It's coming right for us!" Laura screamed.

Helen moaned in Uri's arms. "Don't let them get me . . . please," she cried.

Uri saw two Israeli commandos fall to their faces, unconscious, as the UFO passed overhead. Uri looked behind him and saw that the ring of fire was coming closer every second, turning the area into an inferno. He looked at Laura and said, "We're trapped."

* o *

Mac was doubled over gasping for air. "MacKenzie!" Johanen called from the other side of the wall of fire.

"I'm here." He coughed, choking on the smoke.

"MacKenzie, you have got to make a run for it . . . Try, Mac," Johanen yelled.

Mac struggled to his feet and shielded his eyes from the flames. "Where are you?"

"Here, MacKenzie. Here!" Johanen yelled.

Mac's shirtsleeve smoldered, and he slapped at it with his hand. He looked at the wall of fire in front of him and positioned himself toward where he thought Johanen was. He put his shirt collar to his mouth, took a gulp of air, and then rushed toward the flames.

* o *

Uri was trapped—in front of him the advancing UFO, behind him the ring of fire. More of the soldiers fell unconscious as the UFO advanced. The chopper with the laser cannon had landed just moments before the appearance of the UFO and seemed unaware that the UFO hovered over it.

Uri knelt down, still cradling Helen in his arms.

"What can we do?" Laura asked.

He looked at her and shook his head. He looked toward the ring of fire and spotted Johanen and Enoch. "Look there." He pointed.

"Johanen!" Laura called and waved her arms over her head.

Uri saw Johanen's face fall as he saw the new UFO. Then to Uri's astonishment someone came running through the flames. "It's MacKenzie!" he yelled, holding Helen closer to him.

"No!" Laura gasped. "He's burning."

* o *

Mac felt the hair on his head singe from the heat. His clothes were on fire and he felt the scalding flames lick at his legs. *I can make it,* he thought, and kept running with his hands shielding his face. He felt like he was running in slow motion and wondered if there was ever going to be an end of the flames. His lungs ached from holding his breath, and just when he thought that he would burn alive, he stumbled through to the other side.

Enoch threw his robe over him, rolled him on the ground, and extinguished the flames. Then he dragged him away from the wall of fire.

"MacKenzie, we must hurry, the flames are moving fast," Johanen yelled.

Mac sat up, then he heard Uri calling him. He looked and saw, to his horror, another UFO. But what terrified him was the recognizable insignia—an inverted V with three parallel lines running underneath it.

"I think it's the same craft that my father was taken in. Can't Enoch do something?" he asked Johanen.

"MacKenzie!" It was Uri again.

Mac turned back toward Uri and saw that the UFO had landed. Out of it came a man along with a host of gray aliens.

"It's him," Mac yelled to Johanen. Even from this distance he recognized the man who had emerged from the saucer . . . his father.

The wall of fire towered over them, growing closer with every second. Mac knew that the flames were responding to the will of the Nephilim called Kenson, and were directed to find himself, Johanen, and the others and kill them. Mac saw someone run out of the trailers . . . a human torch. He watched, horrified, as the person made one last futile attempt to extinguish the flames before collapsing on the ground motionless.

Then he heard the voice of Enoch loud and strong and pregnant with command. He saw the man's arms spread out, holding his staff high over his head. Then with both his hands gripped tightly on its end, and adding the weight of his body to the thrust, he brought it down and drove its end several feet into the desert floor. A moment passed, then a deep rumbling noise rose from the depths as the earth trembled under Mac's feet.

Mac saw Johanen and Enoch exchange a look between them, then Johanen yelled, "Run!"

Mac darted after Johanen and Enoch. The ground shook with such a great force that it sent all of them flying. Mac spread his hands in front of him to help break his fall as he hit the sand and rolled. He heard a rushing sound coming from underneath him, and then in the place where Enoch had planted his staff a geyser of water rose up a hundred feet into the air. The water cascaded down onto the ring of fire like a giant fountain, and a cloud of white steam billowed up and spread over the tel.

Mac jumped to his feet and ran to where he had last seen Uri.

The steam was like a thick fog, and after several feet Mac lost his bearings. He saw a silhouetted figure kneeling on the ground in the distance, and thinking it was Uri, headed for it. He was almost upon it when he realized the horrible mistake he had made. The figure rose to its feet, and although several yards away, Mac gasped as he saw the yellow eyes of his father.

"My son, you have come to me at last," Abaris cried out.

Mac was stunned, but he stood his ground and remembered the words that Enoch had shouted a short time ago. "You shall have no peace!" he yelled.

His father let out a torrent of curses, then Mac heard a woman scream. Realizing that it was Helen, he ran in that direction.

He found her being dragged by two gray aliens. A short distance away, Uri and Laura lay unconscious.

"My son! Come back, my son," his father called behind him.

Mac was closing in on the aliens when one of them turned and looked at him. His mind went numb and his legs felt like they weighed a ton each. He recalled what General Roswell had told him about not looking in their eyes. He dropped to his knees, held his head, and moaned, but he was faking. He remembered the flare in his pants. He grabbed it, twisted the cap so that it ignited in a shower of red sparks, then dove at the alien, holding it in front of him so that the flames shot into its eyes. The creature put its hands up to its eyes as it let go of Helen, then let out a piercing wail as it ran away. The other alien backed off. Mac jumped up. "In the name of Jesus of Nazareth you must leave us," he shouted, holding the flare in front of him.

The alien shielded its eyes and started to twist Helen's arm. For a moment Mac felt unsure, then he took a step forward and called out, "In the name of Jesus you must leave us."

The alien let go of Helen, then stepped back so that it was partly hidden in the steam, which acted like camouflage against the gray skin of its body, hiding the creature's form. But Mac could still see the black, almond-shaped eyes watching his every move. He went to Helen and moved her back, away from the alien.

Then two silhouettes appeared less than ten feet away. As they moved closer he recognized them both and felt like the wind had been knocked out of him. It was Kenson and his father, Abaris.

"My son, why have you forsaken me?" Abaris said with mock sincerity.

Mac saw the yellow eyes of his father . . . *the eyes of a demon,* he thought. Kenson held out his hand and pointed it at Mac. The veins on the back of the six-fingered hand rose to the surface of his skin and began to throb.

Then Mac felt a wave of fever and broke out into a sweat. He felt as if his blood was beginning to boil inside him.

Everything is lost, he thought as he fell to his knees. He managed to glance at Helen, thinking she would be the last person he would see before he died. His head pounded from the fever and he hovered on the verge of delirium.

Out of the corner of his eye he saw a robe . . . Enoch's robe. Then strong hands were on his shoulders and he was lifted to his feet. He felt something course through his body, pushing the fever out, and he swayed, but with every heartbeat he began to regain his strength.

"We are strong in the Lord!" Johanen's voice boomed as he joined them. Mac saw that Abaris and Kenson were actually moved backward, as if the force of Johanen's words had lifted them off their feet and moved them. "We are strong in the Lord!" Johanen walked forward and stood protectively in front of Helen, so that he was between her and Kenson and Abaris. Mac heard Kenson snarl and then he saw Abaris back up into the steam.

"There will be another day . . . and she will be ours." Kenson spat at them before he too followed Abaris, disappearing into the steam.

Moments later Mac saw the blinding light from the UFO at the back of the tel create an eerie silhouette as it flew upward through the steam.

Johanen took Helen in his arms. "Helen, I am Johanen, be at peace."

Helen sobbed and clutched him.

Mac looked overhead through a hole in the clouds of steam and saw that the eclipse was over and the starlike cross was gone.

Then he saw something else. It was the same glowing red orb that had created the deadly whirlwind, descending through the steam.

"Oh, no, what's that?" Helen cried.

"Nothing to fear child . . . watch," Johanen said.

The orb came to rest several feet above the desert floor a short distance from the huddled group.

"It's beautiful," Helen exclaimed.

The air was clearing and Mac saw that much of the tel was charred and smoldering. Enoch retrieved his staff, but water still bubbled up from the ground. Then Enoch walked over to the red orb and somehow passed through it until he was inside.

"What's he doing? Who is that?" Helen asked, as the orb began to lift from the ground.

"I think he's leaving us," Mac replied, as the orb hovered near them. Mac saw Enoch lift from his shoulder a cloth sling attached to a clay jar. He tossed the jar at Mac, who caught it. Then with a burst of acceleration Enoch shot up into the sky and was gone.

"MacKenzie," Johanen called, "what about Uri and Laura?"

"They were unconscious the last time I saw them."

Two armed Israeli commandos with Uzis came running up to them. "MacKenzie? Johanen?" one of them asked.

"I'm MacKenzie."

"We have orders to get you out of here as soon as possible."

One of the soldiers slipped on a pair of infrared night vision goggles and scanned the area in front of them.

"There," he said, and the group followed him.

The soldiers found Uri and Laura, who were still unconscious. One of the soldiers knelt and examined them briefly.

"Are they okay?" Mac asked.

The man nodded. Taking his radio, he said, "We've got everybody, we're set to go." He set his Uzi on the ground and shot a flare into the air, and ignited another and set it on the ground next to them.

Moments later Mac heard the sound of the chopper as it crested the hill behind them. It switched on its lights and landed near them.

Mac looked around and saw the smoldering remains of trailers and blackened ground. The megaliths that had withstood the forces of nature for millennia now lay like fallen towers, broken and heaped on top of each other. Several people who had survived the terrible plague of mosquitoes were being rounded up by the Israeli military.

A soldier came up and gave a report to the commanding officer, a man sporting an eye patch. "We've found the remains of at least twenty people that were burned alive in the trailers."

Mac shuddered, realizing that he almost had met the same fate.

"MacKenzie," Johanen called from the tomb's entrance.

Mac slung the jar that Enoch had thrown him over his shoulder and walked over to him.

"It appears that the tomb is destroyed, but I want us to make certain of it," Johanen said.

"There's no way I'm going back down there," Mac huffed.

"That's our job, sir," one of the soldiers said, overhearing Johanen. He proceeded to descend into what was left of the ladder that went into the pit. The soldier produced a flashlight and shined it down into the tomb's entrance. The man was gone for less than a minute before he returned. "It goes for maybe thirty steps and then it's nothing but rubble . . . completely impassable."

The commander came up beside Johanen and MacKenzie.

"What about that?" MacKenzie asked, pointing toward the downed UFO.

"It's been reported and there's a cleanup team on its way, jointly fielded with the Americans."

Everyone was distracted as several of the soldiers came running from the UFO. Several of them were yelling in Hebrew. "What are they saying?" Mac asked Johanen.

"They've discovered two aliens that are alive, but they're badly wounded."

"It's time we got you out of here," the commander said.

Mac helped carry Helen and boarded with Johanen, while other soldiers carried Uri and Laura onto the chopper. He took one last look at what was left of the tel as the chopper rose from the ground.

Epilogue

Art MacKenzie sipped hot coffee and looked at Elisha Ben-Hassen. Uri sat next to his grandfather, and Laura lay on a couch with a wet cloth over her forehead.

Colonel Austin entered the room with a tray of sandwiches. Mac took one and stuffed a corner of it into his mouth.

"Has anyone seen Johanen?" Mac asked.

Elisha cleared his throat. "He told me he was taking Helen back to Naples to see the pilot that flew her from the states. I believe his name was Jack Crawford."

"How is she doing?"

Austin took a bite of his sandwich. "She won't leave Johanen's side, and who can blame the poor girl after what she's gone through."

"I barely got to talk to her," Laura added.

"There'll be another time," Elisha reassured her as he got up out of his chair and came over to the table where Mac sat.

"MacKenzie, are you aware that what you saw was the Merkabah?" Elisha asked.

Mac shook his head. "I had no idea what to call it. It looked magnificent, though."

"The prophet Elisha was picked up by the Merkabah, or a fiery chariot, as the Scripture describes it. I like to think of it as the divine taxi." He chuckled.

"It was beautiful, Elisha, I couldn't take my eyes off it," Mac commented.

"And he just tossed this at you as he left?" Elisha asked, placing his hand on the jar that Enoch had given to Mac.

Mac nodded. "It looks old."

"It is ancient, MacKenzie," Elisha replied.

"It has a scroll inside like the Dead Sea scrolls found at Qumran, only older," Uri stated.

"Can you read it?" Mac asked.

"Not yet, MacKenzie," Elisha responded. "We have to treat the parchment with a special solution so we can unroll it, then we will see about a translation. Uri tells me you saw the body in the sarcophagus up close."

"Yeah, Johanen was with me. It was a very good likeness," Mac said, then realized he had almost given away Johanen's secret.

"What do you mean by that?" Austin asked.

Mac laughed. "Oh, nothing. It looked like some of the pictures I've seen, that's all."

"So when is Maggie coming?" Elisha asked.

"I think she's flying in tomorrow morning," Mac stated.

The door opened and the Major entered.

"We would all like to express our gratitude for your help, Major," Elisha said, going over to him and extending his hand.

"It is I who should be thanking you," the Major replied. "We now know that we have a weapon that can stop their craft."

"Without its use we might not be here now," Elisha agreed.

"Has the Yemeni government made an official statement?" Mac asked.

The Major nodded. "Yes, they're blaming Israel, of course. According to the UPI wire it seems one of our planes was shot down over their air space. They're making a big deal out of it."

"And the unofficial story?" Uri asked.

"We've deployed a cleanup crew with the Americans and we've rounded up what's left of their people. As you know, one of the saucers crashed. We confiscated much of the video from the tel."

Mac raised his eyebrow. "How much video?"

"It's being looked at now, but I was wondering, MacKenzie, once we get it sorted out, if you, Laura, and Uri would comment on it."

Mac looked at Uri and Laura, but remained silent.

"Unofficially of course," the Major added.

Everyone in the room chuckled wearily.

Mac bit into his sandwich. "As long as it's unofficial."

"Another thing you should all know," the Major added. "The star that appeared during the lunar eclipse. We have a preliminary analysis of it."

"What did you find?" Elisha asked.

"It appears that it might have been some sort of a holographic image."

"Created how?" Mac asked.

"We're not certain," the Major answered.

"What's the press saying about it?" Mac asked.

The Major shrugged. "Each country has its own take on it. Some react with fear; others worry more about the stock market."

"But we must not lose sight of who we know is behind it," Elisha stated.

"So they will try again, won't they?" Mac asked.

All eyes looked toward Elisha. "Yes, MacKenzie, I'm afraid this is just the beginning."

"They're not human. They come from somewhere else, somewhere far away…"

NEPHILIM
THE TRUTH IS HERE

L. A. MARZULLI

Two years ago, Art "Mac" MacKenzie was a respected newspaper journalist with a wonderful family and a bright future. Now he lives alone, fighting the temptation to drink and trying to survive as a freelance writer. His faith in God, humanity, and virtually everything else is gone. All that's left is a pile of bills and the ache of his son's death.

Then comes the opening of the multimillion-dollar new wing of the Westwood Center, and a distraught patient's fantastic tale of alien abduction and impregnation. So begins a media story with international implications—and more trouble than Mac has ever imagined.

Hot for a story, Mac follows a lead to Israel, where he comes across the remains of one of the Nephilim—ancient biblical giants sired by demons and born of human women. It's just the tip of a terrifying supernatural iceberg—for the Nephilim are back and will do anything to prevent him from revealing their secret.

Softcover: 0-310-22011-4

Pick up a copy at your favorite bookstore!

ZONDERVAN™

GRAND RAPIDS, MICHIGAN 49530 USA

WWW.ZONDERVAN.COM

We want to hear from you. Please send your comments about this book to us in care of the address below. Thank you.

ZONDERVAN™

GRAND RAPIDS, MICHIGAN 49530 USA

WWW.ZONDERVAN.COM

DATE DUE